IDENTITY

CAMILLE PETERS

IDENTITY

By: Rosewood Publications

Copyright © 2019 by Camille Peters

Rosewood Publications

Salt Lake City, Utah

United States of America

www.camillepeters.com

Cover Design by Karri Klawiter

To my darling sister, Stephanie,
for your constant love, friendship, and for being one of my biggest
cheerleaders.
I adore you.

his was Princess Lavena's riskiest scheme yet—a remarkable feat, considering she'd had plenty of contenders over the years. How could she be sneaking out so close to her wedding, especially with her fiancé only a few corridors away? I peered through the slit in the drapes in Her Highness's bedroom, searching the night for any sign of her. It was nearing midnight, and she'd already been gone for three endless and anxiety-ridden hours.

I paced the perimeter of the princess's elegant bedroom, as if my restlessness could somehow urge her to return sooner, all the while praying Their Majesties wouldn't come check on their wayward daughter. Despite Princess Lavena's claims, I knew they'd never be fooled into believing I was her; the façade only worked for those who didn't know the princess well. If I was caught impersonating a royal...my stomach clenched at the thought.

Why must the princess be perpetually besotted with so many different men and have the habit of sneaking out after dark to meet them?

A familiar and relieving tap on the windowpane interrupted my pacing. *Finally.* I yanked the window open. Cool summer air washed over me, along with sweet relief at seeing Her Highness. She'd returned before midnight, a new record. Perhaps tonight I'd actually get some sleep.

"Welcome back, Your Highness."

She slid expertly through the window before righting herself to pat her still-flawless hair and smooth her wrinkle-free skirts. "Thank you, Anwen. It was a lovely night."

"How so?" I didn't really want to know, but I'd learned early in my service to the princess that she loved to be asked; feigning interest in her exploits was one of my primary duties.

She sighed wistfully, her eyes bright. "My minstrel and I took a romantic stroll beneath the stars. It was like a dream."

I scrunched my forehead. "Your minstrel? I thought you were meeting the stable boy."

"He was last week's interest. Keep up, Anwen."

If she hadn't been royalty I'd have rolled my eyes. "My apologies, Your Highness."

She brushed my apology away as she pattered to her bed and fell onto it with a contented sigh. "Tonight was lovely. I think he's been my favorite."

It was high praise indeed to be the current favorite among the countless men the princess had fancied herself in love with over the years. "He must be quite remarkable."

Another wistful sigh. "He is. It's a pity he's a common man, or I could be engaged to him instead."

The princess's expression twisted at the thought of her unwanted engagement. I bit my lip to suppress a sigh. Here it came: Her Highness's usual fiancé-bashing, which had become more frequent these past few days, considering we were not only visiting his home, the Dracerian Palace, but their union was only three days away.

To my relief, the princess didn't launch into her favorite

stream of complaints. Instead, she spent a moment lost in her dazed "princess who thinks herself in love" expression as she stared unseeing up at her canopy before sitting up.

"Prepare me for bed, Anwen."

I obeyed and retrieved her nightgown from the wardrobe. Princess Lavena stood rigidly as I went through the usual mechanical motions of dressing her. The princess was more talkative some nights than others. Unfortunately, tonight seemed to be one where she had much to say.

"Tonight truly was magical, Anwen, especially compared to the tedium I endured this afternoon."

"You didn't enjoy your time with Prince Liam?"

"Ew no, you know I never do. We got in another fight, of course, and I gave him those juicy insults I brainstormed with you yesterday."

Insults I'd tried and obviously failed to persuade her not to give. As usual, she hadn't listened to me.

"It's been the longest week of my life," she continued. "I've never had to endure him this long before. It's felt like a thousand years."

"You two need to become better acquainted before the wedding."

She wrinkled her nose towards the door, as if trying to send her disgust to its intended victim. "Don't mention the wedding. It's most unfair. Why do I have to marry someone I loathe? Three days until I'm leg-shackled to that ridiculous prince forever." Her hand clenched in a white-knuckled fist.

This time I did roll my eyes, but thankfully I stood behind the princess doing up her nightgown, so she didn't see. I couldn't fathom what the princess's problem with the Crown Prince of Draceria was. He was not only handsome and charming, but he seemed like a very friendly and fun-loving sort...at least when he wasn't around her.

Prince Liam seemed just as disenchanted with the princess

as she was with him. I'd served as their invisible chaperone on multiple occasions and witnessed both their epically long silent treatments and their harsh battles of words. If their marriage actually happened—which at this point seemed inevitable—one of them would surely murder the other shortly thereafter.

"Forgive my saying so, Your Highness, but perhaps you shouldn't sneak out anymore, considering your wedding is so soon. What if His Highness catches wind of it?"

She snorted. "I wouldn't care if he did. I don't intend to stop just because we become legally bound together for the rest of our miserable lives. If we're forced to marry, then he'll discover my habits soon enough."

I gasped. "But Your Highness, it would be wrong for you to continue meeting men when you're married to another."

"Stop scolding," Princess Lavena snapped impatiently. "I'll need to do *something* to make my upcoming sentence bearable. Now stop your worrying; you do it far too much."

At least one of us does. I bit my lip to silence that retort. Handmaidens didn't talk back to princesses, as much as they deserved it.

She pouted. "Besides, don't I deserve a bit of freedom after I become a prisoner to contracts that benefit everyone except me?"

"The alignment of two great kingdoms will be to the benefit of countless people," I recited, having heard the argument many times from Their Majesties during Princess Lavena's frequent complaints about her upcoming match. "It'll not only strengthen trade but also—"

"I know, Anwen, don't lecture." Princess Lavena sighed. "But why should I have to sacrifice my happiness for a bunch of people I don't even know?"

"They're your subjects," I said as I picked up her hairbrush and began her nightly hundred strokes, which would be difficult to keep track of with her current ranting. "As a princess and future queen, you should care."

"Well, I don't. Being a queen sounds terribly dull. Living life with my minstrel would be much more enjoyable. Think of all the places we'd visit and the freedom from responsibility we'd enjoy."

Doubtful. The princess would only enjoy it for a time before finding something new to complain about; nothing would compel her to give up her favorite hobby.

The princess tugged some of her hair away from my brushing in order to twist and untwist it around her finger. "I can't believe the union I've dreaded for so long is nearly here. I can't marry Liam. He's simply awful, Anwen."

Prince Liam could be a saint and the princess would still hate him. Once Her Highness made up her mind against something, there was no dissuading her.

"Lately we've taken to ignoring one another," she continued. "We need to practice for our marriage."

"I truly don't see what you have against him; he seems an amiable sort."

"Spoken by one who doesn't even know him. But even if you did, I'm sure you'd force yourself to find good in him, like you always do. You're so strange, Anwen. Too bad you can't marry him instead."

The princess suddenly froze, staring wide-eyed at her reflection. I could almost see another scheme unfolding in her devious mind. She gasped and twisted around in her chair. "That's it!"

Dread pooled in my stomach. Princess Lavena had that gleam in her eyes that always accompanied words I didn't want to hear. "What is it?"

The princess smirked. "I've just had the most brilliant idea, my most spectacular one yet." She leaned closer, her eyes glistening darkly. "You shall take my place and marry Prince Liam in my stead."

I gaped at the princess, trying to make sense of her words as they jumbled in my mind. "What?" I stuttered. She couldn't have suggested what I thought she had. But by the scheming glint in her eyes, I knew I hadn't misheard.

"You will marry Liam instead of me."

I continued to stare at her. She couldn't be serious. But the longer I searched her expression, the more I realized she was. Trepidation knotted my stomach. "Are you *insane?*"

Princess Lavena's eyes narrowed dangerously in warning, but I didn't care I was speaking disrespectfully to a princess. There were times to remain the silent and submissive servant, and moments when doing so was suicidal. This was such a moment.

"I can't marry Prince Liam," I stammered. "I'm only a handmaiden. I couldn't possibly take your place in a political alliance between Lyceria and Draceria. Not only is it far too important to tamper with, but it would never work; we don't look that much alike."

"You know we do." Princess Lavena motioned triumphantly to our side-by-side reflections in the mirror on her vanity. I stared, silently cursing our uncannily similar looks: same heart-shaped faces and high cheekbones, same dark hair nearly the exact same shade, same chocolate-brown eyes, same upturned nose...even our heights were only an inch apart. Fate had been cruel to me to have me look nearly identical to the princess, a fact that brought me nothing but trouble. But what Her Highness was proposing now was trouble of a far different sort.

I had to reason with her. "We're not twins, Your Highness."

She squinted at our reflections. "I admit we aren't, but

Liam doesn't know me well enough to be able to tell us apart. That's all that matters."

Even though they'd been betrothed for nearly seven years, I knew that to unfortunately be true. I took a deep breath in an attempt to calm my pounding heart and brace myself for what would likely be an arduous battle, one that I had to win at all costs.

"Your Highness, please consider what you're proposing." I fought to keep my voice calm so the stubborn princess wouldn't become defensive; then I'd never win.

"I'm not asking you to undergo torture. Although this being Liam…" Princess Lavena wrinkled her nose. "I'm providing freedom for me and an opportunity for you. You don't want to be a handmaiden your entire life, do you?"

"But if I marry Prince Liam, what will you do?"

She clasped her hands, starry-eyed. "Be with my minstrel, of course."

I narrowed my eyes. "A common man?"

"The life of a minstrel sounds utterly romantic. How adventurous would it be to travel to different places and sing for your keep? I'm an excellent vocalist. We'd make quite the pair."

"But you love your lavish lifestyle," I reminded her. "Why would you throw it all away?"

"I'm currently a prisoner, Anwen. A gilded cage is still a cage."

I knew the princess: she'd rather be trapped in opulence than free in poverty, but as usual, she refused to see any chink in her latest plan. But she would. Eventually she'd want her old life back, and when she did, I'd be the one in trouble.

"You do realize what will happen to me if our switch is discovered. Impersonating a royal is a serious offense. I'd be imprisoned at best or executed at worst." My chest squeezed at the thought and it suddenly became difficult to breath, as if the noose was already around my neck.

The princess rolled her eyes. "You worry too much, Anwen. Nothing will happen to you."

I gritted my teeth. "It's easy to gamble when it's not your own life. I could be sent to the gallows for this."

She frowned at me as if she'd never seen me before, and indeed she'd never seen *this* side of me. I'd never dared be so uncooperative or argumentative before, but fighting for one's life was the greatest motivation for talking back.

"You're not going to the gallows," she said.

"I will when I get caught."

"You won't. I told you Liam won't notice our switch."

That was likely true but I refused to admit it. "But Their Majesties will."

"Perhaps..." She trailed off, and for a moment I felt a flutter of hope that she'd finally seen reason...until she dashed it with her next words. "But I doubt it. My parents don't exactly spend time with me."

"Of course they'll notice. You're their daughter."

"They won't," she said firmly, as if trying to convince herself more than me. "I doubt they'll even visit after the marriage, not after they've gotten their use out of me to fulfill their precious political contract." Sadness filled her voice before her expression hardened with determination.

She clearly wouldn't be dissuaded. But she *had* to be. If she wasn't...panic clawed at my throat as I frantically tried to come up with another argument. "Your Highness, please see sense; this can't possibly work."

"It will," Princess Lavena said. "It's worked before."

"Switching places for a few hours at minor state functions where those in attendance don't know you very well is nothing to switching places for the rest of our lives."

Naturally, Princess Lavena made no acknowledgement of

my logic. "I'm a stranger in Draceria," she pressed. "Thus this will work. It has to."

I gaped at her in disbelief. Was she really willing to risk it? By the determined gleam in her eyes I knew she was. Like always, she seemed to think the entire thing a game. The noose wasn't even a possibility for her, and she didn't seem overly concerned that it was for me. After all these years serving her, I'd hoped my life meant something more to the princess. Obviously she cared only for herself.

She eyed my panicked expression with impatience. "Stop being so difficult, Anwen. You'll make a better match with Prince Liam than I ever would. This is an opportunity for a better life."

"I don't want this kind of life." Who would willingly choose one of deceit?

"It's better than your previous life I rescued you from."

"I was happy as a goose girl."

She scoffed. "No more arguments. I've made my decision —you will take my place and marry Liam."

She nodded, affirming that the matter was decided, but I refused to allow this to happen, not when I had the power to stop it. I lifted my chin. "I'm informing Their Majesties. I've been a silent accomplice against my will in your other schemes, but this is too far. I refuse to let you get away with it."

"You have no choice," Princess Lavena said darkly. "You're my servant and will obey my commands."

"I won't, and you can't stop me." I stomped towards the door, but Princess Lavena blocked my exit, her dark eyes flashing.

"Who do you think you are, handmaiden? I'm a princess, whereas you're a nobody. Thus I'll have my way if it's the last thing I do."

I folded my arms. "How? You can't bind my tongue. I'll

reveal the truth, whether it's tonight or the day of the wedding, but I refuse to go along with such a dangerous and dishonest scheme."

Her smirk became wicked and my heart pounded at the triumphant gleam in her eyes. There couldn't be a way for her to force me into this, could there?

"Poor Anwen, so naive. Do you honestly think I'd risk my happiness and freedom on the chance you'd expose our switch?" She advanced a step and I instinctively stepped away, backing into her bedpost.

"What do you mean?" My voice shook, betraying my fear—fear that seemed to please her.

"I'm surprised you haven't guessed." She pulled a ring off her finger. My stomach sank.

It was the Lycerian contract ring.

I only knew bits and pieces about the enchanted royal heirloom that had been in the Lycerian Royal Family for generations. All one had to do to create an unbreakable contract was speak it out loud while holding the ring before putting it on the victim, who would then be forced to obey it. The centuries-old ring could only be removed by the one who'd put it on, which would break the contract.

I couldn't believe such a powerful object existed. I'd heard enough ancient stories about its rare use to make me certain I never wanted to be a forced wearer of the ring. To my knowledge, the ring hadn't been used in generations, only kept by the royal family for the sake of tradition. Unsurprisingly, Princess Lavena would scoff at tradition and choose to take advantage of such a dangerous object.

"Where did you get that?" I whispered.

She smirked. "I stole it from Mother's jewelry box months ago, thinking perhaps it might come in handy some day... and now it will." She took a step closer.

I stepped back. "You can't use that ring," I stuttered.

The firelight flickered sinisterly off the engraved gold band as she examined it with a thoughtful expression. It was hard to believe something so simple could be so dangerous. "Why can't I?"

"Because it's wrong."

She laughed coldly. "I don't care about that; I only care that it works."

She advanced another step, approaching for the kill like a *reduviidae*—an assassin bug who'd targeted me as its victim. I darted to the side and bolted for the door, but the princess was closer and blocked it once more.

"Stop running, Anwen. Must you be so uncooperative?"

"Don't put that ring on me, Your Highness. I beg you."

"You've left me no choice. I can't allow your ridiculous resistance to get in my way." She leapt forward, but I ducked and managed to make it to the door. I'd no sooner yanked it open than the princess slammed it shut, seized my wrist, and lifted the ring.

"You will take my place and become Princess Lavena." As she spoke, the ring began to glow. I yanked and tugged, but her grip was too strong to break. "You will tell no one you are the handmaiden Anwen, nor show this ring to anyone to reveal you're bound by a contract. Our switch will remain a secret."

I tried harder to wriggle away, but it was as if the enchantment of the ring had given the princess strength beyond her own, keeping me within her grasp whether I wanted to be or not.

"You will behave in such a way that no one will suspect our switch."

"You're insane," I panted, exhausted from the effort of trying to make an escape I now realized with horror was impossible. "This can't possibly work. The switch will be discovered and I'll be forced to take the fall for it."

She merely shrugged. "Oh well."

And she shoved the ring onto my finger. Searing heat encircled my finger as it melded to my skin, sending throbbing pain pulsing up my arm. I yanked away from the princess's now slackened grip and tried to tug the ring off. It wouldn't budge. Instead it tightened further, burning me.

Tears clogged my throat. "Take it off, Your Highness. *Please.*"

But she didn't. She merely watched my struggle with a satisfied smirk, triumph glistening in her eyes at another plot successfully executed. I knew that no matter how much I fought, I was now an unwilling accomplice to her horrible scheme.

And already I felt as if the Anwen in me was beginning to die.

CHAPTER 2

I took every opportunity I could find over the next three days to attempt to pull off the ring now symbolizing my chains, but it remained unyielding. The first several hours after it'd been placed on my finger it hadn't ceased to burn, making sleep impossible. Even without the white-hot pain encircling my finger, sleep would still have eluded me. My mind raced as I frantically searched for a loophole to the princess's contract, but I could see no way out; I was trapped.

But I refused to give up.

I vainly hoped Princess Lavena would eventually come to her senses and become less enamored with either her minstrel or the idea of using him as a way to escape her unwanted engagement. Unfortunately, the princess only became more excited with the thought of ridding herself of her royal duties and political obligations. That didn't prevent me from trying to talk sense into her, but I might as well have been speaking to my insect collections for all the good it did me.

When I wasn't trying to dissuade the princess, I made

several attempts to go to Their Majesties, but the mere thought of doing so would cause my legs to tighten and my tongue to become trapped in my throat, all while the ring burned in reminder of the forced contract to which I was bound.

The princess spent the days before the wedding grooming me for the task of becoming her, not just in looks but in decorum. I'd already received a great deal of training in royal etiquette over the years when she'd forced me to take her place at various court functions, which unfortunately made the short timeframe for the princess's plan possible.

But that didn't mean I would cooperate willingly. Despite the ring's power, Anwen still remained alive and stubbornly resistant inside me, and I'd embrace her for as long as she had left.

"No, Anwen, stop slouching." Princess Lavena pulled my shoulders back to straighten my spine. "A princess must have perfect posture. Do you want to be found out and subsequently thrown in the dungeon?"

I gritted my teeth as once more the princess used her newest weapon against me: since I was unwillingly trapped in the charade, I had to perform it well enough to avoid detection.

"It's hard to stand up straight when carrying a burden as heavy as deceit," I snapped.

She cocked a perfectly manicured eyebrow. "You've gotten a lot bolder. You're usually the embodiment of submissiveness and sweetness."

"Aren't I supposed to be becoming you?"

I expected her to become angry at my rare moment of talking back, but instead she merely smirked. "Excellent, Anwen. Continue to snap at me; you need the practice."

Now I'd lost my only means of fighting against this scheme: my words. I sighed.

The princess lessons continued—how to walk gracefully, carry myself with poise, speak elegantly, and adopt the princess's habits I'd be expected to emulate. Each chipped away at the former goose girl and handmaiden, molding me to fit a part I didn't want to play, all while the thought of my upcoming deceit and danger clenched my heart. There was no doubt I'd eventually be caught as an imposter, and then Anwen wouldn't just be hidden—she'd *die*.

That thought caused me to slip away at every opportunity and try to take off the ring. With each attempt it awakened from its slumber to sadistically inflict pain that felt like searing fire lapping up my arm, a reminder I was trapped and there was nothing I could do about it. To mask my whimpers, I bit my lip so hard it bled.

"I'm pleased you're being so stubborn, Anwen; it's another trait of mine you'll now be expected to emulate."

I spun around to find the princess smirking in the doorway. "Please take it off."

As usual, my pleas were a waste of breath, for she merely laughed. I made another firm tug on the unyielding ring. It remained fused to my finger. What kind of powerful charm was this?

"Keep trying, Anwen," she said cheerily, as if she found my torment truly amusing. "Perhaps this time you'll manage to break the unbreakable enchantment."

I continued tugging through the pain. "I won't give up. I'm not—willingly tricking—His Highness..." I spoke each word through gritted teeth.

Princess Lavena smirked. "It hurts, doesn't it? It wouldn't if you'd stop fighting it."

I gave another feeble tug. Nothing happened except for another flash of pain and the ring glimmering in the light, as if laughing at my failure; its sadistic satisfaction matched the wicked triumph in the princess's eyes.

"Stop this foolishness, Anwen. It's too late. The wedding is tomorrow."

Tomorrow? The wedding couldn't be here already, not when I was still entangled in the princess's ridiculous scheme. "Please, Your Highness, you can't really expect me to—"

"Stop arguing. I've made up my mind, and your ingratitude at my generosity and your constant badgering is wearying me."

"I'm just trying to be you," I snapped again, but instead of being annoyed like I'd hoped, she only laughed and commenced a review of proper princess behavior. I did badly on purpose, hoping my performance would make her realize how unfit I was for her ridiculous charade, but by her triumphant smirk, I knew she saw through my bluff. Despite my resistance now, we both knew that when the time came, I'd do my best not to get caught. Who needed an enchanted ring when the noose was the best motivator?

LATER THAT EVENING, I packed the princess's things into her trunk in preparation for the morrow while she lay on her bed daydreaming about what she was convinced would be a romantic, magical future, one I was certain would be nothing but a disaster.

"Can you imagine sleeping under the stars every night?" Princess Lavena said with a wistful sigh as I carefully folded another gown that would soon be mine—despite it being far too elegant for me—and placed it into her trunk.

"You hate the outdoors, Your Highness. Imagine: you'll quickly be covered in bug bites from sleeping beneath the stars. The *conenose*—or kissing bugs—are particularly nasty;

they like to feed off the blood around people's mouths, not to mention many spiders are nocturnal—"

"That's quite enough, Anwen." The princess actually looked quite green. "Bugs aside, it's still a romantic notion." But she no longer sounded certain. Perhaps I was finally making progress.

But my hopes were dashed when the princess resumed her gushing about all the wonderful things her new life was sure to bring. I turned my back to her and pretended to rearrange the contents of the trunk so I could roll my eyes without her seeing. I immediately stilled. Such behavior was normally unlike me. Already, I seemed to be becoming the princess. My heart clenched at the thought.

"Your Highness, I truly don't think your minstrel will make you happy. Soon you'll want your old life back."

Her responding sigh was less wondrous and more...sad. I paused in my folding to face her. A shadow had passed across the princess's countenance, one I'd seen several times in the years I'd served her.

"Ever since..." For a moment she was silent before sighing again. "Nothing can make me happy, not anymore, no matter how much I search."

I stared at her, trying to make sense of both her words and the pain filling her eyes. "Your Highness?"

She hastily blinked and the emotion vanished as quickly as it'd arrived. "*Anything* is better than marrying Liam and spending a boring existence as his queen—such a dull responsibility, even worse when I have to give up my pleasures for subjects not my own. Why should I sacrifice my freedom for *them?*"

I hated to admit it, but Draceria would likely be better off without her as their monarch...not that I'd do any better; I didn't expect to survive long enough to find out. Cold fear crept up my spine.

"Please, Your Highness, this is foolish. I'm unfit to be queen."

As always, she waved my pleas aside. "Hurry up and finish so I can check and be sure you haven't secretly packed away any of your ridiculous bug things."

I froze. I'd already hidden a few of my favorite entomology books amongst the princess's things and planned to smuggle my entire collection the moment she went to bed. She frowned at me through narrowed eyes, detecting my guilt.

I slumped in defeat. "I'll keep them locked away."

"That's not good enough," she said. "You're supposed to be becoming me and thus can no longer be interested in your creepy crawlies."

She made it sound so easy to kill parts of oneself and become a different person. "I can't just *stop*."

"You'll have to." The princess stepped forward to rummage through her trunk and withdrew two of my favorite insect anthologies, which she tossed aside. "No more of this nonsense. The moment you leave, your entire collection will be thrown out."

I tightened my jaw. We'd see about that. Princess Lavena eyed my hardened expression and her own softened slightly.

"Stop pouting, Anwen. I have a surprise for you. I've arranged for your brother to be appointed to the position of Royal Hunter. Now he'll be occupied and not even notice your absence."

Archer! In all my worrying about myself I'd failed to consider how my disappearance would affect my only remaining family. "Please, I have to tell him, Your Highness. If I disappear without a word he'll be worried sick."

"He'll be much too busy to worry about you since he'll conveniently be out of the picture. See? I've thought of everything."

Everything but the pain of losing my dearest friend. "Just because you and your brother aren't close doesn't mean—"

"Stop whining, Anwen. I'm not completely heartless; I've arranged for him to meet you in the servants' quarters so that you can say goodbye."

And with that she shooed me away. Tears burned my eyes as I trudged from the room. This would likely be the last time Archer and I ever spoke. My heart ached at the thought of his inevitable worry, but I forced myself to blink my tears away. He couldn't see them, couldn't know anything was amiss, not when I was bound by a magical contract to remain silent.

As I descended to the servants' quarters, I silently said goodbye to everything having to do with Anwen: a brother I cared for, my common status, my fellow servants greeting me by name...I said a longer goodbye to each of my character traits and interests before they too were stolen away forever. I felt as if I were killing off parts of myself, slowly casting away my very identity until Anwen no longer existed.

But I refused to let myself slip away completely. Instead, I'd lock Anwen away in a strongbox buried deep in the recesses of my soul. Knowing a part of me was there would give me enough strength to put on my permanent mask and begin my new identity. But not yet. Right now, I was still Anwen with a beloved brother to see.

My breath hooked when I spotted him waiting for me. I studied him, attempting to memorize each of his features to sustain me for however long my new life of deceit would be. Our features were quite similar—same dark hair and dark eyes—only his expression was drawn and serious, his brow furrowed and his shoulders in a stance that revealed he'd witnessed too much heartache in his life.

But he always had a smile for me. He gave it to me now as he held his arms open. "There's my Anwen. Have you heard of my royal appointment? I'll be going on all sorts of adventures and need a hug from my favorite sister to wish me luck."

I ran into his arms and burrowed myself against him, inhaling his woodsy scent as his firm arms held me close.

"Are you going to miss me, Anwen?" he murmured.

I choked back a sob. I couldn't cry. "You have no idea how much, Archer. I love you."

"And I love you, Pillbug." It had been his nickname for me ever since I'd immersed myself in studying insects, one I'd likely never hear again. "But I'll be back soon. Someone has to keep me out of trouble." He cupped my chin.

If only he knew how much trouble *I* was about to find myself in. The secret burned on my tongue as the princess's ring seared on my finger. I tried to make myself form the words to tell him what was happening to me, but my tongue turned to lead and my words became trapped in my throat, the power of the ring forcing my silence.

"Her Highness informed me of your release," Archer continued. "I'm relieved you're finally free from her, Pillbug."

My stomach jolted. Princess Lavena had said *what?* I yanked away with a gasp. "She's releasing me?"

His brow furrowed. "She hasn't told you? Yes, she said after the wedding she'll no longer have need of you."

Had the princess no compassion? If Archer had believed I was still the princess's servant, my remaining behind in Draceria after her wedding wouldn't have alarmed him, but now he'd return to Lyceria following his upcoming hunt to find I'd vanished.

No, I refused to allow that. I opened my mouth to tell him I'd be remaining in Draceria indefinitely, but the ring brandishing my finger thought even this much information a breach of its sadistic contract. It burned once again, silencing me.

Archer lifted my chin, eyes concerned. "Are you alright, Pillbug? Has the princess been horrible to you again?" As usual, he referred to her like an expletive.

If only he knew just how horrible she was currently being. Frustration swelled within me at my inability to tell him. I burrowed myself against him instead.

He sighed at my silence. "She's awful to you. Whatever your new position, I'm so relieved you'll at least be free of her. With my appointment to the royal hunt, I'll finally earn enough coin so that we can soon return home to our meadow and your geese. It'll be alright, Pillbug."

No, it wouldn't. How agonizing I couldn't even tell him so. I bit the inside of my lip to keep my tears at bay.

"Can you say my name?" I whispered, needing to hear it from him one last time.

"You don't like that nickname anymore? I suppose whether or not I want to admit it, you've grown up."

"I love the nickname," I said. "I hope you always call me that. But I want to remember you saying my name before you leave."

"Very well, Anwen." He kissed the top of my head and released me, obviously feeling he'd been affectionate enough to satisfy his brotherly duty. "I'll return to Lyceria within a fortnight. In the meantime, keep your chin up, Pillbug. Anwen." He gave me one of his rare but sweet smiles before cupping my chin again and leaving. I watched his retreating form, my secret fighting to escape but the enchantment holding it back too powerful a barrier.

And then he was gone.

I finally released my tears as I walked slowly back to Her Highness's quarters. She didn't seem to notice or care that I was crying as I helped her get ready for bed before returning to the tiny room attached to the princess's guest suite.

I stood in the doorway and slowly looked around. I'd

stayed in this room multiple times over the years whenever accompanying the princess on her obligatory visits to Draceria. Despite always hating the room, I suddenly didn't want to let it go, considering it was yet another part of Anwen I was about to lose. I said goodbye to it and everything it contained, each farewell stealing another small portion of myself I didn't want to give up.

I knelt beside my bed and reached beneath it. There I stored my entomology things—my books on insects, each scrimped and saved up for with my minimal wages, treasured and reread dozens of times until I had nearly every word and fact memorized; my glass cases of specimens I'd been collecting my entire life, all carefully categorized and organized; and my notebooks of drawings and observations, chronicled from my childhood until now.

I reverently stroked my books and glass cases before tightening my jaw. I refused to relinquish myself completely. I'd keep my treasures close to me, hidden away so they wouldn't disappear, no matter how much of Anwen did.

I carefully packed my entomology things at the bottom of my trunk. As I clicked the lid shut, the first sense of calm managed to penetrate my frazzled nerves. I wouldn't be lost completely, no matter how much I feared I gradually would be as the princess's plot unfolded.

There were some things even the contract ring couldn't take from me.

CHAPTER 3

The soft rosy light of dawn bathed me in warmth as I sat on Princess Lavena's balcony, hugging my knees to my chest as I watched the sun rise. With the way their golden light erased all evidence of night, for me sunrises had always represented promise...until today, for this sunrise represented not a wondrous beginning but an ending, the day Anwen would officially begin to disappear as she was swallowed up by the princess.

I extended my hand and glared at the ring, my ball and chain. Why did I have to bear such an uncanny resemblance to Princess Lavena? If only the princess had never discovered me all those years ago; then I wouldn't be in this mess now.

I still remembered the day I'd met Princess Lavena. I'd lived in a tiny village nestled amongst rolling green hills in our mountainous kingdom, where my days had been spent outdoors in the sun, surrounded by geese, nature, and of course my favorite insects...until the chance encounter that had changed everything, one the princess had always deemed destiny, but which I considered rotten luck.

During a royal tour five years ago, the princess had

ridden through our village on her majestic white horse, nodding to her subjects with a bored, dutiful expression... until she'd spotted me. She yanked on the reins to stop the royal procession in order to stare at me, her eyes wide with astonishment. Shock rippled over me as I stared back. It was almost like looking in a mirror.

His Highness Crown Prince Nolan noticed his sister's distraction and urged her to resume the procession. She obediently did so, stealing several backward glances at me until she was out of sight.

I'd foolishly thought that encounter would be the only one I'd have with Her Highness, but later that day she managed to track me down while I tended my geese in the meadow surrounding our cottage. The darling, mischievous things waddled around me as I sat with my journal in my lap, eagerly sketching a nearby *cicadellidae* I'd just spotted.

Someone loomed over me, blocking out the light of the sun and casting my sketch in shadow. I looked up and was startled to see Her Highness before me, a mischievous glint in her eyes.

"There you are, peasant girl. I've been searching every-where for you."

I gaped up at her. What was the princess doing here, speaking to *me*? I cast a nervous glance at the guard who'd accompanied her, and he made the motion that I was supposed to rise and curtsy. I hastily stood—causing my journal to slide off my lap—and dipped into an inelegant bob.

Princess Lavena bent down to scoop up my journal. She wrinkled her nose as she examined my drawing. "What's this?"

"A leafhopper, Your Highness." A leafhopper that had sadly hopped away at the princess's arrival, leaving my sketch forever unfinished. "A sharpshooter, specifically."

I bit my tongue to keep my usual monologue about all their fascinating features at bay. The princess obviously didn't care for bugs, as was evident by her disgusted scoff as she roughly flipped through my journal. I ached to snatch it back from her; I clenched my hands to resist the impulse.

"Fascinating," she said in a tone indicating she didn't find it fascinating at all. She tossed my journal aside and stepped closer, her expression bright and eager. "We look very much alike."

The similarities were even more striking up close; we could easily pass for sisters. Uncanny. "Indeed we do, Your Highness."

She smiled but it looked more like a smirk, as if she were plotting something. "It's providence. Thus you must become my new handmaiden."

She wanted me to become *what*? "But Your Highness, I'm a goose girl and couldn't possibly—"

"That wasn't a request but a command," she snapped. "It's a great honor to be selected as my handmaiden, especially for a lowly goose girl such as yourself. So I strongly suggest you silence your protests and accept my generous offer."

I clenched my jaw against the arguments eager to burst free. Because she was a princess I had no choice in the matter.

I'd been serving her ever since. It had quickly become clear why Princess Lavena had been so eager for my appointment: I was to be her reluctant accomplice whenever she desired to take advantage of our strong resemblance, forcing me to take her place whenever she saw fit.

And now, these many years later, we'd make our final switch, this one permanent.

I longed to remain lost in this final sunrise before my life changed forever, but as the sun rose higher in the sky, I was eventually forced to stir. I trudged into Princess Lavena's room, where she waited for me with her usual disapproving scowl.

"Watching the sunrise again, Anwen?"

I closed my eyes to bask in one of the last times I'd ever hear my name.

"I hope you enjoyed it," the princess continued. "Because once you become me, mornings will be a thing of the past." As if mentioning the early hour reminded her of how much she hated them, she yawned.

I gritted my teeth. "I won't give up my sunrises." Especially when I was already forced to give up everything else.

"You have no choice. You'll have to accustom yourself to my habits and begin sleeping in. Surely, you've seen plenty of sunrises to satisfy a lifetime."

Her words were a reminder of one of many things I was giving up with this scheme of hers. "Your Highness, do see sense. You can't toss aside your birthright just because of your distaste for your arranged marriage."

"You're so selfish, Anwen. As if I want to spend my life in a loveless union when I can be free with my minstrel."

Her relationship with her minstrel would likely not last a week. It hadn't taken her past beaus long to realize that the princess's pretty face wasn't worth the trouble. "What will you do once you tire of him?"

"I won't," Princess Lavena said. "He's different than the others."

Why? He possessed a higher tolerance? Doubtful. I gave her a skeptical look.

She shrugged. "Even if I eventually tire of him, I'll just find someone else. *Anyone* is better than Liam; he's so childish. You should be grateful for the opportunity I'm providing for you—it's not every day a common girl can become a princess. This arrangement is perfect for both of us."

No, it was only perfect for *her*. Not only was she putting me in danger, but I had no desire to be a princess. I wanted to continue arguing, but the rest of my protests died in my throat as Princess Lavena tugged me over to her wardrobe and began readying me for the wedding that would seal my fate.

The princess pulled off my handmaiden dress. "After the wedding, you'll immediately leave with your new husband for your honeymoon at the summer palace. I'm so relieved you'll be enduring that instead of me. I can't imagine being stuck at that ancient palace with only Liam's company for an entire month." She wrinkled her nose.

My stomach knotted—not because I disliked the prince, but because the thought of pretending to be someone he hated sounded unbearable. "Surely, a month together is enough time for him to notice our differences. Whatever will I do then?"

The mirror reflected the princess rolling her eyes behind me. "How many times do I have to tell you? He won't. Nobody will."

"Why wouldn't he? I've been in his presence several times while serving as a chaperone for you."

"Yes, but you're a servant. No one notices your kind."

Unfortunately, this argument was all too true. As a servant, I was insignificant and not worth the notice of anyone of the upper class, especially a prince. Once again, my attempts to fight against the princess's ridiculous plan had failed.

I stared gauntly at my reflection as the transformation took place—my servant uniform replaced with a gorgeous silk wedding dress, cosmetics put on my face, the sharp stinging pain as Lavena not-so-gently pierced my ears for pearl earrings, my usual handmaiden bun tugged free, and my thick brown hair twisted into an elegant style. Despite my nerves, I secretly loved the feeling of silk against my skin. Would I ever grow used to it?

Princess Lavena stood back to survey her work with a critical frown. "You look ravishing...except for your hair; I don't quite have your talent. No matter, your veil will cover most of it. Liam wouldn't notice it even if it didn't; he never looks at me. That's why this will work."

"Prince Liam may not notice our switch, but Their Majesties certainly will." It was the biggest flaw in her plan.

"They won't. I've already given them my farewells, you'll be veiled during the wedding, and things will be too hectic after the ceremony for them to greet you."

My heart sank; she'd considered everything. But I refused to give up. "Their Majesties will visit Draceria," I said with more feeling than I felt.

Princess Lavena's hands shook as she pinned the veil into my updo. "My marriage won't make them suddenly eager to spend time with me. In truth, they'll be glad to be rid of me."

"They're your parents, Your Highness."

"That doesn't make any difference." Her voice wavered and she fiddled with her hair, a nervous habit of hers. "I'm merely a means to an end. They don't care for me."

Despite my annoyance with her, sympathy washed over me. Could the princess's habits of constantly finding new men merely be her attempts to seek affection any way that she could? She caught my gaze and her vulnerable expression hardened into a cold mask of indifference.

"They do care for you, Your Highness," I said gently. "Thus they'll visit you, and when they do, they'll detect our switch with a single glance. Any parent would recognize their own child."

The princess ignored my comment and surveyed our reflections standing side by side in the mirror, analyzing them with a critical air. While our features were very similar, they were arranged differently enough to make us not identical. Acquaintances—including Prince Liam—might not be able to decipher the subtle differences in our appearances, but her family and those who knew the princess well would definitely notice I wasn't her. It might not be today, but it would happen, that much was certain. I ached to escape that inevitable fate, but the contract ring tightened around my finger at my desire, representing the noose that would one day be around my neck.

I stared at my reflection as Princess Lavena finished helping me get ready, watching the last bits of me slip away, likely forever. My dangerous charade was about to begin.

I WAITED for my cue to walk down the aisle, squeezing my bouquet of daffodils so tightly I was certain their stems would snap. His Majesty stood beside me, ready to escort me, the veil covering my face my only protection from his discovery. Once again I tried to fight against the power of the ring, but it kept me riveted to the king's side.

I stared desperately at the door, silently pleading for Princess Lavena to return and rescue me from her scheme.

She didn't.

The anxiety knotting my stomach tightened. This was really happening, but it had to be a nightmare. *Wake up, Anwen, wake up.* Unfortunately my horrible situation wasn't a dream, but was instead all too real.

The orchestra began playing, notes that sounded to me like the drones of a funeral procession. Icy fear seeped over me and my feet refused to move. The king hesitated when I did, then gently carried me forward with his stride. Everyone stood and watched as I took one shaky step after another down the endless aisle towards the altar, where His Highness Prince Liam stood waiting for me.

I met his gaze and sucked in a sharp gasp. His entire manner was hardened and twisted in pure hatred. With each step closer to him his glare sharpened, ripping me apart.

I yanked my eyes away but I could still feel his skewering gaze. I looked desperately around the attentive audience, hoping that even through the veil my switch with the princess would be discovered before I became trapped forever. *Someone notice*, I silently pleaded.

No one did.

I was nearly to Prince Liam. I stole another peek at his expression, bracing myself for his viciousness. However, he was no longer looking at me but at his parents, his eyes wide and pleading, his own evident desperation to break free from an arrangement he hadn't asked for either.

But they didn't come to his rescue, just as no one came to mine. We were both trapped, mere pawns entangled in words and contracts not of our making, forced to be bound together forever.

Prince Liam returned his attention to me the moment I reached him. He stiffly lifted my veil and his open hostility melted away as he stared into my eyes, his own frustrated but resolved. A strange energy passed between us as he studied my face, raking his gaze over it, as if searching for something he desperately needed to find.

I waited for his perusal to be finished, my heart hammering and my hands shaking. Despite my earlier misgivings, I still hoped that surely *he'd* notice the switch; he'd been around the princess enough times these past seven years to be able to tell the difference. But he too failed me.

He sighed resolutely and held out his hand. I shakily rested mine in his; he held it loosely, barely touching me. With a sideways glance at one another, we knelt at the altar.

The music ceased, leaving behind silence: the audience's one of anticipation, the one between Prince Liam and me fraught with tension.

The priest's words washed over me as the ceremony began, but I scarcely heard him, only aware of the shudders raking over me and Prince Liam's grazing fingers. I peeked sideways at him. He stared straight ahead, his jaw tight.

As if sensing my gaze, he glanced at me in time to witness the single tear that trickled down my cheek. He narrowed his eyes at it before he sighed and briefly squeezed my fingers before turning back to face the priest, an assurance that he understood my pain, for he undoubtedly felt it, too.

All too soon it was time to recite our vows. My heart pounded frantically. This was really happening, but it *couldn't* be. I tried to make myself speak the words that would expose me before it was too late, but they remained lodged in my throat as the ring burned threateningly on my finger. How could mere metal hold so much power?

"I do." Prince Liam spat out the words venomously. The priest's gaze shifted to me and my insides turned to ice.

"Do you, Your Royal Highness Princess Lavena of Lyceria, take this man, His Royal Highness Crown Prince Liam of Draceria, to be your wedded husband?"

My shakes became tremors and my breathing sharpened. I ached to shake my head, but once again the princess's ring prevented me.

The priest prompted me with his eyes, my cue to say the words that would bind me to this prince, no more than a stranger—a stranger who hated me...or rather who he *thought* was me, which was now essentially the same thing. I couldn't live in such a marriage. But my choice in the matter had been cruelly ripped away, and it was impossible to break free.

31

"I—" No, I couldn't do this. Was there truly no way out? "I—"

Prince Liam glanced at me with a wry smile, as if he sensed my internal struggles. Ever so slightly, understanding softened his eyes, erasing a few of the hard lines of his bitter expression. With it I felt a glimmer of hope. Prince Liam might hate both me and our marriage, but he wasn't a bad person. It was enough to give me the courage to succumb to the ring's power and allow it to push me down a path neither one of us wanted to walk.

"I do." My voice shook as I spoke the words. Prince Liam slumped in defeat.

I scarcely heard the priest's pronouncement that we were husband and wife, only his invitation for us to seal the union with a kiss.

I stiffened and Prince Liam gave me a look like he'd just been asked to kiss a porcupine. With a twisted expression, he leaned over and brushed the briefest touch of his lips along my cheek—scarcely a kiss at all—before he yanked away. We both stood, and still maintaining our loose contact, turned to the applauding crowd.

"Lavena?"

I winced at the new name and turned to face Prince Liam, responding to it for the first time of many to come. "Yes, Your Highness?"

He smiled mockingly, whatever sympathy I'd caught a glimpse of during the ceremony long gone. "Our sentence begins."

Dread pooled in my stomach as he snapped his gaze away. Mere minutes into my forced marriage and it was as awful as I'd feared.

CHAPTER 4

*T*he reception was a lavish affair that took place on the vast grounds of the Dracerian palace, but the elegance, laughter, and delicious food failed to dissipate the suffocating panic squeezing my heart. Thankfully, Prince Liam effortlessly interacted with the well wishers, allowing me to remain silent at his side. I miraculously managed to avoid speaking with Princess Lavena's family—Their Majesties, the King and Queen of Lyceria, and her brother, Crown Prince Nolan—while also failing to be recognized as an imposter by the other guests. But surely it was only a matter of time.

After our obligatory greetings, Prince Liam and I sat together at a private table in stony silence, my new husband looking everywhere but at me. He made no effort to mask his disdain for our match; each stolen glimpse was hardened with cold indifference. When the King of Draceria stood to formally express his pleasure at the union of our two kingdoms, Prince Liam's jaw became taut.

"Prince Liam?" I asked tentatively when his father had sat

down, unable to bear the tense silence any longer. "Are you alright?"

His devastated gaze snapped to mine, sharpening into a glare. "Isn't it obvious how pleased I am with this forced prison sentence?"

I flinched. "But—"

"Don't talk to me," he spat. "Let's not make this any more unbearable than it already is."

I lowered my eyes and obediently fell silent, all while my unhappiness swelled. I remained in this position until the King and Queen of Draceria and Prince Liam's three sisters —the Princesses Rheanna, Aveline, and Elodie—approached our table.

The queen stroked Prince Liam's hair. "How are you holding up, dears?" She glanced towards me, extending the question to both of us.

Prince Liam's jaw tightened but he said nothing. The queen nibbled her lip and cast the king a worried look, who patted his son on the shoulder.

"I know you're unhappy, Son, but we're so proud of you for doing your duty to your kingdom. The union will be a great benefit to the future of the monarchy as well as to our people."

"Oh yes, it'll be a huge benefit to everyone, everyone except *me*."

"Liam, really." The queen cast me an anxious glance before I could hide my wince. Prince Liam glanced at me with a small frown, as if surprised by my reaction. A look that almost seemed like regret flittered over his face before it disappeared.

"I'm only speaking the truth. Lavena feels the same way I do, so there's no sense pretending either one of us is happy about this marriage."

The king cast me an awkward glance. "A piece of advice,

Son: the happiness of a union is mostly determined by the wife, so despite the circumstances, do try to please her as much as possible."

Prince Liam said nothing, but remained rigid as his family hugged him goodbye and wished us a pleasant honeymoon with doubtful tones.

"They look on the brink of murdering each other already," Princess Elodie whispered unquietly to her sisters as they left. "Who do you think will act first?" They faded into the crowd before I could hear their bets.

With an unhappy sigh I returned to picking at my food, the nausea swirling my stomach making it impossible to eat any of it. It escalated the longer the silence festered between us. The few feet of distance between me and the man I now called husband felt like miles, insurmountable to cross. Occasionally, I caught Prince Liam watching me, brow puckered. There was one moment when I was certain he was bracing himself to speak, but before he could, Crown Prince Deidric of Sortileya and his wife, Princess Eileen, approached.

Prince Deidric glanced warily at me before forcing a smile for his friend. "I'm uncertain what greeting to extend when congratulations are clearly not welcome. How are you doing?"

Prince Liam sent me another skewering glare, causing me to sink several inches in my seat. "What do you think?" he spat.

"I see." Prince Deidric exchanged a wary glance with his wife, as if seeking guidance on how to proceed. "I'm truly sorry, Liam."

"Being sorry doesn't change my fate."

"I know." He patted Prince Liam on the back and leaned down, lowering his voice to a whisper. "Perhaps you can simply avoid each other, one of the advantages of living in a palace."

Misery clawed at my heart at the suggestion. Being forced to play a part the rest of my life would be even more unbearable if I had to do it while being ignored and unloved.

"I can't believe it actually happened," Prince Liam continued, talking as if I wasn't even there, obviously practicing for our marriage. "It's going to be torture, for I'm the prisoner and she's the jailer."

Princess Eileen gasped at the biting insult, and even Prince Deidric winced. Prince Liam gave me a challenging look that clearly said, "your move" in this twisted game he and Princess Lavena often played.

The ring promptly stirred. I felt it take control of my tongue and try to force me to return his attack...but my resistance kept the retort temporarily at bay. No, I wouldn't give in. I felt as if I stood at a crossroads in impersonating Princess Lavena: I could either succumb to the ring's power, changing everything about myself in order to fit her character completely, or change only enough to ward off suspicion. The ring might force me to insult the prince should I open my mouth, but it couldn't fight against my silence.

I tilted my head at Prince Liam before looking away without saying anything. The ring throbbed in protest, but the pain was bearable enough to be worth enduring, considering it meant I'd won this particular battle between us.

Princess Lavena would have never backed down from the opportunity to insult the prince with biting words of her own, but despite being forced to pretend otherwise, I wasn't Princess Lavena, and she wasn't the one experiencing this marriage. How I navigated these raging waters would determine how rocky the relationship with my new husband would be, and the Anwen still alive within me wanted to make them as smooth as possible.

After Princess Eileen gave her goodbyes and Prince Deidric extended a small nod, they departed. I summoned enough bravery to risk another glance at Prince Liam. He was frowning at me, brows furrowed, before he looked away with a puzzled shake of his head.

I returned my attention to nervously watching the Lycerian Royal Family sitting only a few tables away with the Dracerian Royal Family, all seeming pleased that the coveted union between their kingdoms had finally been accomplished. Although Princess Lavena had assured me she'd already given her family her goodbyes, I wasn't convinced they'd avoid the opportunity to see their daughter one last time before the honeymoon. If they did...this charade would end before it'd even begun.

They rose and I stiffened. Were they coming over? I twisted my napkin in my lap as I watched them smile and greet their guests, my pulse palpitating as they inched ever closer to us. At first Prince Liam ignored my wriggling, but soon my nerves caught even his indifferent notice.

He sighed. "Come now, Lavena, do stop fidgeting. Despite our beliefs to the contrary, this isn't a death sentence."

I tried to relax but stiffened all over again as Crown Prince Nolan broke away from the king and queen and approached. Surely he wasn't coming to greet me? My stomach plummeted. He was.

A tight, overly polite smile penetrated his usual serious expression. "I'd be remiss as an older brother if I didn't come to wish the newlyweds well, even though I know such a sentiment has no place in this union." He rested his hand on Prince Liam's shoulder and gave him a sympathetic look, which was returned with a grimace. "My sister fights dirty, but I'm placing my bet on you. Will you be challenging that, Lavena?" He turned to face me.

At first he merely stared, expression bewildered, before

his eyes widened in shock. Unsurprisingly, he'd noticed our switch, just as he always had at the court functions where the princess had forced me to take her place. He'd gone along with those past schemes, kindly helping me navigate the world of protocol and elegance so I wouldn't get caught.

I wasn't sure what his reaction would be now. Pretending to be Princess Lavena for a few hours was nothing compared to taking her place in an arranged marriage created by a political contract between two kingdoms.

A long, tense moment passed between us, during which I could see Prince Nolan's thoughts racing as he scrambled for his next move.

Prince Liam's gaze flickered to him. "What is it? You're acting as if you've never seen your sister before."

Prince Nolan managed to snap his mouth shut, but even then it took him a moment to find his voice. "*Anwen?*"

I squeezed my eyes shut with a groan. As predicted, my exposure hadn't taken long.

Prince Liam frowned. "Who's Anwen?"

Prince Nolan forced a smile for my new husband. "No one of consequence, just someone I spotted in the crowd. I'll greet her after extending my congratulations."

Understanding filled his gaze as it lowered to the ring adorning my finger. Surely he'd free me from this mess now that he realized my plight. After all, he had a duty to his family, his crown, his kingdom, and the contract that would benefit his future reign. Thus he'd find Princess Lavena and switch us back. Nobody would ever need to know what had happened.

I held my breath as Prince Nolan considered, studying first Prince Liam, then me, his look thoughtful. I stared back with wide eyes, silently pleading for him to help me. Mischief filled his gaze. He nodded to himself before offering me a wink and a smile. What did *that* mean?

He turned to Prince Liam. "Actually, I was merely jesting before about placing bets on which of you would murder the other first."

Prince Liam cocked an eyebrow. "You don't think we'll kill one another? Because I believe it. Widowhood sounds more ideal than a life with *her*." He glared at me. I flinched at the attack.

Prince Nolan cast me a sympathetic glance. "Don't talk about my sister that way. Despite your assumptions, Lavena is actually a charming and sweet girl."

Prince Liam snorted. Prince Nolan gave me a "this will be quite the challenge for you to prove him wrong" sort of look.

"You'll see soon enough. Lavena's hostile behavior came from wanting the freedom to choose whom to marry and thus she pretended to be...not herself. But now that this union has gone through, you'll discover that your new wife is quite different from the woman you believe her to be."

He winked again. In that wink I fully realized what Prince Nolan was doing. Panic tightened my chest. He had no intention of rescuing me; he was *playing along*. Oh no, he couldn't. He was my only chance of escaping both this scheme and the noose and I wasn't going to lose it.

"Prince Nolan," I said through my teeth, my voice pleading.

He cocked an eyebrow. "*Prince* Nolan? Come now, Lavena, there's no need for formality, despite this being a formal event."

"*Nolan*," I said, hating to drop his title but having no choice. "Please, Nolan. *Please*."

"I know you're nervous about this arrangement, dear sister." Another conspiratorial wink. "But not to worry; I have a good feeling about it."

Prince Liam rolled his eyes. "You're delusional."

"Not in the least. I promise you'll soon find yourself

pleasantly surprised." Prince Nolan glanced between us once again before nodding. "Yes, I truly believe you two will work."

Prince Liam glared at me once again, his protest against such a statement. I withered, sinking a few more inches in my seat.

"Be good to her," Prince Nolan said firmly. "She deserves nothing but kindness." He started to depart but paused, eyes widening as he stared into the crowd. "Mother and Father are coming to say their goodbyes. I advise you take your leave while I make your excuses to hold them off. Good luck, you two, especially you, *Lavena* dear. Trust me: all will be well, you'll see."

With that, he hurried off to intercept the King and Queen of Lyceria, leaving me staring after him in disbelief and frustration that my only source of escape had slipped away without coming to my aid. What could his motive possibly be for playing along? Did he really think now was a good time to play matchmaker? Surely it'd be in his best interest to expose the charade before it went any further.

I was tempted to go after him and demand not only an explanation but that he help me wriggle out of this mess before it was too late, but he'd already disappeared in the crowd. True to his word, he managed to stave off the king and queen, and soon an announcer informed the reception guests that we were leaving for our honeymoon.

Prince Liam sighed and swiveled around to face me, his expression no longer hard but weary, as if the reception had been just as draining for him as it'd been for me.

"Are you ready to leave?" His tone was absent its earlier venom, a small miracle. He didn't wait for me to respond before motioning me towards the carriage that would take us to our month-long honeymoon, the beginning of what promised to be a rocky marriage.

Liam pressed his hand against the base of my back as lightly as possible in order to escort me to the awaiting carriage. He briefly took my hand to help me inside—releasing it the moment I'd settled—before scrambling in after me.

The carriage clattered out of the palace gates. The moment we passed them, I released a pent-up breath at the same time he did. Our gazes briefly met before we both hastily looked away, him with a disdainful twist to his mouth, me with an embarrassed blush tickling my cheeks.

Silence filled the chasm between us, magnified in the confines of the carriage. I ached to do something to bridge the distance and dissipate the suffocating tension, but Prince Liam appeared content with the quiet, seeming to have lost all motivation to pay me any attention now that we found ourselves away from prying eyes.

I sat rigid in my seat, clutching at the velvet upholstery with my sweaty and shaking hands, all while fighting the moisture stinging my eyes. I stole several glances at Prince Liam—so cold, formidable, and unapproachable. I soon noticed him stealing several glances towards me in return, the hard lines of his face growing more and more stern with each one.

He finally fully faced me with a long sigh. "You seem a bit tense and much more quiet than you usually are. It's not often you miss an opportunity to fight with me."

I said nothing, certain if I opened my mouth, the sob I'd been fighting to suppress would tumble out.

The prince's brows squashed together as he studied me more closely. "Are you...frightened?"

Yes, but not of him, despite his open hostility. During my service to the princess, I'd had many opportunities to observe Prince Liam, enough to know that he was a kind and good man. Whenever he wasn't around Princess Lavena, he was an entirely different person—one who was full of life and laughter. Princess Lavena was the only person I'd ever seen him behave differently towards.

And she was the person he believed me to be, a fact which only intensified my fear of our future together. I was a handmaiden who'd married a prince in a princess's place. I felt I was drowning.

His sigh tore me from my thoughts. "So it's to be the silent treatment? Is that the game you want to play now? It's always one with you. Only a few hours into our marriage and already it's oh-so-pleasant. I knew you'd be difficult."

My whimper escaped, as did a single tear that trickled embarrassingly down my nose. His breath hooked but I didn't await his response.

I scooted into the corner to rest my head against the windowpane to stare out at the rolling hills of the Dracerian countryside, scenery that reminded me of the cottage nestled in the meadow where I'd grown up. Fierce homesickness for my old life pierced my heart. I wanted my childhood home, my simple life, Archer and my long-deceased parents, my geese...but most of all I wanted my identity, already gone, considering my sole companion knew me by a different one entirely.

"Lavena?" He said my new name hesitantly, as if he was doubting my identity along with me. I peeked at him and was startled by the remorse filling his features. "Are you crying because of...*me*?"

I knew the silent treatment was unfair. "This isn't a game to me. Truly, Prince Liam."

His lips quirked up on one side while he cocked a single eyebrow on the other. "*Prince* Liam? Goodness, such formality between husband and wife."

"I'm sorry," I said hastily, silently cursing myself for my faux pas. I twisted the ring Princess Lavena had forced onto my finger, aching to yank it off. I was already weary of the tension festering between us, and the charade and only just begun. Could I survive this?

He frowned. "You apologized." His brows squashed together but he seemed to have no further comment.

I turned back to the window. Several more moments of silence stretched between us, measured by each turn of the carriage wheels carrying us towards our new life together, one that had already started off all wrong.

"I'm sorry, too."

I glanced back over. "For what?"

He clenched and unclenched the ends of his shirt, his knuckles white. "For being rude. I'm always rude to you."

"As am I." For I'd heard enough stories about his and Princess Lavena's interactions—not to mention witnessed several confrontations myself—to know she held equal blame for the contention in their relationship.

He tilted his head, studying me closely. "You're…different."

I stiffened. Oh no, he'd already discovered I was an imposter. I knew this scheme wouldn't work; the princess was a fool to believe it possibly could. It was impossible for anyone to become another person.

My heart pounded wildly as I braced myself for his accusations. Prince Liam continued studying me closely, as if trying to pry my secrets from the recesses of my soul.

"Yes, from the moment of our wedding, you've seemed…altered."

I swallowed, not trusting myself to speak.

"I can't quite pinpoint how, exactly." He drummed his fingers on his knee as he continued to peruse me. "But something is…off."

"Really?" I could barely squeeze the word past my dry throat. My shaking hands groped for the carriage door handle to steady myself. He leaned forward and rested his hand over mine to pull it away. An unexpected jolt rippled over me at his touch. He hastily withdrew his hand.

"Perhaps this marriage, as undesirable as it is, will hopefully not be as bad as we both fear."

"I hope so too, Your Highness, but—"

"*Your Highness?* Lavena, please, this formality must stop."

Another mistake. I leaned on my elbows to bury my forehead in my hands. "This is such a disaster."

He actually chuckled. "It is, isn't it? Two enemies bound together forever."

"*Enemies?* Is that what we are? Are we to draw up battle plans and spend the rest of our marriage at one another's throats?"

His eyes widened. "Don't you hate me?"

"*No!* Do you hate *me?*" The tears I'd fought so hard to keep back finally escaped. Prince Liam scrambled to my seat and hovered over me before awkwardly patting my back.

"I'm a dunderhead," he murmured. "A few hours in and I make my wife cry."

"A few hours in and my husband hates me."

"I don't hate you," he said hastily, his tone making his words sound like a question. "Really, Lavena. I thought you hated me. We've never exactly gotten along."

"Because we've never even tried."

To my amazement, Prince Liam cupped my chin to tilt my head up and carefully dried my eyes with his handkerchief. The gesture was so incredibly sweet my tears nearly overcame me again.

"We haven't, have we? We've done a pretty good job of avoiding one another. I've never wanted this arrangement, Lavena. You were never meant to be my wife, but Kian's."

It took me a moment to remember that Kian was the deceased Crown Prince of Draceria—Liam's older brother and Princess Lavena's original fiancé. "I didn't want this arrangement either." Especially since it placed me in such a dangerous situation.

He managed a wry smile. "I know. You've made your opinion clear many times."

"As have you." I shuddered as the Lavena-like accusation escaped, causing the ring to purr in approval. Already parts of her identity were eclipsing mine. "I'm sorry," I said hastily, as if my apology would allow me to snatch whatever portion of myself remained before I disappeared forever. "I didn't mean that."

Prince Liam stared at me as if he'd never seen me before. "You apologized again. I mean…" He pressed his fingers to the bridge of his nose, as if trying to ward off a headache. He took a deep breath. "Right. Let's confront this arrangement head on."

I wrinkled my nose. "Head on?"

"Yes, we must face the situation directly. Fact number one: you and I don't like one another."

"I don't hate you," I contradicted, ignoring the flash of pain my rebellion against the ring caused.

"I didn't say hate, but you must admit we haven't exactly been hiding our dislike for one another."

I ached to deny it, for it was *Princess Lavena* who didn't like him, not me. I hated being so misrepresented. It was all I could do to bite my tongue to stifle my protests.

"Now." He playfully tapped my nose. "Fact number two: You and I are stuck together, whether we like it or not. But while I'm many things, I'm not dishonorable. I'll be faithful to whatever *this* is. Will you? I know you're rather…" He bit his lip.

Heat flashed through me. Yes, Princess Lavena was *that* way, but that was not a trait I'd pretend was mine for one moment. "I'm honorable, too. I've not had exploits before you, and I certainly won't have them now that we're married."

The ring heated once more, warning me to watch what I said. I swallowed the rest of my adamant denial.

"That would be wrong," I finished weakly.

He gaped at me for a moment before blinking rapidly. "I see." He cleared his throat awkwardly. "So, we both intend to be faithful to whatever *this* is." He waved his hand between us.

"Of course."

Up went his eyebrow. "So we have that in common, at least. It's a start. I'm still not happy about this, but I'll do my best."

"As will I." For whether I was Princess Lavena or Anwen, I couldn't live in a loveless union for as long as it took the princess to come to her senses.

"Then it's decided." Prince Liam turned towards the window, signaling the end of our conversation.

I pressed my face against the glass and spent the rest of the carriage ride watching the sun lower over the rolling hills. My breath caught when the Dracerian summer palace loomed into view, a vision of white marble and splendor, cast in a sheen of ruby and gold from the setting sun. The carriage clattered through the gates and rolled to a stop in front of the towering oak front doors. Prince Liam descended and helped me down, looping my arm through his to escort me up the steps.

A bowing footman opened the door for us. "Welcome, Your Highnesses."

I stiffened at the address and forced myself to nod in reply.

Prince Liam led me upstairs towards the bedrooms, and too late I remembered that with marriage came...my stomach jolted. *Oh no.* We couldn't. I wasn't ready, we were still strangers, and I wasn't even sure we were legally married. No, no, no, no...

Prince Liam paused outside a door and gave me a shy and awkward look. My chest tightened. "This is where I leave you."

"You mean we're not—"

He shook his head. "Not tonight. We should wait until we can at least tolerate one another."

I released my sigh of relief in a whoosh. "Thank heavens."

He actually laughed, a light, bouncing sound that filled me with warmth. "I thoroughly agree. I told you I was honorable, Lavena. You really think I'd..."

I shrugged. "You're a man."

He pursed his lips, obviously to contain his laughter. "Not so much so that I'd ever consider...I mean, I've waited this long, I'd rather wait longer so it might at least be bearable. Wouldn't you?"

"Do you think it ever could?"

"Well, I'll need an heir eventually..." He blushed and seemed to take great interest in the ornate rug lining the marble corridor. "But I don't need one now. So we should wait. I'm not asking for a miracle, but for the first time, I feel a glimmer of hope that this won't be as torturous as I anticipated."

I managed a small smile, my first since this entire nightmare had started. "I have hope, too. Only a sweet man would dry one's tears."

He seemed startled by my compliment before he slowly returned my smile, a crooked one that lit up his eyes, and in that moment I felt something pass between us, something warm and bright.

"Thank you, Lavena. I wish you a pleasant night." He bowed before entering his room. I slipped into the adjoining one and leaned against the closed door, trying to settle my

frantic heartbeat as the emotions from the day finally overcame me.

I collapsed face-down onto my bed and broke into shuddering sobs. I felt hopelessly lost and unsure how to navigate
the waters ahead, while another part of me remembered
Prince Liam's smile, the way he'd dried my tears, and his
contagious laugh. If that Liam could always exist, then could
this arrangement possibly not be as unbearable as I'd feared?

CHAPTER 5

*W*hen I first awoke the following morning I forgot where I was. I stared up at the lacy canopy hanging above me as I ran my fingers across the satin sheets. The bed was incredibly soft, like lying on goose feathers. When had I ever slept so soundly? I blinked sleepily before rolling over. Rosy, golden dawn tumbled from the window in shimmering dappled patterns across the lush rugs and spacious room. Where was I?

And then I remembered.

Disoriented, I sat up with a gasp and found a maid stoking the fire, a job that, up until this morning, I'd always performed for Princess Lavena. She startled at my sudden movement and blinked at me in surprise before sweeping into a grand curtsy.

"Forgive me, Your Highness, I didn't mean to disturb you. I was informed you were a heavy and late sleeper."

She said it like a question, obviously doubting herself at seeing me awake so early. While that was true for Princess Lavena, I was used to rising with the sun in order to begin a long day serving Her Highness. But that time had passed;

now servants were serving *me*. Being a princess would take some getting used to.

The maid wrung her hands as she anxiously awaited my reply. By the stiffness in her posture, she'd undoubtedly been informed of Princess Lavena's foul temper when woken too early—a temper the ring encouraged me to unleash. But despite its insistence the words wouldn't come, for I was not Her Highness. Even though I knew I had a part to play, I couldn't bring myself to be outright rude.

"It's quite alright." Confusion lined the maid's brow at what was likely a much softer answer than she'd expected. The ring flared in protest, and I found myself narrowing my eyes. "See that you exercise caution in the future."

I gasped at the words and the cold tone that had accompanied them, both of which seemed to have tumbled out beyond my control. I gave a dismissive wave of my hand, cringing when the gesture was obeyed. Only hours into the charade and I already loathed it.

She paused in the doorway. "Will you be returning to sleep, Your Highness, or would you like me to bring you a breakfast tray?"

Despite the unusual drowsiness suddenly pressing against my senses—undoubtedly the ring's doing as it encouraged me to adopt the princess's late-lie-in habits—I wouldn't waste another moment in bed. "I fancy an early morning stroll before breakfast." The princess had occasionally gone on those for it to not be entirely out of character...although her definition of *early* greatly differed from mine.

She blinked in astonishment. Whatever warnings she'd received about Princess Lavena, I was doing a terrible job of living up to them. But my nerves were too frazzled to even try to pretend. Perhaps a brisk walk in the crisp summer morning followed by a good breakfast would grant me the motivation to better play my part.

The maid bustled towards the wardrobe for a gown. Great, now it was my turn to be dressed up. It turned out to be as awkward as I'd always imagined. Luckily, the maid worked quickly and efficiently, dressing me in a fern-green satin gown—and while it fit me perfectly considering Princess Lavena had put me to work doing up all her hems to make up for my slightly shorter height, I wasn't used to its tight and confining feel. I pressed a hand to my chest and struggled to breathe. How would I ever get used to such an outfit?

After the maid styled my hair in a simple but elegant twist, I escaped the confines of my room and managed to find my way outside. I tipped my head back and breathed in the brisk air, full of the scent of blossoms and morning dew. I basked in the sun warming my face and the cool breeze caressing my cheeks. The early morning stillness had always been my favorite time of day, when the world was awakening and the day was fresh and new.

I managed to stir in order to explore the pathways that twisted through the magnificent gardens, observing not the flora but the insects. Morning was the best time to study them, for the cooler temperatures of night combined with the dew covering their wings prevented them from flying away, thus allowing me the opportunity to examine them more closely.

I paused when I spotted a dragonfly resting on a leaf, its wings lightly coated in moisture. From its coloring, I could tell it was a species I'd never seen before. Fascinating. As I debated whether I could get away with sitting on the damp lawn in my fancy dress in order to get a closer look, footsteps sounded on the cobblestones behind me. I swiveled around just as Prince Liam appeared at the end of the path.

He froze when he saw me, looking startled. "Lavena?" No

"good morning," no inquires on how I slept, just my name given like an expletive. I smiled anyway.

"Good morning, Prince Liam." I had to catch myself before I curtsied out of habit.

He eyed my smile suspiciously before he frowned. "*Prince* Liam? You do love riling me in the most subtle ways."

My smile vanished. *Wait, what?* "You think I'm trying to upset you?"

"You always do."

Awkward silence choked the chilly air, making it feel as if miles existed between us rather than mere feet. I fidgeted with my ring, desperately trying to find something to say to dispel the brewing tension. I thought we'd made progress yesterday. Now that hope was rapidly evaporating.

"I don't understand," I finally managed. "Last night in the carriage—"

He gave me a mocking smile. "Oh yes, the carriage ride. I did fall into your trap quite easily, but the morning has put everything back into perspective. The more I think about it, the more I realize how out of character you were behaving. There's only one explanation for it: it was all an act."

I frantically shook my head. "No, Prince Liam."

"See? Calling me *Prince* Liam is only a continuation of this new game of yours." He furrowed his brow. "Why are you awake so early? Can't wait to get started on finding ways to make me miserable, *Princess* Lavena?"

I winced. "I know you rise early," I said slowly, analyzing each word before I spoke, trying to discern if he could twist it to fit his dark perception of Princess Lavena, now *me*. The fact he thought so ill of me was torturous.

He shrugged. "Don't get up early on my account. I was actually pleased at the thought of not having to hide from you during the blessed hours you slept in."

Once again I cringed. I struggled to speak past the tears

clogging my throat. "I was hoping to see you. I thought we could have breakfast together."

He shook his head in a jerky movement. "I've already eaten."

My heart sank. "Oh."

He studied my expression with a thoughtful pucker. "You really thought I'd want to eat breakfast with *you*?"

"I just thought...we could at least try to..." I trailed off.

He folded his arms and surveyed me with a sharp, penetrating look. "This is another example of your behaving entirely out of character. The Lavena I know would be avoiding me as much as I'd be avoiding her. You're definitely up to something, but I'm on my guard now and won't fall for it."

My panic swelled. "You think I've been pretending?"

He smirked. "Surprised? I'm certain you think me gullible enough to fall for your tricks, but I've won this round. But don't fret, you're still emerging from this confrontation with a prize: congratulations on ruining my morning. I'll take my leave before you make any more of my day unpleasant." He performed a stiff, mocking bow and began walking away.

Desperation caused me to step forward. "When do you take lunch?"

"I don't want to eat lunch with you."

"Dinner, then?"

He released a long breath through his teeth and considered. "I expect my parents will want a report on my *efforts* in this blasted arrangement. Fine, I'll see you at dinner, though I'm not looking forward to it."

He left the garden without another word. My heart twisted as I watched his retreating form. I supposed it'd been unrealistic to expect to erase seven years of animosity between Prince Liam and Princess Lavena so easily, but now I realized it would be far more difficult than I'd anticipated.

Not only did I have to pretend to be someone else, but I now had to take responsibility for all the hurt, anger, and hatred that had festered between the prince and princess for years and somehow make up for it.

The beginnings of a headache pulsed against my temples. The task felt utterly impossible.

~

GROWING UP, whenever I'd imagined marriage, I'd envisioned a union full of love and happiness like my parents shared, not the torturous experience this was. It grew so unbearable I actually tried several times to leave, testing the limits of the ring, but each attempt caused immobilizing pain that kept me ensnared within the palace grounds.

The first several days of our marriage were horrible—full of loneliness, tears, and tension, each day nearly impossible to endure. I alternated my time between trying to bridge the vast distance between me and my husband and frantically raiding the library for any information about the contract ring binding me to this union.

My research proved futile. The books in the summer palace were mostly antiquated, obsolete volumes from when the palace had been the primary residence of the royal family several hundred years ago. Many of the books contained information on the surrounding kingdoms, including Lyceria, as well as details about ancient contracts, but I could find no information on the centuries-old contract ring. Still I forged ahead, spending several hours a day searching for any way to escape my sentence.

After several days combing the shelves, I finally gave up trying to find a way to overcome the ring's power and instead spent all my efforts trying to soften my new husband —a quest made more difficult since he didn't seem bothered by the tense state of our relationship. He couldn't seem to let go of his assumption that my efforts were insincere and calculated to hurt him. Thus he responded to each of my attempts with coldness, sharp glares, or ignoring me completely.

Feeling more trapped than ever, I locked myself in my room and wrote a desperate letter to Prince Nolan demanding an explanation for his playing along with the princess's scheme and requesting his assistance in getting me out of it. I pleaded for him to find Princess Lavena and help us trade places before Prince Liam or anybody else became suspicious. I sent the letter with little hope, but it did ease some of the anxiety tightening my chest to have done *something* to try and escape my predicament, no matter how small.

Despite Prince Liam's continued animosity, my resolve to improve my marriage remained. I fought against the ring's attempts to get me to sleep in and managed to wake up early each morning to take breakfast with him. Rather than the gesture improving our relationship, he viewed it as another move in what he considered our cruel game and retaliated by getting up even earlier in order to avoid me. Even on days I managed to eat with him, all my "good mornings" and attempts at conversation remained stubbornly unacknowledged.

Prince Liam wasn't the only source of contention. I felt as if the ring and I were engaged in a constant tug-of-war between emulating the princess's rude behavior and my fighting to maintain any sense of myself. I faltered several times, and with each biting retort the ring forced from me, the more Prince Liam became convinced my kindnesses were nothing more than an act.

But the more I fought to resist the ring's power, the more I emerged as conquerer in our battle of wills, and the less the ring seemed to fight me, as if my determination to maintain myself was causing it to lose strength. Yet this success didn't fully usurp its control over me and did nothing to lessen the contention between Liam and myself.

Still I pressed forward. I watched him at every opportunity, trying to glean any information about my husband that I could and showing kindness to him whenever possible. My favorite place to observe him from was the window seat of my bedroom, where I could watch him in the garden below. During those times and while witnessing his interactions with the servants, my earlier conclusions were confirmed— he was a kind, thoughtful man, always ready to offer others an easy smile. He was also full of life and boundless energy, which he tried to expend in his frequent outdoor walks, hours of horseback riding, and restless pacing of the corridors after long periods of sitting.

These glimpses—as well as my favorable memories of him prior to our marriage whenever he hadn't been around Princess Lavena—gave me hope and renewed my determination to forge a friendship with my husband. This was the true Prince Liam, a man I ached to know personally—a wish that would be impossible with his determination to remain distant from me.

But despite his open disdain, I couldn't help but admire him. Like myself, he was trapped in a loveless and forced union, an arrangement likely more suffocating for one who loved life as he did than it was for me. Although he was clearly unhappy about the arrangement, he did offer me occasional moments of softness--respecting me enough to stand when I entered a room, helping me with my chair, and never raising his voice or physically hurting me.

Yet these few tender mercies didn't dispel his coldness, the hatred filling his eyes, and his mocking smiles whenever he delivered a particularly biting blow with his words. I endured all of this along with our tense, silent meals and his continued avoidance. I felt like I was slowly dying from neglect with each passing day. I couldn't live like this.

Eventually, Prince Liam grew tired of the silent treatment and came up with a new game. The evening that marked our week anniversary, I entered the dining room for dinner to discover parchment, quill, and ink midst the dishes of steaming food.

"Good evening, Liam." As usual I didn't expect a response. To my surprise, one came—in the form of a scornful smile.

"For once it is a good evening, Lavena, for now it's *my* turn for a move."

I crinkled my nose. "A move?"

"Yes, one for this game we're playing. Have a seat and I'll explain."

Trepidation knotted my stomach as I shakily accepted his invitation. The look in Prince Liam's eyes was calculating, with no sign of the sweet, jovial man I'd caught glimpses of whenever I spied on him.

He steepled his fingers and leaned forward. "You've tried to best me with your own game of supposed sweetness, but as you are about to find out, I don't go down without a fight. Thus it's my turn to play one with you. Seems only fair in this war of ours, wouldn't you say?"

"Please, Liam, I don't want to play these games with you." Even in my desperation I managed to remember to omit the *prince* before his name, hoping doing so would appease him. Unsurprisingly, like all my efforts, this one too proved futile.

"Come, Lavena, stop pretending. We both know what you're really doing."

"I'm sincere in that I don't like fighting with you. Really, Liam."

He snorted. "You truly think that after seven years I'll believe you've had a sudden change of heart?"

No, I didn't, but I still hoped. I couldn't bear the thought of being trapped in a loveless union with a man who hated me just for the sport of it. But I was. Everything was such mess.

I twisted the ring, aching to yank it off. "Things are different now. I want us to work. Please believe me."

"I can't. What are your words now compared to your past actions?"

"But what of my current actions?" I asked. "Do they mean nothing? I'm trying to show you I feel differently, that *I'm* different. My actions before the wedding don't matter."

"You're wrong; they do, for I remember all of them." He tapped the side of his head. "Believe me, not a single memory is pleasant. Now, shall we begin?"

He gestured to the parchment in front of me, which contained a map of the summer palace. Liam twirled his quill between his fingers with another mocking smile that didn't at all light up his eyes.

"Before our *marriage*"—his mouth twisted on the word —"we engaged in a war simply for the pleasure of hurting one another. Now that we're forcibly *attached*"—he spat this word like a curse and my heart constricted—"I thought it time we change tactics on how we fight this war of ours."

I shook my head. "Please, Liam."

As usual he ignored me. He dipped his quill into the inkwell. "I thought we could draw up battle plans. First, let's select our weapons. Mine up until this point have admittedly been rather weak: silence and avoidance, whereas yours has been fake kindness." He scribbled these down. "Do you have anything to add, Lavena?"

I bit the inside of my lip to keep my burning tears at bay and shook my head.

"Let's discuss strategy." His tone was that of a military general discussing plans for going into battle. "I've wielded my weapon of retreating in order to survive, but you seem determined to track me down in my strongholds, obviously luring me into a false sense of security before going in for the kill. You're a formidable opponent, Lavena, I'll give you that."

My escalating tears clogged in my throat, making it difficult to breath. I bit my lip harder until it bled.

"Shall we divide our territory?" He snatched the map and began to draw rigid strokes. "I'll take the west side of the palace and you can take the east. The only neutral territory is this dining room, where we're forced to interact at least once a day, but after that, we agree not to cross enemy lines. I'll draw up a formal contract and we can—Lavena?"

Liam had been so caught up in his speech that he hadn't even realized until now that I was crying, having lost the battle against my emotions as Liam discussed the battle plans for our marriage. His quill slipped through his fingers as his gaze followed each tear that trickled down my cheek.

"Lavena?" He hesitated. "Are these tears real or are you just trying to manipulate me into giving you a bigger area of the palace for your territory—"

"Are these tears *real*?" My voice shook. "How can you even ask that?"

Liam swallowed. "Then they're—"

"How can they be anything *but* real with the cruel way you've been treating me?" I stuttered. "But you don't want them to be real; you only want to believe they're merely a ploy in this ridiculous game you think we're playing. But I can't live like this anymore. I've shown you nothing but kindness since our wedding, but you seem determined to make our marriage miserable. Why does it baffle you that I want more than to be enemies with my husband?"

"Lavena, I—"

But I couldn't hear any more of his biting words. I'd finally had enough. I jostled the table as I stood, knocking over a pitcher of water, which soaked his battle plans, smearing the ink so that the territory lines began to disappear. He also stood, reaching for me, eyes wide with remorse.

"Lavena...I'm sorry."

I picked up my napkin and flicked it in the air like a white flag. "I surrender. You've clearly won the war. I hope you enjoy your prize. I'm not even sure what you were fighting for. Loneliness? Misery? A loveless, tense union? If so, then I've clearly won, too, because that's all this is and apparently all it ever will be."

I threw my napkin on the table and strode towards the door.

"I don't want this," Liam called after me. "I've never wanted *this*."

I turned to see his wide, glassy eyes, full of vulnerability and his own fierce unhappiness.

"Neither do I," I said. "But now that we have this, you don't seem to want to make it anything different."

I left the dining room and pressed myself against the wall near the doorway to take several shuddering breaths, allowing my pain to wash over me. When I finally stirred, I risked a single glance back into the dining room. Liam had sunk into his seat and buried his forehead in his hands, his face twisted in despair. Despite the hurt still encasing my heart, sympathy for him pierced my defenses.

CHAPTER 6

The following morning, I startled when I opened my bedroom door and discovered Liam nervously waiting for me. He blushed the moment he saw me and lowered his eyes.

"Good morning, Lavena."

I stared, trying to discern whether the husband who hated me was really standing here now. When I'd been silent too long, Liam raised his gaze, his own filled with exasperation.

"The silent treatment again, Lavena?"

Oops. "I'm sorry, I'm just surprised to see you. Good morning, Liam."

He managed a wry smile. "If you think *you're* surprised, imagine how I'm feeling." He glanced uncertainly down the hallway in the direction of the dining room. "I thought perhaps you'd like to have breakfast with me."

"Really?"

Still not looking at me, he nodded.

Well, this was a surprising turn of events. I took his arm,

which he'd extended somewhat reluctantly. Still, it was a start.

He escorted me in silence, one much different than the kind that had filled our first week of marriage, as this silence was filled with awkwardness rather than tension. He cast me many sideways glances and kept frowning down at our connected arms, as if to discern whether or not we were really touching.

"How did you sleep?" I asked when the silence became too much. He startled before relaxing.

"Well enough, thank you." We'd turned a corner, walked an entire hallway, and had just begun our descent down the stairs before he added, "I dislike sleeping. Too much else to do."

I smiled. As I'd suspected, Liam craved activity. "You must enjoy dreaming, then."

He managed a half smile in return. It really was an adorable smile, dimpled and slightly crooked. "I do. Dreams allow me to go on adventures even while lying still."

We reached the dining room, where he helped me with my seat before taking his own across from me. He picked up his fork and was about to dive into his eggs and bacon when he paused and peeked up at me.

"Did you sleep well?"

I hadn't. I'd spent half the night crying, but I couldn't tell him that considering he'd been the source of my tears. So I settled for, "Well enough."

He nodded, and when he returned to his breakfast, the silence that settled over us was no longer tense but calm and full of promise. Liam cast me several glances throughout the meal, staring longer each time. Conscious of his attention, I tried to eat as daintily as possible, but it was difficult to maintain table manners while being analyzed.

So it was no surprise when I tipped over the jar of marmalade. "I beg your pardon."

Liam picked it up. "There's no harm done, unless the marmalade is offended." He gave it a friendly look. "Will you forgive Lavena for knocking you over?" He raised it to his ear and "listened" with the utmost concentration, as if the marmalade was truly speaking. Liam's eyes met mine as he lowered the jar. "Good news: it's not upset. Looks like you're forgiven."

For a moment I simply stared at him, Princess Lavena's assessment of Liam swirling in my mind: *immature*. Certainly if she were here, she'd roll her eyes at his antics, but that was the last thing I felt inclined to do. Instead it was all I could do to keep my threatening smile at bay.

Liam hesitated before tentatively pressing his finger against the corner of my mouth. "I see that smile you're trying to hide. Won't you give it to me?"

I allowed it to fully emerge. "I didn't want you to think I was laughing at you."

He wound his fingers together and rested his chin on top of them. "I'd thoroughly deserve it if you did."

"Perhaps, but I couldn't offend the marmalade, especially when I was seeking its forgiveness."

His grin widened, causing my stomach to flip. Goodness, he really had an adorable smile. My cheeks warmed as my gaze caressed his face. *He* was adorable.

"Why are you blushing?"

I became preoccupied searching for my knife and for something else, my current fluster causing me to forget what it was...until Liam calmly handed me the marmalade. My blush deepened.

"Thank you," I stuttered.

"You're welcome, Lavena."

I flinched at the name. Would I ever get used to being

addressed by it? Doubtful. As I spread marmalade on my toast, I silently chanted my own name to myself. *Anwen, Anwen, Anwen...*

"Are you alright?"

I jolted, shaking the cutlery. "Of course."

"You shouldn't be." Whatever good humor had settled over the prince slipped away. He leaned back in his seat with a heavy sigh. "My behavior this past week has been inexcusable. I sincerely apologize."

"I don't hold it against you," I said.

His brow furrowed. "How can you not?"

"Because I understand your reasons for it."

He tilted his head thoughtfully. "Nolan was right—you're really quite different now that we're married. I never would have believed it."

I stiffened. I was doing a terrible job playing the part I was expected to. I scrambled for an excuse to excuse my poor performance. "Before the wedding I fought against the arrangement because there was still a chance we could avoid it. Now that it's done I want to make it work. Can we at least be friends?"

He studied me for a long time, his gaze searching. "Friends..." He seemed to be testing the word to see whether or not he liked it. By his smile, it seemed that he did. "I'd like that. I can't live like this anymore. Being enemies is torture."

"I don't want to be enemies with you."

"Even though a few days before our wedding, you informed me in no uncertain terms that you did?"

"I did not." But even as I made my defense, I realized that Princess Lavena likely had, which meant I'd have to take responsibility for not only this, but for every biting comment she'd ever made to Liam. I gritted my teeth. This wasn't fair. "Did I?" I asked tentatively, wanting to be sure before I unwillingly took the blame.

"Yes. It was the day we went riding and were alternating between not speaking and going at one another's throats. You were the first to decide a battle of words would be an excellent way to pass the time."

I groaned. Yes, that sounded exactly how Princess Lavena would have treated her intended. *Curse you, Lavena.*

"I beg your pardon?"

I stiffened. "Did I say that out loud?"

He offered another crooked smile that somehow calmed my frazzled nerves. "You did. Scolding yourself?"

Scolding *her*, the one who'd gotten me into this mess. "I fully deserve it. I didn't mean a single word of...whatever I said." I leaned forward, paranoid. "What exactly did I say? I don't remember."

"Nothing that bears repeating."

"Oh, dear." I buried my face in my hands. That meant it had undoubtedly been extremely rude. My frustration over my inability to explain away all of Liam's past hurts pressed against my heart. I took a deep breath and looked directly into his deep blue eyes. "I'm sincerely sorry for all the cruel things I've ever said and for any pain that those words may have caused you. I promise never to speak to you in such a way again. Please forgive me."

His eyes widened and his mouth fell agape before his entire manner softened. "Oh Lavena, it's quite alright. Thank you for your apology. I'm sorry, too, for how I've spoken to you in return."

Thank goodness I didn't have any negative memories of Liam's rudeness towards Princess Lavena. I smiled my forgiveness. He returned it, and with it I felt healing begin to settle over us, melting away the hurt from the contention that had festered between us since we'd taken our vows, giving us a fresh start.

I returned to my plate with a much lighter heart, which

allowed me to finally enjoy my meal. The food was delicious, far more satisfying than the porridge I'd spent every morning of my life up until this marriage eating. I ate each item eagerly and likely a bit too messily, but paused with my fork halfway to my mouth when I noticed Liam watching me.

"What is it?" I squeaked.

His lips twitched. "Your appetite is much heartier than it used to be. You usually pick at your food, claiming it isn't to your liking."

I froze, too late remembering the princess's finicky tastes. "It's impossible not enjoy it; I've never eaten such fine food."

The ring burned in protest at this second mistake. Liam's eyes narrowed, causing my heart to beat wildly. Did he suspect? "Haven't you? Strange…I haven't found the food on our honeymoon to be anything special." He continued studying me thoughtfully before he shrugged. "Perhaps the method of preparation is superior in Draceria; I must be sure and give my compliments to the royal chef."

I took a deep breath, urging myself to relax. I needed to be more careful so as not to crack the façade, especially now that, thanks to our tentative friendship, Liam was paying better attention to me. I fiddled with my hair—something I'd seen the princess do a multitude of times—as if the gesture could better conceal the fact I was a fraud. It felt so foreign. Would I ever grow accustomed to my mask?

Liam finished breakfast first but made no move to leave the table to escape my presence, a promising sign. Instead, he began stacking his empty dishes. Princess Lavena had frequently complained about this habit of his. Although she thought it quite immature behavior for a prince, I found the expert way he balanced each dish to form a pyramid rather impressive.

He arranged the dishes carefully and with exaggerated

concentration, his hands shaking slightly with each movement, as if the seemingly confident prince was nervous. He began to place his goblet at the very top but paused, his cheeks darkening as he shyly lifted his gaze to mine.

"You hate when I do this, don't you?"

I rose from my seat and rested my hands on the plate at the top. "I'll hold it steady."

His eyes widened before he managed a crooked grin. He balanced the jeweled goblet with a steadiness that undoubtedly came from many hours of practice. "There, the pyramid is complete." His fingers brushed against my hand as he withdrew, causing me to nearly flinch and ruin the pyramid.

"An impressive structure, clearly made by an expert. How long have you had this hobby?"

"Ever since I was a boy. I like the challenge."

"Are you brave enough to make this pyramid even more impressive?" I handed him my cutlery. "I challenge you to put this on top of the goblet."

He stared at me for a moment before chuckling. "Once again, you surprise me. You really are different, Lavena. I clearly never really knew you before our marriage. I suppose I never really tried." He gingerly placed the cutlery atop the goblet and sat back. "There."

We both admired it before our gazes met and we exchanged shy smiles.

"Do you still find this unconventional hobby immature?" Uncertainty filled his eyes. My heart wrenched. The princess's insults had clearly bothered him, even if he'd always pretended they hadn't.

"Not at all."

He frowned. "Why the change of heart?"

I bit my lip, considering how to respond. "Because we're friends now."

He reached out, almost as if he were going to take my

hand, but instead he laid his inches from mine, so close I could reach out and touch it with my fingertip if I wanted to.

"You were never wrong, although at the time I refused to admit that. It *is* immature. When I was younger it never mattered, for back then I was the spare, not the heir. But ever since Kian died, the goofy prince is expected to change in order to become someone he's not: a future king. But I don't want to let go of who I am, even though I know I'm supposed to."

"You're afraid of losing yourself." I understood that fear all too well.

He lowered his eyes. "I don't want Prince Liam to be swallowed up by Crown Prince Liam, a role I never asked for."

I smiled gently. "If it means anything, I think I like Prince Liam better. Because we're now friends, you can be whichever Liam you want to be for me."

His smile lit up his eyes. "That's rather...sweet. Thank you for listening. I never expected to share this part of myself with you—or *any* part, for that matter—but you're easy to talk to." His brow furrowed. "I don't quite understand it."

My heartbeat escalated. "Understand what?"

"This." He motioned between us. "It's the opposite of what I imagined our marriage would be like."

"I hope our marriage continues to be better than our previous expectations."

"As do I." He sighed. "In my displeasure for our union, I allowed my bitterness to manifest in hatred. I've said so many horrible things to you."

I sent up a prayer of gratitude that I had no memory of those bitter fights between Liam and Princess Lavena; our first week of marriage when his attacks *had* been directed towards me—or rather, who he *thought* was me—had been bad enough.

"I'm so sorry for my own words," I said. "I can't even convey how deeply I regret the pain they caused you."

He studied me, expression pensive, before he shook his head. "I still can't get over how different you are."

I instinctively tensed.

"It's almost as if you're a different person." He laughed, as if the thought were ridiculous, not realizing just how true his words really were. His humor quickly faded and he became serious once more. "Can I ask you something?"

My mouth had gone dry. "What is it?"

He leaned over the table. "This last week—were you playing a game or were you sincere?"

I met his gaze directly so he couldn't miss my earnestness. "I was sincere."

He released a relieved sigh. "I'm glad, although admittedly rather confused, which leads me to ask again: why the sudden change of heart?"

I nibbled my lip. How to answer? The way I was choosing to handle this marriage was the opposite of the role I was meant to play, but if Princess Lavena meant for our switch to be permanent, then it was *me* who'd spend the rest of my life with Liam as my husband, not her. Thus I had to handle the marriage in the way *I* wanted rather than the way she expected.

"I can't live the way we have been this past week. I've always dreamt of a happy marriage. Just because my choice of spouse has been stolen from me doesn't mean my choice to make our marriage work has."

"I feel the same way," he said. "I originally grew up knowing I had a choice, only for that choice to be ripped from me when I inherited not only my deceased brother's title but his fiancée as well. It all felt horribly unfair to be forced into a situation not of my choosing. I thought if I despised the arrangement enough, my parents wouldn't make me go through with it. But it didn't work. Instead, it just created hatred between us."

"I don't hate you," I said hastily. "I swear, Liam."

He considered. "And I no longer hate you. It's a start, at least, to mending the mess I've created. I'm sorry my resentment towards the situation started the hostility between us. I should have thought less of myself and considered your feelings at suddenly becoming engaged to me after having grown to care for my brother. No wonder you resented me."

I wasn't sure who'd started it, considering I didn't doubt Princess Lavena had enthusiastically gone along with Liam's desire to be enemies. It didn't matter anymore. "I'm sorry, too."

He smiled. "A fresh start to try and make our marriage work. I admit that I'm still wary; it'll take time to build my trust and believe you've really changed. But in time, I do think we can at least be friends."

Friends…it was both a beautiful thought and a painful one that our arrangement would likely never be anything more. Still, if I could at least have his good opinion and his friendship, then this charade would not only be easier to endure, but it might actually become more than bearable, for the more time I spent around this prince, the more I realized how much I liked him.

He wanted to be friends. I needed to accept that, all while doing my best to school my heart so that I wouldn't risk losing it further to a man who was uninterested in anything more.

CHAPTER 7

That tentative morning marked a shift in our relationship. At first I feared our apologies would change nothing, that like the first morning of our honeymoon Liam would think me insincere and revert back to his cold behavior, which I now realized had served as his protection from getting close to me and opening himself up to the possibility that our relationship could be something more than duty to a political contract.

Thankfully, my fears proved unfounded. We chatted together the remainder of breakfast, after which Liam excused himself with a friendly smile and a bow, leaving for whichever adventure he'd planned for today. I fought to quench my disappointment as I watched him disappear down the corridor before firmly reminding myself that distance was for the best. It'd help prevent me from becoming too attached to a man who wasn't mine, for Princess Lavena would undoubtedly one day grow tired of her current beau and want Liam back.

Outside was grey and drizzly. Normally, I'd have

embraced both the weather and the opportunity to study the insects that only emerged when it rained—especially since I had a half-completed study of *dytiscidae* diving beetles that I was eager to complete—but unfortunately, behaving like Princess Lavena forced me to remain indoors.

I aimlessly wandered the various palace rooms before reluctantly settling in the parlor with my embroidery, a hobby for which I lacked both the patience and the skill. My threads quickly tangled to form a rather hideous picture. I set it aside with a sigh and instead stared out the rain-splotched window. If only I could instead spend the morning outside searching for aquatic insects. Would venturing outdoors be forbidden by the ring even if no one caught me?

"Do you like the rain?"

I startled at Liam's voice and swiveled around. He leaned against the doorframe with a tentative but still friendly smile. He straightened and after a moment's hesitation he stepped into the parlor. He motioned towards the window with his chin.

"Do you like the rain?" he repeated.

"I love rain," I said, in my shock straying from my Princess Lavena script. But the ring didn't seem to protest, and Liam took no notice.

His grin widened. "I love the rain, too. We have something in common."

As if this revelation gave him courage, he took another step into the room, followed by another, each one bringing him closer until he stopped in front of me. There he shifted his weight from one foot to the other and looked around, as if searching for something more to say.

His gaze settled on the needlework in my lap. "You enjoy embroidery?"

Princess Lavena had embroidered too often in his presence for me to be honest in this particular answer. "I do."

He tilted his head to study the picture more closely. "What is it?"

I lowered my gaze to my tangled mess of threads. Hopefully, Liam didn't realize how talented an embroiderer Princess Lavena was compared to me. "I don't really know."

He snorted, the beginnings of a laugh lighting up his eyes. "I haven't the faintest idea either."

I pretended to be affronted. "Making fun of my embroidery?"

He stiffened, suddenly wary, as if afraid his teasing would lead to another fight, but when I continued to smile he visibly relaxed. "Not at all." His twitching lips gave him away. At least he was polite enough not to laugh outright at what was undoubtedly the ugliest piece of embroidery that had ever been created.

"It's unfinished," I said, as if this excused how horrendous it was.

"I can see that."

I raised an eyebrow. "Are you an expert in embroidery? What an interesting fact about my husband."

He held up his hands. "Even the most manly prince such as myself can become such when he has three sisters." Laughter filled his eyes as he stared at my monstrosity. "I'm still new at this husband thing and am unsure what my primary husbandly duty is: to lie and say it's lovely, or to be brutally honest and advise you never to show that to anyone other than our most boring diplomats with the hope that it will encourage them to cut their visits short."

I stifled a smile. "I prefer your honestly. But it's most unfortunate that you feel this way about it, as it was intended as a wedding gift for you. I thought we could frame it in a place of honor. Perhaps the throne room?"

His eyes widened in horror. "You want me to hang it in the throne room?"

"Didn't your father tell you to keep your wife happy?"

Liam gaped at me as if trying to discern whether or not I was serious...until I started giggling. Relief flooded his face and he broke into a wide grin.

"You had me worried there for a minute, for I always thought of you as serious and devoid of any humor. To avoid the fate of being the recipient of such a gift, I must work to get into your good graces." He lowered his eyes and crunched the hem of his shirt. "That's actually why I'm here. It occurred to me that solely spending mealtimes together isn't enough to become friends, so I've come to see if you wanted to spend the day with me."

I smiled. Instead of me attempting to seek him out like I'd done our first week of marriage, he was now coming to *me*.

"However, the situation is more dire than I thought," he continued. "I expected you to be engaged in something amusing that I'd have to cajole you into abandoning. But what do I find?" He wrinkled his nose at my embroidery. "Your working intently on whatever *this* is."

His eyes twinkled, causing me to warm. This teasing was so different from the coldness that had previously filled our interactions. I basked in his friendly efforts to make our marriage work.

"It appears I've been caught; I'm actually a spy who weaves encrypted messages into her embroidery, hence it's so ugly."

"I'm relieved to hear there's a logical explanation for how it looks; I'd hate to think you wanted it to look like that on purpose."

Again, lightness filled both his tone and his eyes, as foreign as it was welcome. He closed the remaining distance between us and gently took hold of my hands. He normally didn't touch me outside of escorting me, so I was unprepared for my body's response. A flutter began at my fingertips as they curled around his and rippled up my arm. The effect of his touch seemed lost on him as he tugged me to my feet.

"What are your plans?" I managed to stammer.

"I was going to invite you to take a stroll through the gardens, but since it's raining, perhaps a grand tour of the palace would be better. I'll make it worth your while by sharing my own spin on the tales of the palace's grand but rather stuffy history. Shall we begin with this room?" He gestured grandly around it. "Now, it may look like an ordinary sitting room, but in reality it harbors a secret hidden beneath the floor. Some claim it's a centuries-old cursed treasure stolen from a dragon. If you listen carefully, you can occasionally hear his nocturnal visits as he pokes around the room in search of it."

He led me from the parlor, where he continued his inaccurate but rather enthralling tour, sharing both exciting and spooky stories about each room, many of which soon had both of us laughing.

I loved his laugh—a deep, contagious sound that was full of pure joy. I'd never heard anyone laugh with so much abandon and pleasure. The sound seeped over me, not only dispelling the last of our tension but causing my heart to stir. With it and his company, the afternoon melted away.

THE FRIENDLINESS and ease between Liam and me continued for the remainder of the week. Each day we spent more and more time together, gradually building a beautiful trust and friendship between us; my unease slowly began to slip away, and I came to treasure being with the man I never would have known if not for the princess's scheme.

But things couldn't remain so pleasant for long. At the end of our second week together, dinner was interrupted by the arrival of a footman. Liam paused in his animated story about some mischief he'd entangled himself in as a boy and reluctantly turned his attention to the servant, who executed a crisp bow.

"Forgive the interruption, Your Highnesses, but I must inform you of an unusual occurrence that just took place belowstairs."

Liam raised his eyebrows as he leaned back in his seat. "An unusual occurrence? That sounds intriguing. The dragon hasn't escaped the dungeon, has it?" He gave me a sly smile.

The footman's expression didn't even falter; he was undoubtedly used to Liam's antics. "No, Your Highness, he's fed and chained for the night."

"What a relief." Liam winked at me before turning back to the footman. "What is the real situation?"

"A servant from the Lycerian palace has paid an unexpected visit, making inquiries. He now requests an audience with Her Highness." The footman's gaze flickered towards me.

I jolted and my breath caught as horror eclipsed my previous curiosity, for I had no doubt who this Lycerian palace servant must be. *Archer.* As I'd feared, he'd returned from his hunting trip to discover me missing and was now frantically searching for me.

Puzzlement furrowed Liam's brow at my reaction. I took a steadying breath in an attempt to remain calm, a near impossible task with the wild way my heart pounded in my chest. "Who is this servant?"

"His name is Archer, Your Highness, a member of the Lycerian Royal Hunt. He's looking for a handmaiden named Anwen, whom he says used to be in service to Princess

Lavena. I informed him there's no servant here by that name."

Liam frowned. "How peculiar. You don't have a servant named Anwen, do you, Lavena?"

"I used to, but she's no longer my handmaiden."

The footman was still awaiting further instructions. "What should I tell him, Your Highness?"

My chest tightened as I frantically scrambled for what to do. Archer was here. I couldn't just send him away without easing his worries. Could I possibly manage to change undetected into my handmaiden outfit and meet with him in order to assure him I was alright? But even if I managed to convince him that Princess Lavena had decided to keep me in her service, he'd undoubtedly try to get a position serving the Dracerian royal family in order to remain near me, which would undoubtedly lead to his discovery of the role I now played before long.

My heart lifted. Archer learning of the switch would finally grant me the escape I'd been desperately searching for without my breaching the ring's contract. He could petition Prince Nolan, and then—

A flash of heat shot through my hand, grinding the remainder of this tentative plan to a halt. The ring would forbid me from seeing my brother if it exposed the switch.

But I couldn't give up; I couldn't bear to think of Archer's worry should he never learn what had become of me. I had to at least meet with him, all while carefully choosing the words that would both ease his heart and appease the sadistic ring.

"Your Highness?" The footman eyed me, awaiting my instructions.

I shakily rose from my seat. "If he requests an audience, then I should see him."

Liam immediately stood as well. "I'll accompany you."

I stiffened. "There's no need." I forced a smile. He narrowed his eyes at it, his look suspicious, and too late I remembered the rumors that the Lycerian princess took too much interest in her male servants.

My face burned at how my desire to speak with Archer alone appeared—not as a concerned sister who needed to ease his frantic heart, but as a princess with an unsavory reputation spending time with a servant she had no business interacting with.

"I insist." Liam's tone left no room for argument. I fiddled with the ring as I frantically tried to think of a way out of this predicament, but the only path I could see was the one that would break my brother's heart.

I slumped in defeat and turned back to the footman. "On second thought, I won't see the hunter. Inform him that there's no servant by the name of Anwen currently serving at the palace."

The footman nodded. "What should I tell him should he inquire for further details? He gave the impression that she's missing and seemed to believe you'd know of her whereabouts."

"Inform him that I haven't seen her since she left my service." Guilt squeezed my chest at the torment my words would bring to my worried brother. I hastily blinked away the tears burning my eyes. I had to remain calm, even while my heart was breaking.

The footman bowed and departed to carry out my instructions, and I collapsed back into my seat, utterly spent.

"Lavena?"

I startled and swiveled to face Liam, frowning at me. "What is it?" I squeaked.

Liam's suspicious look softened into concern. "You seem

troubled. Are you alright?" He hesitated. "Do you know this Archer?"

I sighed. I couldn't ease Archer's worries, but I could at least attempt to ease Liam's. "He's the twin brother of my former handmaiden." How strange it was to talk about my real self with him.

Liam frowned. "The handmaiden he believes to be missing?"

"I felt it was my duty to ease his mind concerning the matter, considering she used to be under my charge."

Liam considered this explanation before nodding to himself, accepting it. Relief spread over me, but it was short-lived. It was impossible to focus on Liam when he resumed his animated story, my thoughts eclipsed by dear Archer. The guilt that I'd sent him away without news of me weighed heavily, pressing against my chest until I could scarcely breathe.

No, I couldn't do that to him. The ring might forbid me from telling him the truth, but I had to at least try speaking with him, no matter the consequences.

I jolted to my feet, rattling the table in my haste. "I need some fresh air."

"Do you want me to accompany—" Liam began, but I cut him off.

"No, thank you," I said breathlessly. "I want to be alone."

He started to stand, as if to follow me—he undoubtedly didn't trust me—but before he could, I hurried from the dining room. As soon as I was out of Liam's sight, I lifted my skirts and darted through the corridors, hurrying past many startled servants before making my way outside.

The light was beginning to fade, the lowering sun bathing the sky in sunset. I searched the grounds for Archer, but there was no sign of him. Undeterred, I ran across the grounds towards the gate. Ignoring the surprised and baffled looks from the flanking guards, I pressed my face against the bars and searched the dusk for him.

Nothing. He'd gone. The disappointment returned, squeezing my heart. I should have ignored my fears and insisted on speaking with him the moment the footman alerted me of his arrival and smoothed it over with Liam later. Now I'd lost my chance.

With a sigh I trudged away from the gate, but I didn't return to the palace. Instead, I wandered the manicured grounds until I arrived at the nearby meadow, where the familiar honking of geese made me pause.

I squinted through the fading light to see a goose girl rounding up her geese to return them to their pen for the night. Naturally, the mischievous birds didn't seem inclined to listen to her, more content to graze for the remainder of the evening.

I stared hungrily at the birds as I inched forward; they were so similar to the geese I'd tended at home before the princess had forced me into her service. Aching homesickness filled my breast. I yearned for the days of being a goose girl, spending all day outside tending my delightful birds, a life so much simpler than the one in which I was currently entangled.

A goose escaped the gaggle and wandered over to me. I crouched on my heels and extended my hand. It tilted its head, as if discerning whether I was friend or foe, before slowly waddling close enough for me to pet it. For the first time since Archer's unexpected arrival a wave of calm washed over me, dispelling the tension that had knotted my stomach.

The goose girl noticed her goose's mischief and hurried over with a gasp, her eyes wide. "No, Minnow, you can't approach the princess."

I smiled reassuringly. "It's quite alright. I'm fond of geese."

The goose girl gaped at me. "You're fond of geese, Your Highness?"

I nodded as I turned back to the goose called Minnow and tickled beneath its beak. More unease slipped away with each stroke, and with it I felt a part of Anwen which I'd securely locked away emerge, a reminder that even though I'd lost my brother once more, *I* was still here. It was such a comforting thought.

"Lavena?"

I startled at Liam's voice and swiveled around to see him approaching. So he had followed me. Unsurprising. He arrived and sat on his heels beside me, looking first at me and then Minnow, now waddling after the goose girl to join its gaggle.

"What are you doing?"

"Just...petting a goose."

He raised his eyebrows even as his lips quirked up into my favorite dimpled smile. I ached to reach out and press my fingertip in his adorable dimple; I clenched my hands to resist this impulse.

"I didn't know you had an affinity for geese," he said.

Oops, Princess Lavena certainly wouldn't. In my need to connect with my real self I'd allowed my role to slip. I forced a smile. "When the goose waddled over to say hello, I couldn't resist her charms; a princess must treat all her subjects with respect."

Liam chuckled as he settled beside me, so close we were practically touching. "Forgive me for following you, but I wanted to see whether you were alright. You still seem a bit unsettled by the news of that servant's arrival."

"I'm fine," I lied.

His frowned deepened, clearly unconvinced. "What was his name again?" He scrunched his forehead, trying to remember. "Oh yes, Archer. You say you've met him before?"

A peculiar look filled his expression, as if he'd formed a theory about my interest in Archer that he was desperate to disprove.

"Only a few times when he visited Anwen."

Liam perused my expression, as if gauging my sincerity, before his countenance softened. "I'm relieved that there's an explanation, because for a moment, I feared…"

I stiffened. I knew exactly what he'd suspected.

He studied me for a moment more before he shook his head and forced a smile. "Forgive my suspicions. I'm doing my best to forget our past and trust that things have changed. It's getting easier every day, especially the more I come to know you."

"I'm sorry that my worry for my former handmaiden gave you cause to be suspicious. I'm merely upset she's missing. What could have happened to her?" I fought to keep my voice steady while the lie wrenched my heart with guilt, especially considering *Anwen* was in reality sitting right beside him.

He reached out a hesitant hand and, after a moment's pause he rested it over mine. "It's touching that you're worried for her."

"Of course. She was in my service for five years." I ached to say more, to share not only parts of myself I'd hidden away but my guilt for Archer's distress, the difficulty of pretending to be a person so different from myself, my fear of being discovered…all my thoughts, secrets, and burdens. What better man to do so with than my husband? The fact that I couldn't was agonizing.

The ring throbbed threateningly, reminding me once more that I had a part to play. But after this week of this new friendship with Liam, I realized hiding myself would be far more difficult—and painful—than I'd initially anticipated. Maintaining distance would be wise, for when the princess returned, I'd lose him. My heart ached at the thought, and for the first time since the charade began, a part of me never wanted it to end.

Liam was still watching me, his look both curious and incredibly sweet. Even if I couldn't confide my fears and worries to him, I yearned to give him any piece of Anwen that I could. I glanced at the retreating geese now at the edge of the meadow.

"Would you like to know a secret? I'm quite fond of geese. Isn't that shocking for a princess?"

Liam smiled. "Quite shocking. A bribe may be required for me to keep such a scandalous secret quiet." He scooted closer and once again reached out to touch me, this time lightly resting his hand on my arm. "As interesting as that secret about my wife is, I've made an even more important discovery about you."

I held my breath, waiting. He leaned forward, eyes aglow. I naturally leaned closer, drawn to him.

"You're incredibly kind," he whispered, his voice tender. "Why did it take me so long to discover that?"

"How do you know I'm kind?"

"I've been watching you these past two weeks," he said. "You're sweet and gentle with everyone you interact with— you even treated me the same way despite my trying to push you away—and you're the type of woman who notices those whom others deem insignificant." He motioned towards the geese as they waddled from the meadow. "So it doesn't surprise me that you're concerned for your former servant, even though most in your station wouldn't give her a second thought."

His compliment warmed my heart. Princess Lavena wasn't kind; *Anwen* was, and despite the mask I was forced to wear, he'd discovered a portion of the real me, no matter how small. Would the ring allow me to show him more? It was a dangerous desire, one I shouldn't risk acting on, no matter how much I yearned to...yet I knew that throughout our charade together, I would at least try. Could I do so while also guarding my heart against the pain of our inevitable separation?

CHAPTER 8

I treasured each day and every moment I spent with Liam, all filled with warmth, as if Liam were the sun and I were a flower that blossomed from his easy smiles, contagious laughter, and fun-loving personality. Although our relationship didn't go deeper, I cherished the friendship we'd developed so far.

The chill and tension that used to fill the stretches of suffocating silence between us had vanished, so now whenever there was silence—something that became less common with each passing day—it was a comfortable sort, as if unspoken conversations were filling the space instead. Liam often paused to watch me with a peculiar look, as if not only seeing me for the first time, but also as if searching for something he'd lost and was desperate to find.

One evening after dinner, we adjourned to the library, where Liam strode purposefully to a shelf and yanked out a book without even looking at it. He noticed my raised eyebrow and grinned.

"Reading a random book is more of an adventure than purposely choosing one. I believe the book you're meant to discover next will always find you." He plopped down on the rug in the center of the room and opened his book to the middle.

I fought my smile as I watched. "Do you always begin in the middle of a book? Is that because you like to imagine what the story could be rather than what it actually is?"

As was becoming more and more common, he grinned widely. "Exactly. This way I can come up with my own possible beginning. It's like a game."

"So what do you imagine for this story?"

He read a few sentences from his place in the middle of the book. "Hmm, I'm imagining a murder mystery full of political intrigue. Let's see whether I'm correct." He flipped the book to its cover to read the title: *Quest for the Lady's Heart*. He wrinkled his nose. "A *romance*? Ugh." He unceremoniously tossed the book over his shoulder and stood to retrieve another.

"Oh no, you don't." I scooped up his discarded book. "You told me the correct book always finds you. Choosing another now would be cheating."

He scowled, but by the dancing filling his eyes I knew he wasn't truly upset. "It appears I'm forced to endure a sappy tale. If you hear me sniggering, you'll know why." He re-examined the cover. "On second thought, perhaps this *is* the book for me...if it'll provide the tips I need to succeed in my newest quest."

My heart flared to life at his words. What did he mean by that? He smiled softly, as if my deepening blush in response to his words pleased him.

"What book will you read?" he asked. "Shall I find one for you?"

"And ruin my own adventure? Finding the perfect fit will only come from searching myself."

I took refuge in the shelves, using their cover to wait for

my warm cheeks to cool before perusing the titles. I sensed the heat of Liam's gaze and glanced over to find him watching me, his expression soft. He offered me a mischievous smile before returning to his book, only to look up to watch me again. My heart pattered wildly each time our gazes met.

It took fifteen minutes of exploring the shelves for me to find something to read. I passed the entomology books half a dozen times, each time forcing myself to resist the intriguing volumes. It wasn't until I promised myself I'd return later and smuggle a few to my room to read them in secret that I settled on a book of fairy tales.

Liam was where I'd left him, but now lay propped on his side as he mindlessly turned pages, stopping occasionally to read passages.

"How's the story?" I asked.

"Mushy. Do women really like this stuff?"

I shrugged. "I've never read a romance."

He cocked an eyebrow. "Then allow me to demonstrate. Come here." He patted the spot next to him. I hesitated, unsure if it'd be wise to abuse my heart by sitting so close to him. "Don't be scared, Lavena. I don't bite…usually." He wriggled his eyebrows and patted the spot again.

With a steadying breath I settled beside him and immediately became enveloped in his cinnamon-scented warmth, like I was sitting in front of a hearth. I resisted the impulse to scoot closer.

"The characters spend an inordinate amount of time doing mushy things, such as gazing into each other's eyes, as if that could tell them anything about a person." He frowned, pondering. "Not that I would know, considering I've never done it. Shall we experiment?"

I immediately lowered my eyes to my lap, but he hooked his fingers beneath my chin to raise my gaze to meet his. His lopsided "this is so ridiculous I can't believe we're actually doing it" smirk quickly slid from his face, replaced by a flicker of surprise. He scooted closer and I did too, leaning forward to quench my sudden need to be close to him.

His gaze seeped into mine. His eyes were the most beautiful shade of blue, just like a summer sky, completely fitting for his sunny personality. A multitude of emotions resided in them, as if they were the windows to his soul, reflecting both his usual contentment and a bit of uncertainty.

He blinked rapidly and hastily tore his gaze away. "Your eyes are brown."

"They are." A strange disappointment filled me at his words. After such an intense, beautiful moment, I'd expected something *more*.

"They're really pretty and...oh bother. Books never mirror real life." He held up the one that had started us down this strange path with an accusing glare. "The hero in this book constantly gushes accolades to his fair maiden, as if spouting poetry on a whim is effortless—it's not; believe me, I know—and I can't even say anything about your eyes that doesn't sound like...well, like a prince who has no command of his tongue."

"Not every maiden likes poetic accolades," I said hesitantly. "I, for one, prefer sincere compliments."

The corner of his mouth lifted. "I suppose that means this book won't help me in my quest after all. It appears I'm on my own."

My pulse pounded rapidly. What did he mean by that? "Perhaps you simply need to read more of it; you may find yourself surprised."

He sighed as if I'd suggested braving a monstrous beast rather than a romance novel. "I'll press forward and see if I can glean any useful tips. I hope you enjoy your own book."

He glanced at the cover. "Ah, fairy tales. Excellent. Imagine me in every heroic role."

He winked, thoroughly disarming me, before opening his own book to another random place and resuming reading. Feeling slightly dizzy from our proximately and conversation, I went to the nearby settee. I'd no sooner settled than Liam spoke again.

"Lavena?" Crimson stained his cheeks and his look was bashful. "Your eyes really are very pretty, even if I can't use a lovely phrase to explain why. I never noticed you had brown eyes. I must have been blind, for they're striking."

He laughed nervously as he rumpled the back of his hair and returned to his book. My heart fluttered as I stared at him, and it took several minutes for me to gather myself and open my own book.

After only a few pages, Liam grew restless. He wriggled about, shifting into a new position every few minutes, seeming unable to get comfortable.

I nibbled my lip. "Are you bored? Would you prefer we do something else?" I didn't particularly care what activity we did, as long as we were together.

"I'm not bored." He rolled onto his back, propped his feet up on the settee so they were elevated above him, and held the book above his head. "I haven't the faintest idea what this story is about. It's fantastic."

Liam's restlessness continued. Soon he was pacing the floor as he read, then he was circling my settee like a hawk, and finally he leaned over the back of it. "I'm feeling a bit fidgety. It's likely the story. Time for a new plan." He scampered to the nearest shelf and yanked out an armful of books. "I'll read a page of each and see what story emerges."

He dumped them on the floor, arranged them in a circle around him, and opened each book to the first page before lying on his stomach in front of the first and beginning to read. My own fairy tale was entirely forgotten as I watched him scoot from one book to another.

"You're eager to experience as much of life as possible," I said.

He looked up with a grin. "There are so many wonderful things in life to enjoy. I don't want to miss out on a single moment."

That was definitely Liam. It was amazing how well I felt I knew him even though we hadn't known each other long.

A peaceful silence settled over us, filled only with the rustle of our turning pages and the sounds of Liam scooting from book to book...until it seemed he couldn't stand being still a moment longer. I sensed his wicked grin even before I looked up and saw it was aimed at me.

Trepidation filled my stomach. "Uh oh..."

He chuckled. "*Uh oh* is right. I've just had a fancy and I must humor it. Whatever you're reading has you quite engrossed. Perhaps I should investigate why so I can get to know you better." He crawled over to tug my book from me.

"Liam, I was reading that."

He leaned close until he was inches away, so that I could see every freckle that dotted his nose. "Please?"

I immediately melted. Goodness, he was dangerous. "Fine, but only if you imagine yourself in the role of the villain."

"Success!" He pumped his fists in the air before giving me a heart-stopping smile that instantly earned my forgiveness. "Thank you for humoring me. As a token of my gratitude, I'll let you read one of my books." He picked one at random and handed it to me with an exaggerated flourish. "Your book, milady."

My heart lifted at the title. "This is a book about insects."

"Oops, not a very appealing subject for a lady. Shall I choose another?"

He made to take it but I clutched it protectively. The book he'd given me at random had been the exact book I'd wanted to read. Perhaps his theory was correct: the right book had a way of finding a person at the right time. Now was the best time to immerse myself in my favorite subject, especially when with each passing day I felt bits of Anwen slipping between my fingers no matter how hard I tried to hold on to myself.

"According to your rules, this book has chosen me. I must read it."

"Brave girl. Very well, if you want to." Liam returned to his previous spot on the rug before casting me a suspicious look over his shoulder. "You're not reading it just to find the perfect bug to sneak into my bed in revenge for my stealing your book of fairy tales, are you?"

I giggled. "You'll be happy to note that revenge isn't in my nature."

"Of course it isn't." He spoke this quietly, as if I wasn't meant to hear the words. But I had, and they filled me with the warmth that was becoming a common feeling whenever I was around Liam.

I immersed myself in the book of bugs, feeling more myself with each turn of the pages. Memories filled every word and sentence, transporting me back to my childhood when, as a young girl, I'd first noticed a spider weaving a web in the rafters above.

It wasn't the first time I'd seen a spider, but it was the first time I'd seen one at work. I'd stared, transfixed, as it wove its web in an artistic pattern. What a fascinating process. Questions filled my mind. How did a spider accomplish such a remarkable feat? Why? Did other spiders create similar webs, or were they all different, unique to the type of spider itself?

I'd begun searching for spiders earnestly in hopes of watching them build their homes from their silky thread.

Soon I was capturing them to study them more closely, sketching them, and scribbling my observations in my journal. It wasn't until I caught one in front of my shrieking mother that I realized my fascination was unique to me.

She'd made me release all my spiders—saying goodbye to those I considered my pets was one of the saddest moments of my childhood. Luckily, insects were in abundance around my home in the meadow, so I searched out others to study. A new world had opened up to me. There were so many bugs—small and seemingly insignificant, undetected by the casual observer—but the more I studied them, the more I came to realize just how much they influenced the world around us, changing it in ways that, like them, went unnoticed.

Just like me, a common goose girl.

It wasn't until I once again held a book about *pterygota* insects that I realized how much Anwen had been wilting as she was slowly smothered by Princess Lavena. I held the book inches from my nose as I devoured every word, each fact breathing new life into me, into *Anwen*. My passion was like water for a plant, nourishing me and allowing me to blossom.

I was jolted from my reverie of insects and their interesting habits by Liam's sigh. I looked up in time to see him toss aside the book of fairy tales he'd stolen from me. "That book is the worst of the bunch I've read."

"Why is that?" I asked.

"It's full of perfect princes who grow up to be perfect kings. Totally unrelatable. Life's too short to read such nonsense."

He pulled his knees up to his chest, insecurity cloaking him. I snapped my book shut and knelt in front of him. "What's wrong, Liam?"

He traced swirls in the rug. "You seemed rather engrossed in your own book."

I shrugged in what I hoped was an offhanded way. "It's quite different from fairy tales." Different and absolutely *wonderful.* "I was just reading about queen bees and their hives." I couldn't quite disguise my enthusiasm.

He raised an eyebrow. "You sound as if you enjoyed the account. Will you share why?"

Little did he realize his invitation would unleash a monologue about my favorite subject. "A queen bee is an adult mated female who is the mother of most—if not all— the bees in her hive. Her sole function is to reproduce, and she can lay up to fifteen hundred eggs per day, which is more than her own body weight. Not only that, but she controls the sex of the egg, allowing her to tailor-make her hive."

I paused to take a breath and cast him an uncertain glance. I expected to find him wearing the same bored expression every victim of my exuberant recitations wore, but instead he listened, head tilted, appearing almost...*interested.*

"Sounds productive. The best I can do on any given day of royal duties is to not fall asleep during meetings." He searched my expression. "You're lighting up. Did you actually enjoy the book I forced upon you?"

"It was just so...*fascinating.*" I hugged the book to my chest. What I wouldn't give to find a hive, identify a queen bee, and watch her process of expanding her hive. I sighed wistfully.

Liam misunderstood it. Sympathy filled his expression as he rested his hand on top of mine. "You were bombarded with unrealistic royal expectations, too?"

Sadness and bitterness laced his voice. I forced myself to float down from my fascination. Queen bees were nothing compared to the distressed prince in front of me. He seemed so vulnerable in this moment; it wasn't until his usual light was missing that I realized how much it'd been a constant part of him.

Princess Lavena wouldn't have comforted him, but she wasn't here. I rested a gentle hand on his arm. He jolted but made no move to pull away. Instead he stared at where I touched him, as if confused by my hand's presence.

"Are you afraid you're not fit to be the crown prince?"

"I know I'm not," he said. "I was never meant for this role; it was Kian's title and responsibility, not mine. I've inherited everything that was meant to be his—the crown and you—and I'm unfit for both."

I flinched. "You seem to be handling me well enough."

His brow furrowed. "What's wrong?"

"Nothing," I said hastily.

He groaned. "Father warned me about this."

"About what?"

He leaned closer, as if to share a secret. "*Wives.* He said there are certain words and phrases that don't mean what I think they mean, like a secret code. When a woman says *nothing* is wrong, apparently that means *everything* is." He straightened, as if bracing himself for battle. "But I will not be conquered. No code, Lavena. Just tell me what's bothering you so we can face it head on."

His determination softened me. I didn't want to play games with him. "I don't want to feel like a duty you inherited."

He was quiet for a moment. "I admit I felt that way in the beginning, but please be assured: you don't feel like a duty any longer."

My heart warmed at his words, ones whose sentiments I now shared—this arrangement felt nothing like a duty. I flipped my hand over so our palms touched.

"I feel the same," I whispered. "So please talk to me. Don't hide your feelings from me; let me share your burden."

He tapped the cover of the book of fairy tales with a wry smile. "Aren't princes supposed to be heroes? We're gallant and noble and not afraid of anything, not even dragons."

"Everyone—prince or not—is afraid of dragons. The secret is to face them despite our fear and defeat them before they consume us."

He swallowed. "Not all princes slay dragons."

"Prince Liam does. He faces life head on."

The words seemed to lend him courage, for he took a deep, wavering breath before his pent-up dam of emotions came tumbling out.

"Kian was everything I'm not: serious, responsible, mature...the perfect crown prince, born to be king. He embodied his role, just as I embodied mine as the extra prince whose sole function was to be an ornament. I always knew I was the spare, but I didn't mind. I never imagined I'd actually be needed. But then he fell ill."

Pain twisted his expression. He took another long breath and continued.

"It was so unexpected. He'd always been healthy and then suddenly he wasn't. It was the scariest time of my life. Although I loved Kian, it wasn't the thought of him dying that terrified me, but the thought of having to take his place." He squeezed his eyes shut. "Isn't that terrible? I cared more about what losing Kian would mean for me than about losing him."

"I can see you loved your brother," I said.

"I did, but not enough. I wanted him to live for selfish reasons." He took another wavering breath. "But he didn't. Despite my prayers, he got sicker and sicker. And then he died. I'll never forget the moment I heard the news—the ache at losing my brother eclipsed by the fear of losing all that I was in order to take his place.

"But I'm not good enough to take his place. I never will

be, no matter how hard I try, so what's the point in trying at all? I wasn't meant to be king; *he* was. Who I am no longer matters; I'm only measured by the role I now fill. I've seen enough of my parents' disappointment and the disapproval of visiting royals and dignitaries to know I'm falling short. I fear they wonder why *I* didn't fall ill instead of him."

My heart wrenched at the heartache and insecurity Liam had carried all these years. I squeezed his hand. "I understand your feelings of losing yourself, but you don't need to in order to be a wonderful king. I like who you are."

He frowned. "There's no need to lie. You've constantly reminded me over the years that I'm not the man Kian was and that you wish you could have married him instead, like you were supposed to."

I gasped. Princess Lavena had told him *what*? "I don't think that."

"But that's what you've *said,* many times." Pain filled his eyes at the memories. I silently cursed Princess Lavena for hurting him so deeply. I'd never hated the princess more than I did now.

I cradled his face. "I'm so sorry I ever said such a thing. Please believe me when I assure you that I didn't mean it. I wouldn't want to be married to anyone but you." The truth of my own admission washed over me, causing me to lean forward to fulfill my heart's desire to be closer to him.

"Really?" He scooted closer too, eyes pleading.

"Yes, Liam. Really."

"Then why did Kian's death change you? You were so much kinder before, but the moment you and I became bound by his contract, you became so…hardened, and the battle between us began. I always thought it was because you couldn't bear the thought of marrying the inferior spare." His expression twisted.

My heart ached for his pain while also sympathizing for

what Princess Lavena must have been experiencing to have led her to treat Liam the way she had, for I was now starting to realize just how much she must have cared for Kian.

"I'm so sorry, Liam. Grief can do horrible things to a person. But please believe me that the Princess Lavena who hurt you so deeply is not the Princess Lavena who sits before you now. Please forgive me for how I've treated you in the past and allow me to make it up to you."

He searched my expression, gauging my sincerity. "Really?" Desperation filled his tone, as if he wanted nothing more than for my words to be true.

"Really."

"And you don't resent having to marry *me* instead of Kian? I know you cared for him."

"I don't resent it." It was not only true, but it was becoming more so with each moment I spent with him. "Please don't try to change yourself. I don't want to be married to Kian; I want to be married to *you*."

His crooked grin slowly emerged, and it did wonders for me to see his smile again. "As strange as it is, I'm finding I may just want to be married to you, too. You make me believe that perhaps I can bear the responsibilities placed on my shoulders—if I have you by my side."

He lifted a hesitant hand to slowly stroke my cheek before leaning closer. I kept totally still as he softly pressed his lips to my brow. It was such a gentle kiss, one that sent warmth over me and left my heart pounding.

With that simple kiss, Anwen stirred within me once more, and I felt even more alive than I had when reading about insects. A new passion filled me—one both foreign and slightly confusing, yet beautiful...and entirely forbidden.

CHAPTER 9

*L*iam was being unusually quiet as he picked at his breakfast, our usual flow of conversation that had been increasing each day suddenly dammed. The memory of the insecurities he'd shared the evening before filled my mind as I studied him. Did he regret baring his heart to me?

Liam finally excused himself—leaving behind his untouched plate—and locked himself away in his study, leaving me in worry; it gnawed at my heart as I wandered the gardens.

Soon I couldn't bear the thought of Liam's melancholy any longer. I went to the kitchens, which were in a swirl of cleanup from breakfast and preparations for lunch. I waved away the excited kitchen girl who bustled over to serve me and prepared a cup of tea. She bounced on her toes beside me, anxiously wringing her hands.

"Please allow me to assist you, Your Highness."

I shook my head. *I* wanted to make tea for my husband. I prepared it the way I knew he preferred—a large dose of cream with three spoonfuls of sugar. My lips twitched. He certainly adored sweets. When I finished, I spotted a tray of freshly baked cherry tarts, a treat he was partial to.

"May I take some of these?" I asked the frittering kitchen girl.

She curtsied. "Certainly, Your Highness. Would you like me to—"

I shook my head and placed four on a plate before carrying it and the cup of steaming tea to Liam's study, where I rested the tray on my propped-up knee so I could raise a hesitant hand and knock.

"Come in."

I pushed the door open and found Liam leaning back in his seat at his empty desk, staring out the window. He glanced over and raised his eyebrows in surprise.

"Is there something you needed, Lavena?" I set his treats down on the desk. He blinked at them. "What's this?"

"I—" Heat filled my cheeks. "You seemed out of sorts, so I wondered…perhaps you might like some tea?"

He gaped, first at the tea, then up at me, his brow furrowed. He slowly took a sip and his eyebrows rose further. "How is this prepared?"

"A large dose of cream, three spoonfuls of sugar."

His eyes widened. Once more he stared at the tea, followed by the plate of treats. "I love cherry tarts," he said.

"I know." I smiled and turned to leave.

"Lavena?"

I paused in the doorway and glanced over my shoulder. Confusion filled his expression, but it softened as our gazes met. "Thank you, this is very sweet." His forehead puckered. "You're so…*nice*. Why didn't I realize this about you sooner?" He buried his face in his hands with a sigh. "I'm so daft. Of course you're a kind person, despite how horribly I treated you all throughout our engagement."

"You're not the only one at fault, Liam; I hate the thought of how much I hurt you."

His slow smile was almost…sad. "See? You're extremely sweet and forgiving. I wish I'd taken the time to learn more about you before our marriage rather than determinedly pushing you away. Thankfully, it's not too late to remedy that oversight." Shyness filled his eyes as he motioned to the seat across from him. "Won't you sit down?"

I returned his timid smile with one of my own as I closed the door and approached. Liam moved his seat around the desk closer to me so that when I sat down our knees were practically touching. He pushed the plate of tarts towards me.

"I brought them for you," I protested.

"I know, but I want to share them with my wife." He tilted his head rather adorably. "You knew these were my favorite, didn't you?"

I shrugged and his grin widened.

"You've been paying attention. And you're not the only one." He snagged a cherry tart and shoved the entire thing in his mouth. "Your favorite dessert is blackberry pudding."

It was actually anything with strawberries, particularly shortcake, but strawberries had been entirely absent from our meals considering Princess Lavena was deathly allergic to them. But blackberry pudding was admittedly the dessert I'd most enjoyed since our marriage, and I was pleased he'd noticed. "You've been observing me?"

He nodded as he licked his fingers and urged me with his eyes to take a tart. I did and began nibbling at the ends. He studied me. "You always eat everything so slowly. I can tell you take pleasure in it."

"Shouldn't wonderful things be made to last?"

Liam gave me the sweetest, most knowing look, as if he

could see straight into my heart. "Indeed. You love life. We're similar in that way, even if we express it differently."

"You jump into life with both feet and live each day to its fullest potential."

"Whereas you take time to appreciate every experience."

We exchanged another smile and I felt something pass between us, a thread pulling us closer.

"We're rather…compatible." Liam's expression was dazed.

My heart warmed at the word. I loved discovering similarities between us, ones that only existed because I wasn't Princess Lavena.

Liam took a sip of his tea as he leaned back in his seat, his gaze flickering towards the window. "I saw you pacing the gardens. Are you alright?"

The warmth already within me grew, every word he spoke stoking the fire in my heart—he'd noticed me just as I'd noticed him. "I was worried about you. You've been rather pensive this morning."

"And you expected an imposter, I take it?" His teasing grin lit up his eyes, dispelling the melancholy that had been present earlier. "I know it must have been rather shocking for you to see the goofy prince so somber. It's been known to happen." He drained the rest of his tea. "I've been thinking about last night…and about us."

I'd been thinking obsessively about last night, too, especially the kiss he'd tenderly pressed against my brow, a kiss whose shadow still lingered. I leaned closer. "What about us?"

His cheeks darkened, but his blue gaze smoldered with an intensity that hadn't ever been present between us. "As much as I've enjoyed our growing friendship these past few weeks, I want us to be *more* than friends. I want us to be…a couple."

My breath hooked. Was he really saying…?

"I know it may take time," he continued hastily. "We both

need to heal from the pain we caused one another before our marriage, but I'll never give up until I've atoned for it. I'm so sorry I never gave you a fair chance. I not only created a false image of you, but I kept you at arm's length. I think I was afraid about what would happen should I open my heart up to you." He took a wavering breath. "But no longer."

My own heart pounded at his tender words even as uncertainty tightened my chest. How could I allow Liam to open his heart to me when who he thought I was...was all a lie? It'd make it so much harder when Princess Lavena returned to take back what was hers. But the more I came to know Liam, the more deeply I cared for him and the more I wanted to open my heart to him in return.

He looked at me expectantly, his eyes full of hope. I rested my hand on his knee. "You want to be more than friends?"

"I want to *try*. After all, you're my wife, and thus I want to care for you. You deserve to be loved, not merely put up with."

Wife...my heartbeat escalated, both at hearing such a beautiful word applied to me and at his sweet desires to care for me, even though doing so would make our eventual separation all the more unbearable. Joy and despair raged war within my heart. But joy won, causing me to smile. "Does that mean you like me?"

He nodded. "I like you *a lot*."

I sighed contentedly. The only explanation for his changing feelings was that I wasn't Princess Lavena. Despite the mask I was forced to wear, bits of Anwen were emerging. Perhaps he'd discover more during our time together. I'd happily give him as many parts of Anwen as I could.

"I really want us to work," he continued shyly. "Do you?"

"More than anything," I whispered, answering not for Lavena but for myself.

He smiled tenderly and stood. "Then will you spend the rest of the morning with me?"

At my nod, he extended his hand and helped me to my feet, pulling me so close we stood nearly pressed against one another. The warmth from his body enveloped me like an embrace as our eyes remained locked, allowing dozens of wordless conversations to pass between us, conversations I ached to explore forever. I desperately hoped I had a lifetime to do so, even though such a wish was surely impossible.

His soft touch trailed down my arm until he reached my hand to gently wind my arm through his. My fingers curled at his elbow. He stared at where my hand rested before raising his gaze to mine, his own filled with an intensity that made me slightly weak in the knees.

"Will you accompany me on a stroll?" He escorted me from the study and outside to the manicured grounds. "Have you tired of the gardens after having spent most of the morning walking them?"

"I could spend all my time outside; I adore nature."

The ring flared, a warning for me to watch my words. I bit my lip to suppress a sigh. There were so many memories I ached to share with Liam from my time spent as a goose girl before Princess Lavena had discovered me, when I'd spent every single day outside, no matter the weather. Going from such a life to being cooped up indoors as the princess's hand-maiden had been suffocating. But I couldn't share any of this.

Liam paused halfway down the stone steps to search my expression, his own concerned. "Are you alright, Lavena?"

I flinched at her name. "I'm fine." But it was a lie.

Liam cupped my chin to lift my gaze. "I know I'm rather new to this husband thing, but you don't *seem* fine. What's bothering you?"

There were so many things I wanted to tell him—so many I would never be able to—but I couldn't bear the thought of keeping every part of myself hidden from him. Perhaps I could explore the ring's limits and see how much it'd let me reveal.

"Until I was fourteen, I spent the majority of my time outside, no matter the weather."

The ring made no protest.

He chuckled. "I never thought of you as one who spent so much time outside."

We strolled down a path that twisted through rows of blooming irises on one side and a hedge along the other. I ran my fingers along the green leaves as we passed by.

"Princesses aren't supposed to like the outdoors; the sun ruins our complexions." That had been Princess Lavena's primary reason for avoiding being outside, which made her choice of a traveling minstrel all the more ridiculous.

It definitely wouldn't last, which meant Liam and I wouldn't be together long. Perhaps the princess was even now waiting at the Dracerian palace for when we returned from our honeymoon. My heart constricted at the thought.

Liam tilted his head to study my face. "Ah, you have freckles." He lightly brushed over them with his fingertip.

"I freckle in the sun."

"And princesses aren't supposed to freckle?" His mouth quirked into one of his adorable dimpled smiles. "Your freckles are cute. They're making me want to play connect-the-dots." He traced his finger from one to another.

I giggled. "Perhaps I can be persuaded to humor you."

His eyes widened before his usual grin broke free. "Excellent, another husband perk. I'm surprised you're so willing to let me exhibit my childish antics in such a way. I used to think you rather vain." A blush caressed his cheeks at the admission, and goodness, he was even more adorable when bashful. "But you're not that way at all. Was pretending otherwise merely a charade?"

I sighed. "Yes, everything is a charade."

"I like you better when you're not playing a part," he said. "I'm grateful I'm finally coming to know the real you."

My stomach knotted. He was wrong; he didn't know me at all. I ached to tell him the truth, but the princess's ring tightened around my finger in warning. He must have sensed something had distressed me and allowed silence to settle over us. Walking arm-in-arm with Liam soon calmed my anxiety.

After several content minutes, he stirred to slowly unhook our arms. I peeked curiously at him and found him blushing once more. "Lavena, can we--"

His look became shy as he wove our fingers together. My breath caught and my hand instinctively tightened around his. *Liam is holding my hand.* I'd never held a man's hand before except for Father's and Archer's, and that hadn't been since I was a little girl. This experience was vastly different and far more wonderful.

"Is this alright?" he asked.

"Yes," I managed breathlessly.

I vaguely realized we'd stopped walking. I was grateful, certain my wobbly legs were too weak to continue our stroll. At first Liam only held my hand, but then he began to stroke the back of it with his thumb, each touch sending a pulse of heat up my arm.

"This alright?" he asked again.

This time I couldn't speak, so I only nodded. Liam lifted our hands and pressed them to his chest, right above his beating heart, a heart I wished I could keep forever. He leaned down and pressed a soft kiss on each of my fingertips.

"Such beautiful hands, just like the woman who possesses them." His smoldering gaze rose to meet mine. "Shall we continue our stroll?"

"I don't think I can walk," I admitted. His entire manner

lit up as he stepped closer, his fingers caressing up and down mine.

"Why? Am I...affecting you?"

Heat tickled my cheeks but I was unable to look away. There were no words to describe the sensations filling me from each of his touches, the strong need I felt for him to never pull away. "I've never felt this way before," I admitted.

"Neither have I." He raised my hand once more to press a soft kiss on my palm. "But I like it."

"So do I."

We stood for several minutes in this manner, Liam attentively playing with and kissing my hand, until he eventually tugged me gently after him to continue our walk. Our hands stayed intertwined as we playfully swung our arms back and forth. I felt as if I floated rather than walked down the path. Who knew such a simple gesture could fill me with so much joy?

I suddenly paused when I spotted a *chrysis ignita,* a ruby-tailed wasp, an insect I'd read about but had never seen before. I gasped. "Oh! *Oh!*" The wasp buzzed several yards away, silently pleading for me to study its vibrant colors more closely. I instinctively stepped forward, taking Liam with me.

"What is it?" Liam looked around quizzically, having not spotted the marvelous insect buzzing around the primroses.

"Look!" I pointed and his eyes widened, but not with awe.

"What is that?" He pulled me away. "Don't worry, my dear, I shan't let the pest harm you." And just like that, I lost my opportunity to study one of the insects I'd always ached to see. I dug my heels into the path, too annoyed to even savor the fact that Liam had just called me *my dear.*

"No, wait—"

He paused, eyebrows raised, but before I could explain, a searing pain encircled my finger, a reminder to act like

Princess Lavena, which meant I wasn't supposed to like insects. Frustration and confusion welled up within me for the ring's fickle demands. It had allowed me to tell Liam that I'd enjoyed the book on insects, so why couldn't I study them now? Perhaps it had been my exuberance that had triggered it this time. I gritted my teeth as I cast a longing look back at the wasp, no longer in sight.

"What's wrong?"

"Nothing," I snapped, far more sharply than I intended, even though it wasn't his fault I had an unwanted part to play. It was torturous having to keep so many parts of myself hidden, no matter how small. The realization caused the beautiful moment that had been between us to all but shatter, so much so that even his hand holding mine seemed to burn, but not enough for me to pull away.

"You're upset." He sounded perplexed. "I suppose I figured it was too good to be true to think we'd completely gotten past our usual contention. Won't you tell me what's wrong?"

"I saw a ruby-tailed wasp," I said. "That's what's wrong."

"Okay..." The poor man seemed thoroughly confused. "And it frightened you?"

"Heavens, no. It was...lovely, wasn't it?" I said the words tentatively as I nervously fiddled with my hair, wanting to share *something* about Anwen—if we were going to work at all with this ridiculous deception, I couldn't hide *every* part of me away, especially my feelings—but not wanting to upset the sadistic ring. Thankfully, it made no protest. I relaxed.

"Lovely?" He wrinkled his nose. "You're upset because a garden pest was *lovely*?"

I sighed. "No. I'm sorry, Liam, this isn't important."

"But it is." He cradled my hands within his. "I admit I don't understand, but I want to. Please help me to."

I pressed my hand against his heart, relishing each beat it made against my fingertips. His sweet concern did wonders for my disappointment. "I was disappointed about something, but the moment has passed. Thank you, Liam."

He gave my hand a gentle squeeze. "I admit I'm still confused. What did I do to help? Please tell me so I can write it down for next time."

I managed a smile, which he tentatively returned. "You were simply you."

"And you like me being me?"

I tipped my head back to stare deeply into his blue eyes. "Very much."

"Thank heavens the remedy to a sad Lavena is so easy; I just have to be myself."

He winked before he proceeded to do just that, spending the remainder of the walk telling me humorous stories, pointing out anything to make me smile—such as a bird's nest full of baby chicks—and tucking a flower that matched my dress behind my ear.

Each sweet, playful gesture only made it more difficult not to fall in love with him. I couldn't allow myself to do that, not when the princess would eventually return to take back what was rightfully hers.

But I was powerless to fight the process, and it frightened me. As Liam managed to cheer me up and make me laugh, I clung to his hand all the more tightly, afraid to let go and lose him, even though in my heart I knew our separation was inevitable.

CHAPTER 10

M y Dear Sister,

Thank you for your recent letter. I know you're confused by my actions at your wedding, but allow me to reassure you that I have nothing but your best interests in mind. I'm fully aware of your situation and won't allow you to come to any harm. Don't be afraid; all will be well.

I'll visit soon. I have a good feeling about this union. Trust me.

Your brother, Nolan

I SIGHED as I crumpled up Prince Nolan's letter and tossed it aside. Short, vague, and pointless. He was the only one who could help me, and yet my plea for assistance had fallen on deaf ears.

I pressed my forehead against my desk in defeat, a headache already pulsing behind my temples. What could His Highness's motive possibly be for not intervening? Didn't he realize that the longer we waited, the more difficult it'd be to untangle me from this mess? It was likely impossible now, for surely Liam knew me well enough at this point that he'd notice if the princess and I switched back; I was completely trapped.

Strangely, the more I came to know Liam, the less distressing that thought became.

I released a long sigh as I forced myself to straighten. My gaze lingered on the offending letter once more. I'd waited so long for a reply, hoping it'd be good news, but instead it'd been utterly useless. I retrieved it and smoothed out the wrinkles marring the parchment so I could reread it, not just once, but twice.

My brow furrowed over a particular line: *I have a good feeling about this union.* What did the prince mean by that? Did he truly think this arrangement was for the best? Would he do nothing to wriggle me out of the princess's tangled web? He had to realize that his sister would eventually return to claim what was hers. Surely he'd do *something* to help me, wouldn't he?

But from his letter, I could see that that *something* would be very little—possibly nothing. I sighed as I re-crumpled it, this time tossing it into the fire, where the flames consumed it, and with it any chance of someone stumbling upon this rather unconventional letter from a brother to his supposed sister.

My thoughts automatically drifted to my own brother. Archer had never been far from my mind, especially after his unexpected visit the week before. I'd tried not to think about him too much, a task made easier considering how well things were going with Liam. My heart wrenched with guilt at just how easy it'd been not to dwell on my brother's worry.

My mind repeatedly drifted to Prince Nolan's letter and my own brother's distress all throughout breakfast, where I scarcely touched my food and listened to Liam's charming conversation with only half an ear.

He paused in his current story of mischief he'd entangled

himself in as a boy to search my expression. "Are you alright, Lavena? You seem out of sorts this morning."

I was pleased he'd noticed. I fiddled with the ring on my hand, trying to find an adequate excuse, but before I could, we were interrupted by a footman, a timely rescue.

He bowed crisply. "Forgive the interruption, Your Highnesses, but I've been informed that a family in the nearby village has just lost their home due to a fire."

Liam's expression became solemn immediately. "Was anyone harmed?"

"No, Your Highness."

"And were any other families affected by the fire?"

The footman shook his head.

"I'm relieved no one was hurt, but what a tragic event for the family who lost their home," Liam said. "Of course we'll lend our aid. Prepare for supplies to be sent immediately."

The footman bowed again and left to execute Liam's orders while I gaped at my husband. Supplies? Was that all he would do? Surely, there was more we could do in our position. My heart immediately reached out to this family I didn't even know, even as a memory from my childhood returned: when I'd been a young girl, our village's crops had flooded from a season of unusually heavy rains, resulting in a long, hungry winter. While the Lycerian royal family had sent some aid, it had done little to ease our physical suffering, let alone our emotional distress at our dire circumstances, leaving the entire village feeling neglected by our monarchy.

I refused to allow this family to endure the same experience, especially now when I could finally do something to help. I stood. "We'll go at once to see how we might offer our assistance."

Liam blinked up at me from where he sat unmoving in his own seat. "Wait, what?"

I was already halfway to the door. "We're going to help the village family whose house has burned."

I glanced over my shoulder to see whether or not he was following. Liam stared after me for another baffled moment. "We're already helping. I'm sending servants and supplies to--"

"Sending servants and supplies is *helpful*, but there's more we can do to assist. We must survey the situation ourselves."

His forehead furrowed. "But it's our honeymoon."

"Your duty to your subjects comes first. There's a need for our service now and we should provide it, despite any personal inconvenience." I gave him a teasing smile. "Besides, isn't dealing with the aftermath of a fire a grander adventure than another garden stroll or afternoon in the library?"

He gave me a rather desperate look, as if he didn't want me to leave without him, but also as if he wasn't sure whether he wanted to go.

"Don't you want to come along?" I asked. "You should. You're the crown prince, and the members of that family are some of your subjects, *our* subjects."

I briskly left the dining room to go to my room to change, wondering whether or not he'd follow. To my delight he did, easily catching up to me and maintaining my rapid pace with his own longer stride. As we walked, he peered into my face with a look like he was trying to decipher a complicated puzzle. I raised an eyebrow and he grinned.

"We're to jump into the heat of it, are we? Get our royal hands dirty doing something useful for a change? Excellent." His eyes lit at the prospect of an adventure, even though the day that lay before us would likely be anything but adventurous. My heart swelled. He was such a good man.

"You really want to come?"

"I want to help our people almost as much as I want to spend the day with you." He blinked rapidly—as if his words surprised him—before he nodded to himself. "You could drag me anywhere and I'd come."

I smiled at his sweet declaration. If only I could spend the rest of my life with him at my side. I bit my lip to hold back a sigh, determined to enjoy the time we had together while it lasted.

We separated at our bedrooms to change into simpler clothing. Before emerging from my room, I glanced into the mirror and frowned at the fake princess staring back at me, all signs of Anwen completely hidden away. Even after several weeks, the thought that I couldn't see myself still bothered me. How much longer would my true reflection remain hidden beneath this mask?

I met Liam in the hallway, and together we went down to the servants' quarters to organize the labor force and supplies. Despite his sweet willingness to help, poor Liam seemed at a loss as to what to do for a peasant family who'd just lost everything. So I took charge of gathering the supplies—blankets, clothing, cooking dishes, flour, dried fruit and potatoes—as well as arranging for a labor force that would help rebuild the family's destroyed home.

Since the carriages held the supplies, we opted to walk, a half-hour journey on foot. Liam made no complaint about walking. He merely wove our fingers together and whistled cheerfully as we went. I glanced down at our connected hands and then up at him. He paused mid-whistle, a blush filling his cheeks.

"Is this alright?"

"Of course." His inquiry surprised me. After all, we'd been holding hands on all our strolls for several days now.

He released a breath of relief. "I was afraid my attentions wouldn't be welcome, considering you're coming to discover they come from a useless prince." A frown tugged at his mouth.

"You're not a useless prince, merely an untrained one."

"Perhaps, while you're obviously already a dutiful and compassionate princess." The look he gave me was admiring.

My cheeks warmed. "Isn't it my duty as a princess to help?"

"This is more than a duty for you," Liam said gently. "I can see it in your eyes. You're relishing the thought of helping this family. You'll make an excellent queen."

"And you'll make an excellent king." By his solemn expression, I could tell he still doubted himself. I squeezed his hand assuredly. "I think you're going to surprise yourself today. You claim you didn't really know me before our wedding, but you clearly don't know yourself either."

His brow furrowed. "What do you mean?"

"You're a good man, Liam; you just haven't allowed yourself to embrace your new role as the crown prince. But you will, starting now. I'll help you."

After all, Liam would one day be king, no matter who stood at his side. If I did nothing else in our precious time together, I'd help him see himself clearly and embrace who he was so that when the time of his reign came, he'd fulfill his role with confidence.

We soon reached the tiny village, comprised of small wooden homes and a bustling market of villagers. They blinked in astonishment at our presence before sweeping into bows and curtsies, each villager greeting us with a reverent, "Your Highnesses" or "Prince and Princess."

I blushed at the gestures I didn't deserve, and I felt even more an imposter now than I had during this entire façade thus far. If only they knew I was really one of them.

With our carriage rattling behind us, we wove through the crowd, following the scent of smoke that still blistered the air to a tiny makeshift house burned almost entirely to the ground. The laborers we'd sent had already arrived and had been joined by several villagers to help remove the charred remains. I could do little to help with that. I found my purpose the moment I spotted two little girls clinging to their mother's skirts, their faces tear-stained and covered in soot.

I choked back a sob. "*Oh*." I released Liam's hand and knelt before them, ignoring the soot already marring my dress. I took the little girls' hands. "Hello, darlings, are you alright?"

One immediately buried her face against her mother while the other gaped at me before offering a shy smile. "Are you Crown Princess Lavena?"

No. But I forced myself to nod. "I am. What are your names?"

"Erin, and this is my little sister Anea."

The girl didn't even peek out from her mother's dress.

Erin's lip trembled. "Our house burned."

I removed my handkerchief and gently wiped away the tears and soot streaking her cheeks. "I know, and I'm terribly sorry. But Crown Prince Liam and I are here to help you."

Erin's eyes widened further as her gaze darted towards Liam, who'd already crouched down beside me with a sweet look as he stared at the girls. "You want to help *us*?"

He gave her his usual charming smile. "Of course. It's a prince's privilege to help two fine maidens in need of assistance."

Erin blushed and tugged on her mother's skirt. "Hear that, Mama? The prince and princess want to help us."

She smiled through her own tears. "Thank you kindly, Your Highnesses, we're ever so grateful."

"We'll help in whatever way we can." My most pressing concern was these two little girls. I focused my attention on washing their sooty faces, hands, and bare feet before arranging for their breakfast and ensuring they had what they they needed. As I worked, I strove to lock my emotions away so they wouldn't overcome me, but soon the heartache and worry filling their faces became too much. My eyes began to burn, and not from the smokey air.

I needed a moment. I excused myself and hurried a few paces away to lean against a nearby cottage, taking several shaky breaths that did little to quell my tears. They escaped to trickle down my cheeks.

I fumbled with my handkerchief before remembering it was dirty after I'd used it to wash the girls' faces. Liam appeared at my elbow with his own, but rather than handing it to me, he used it to gently dab at my teary eyelids.

"Are you alright, Lavena?"

I glanced towards the family, who were eagerly accepting the supplies we'd brought, even as the two little girls looked on in wonder at the laborers already rebuilding the walls of their home. "They'll be alright, won't they?"

"Of course they will."

"Really? Because I need them to be."

Tenderness filled Liam's gaze. "Oh Lavena, you compassionate, remarkable woman."

He gathered me in his arms and I nestled against him, burrowing against his cinnamon-scented warmth. He pressed a soft kiss on the top of my head.

"This is my favorite day of our honeymoon thus far," he murmured. "It's allowed me to come to know you even better." He gently cupped my chin and lifted my teary gaze to meet his own, which glistened with an incredibly special look, one I couldn't put into words but which made me feel cherished. His thumb lightly caressed my wet cheeks. "You're so sweet, Lavena."

His caressing gaze lowered to my lips. Fear compelled me to reluctantly extract myself from his embrace before he could act on the desire filling his eyes.

"We should return to work."

We spent the remainder of the day in the village. While I remained with the women volunteers sewing and cleaning, Liam rolled up his sleeves and jumped into the process of rebuilding the ruined home. Sweat and dirt quickly lined his brow as he lent his assistance with contagious cheer and enthusiasm, immediately putting the village men at ease as they worked together on the cottage. Laughter and banter soon filled the air, along with shouts of, "Hey, Prince, pass me that log," and "Who knew a prince could wield a hammer?" By Liam's wide smile, I could tell he was enjoying himself immensely.

He only took an occasional break to dote on all the little village girls, who were drawn to him like bees to honey. Liam made it his personal mission to get every child to laugh and smile. Each of his tender gestures caused me to lose more of my heart to him. I tried to ignore him and concentrate on my tasks in order to protect myself, but I couldn't close off my ears to the sound of his sweetness and laughter with the children and his good-natured ribbing with the laborers. Several times throughout our work we exchanged shy looks, always smiling before hastily looking away.

As I washed what had survived of the family's sooty laundry, Erin sidled up to me with a mischievous grin. "You love the prince, don't you? You keep staring at him with a mushy look in your eyes."

My pulse quickened, especially considering we were close enough to Liam that he could hear our conversation. *Love...*I forced the word from my mind. No matter the role I played, I was still a handmaiden. As such, loving the crown prince would only lead to heartache.

Erin was still waiting for an answer; by her expectant smile, it was clear she didn't doubt what it'd be. The heat in my cheeks deepened. "He's a good man. I'm very fortunate to have him for my husband."

I glanced shyly at Liam again, desperate to see his reaction to my words, and was pleased to discover him staring at me with his usual tender look. What did that look mean? I was almost afraid to analyze it. Shy little Anea—whom Liam had managed to convince to sit snugly on his lap—was also watching me, her eyes wide with innocence.

"Your princess is really pretty," she whispered loudly to him. Liam beamed, his tender expression growing even softer.

"She is, but more importantly, she's the sweetest woman I've ever met."

My heart lifted before I could school its reaction. At this point, losing it to Liam was inevitable, though it would make our eventual separation all the more torturous.

As the sun began to set, we bid our goodbyes to the family and other villagers and made our way back to the palace. Despite the carriage now being empty of supplies, I wanted to walk and Liam made no objections. He sent the carriage on ahead and we strolled in silence for several minutes, allowing the settling dusk and the day we'd shared together to enfold us in reverence.

Liam broke the stillness first. "I'm surprised how much I enjoyed helping that family and interacting with the villagers." His gaze met mine in the golden-rose light. "It must have been because we did it together."

"Partly, but it's also because you're so naturally generous and enjoy helping your subjects—not to mention you're exuberant and love doing new things and staying busy. You really will make a wonderful king."

"That was the hardest day of labor I've ever done, but also the most satisfying." He tugged us to a stop and cupped my cheek. "You helped me take a step forward in fulfilling my future role of king. Together, we'll make such a difference in our kingdom. I caught a glimpse of that potential today."

I stared up at Liam with his sweat-caked face and dirty clothes. He'd never looked more handsome to me than he did in this moment.

I ached for a future together—to be by his side and witness firsthand all the good he'd do for his people—but I knew that was impossible. For now, I just needed to help him realize that he was capable of standing on his own.

"You're an amazing crown prince because of who you already are," I said. "You once confided that you're afraid your role will change you, when in reality you already possess the traits that you need to fulfill it. You're incredibly compassionate."

"Not as much as you." He enfolded both my hands in his. My heart flared to life at the contact. "In addition to teaching me how to be a king, you're also helping me realize what marriage really is. Before, I only saw it as something to be endured, whereas now you're showing me it's a partnership where we help better one another and work side by side. I'm already a better man because of you. It'll be a privilege continuing to come to know you more." He pressed a soft kiss to each of my hands.

The energy between us hummed. My pulse pounded painfully, especially at the tender look filling his eyes. He wrapped his arms gently around my waist, drawing me closer as his gaze, now lit with purpose, flickered down to my lips.

For a moment I almost gave in, but I couldn't allow myself to become any closer to the man who wasn't mine to keep. I pulled out of his arms.

"It's getting dark," I whispered.

He didn't move at first, and when he eventually stirred it was with obvious reluctance. I risked a glance at him, and my heart wrenched at the disappointment filling his expression, his anguish matching the emotion tormenting my own heart .

It had been the right choice, but that didn't keep the regret away.

CHAPTER 11

*W*hen I arrived for breakfast the next morning, I found a daisy resting beside my plate. I grinned girlishly as I picked it up and breathed in its sweet floral perfume. *Liam...*

He'd been offering simple, sweet gestures for me every day this week, ever since our garden stroll when we'd first held hands. Small tokens, really, but all of which felt monumental to me—from asking the cook to prepare blackberry pudding as a surprise, to leaving hidden notes for me to discover, and now flowers. If this was Liam courting, he was doing a remarkable job of it.

I didn't hear him come in but I sensed his presence after he'd approached. He leaned over my chair, enveloping me in his cinnamon warmth. "Good morning, Lavena."

I shuddered as his warm breath caressed my skin. "Good morning, Liam."

He twisted around to playfully rub his nose against mine. I clutched the arms of my chair in an attempt to ground myself. Goodness, he was getting more forward; as much as I loved it, I couldn't continue to allow this to happen between us.

I'd spent most of the night reliving yesterday's excursion to the village in every detail, dwelling on each look, smile, and tender word Liam had given me. Each reminder caused my heart to flutter in a way that was foreign but which I recognized all the same—it was the early signs of falling in love, I was sure of it. And falling in love was something I couldn't do.

Oblivious to the battle raging within me, Liam smiled warmly. "It is a wonderful morning, isn't it?" He withdrew and walked stiffly over to his seat, wincing as he went. "It appears my princely stride has been replaced with the waddle of a goose. I wasn't sure I'd be able to get out of bed this morning, considering yesterday I used muscles I didn't even know I had."

"It's a good thing I like geese so much." The words escaped before I could check them. Already trying to resist my affections for Liam was proving difficult.

He grinned as he plopped into his chair and turned his soft gaze to me. "You look lovely today, just as you did yesterday with your soot-covered dress and messed-up hair. You were amazing with the villagers."

"And you were never more a crown prince than when you were working with the men to rebuild the cottage." I lifted the daisy to my nose again. "Thank you for the flower; I love daisies."

"Is that a daisy, then?" He slumped in relief at my nod. "Thank goodness. You've frequently noticed a specific white flower during our daily walks, but this morning when I rose early to track one down for you, I realized just how many white flowers there were and was afraid I'd plucked the wrong one."

"Even if you had, the gesture would have been equally

appreciated." Achingly sweet, just like everything about him. Regardless of what happened between us, I felt quite fortunate to have the opportunity of knowing this wonderful man.

Conversation flowed easily as we began breakfast. Liam was his usual animated self, laughing boisterously as he talked with his hands while occasionally grimacing as his stiff body moved. His laughter washed over me and each tender smile sent a flutter straight to my heart. If only this moment could last forever.

Liam shoved his last bit of toast into his mouth and leaned back in his seat. "What are your plans for today, dear?"

Dear...he'd been using that endearment more and more often, and it never ceased to make me smile. "Is there a reason for your curiosity?"

Crimson dotted his cheeks as he ran his fingernail along the table seam. "I was hoping you'd want to spend the day with me."

He made the same request every morning, always with shy uncertainty, as if afraid I wouldn't want to. But how could I not when being in his presence was like basking in the sun? "I'd like nothing better than to spend more time with my husband."

He brightened. "Really?"

"Yes, really."

"Then we shan't waste another moment." He bounded from his seat with his usual exuberance and took my hands to tug me to my feet.

"Can't I finish breakfast first?" I asked.

"Ah yes, provisions." He picked up my napkin and dumped the entire basket of fruit inside. "Now we're ready."

I grabbed my last piece of toast and allowed him to lead

me from the dining room. "What adventure do you have in mind for today?"

It turned out to be a trip to the fountain. Liam sent a servant to retrieve a small stack of rather important-looking documents before taking one with a reverence that I doubted was for its content.

"Have you ever folded a paper boat? Why are you shaking your head? This is blasphemy, Lavena."

I dipped my hand into the cool fountain and splashed him. "I've always been too busy to fold paper boats."

He arched an eyebrow. "Busy doing what? You're not the heir."

Oops. I silently cursed my mistake. While the handmaiden Anwen worked from dawn until dusk, Princess Lavena was one of the most idle people I knew. "I don't like being idle."

"It's true you never sit still for long...like me. Another compatibility." His grin was hesitant at first, but at my returning smile he brightened. "Now, shall I remedy this appalling lapse in your education? The art of making paper boats is far more important than any princess subjects you've studied. Kian and I spent many hours perfecting the process when we were children." He handed me one of the documents. "Now, watch closely..."

"Wait, Liam, we're using *this*? Isn't it important?"

He took it and studied it with a furrowed brow before shrugging. "Not really." He returned it, his touch lingering on mine. "Now watch the master."

He set his document on the rim of the fountain, pulled up his sleeves, and went to work, his tongue half-sticking out of his mouth as he made each fold with practiced precision. I watched, fascinated, as the boat took shape.

He held it up triumphantly when he finished. "I dub this ship the *HMS Lavena*. May she sail the seas and experience grand adventures for many years."

I winced to hear *her* name used in place of mine. "I hope I don't sink; I have no experience captaining such a seaworthy vessel."

"As your first mate, I'd never let you perish in a shipwreck." He placed the boat in the fountain and gave it a gentle push. Sure enough, it floated. He wriggled his eyebrows. "I'm ready for my accolades."

I stood to sweep into an exaggerated curtsy. "Oh Master Shipbuilder, please teach your humble apprentice all your knowledge."

He stroked my cheek with his knuckles. "I thought you'd never ask."

He scooted closer to me, whispering instructions as if he were imparting great shipbuilding secrets, all while finding any excuse to touch me—from brushing a strand of my hair aside so I could better see, to guiding my hand, to helping me make each fold. I cherished each touch and soon found myself doing poorly on purpose.

"I know what you're up to," he whispered in my ear in a singsong voice.

Heat tickled my cheeks. "I—" I had no words.

He chuckled. "I see I've rendered you speechless." He hesitated before running his fingers through my hair, and even though I was determinedly avoiding his eyes, I still sensed his soft smile. "I don't mind, Lavena dear. Too bad we've almost completed this boat's construction. Perhaps the ship will sink so we're forced to start over."

The blush filling my cheeks deepened. "But then the *HMS Liam* won't be able to go on its own adventure."

"Perhaps the *HMS Liam* likes this one better." He playfully tapped my nose. "Despite that, I do want to accompany the *HMS Lavena* on her own voyage."

We returned to constructing his boat, and after more touching and giggling between us, the *HMS Liam* was at last ready to launch. I placed it in the fountain, where it immediately capsized. "My apologies, Captain, but your boat is sinking."

Liam watched the ship slip beneath the water before sighing. "It appears I distracted you a bit too much. Thus ends the days of the *HMS Liam*." He placed his hand over his heart and bowed his head solemnly.

"Not to worry, I'd never leave my husband to such a fate. The *HMS An—Lavena* rescued you before you could perish. Perhaps you can repay my generosity with a grand adventure."

He stroked his chin before a rather wicked grin filled his face. "I have the perfect one in mind."

My heart hammered, but not in fear. "I recognize that mischievous gleam. What plot have you just concocted?"

He slowly leaned forward. "This." He pushed me, sending me tumbling backwards into the fountain with an icy splash. My shriek was eclipsed by his boisterous laugh. I gaped at him through my dripping hair.

"You *pushed* me?"

"Not a very husbandly thing to do, is it? I'm sorry, my dear, but you did sink my ship." He laughed again.

I pushed aside my wet hair. "It appears I mistook you for a gentleman."

He bowed slightly. "I *am* a gentleman and will thus render my assistance immediately." He extended his hand to help me out, but instead I yanked him into the water with a spectacular splash. Sputtering, he scrambled to his knees and gaped at me in shock before he grinned.

"I probably deserved that."

"No doubt, but I'll still apologize." I leaned over and pressed a kiss on his cheek, finally acting on the impulse I'd felt for days. So much for distance.

He stilled, and for a moment he stared at me blankly before his smile widened. "Wow, I like your apologies."

I smiled shyly. "Does this mean you accept it?"

"I certainly do. In fact, I may need another apology as I think I bumped my knee when I fell in." He tilted his cheek towards me expectantly, but instead I splashed him. He chuckled. "I deserved that, too. Now, allow me to do my husbandly duty and warm you up." He pulled me against his wet chest and rubbed his hands up and down my arms. "Pushing you was beyond the lines of my usual immaturity. Are you alright?" His gaze softened in remorse.

"I'm fine." If holding me was Liam's way of saying sorry, it'd always be easy to accept his apologies.

I shyly snuggled deeper into his toasty embrace, telling myself I was only doing so because he was a welcome respite from the cold water soaking my skirts. I soon found my fingers stroking the nape of his neck. His breath hooked and he started to lean closer...until my shiver shattered the spell.

"Are you cold?" he whispered.

"No," I lied.

"We should go back inside and get into some warm clothes."

"I don't want to." The water rippled as I nestled closer, not wanting to end this moment with him.

"I don't want you catching a chill. But don't worry, today's adventures aren't over." He helped me out of the fountain and escorted me to my room to change.

I emerged several minutes later to find him waiting for me, already in a fresh outfit himself. His gaze lingered on my hair, which I hadn't bothered styling despite the insistence of my maid, so it now lay in dark clumps plastered down my back. The princess would have had a fit if she'd seen how I was representing her. I smirked at the thought. *Excellent.*

"Are you going to tell me the story behind that smile?" Liam asked. "I'm quite anxious to know."

"You seem quite invested in my smiles."

"They show me you're happy, which means I'm being the husband you deserve."

Despite my lingering chill, his words warmed me through, a warmth that only grew as he continued staring at my hair, his grin widening with his perusal.

"You look even lovelier than before, Lavena, if such a thing is possible." He ran his fingers through my hair. "I like this look on you."

"I thought I'd leave my wet hair down so that you'd be reminded of your crime of pushing your wife into the fountain and feel the proper guilt."

He chuckled before lowering his hand, running it down my arm to weave his fingers through mine. "It appears I must still earn your forgiveness. Perhaps we can limit our next adventure to a more land-based activity, such as spending the afternoon in the library together."

"Unless I'm in the mood for you to grovel for a bit longer."

He chuckled again before escorting me to the library, where we each selected books and settled beside one another on the settee, which I quickly realized was a mistake. His proximity made it impossible to concentrate; I read the same sentence half a dozen times before closing my book in defeat.

He glanced up. "Finished already?"

"You're distracting me," I said. "I can't concentrate with you sitting so close."

"You're not the only one who's distracted. I haven't the faintest idea what I'm supposedly reading." He studied his book's cover. "Well, this is embarrassing; it's actually upside down." He laughed but stopped when I stood. He caught hold of my skirt. "Where are you going?"

"I can't read while trying to resist touching you."

"You mean you've been just as tempted? I've been fighting the desire to put my arm around you ever since we sat down."

He'd been as tempted as I'd been? For I'd spent the entire time clenching the folds of my skirt to resist taking his hand. Perhaps distance would be best.

"I'll just be in the window seat." But I'd only taken a few steps before he tugged me back, expression imploring.

"Please stay, Lavena. The settee is rather frightening when one is alone on it."

I raised an eyebrow. "The settee is *frightening*? What's the story behind that?"

"I'll tell you if you stay." His eyes became pleading and I felt dangerously close to relenting. But as much as I welcomed his attentions, they placed my heart in greater jeopardy.

I made a show of considering his offer, tapping my lips thoughtfully, before shaking my head. "Maybe later." I tugged myself free and pattered towards the window seat. I'd no sooner settled than he bounded over, expression lit with mischief.

"Is your book really more interesting than me?"

"Hard to say. Are you interesting, Liam?"

He crawled onto the seat beside me, so close our sides touched. "I'm *very* interesting. Let me prove it to you." He stroked my cheek. At my body's responding shiver, I realized what he was up to.

"Are you flirting with me?"

He grinned. "I suppose I am." His fingers lightly trailed up and down my neck. "Are you enjoying it as much as I am?"

It was becoming difficult to breathe. All that was happening between us was too new and somewhat frightening, despite it also being wonderful. "I—" My head felt foggy but in a pleasant way. I liked this feeling, but nowhere near as much as I adored the tender way he smiled at me.

"Speechless again? I love knowing I'm affecting you in even the smallest way, as you always affect me with just a single look."

My heart felt on the brink of soaring if he continued looking at me like that. I raised my book and held it in front of me like a shield, but he merely removed the barrier between us, raising his eyebrows at the cover.

"*The World of Insects?* It appears I'm not the only one who grabbed a random book." He set it aside. "With that obstacle out of the way, shall we resume our *flirting?*"

"I'm not very good at it," I stammered.

"I disagree, because whatever you're doing, it's definitely working."

His own flirting nearly undid me completely. I pressed myself further back against the seat even though I wanted nothing more than to bridge the distance between us to discover what lay on the other side. "Liam…"

He reached out to caress my face, but I ducked beneath his arm and scrambled from the window seat. He chuckled. "Oh, so you want to be chased? I'll happily accommodate."

He came after me. I darted from his reach and ran to the other end of the library, where I found myself wedged between two bookcases. Liam cornered me and rested his arms on either side of me like a cage, but I didn't feel trapped; instead I felt moments away from floating.

"Gotcha," he said with a triumphant smile. "Now that I've captured you, what shall I do to you?"

"Let me go?" I squeaked, both wishing for him to and desperately hoping he never would.

"Ah, Lavena, I couldn't do that. When one discovers a treasure, they keep it in order to cherish it."

He ran his thumb across my cheek before tracing it along

my jaw to cradle my face, tipping it at the perfect angle, his gaze on my lips. A purposeful glint filled his eyes as he dipped down. I immediately knew his intention. And I almost let him, but at the last moment...

"Please don't," I pleaded breathlessly.

He paused inches away, close enough that I could feel his warm breath caress my mouth. It would be so easy for one of us to close the remaining distance. I ached to, needing to feel his lips press against mine. But he heeded my plea and immediately released me, stepping back to give me space. I released a pent-up breath I hadn't realized I'd been holding.

"I'm sorry," he whispered. "I didn't realize you didn't want..." He trailed off, cheeks crimson. I felt horrible for hurting him. Again. Regret for stopping the kiss already gnawed at my heart.

"I'm not ready, Liam." Another lie, one of many. I hated being forced to lie to him.

"I'm sorry, I didn't mean to rush you. I thought you were flirting back, that you welcomed..." He dug his fingers in his hair, looking so lost and uncertain.

"I do welcome it," I said.

He misunderstood my words and, with an ecstatic grin, he leaned down to try and kiss me again. I jerked away, this rejection more painful to give than the last. "No."

He frowned. "But you just said—"

"I'm sorry," I said hastily.

He looked at me suspiciously. "Is this another game?"

I flinched. No matter how many steps forward we made together in this relationship, there were moments Liam still doubted me, causing us to retreat several steps back. I couldn't blame him—Princess Lavena had much to atone for in her past treatment of Liam, and I was paying for it now.

I took his hands. "Of course it's not a game. I only meant that while I welcome your affections, I'm not ready to go as far as a kiss quite yet." I wasn't sure if I ever would be. Surely kissing Liam would make it all the more difficult to eventually let him go.

His gaze snapped to mine, eyes hopeful. "Really?" He seemed encouraged by the blush warming my cheeks and his lips quirked up in a tentative smile. "You mean it?"

I shyly peeked up at him. "I do."

Even though I knew it was unwise to encourage him, the battle between yielding to him and resisting him was already so wearying. How long could I fight it when it seemed obvious which side was destined to win?

I shifted restlessly. "I should go. It's been a long day."

He nodded, as if he'd expected me to run away after he'd pushed me too far. He took my hand and kissed it, his lips lingering. "I hope to see you soon."

Despite my own longing to stay with him, I was too frazzled to do so tonight. I took dinner in my room, but rather than eating any of it, I sat picking at my food as I relived that moment in the library—the smoldering look filling Liam's eyes, his leaning into me and enveloping me with his intoxicating warmth, and especially the fact he'd almost *kissed* me. My heart ached, and even though I knew it had been for the best, I wished more than anything I hadn't stopped it.

CHAPTER 12

I fought off a yawn from my restless night as I pushed my eggs around my plate at breakfast the following morning. Rain pattered against the dining room windows, the only sound filling the awkward silence between us, a silence seeming more unbearable after we'd gone so long without it.

I stole a peek at Liam sitting across from me. He wasn't eating either but was instead building an elaborate tower with his toast. He completed the structure and met my gaze with a shy smile. "I know what you're hoping for."

I'd been lost in thought, bemoaning the fact I hadn't let him kiss me yesterday while trying to imagine what it would have been like. I startled at his statement, jolting the table and knocking over his toast structure. He blinked at it in shock.

"Oh my goodness, I'm so sorry."

He chuckled. "For what? For knocking my amazing tower over or for not kissing me?"

"Both. I mean for ruining your tower. I mean...*oh.*" I buried my flaming face in my hands.

He reached over and gently pried my fingers away. "I'm sorry for teasing you. I just found it amusing that you knocked over my tower when I was just about to invite you to do so. It was as if you'd read my mind."

I took a steadying breath as I fidgeted with the ring, waiting for my cheeks to cool. Liam watched me with a sweet look before it melted into a frown.

"You didn't eat dinner with me yesterday."

I continued twisting my ring. "I didn't eat at all."

"Why? Was something on your mind?" He tilted his head. "Please say it was me."

I was caught. "Can you read my thoughts?"

"It appears I'm getting better at it. I must have affected you deeply yesterday." His responding smile was triumphant.

He had no idea just how much, both then and now. I found myself staring at him, lingering on his gorgeous blue eyes, aglow with good humor. Oh dear, I was gawking. I hastily tore my gaze away.

He chuckled. "You know, Lavena, for claiming you don't know how to flirt, you're remarkably good at it."

"I'm not *trying* to flirt."

"You're still succeeding."

I traced swirl after swirl on the table with my fingertip to avoid meeting his eyes again.

"I wish I knew how to flirt," he continued seriously. "Then perhaps I could win you over like I'm so desperate to. Though perhaps I'm more skilled than I think. Lavena, you're blushing rather adorably. You'd best stop if you want me to slow down."

I finally raised my gaze. "What are you doing to me?"

"I'm trying to make you smile and am disappointed I'm failing."

I managed a smile. He studied it for a moment before shaking his head.

"A *real* smile, Lavena, not one to humor me."

"If you want to see it so badly, then you should give me something to smile about." Which, knowing him, wouldn't be difficult.

"A challenge." He rubbed his hands together, his eyes already brightening with an idea. "I mentioned yesterday while we were in the library that the settee is frightening when one sits on it alone. Last night while I was tossing and turning, I refined the story about the potential dangers of that particular settee. Do you want to hear it?"

He gave me such a heartbreakingly hopeful look that I couldn't resist him. It was difficult even at the best of times, but nearly impossible now with my defenses weakened by the lingering memory of our almost kiss, a memory almost unbearable to recall when its most charming subject was staring at me from across the table.

"Will it make me smile?" I asked.

"I hope so." He frowned. "Although perhaps not. My theories never make anyone smile. Whenever I spout any off, people always give me a look of forced endurance."

"I understand that all too well." I never failed to receive blank stares whenever discussing insects.

Liam leaned closer, as if trying to cross the table keeping us apart. "Do you? How so?"

His bright eyes were rather dangerous. I could feel them reaching inside me, attempting to extract my secrets. The ring warmed on my finger, an unwanted reminder for me to be careful. "Perhaps one day I'll be brave enough to share that secret."

The tender look in his eyes intensified. "I hope one day you'll share every part of yourself with me."

The promise I ached to give burned on my tongue, but I knew I could never share Anwen's interest in entomology, which was a shame, because I not only longed to share this part of myself with Liam, but I had a feeling he'd be one of the only people who wouldn't laugh.

His sigh tore me from my reverie. "Another frown. I'm not very good at making you smile today."

"That's only because you haven't shared the theory you came up with. I really do want to hear it."

He fidgeted nervously. "You'll think me childish."

"Never."

He searched my expression to gauge my sincerity before leaning close and lowering his voice. "I'm convinced certain objects within the palace are *haunted*, and not just any objects, but the favorite objects of past royals. One of the settees in the palace—which I'm pretty confident is the one in the library—happened to be the favorite lounging place of the insane King Claude the Second, dead these past five hundred years, whose spirit still lingers near his prized settee. Should one find themselves alone on it…"

He trailed off mysteriously before giving me a look that dared me to laugh. But I could never laugh at him. Instead, I felt inclined to do something else: play along.

"Well, there's only one thing to do." I stood to leave the table.

Liam's brows furrowed in confusion. "Where are you going?"

"On a quest, of course. We need to track down all the haunted objects in the palace, beginning with that mysterious settee. I don't know much about this insane King Claude the Second, but I wouldn't be surprised if his haunted settee swallowed its victims the moment they sat down on it alone. We must find it…unless you're too scared."

I began heading for the door and he scrambled after me with a wide smile. "You're initiating an adventure?"

"You can't be the only adventurer in this relationship."

He seized me around the waist, tugging me to a stop. "Just when I didn't think you could be more perfect for me…"

Flutters filled my stomach. "Am I perfect for you?"

"Extremely. You never cease to surprise me." His grin widened. "I like surprises." He started to lean in, as if he meant to once again try to…but no. He blinked and jerked back, cheeks crimson. "I'm sorry, I'm distracting us from our quest: tracking down haunted objects. Shall we go?" He offered me his arm, which I happily accepted with a smile. He lit up. "At last, my Lavena's smile. I've been waiting for it all morning. I shall treasure its memory, for I'm afraid the rest of the day is going to become rather frightening as we seek out every spooky object in the palace."

"Beginning with the settee in the library."

We walked there together, and once we arrived, Liam got down on his hands and knees and examined the settee with the concentration of an investigator searching for clues.

"Have you discovered anything?" I asked.

He settled back on his heels with a sigh. "Nothing. Perhaps what we need is live bait." His gaze flickered towards me with a rather wicked grin.

I held up my hands and backed away. "Oh, no you don't."

He stood and slowly approached, stalking me like a *salticidae*—a jumping spider on the prowl for its prey. "Now who's the scared one?"

"I'm not inclined to be attacked by a haunted settee. Aren't you supposed to be the gentleman protecting your lady from such a horrible fate?"

"One of us must be sacrificed in order to figure out whether this is the haunted settee, and *I* certainly can't do it," he said with feigned solemnity. "I'm sure the trap is only sprung on beautiful maidens. But not to worry; I'll be sure to have a lovely funeral for you, and I will see that your legendary sacrifice lives on in royal lore."

I took another step back. "It'll look like murder should I be knocked off during our honeymoon when there's no other suspect but you. No one will believe I met my demise via the royal furniture."

He paused and stroked his chin. "True...but all suspicion will drop from me when I play my role of the grieving husband. You'd be surprised at how convincing I can be as an actor."

"So your grief will be insincere?"

"Of course not, darling. You're my wife and I'll miss you terribly, but the mystery of the haunted settee must be solved no matter the cost."

"Even the cost of offering your new wife as live bait?"

He flashed me another wicked smile and I realized he was about to spring. I bolted, but he was quicker. He pounced with so much force he sent us crashing to the floor, but at least he was gentleman enough to absorb most of the fall with his body. He *oofed*, both from the landing and from when I elbowed him in my scramble to escape the confines of his arms...never mind it felt amazing having them enfolding me.

"I can't believe you actually *attacked* me." He really was just like a jumping spider. How delightful.

"All in the name of proving a theory, my dear. Hey, where do you think you're going? Come back here." He tugged me back into his hold, keeping me pinned to his comfortable chest with a rather affectionate snuggle. "Mm, much better. You shan't escape me."

Escape was the last thing on my mind, not when every touch from him felt like fire. "Imprisoning a lady? And here I thought you were a gentleman."

"You doubt me, milady?" He tried to sound affronted. "Such ingratitude, especially after my demonstration of gentlemanly behavior in protecting you; my shoulder will be sore for days from breaking our fall."

"All in the name of proving a theory, my dear," I quoted back to him. "And considering you're keen on sacrificing me to the settee, forgive me for not being more sympathetic."

I made a half-hearted effort to wriggle free, but I wasn't inclined to fight too hard, given the incredible feeling of his arms wrapped around me. He sat us up and gave me another affectionate squeeze.

"I'm rather enjoying this. It almost makes me want to spare you your fate...but not quite."

With another wicked grin, he stood and swept me into his arms. I made more of an attempt to escape, flailing everywhere, but he was too strong. He carried me over to the settee and gave me a rather somber look, marred only by the light dancing in his eyes.

"Well, my dear, this is it. Please visit from beyond the grave to let me know how you are." He leaned down to tenderly kiss my forehead and I froze. "Mm, so this was the secret to making you more cooperative? I should have done it sooner. Too late now. Goodbye, darling."

He dropped me onto the settee and scrambled back, watching with wide eyes, as if he truly expected the cushions to swallow me whole. Nothing happened except for me sitting up to glare at him.

"It appears this settee isn't haunted after all, leaving you with a rather angry wife who was just given up so freely by her husband to a piece of furniture."

He held up his hands. "Now, my dear, let's not be rash; it was all for a good cause."

I crawled off the settee, glaring, all while fighting my smile threatening to emerge. "Here's a lesson that you'd best learn early in our marriage: I don't take kindly to death threats." I raised my eyebrows when he chuckled.

"You're delightful," he said fondly. "I'm quite enjoying this."

I was too, but I refused to break out of character. "Don't try to humor me out of my revenge. First you tried to drown me in the fountain, and now you've attempted to sacrifice me to the settee."

"If you want to exact revenge, you'll have to catch me first." He turned and bolted. I immediately gave chase. At first he stayed within the confines of the library—ducking beneath tables and darting around the shelves—but then he escaped into the corridors. I followed as he darted into a sitting room, passing several gaping servants.

"Shall we see if *this* settee is the haunted one?" he asked.

"Excellent idea," I panted when I finally caught up. "This time *you* can be the sacrifice." I pushed him onto it and stood back to wait. Again, nothing happened. "Oh dear, this haunted settee is proving difficult to track down."

"Giving up already? We still have dozens of settees in the palace to investigate."

I gaped at him. "Are you serious?"

His look became challenging. "Am I ever."

My lips quirked up. "I'll join you on this quest on the condition that we take turns being the required sacrifice."

"Deal." He took my hand and hurried me from the room, where we spent the remainder of the morning exploring every nook and cranny of the palace.

In the end, we never found the haunted settee, but we had a spectacular time looking all the same, ending our search only to take lunch, after which we spent the remainder of the day in each other's company. As evening settled we found ourselves back in the library where the adventure had started.

I gaped at the clock on the mantle. "Is it really that late?"

"Time flies when you're romping around the palace most

of the day." He tugged me down onto the rug in front of the fireplace. "Won't you join me?"

"Are you going to push me into the fire?" Our death threats had only increased with each failed attempt to find the haunted settee, and I saw no need to stop now.

"Silly Lavena, if I were to truly knock you off, I'd do it in a more stealthy way—like in your sleep."

"Then it's a good thing we don't share a room yet." My cheeks enflamed the moment the words left my mouth.

Liam grinned as he leaned towards my ear. "The operative word being *yet*." He traced my blush with his fingertip. "I love how you blush for me."

I had never been much of a blusher, but something about Liam made me hyperaware of every response of my body.

The rainstorm continued raging outside, thunder rumbling and wind lashing against the windowpanes. I watched the swirling grey sky and the rain splattering the glass.

"Are you scared of rainstorms, Lavena?" I shook my head and he sighed. "Can you pretend that you are?"

My brow furrowed as I tore my gaze away from the storm. "Why?"

"So I can propose warm tea and a snuggle with me beneath a blanket in front of the fire and be your doting husband by comforting you from your fears."

"I can't keep up with you," I said. "First you want to sacrifice me to a piece of furniture, and now you want to comfort me from the storm?"

He flashed a mischievous grin. "I'm a husband of many talents."

My lips twitched into another grin. "You certainly are. But must I be the scared one?" I scooted closer, arranging my expression into one of concern. "Why Liam dear, you're trembling. You must be frightened out of your wits."

I expected him to play along but he missed his cue; instead of acting frightened, he smiled. "You called me *dear*."

My stomach jolted. So I had. "You started using the endearment for me several days ago."

He tucked a strand of hair behind my ear, his gaze intensifying. "It seems appropriate for you. As such, I'm quite eager for an excuse to snuggle with my wife."

"Then pretend to be scared so I can be your adoring wife and comfort you. If you promise you'll no longer threaten to sacrifice me to haunted settees, I won't tell our servants that the crown prince is afraid of storms."

He sighed. "I'm rather disappointed that my theory turned out to be false. This palace is centuries old; I felt certain it was haunted."

I playfully shoved my shoulder against his. "Giving up already? Perhaps the settee only comes alive at night."

"Excellent hypothesis. Sometime before our honeymoon ends, when you least expect it, I'll sneak into your bedroom, scoop you up from your bed, and dump you on every settee in the palace. You've been warned."

The thought of Liam in my room at night caused my stomach to both twist in nerves and flutter in anticipation. "I'll be on my guard. Now I shall fetch some tea and we'll both comfort one another from the storm."

He grinned. "A compromise. We make a fantastic couple, don't we, dear?"

My cheeks warmed in pleasure as I went to pull the cord that summoned a servant. A maid promptly arrived and swept into a curtsy. I arranged for tea and blankets, and when the maid returned, I tucked the blanket around Liam.

Before I could settle beside him, he tugged me over. "Where are you going? I still need to be your doting husband." He wrapped his blanket around the both of us.

"I'm actually not cold."

"Then humor me and pretend you are."

The thought of spending the evening beneath this blanket with Liam was too wonderful to pass up. With the blanket, the fire, and Liam's body heat, it was unnecessarily warm, but it was extremely cozy. For a beautifully long time we stayed in this comfortable embrace until Liam's murmur broke the reverent stillness. "This is nice. Shall we make the experience even better with some tea?" He kissed the top of my head—causing my breath to hitch—before pouring me a cup and passing me the plate of cookies. "I had fun today."

"I did too."

"And not just today; I'm enjoying our marriage more and more with each passing day."

I blew on my tea and took a sip. "Same. I enjoy being married to you, Liam." But it was more than that. The feelings that had been growing within me were far stronger than merely *enjoying* his company.

Feeling brave and needing to be even closer to him, I laid my head on his shoulder, a gesture that felt incredibly natural. To my delight, he rested his head on top of mine as his arm looped around my waist.

I marveled at the remarkable feelings rippling over me as we sat cuddling, staring at the popping embers and the dance of the flickering flames. Soon his fingers began caressing up and down my arm. I tipped my head back to stare up at him and his gaze met mine. In that moment, I finally understood all the feelings that had been stirring within my heart ever since meeting this wonderful man.

Despite promising myself it wouldn't happen, I'd fallen in love with him. This beautiful realization mingled with my fierce desire for him to feel the same way towards me. But he could never love Anwen, for she was a woman he'd never even met.

The thought broke my stolen heart.

CHAPTER 13

"Are you ready, Lavena?" Liam poked his head into the parlor, finally returning after he'd scampered off nearly half an hour ago with an exuberant, "I have a brilliant idea."

I looked up expectantly from the tangled knots of my embroidery. Ever since realizing my deeper feelings for him two nights ago, I hated being apart from him, especially considering we only had a few days remaining of our honeymoon. My cheeks warmed at seeing him again, an unfortunate effect from my realization—he merely had to look at me and I became a blushing mess, even more than usual.

He grinned crookedly. "You're blushing again," he said, his tone singsong; he'd developed the habit of pointing out all my blushes whenever they occurred.

The heat in my cheeks only deepened, causing his grin to widen. Odious man. I adored him. "Am I ready for what?" I stammered.

"A surprise. Will you do me the honor of accompanying me to the gardens, my dear?"

He bounded into the room to take my hands and gently

pull me to my feet before hooking my arm through his and leading me outside. The day was lovely, full of bright sunlight that glistened off the manicured palace grounds in golden streams. As we walked, Liam rubbed gentle circles along the back of my hand, causing me to shiver.

"Where's this surprise of yours?" I asked breathlessly.

His eyes twinkled mischievously. "A surprise is more satisfying after the anticipation for it builds."

"So you're purposely delaying it in order to torture me?"

He laughed, not seeming bothered that his current scheme had been exposed. "You're beginning to know me well. Alright, I'll stop teasing you." He changed course and led me into the rose garden, where the rainbow of blossoms were in full bloom. In the center of the garden, surrounded by carefully manicured hedges, was a picnic spread.

I gasped in delight. "Oh, Liam..."

"I know, who knew I could be so romantic?" His smile faltered. "This is what ladies consider romantic, right?"

"Seeking compliments, dear? You know this is utterly romantic."

"True, but I love hearing you say so all the same."

I giggled and stood on tiptoe to kiss his cheek. A boyish grin slowly spread across his face.

"Wow, that alone was worth the effort to please you. I'll surprise you with a picnic every day for such a reward. Ah, there's my blush." He caressed my heated cheek before his hand trailed down my arm to connect our fingers. "Shall we, my dear?"

We settled on the lawn. As Liam made me up a plate, my attention was captured by a *plebejus argus* that had settled on the nearby heather. My excitement swelled as I eagerly crawled over for a closer look at the butterfly.

"Darling?"

I glanced back at my husband with a wide smile. "Come see! It's a *plebejus argus.*"

His brows squashed together as he came over and crouched down beside me. "A…what?"

"A silver-studded blue butterfly." The familiar enthusiasm that came from sharing about insects enfolded me. "This butterfly is more sedentary than other species, only flying a few short distances a day, meaning it'll likely let us observe it for awhile. Its vibrant colors means it's male." I pointed to its bright blue wings, rimmed in black with white edges and silver spots. So lovely. I sighed contentedly.

Liam stared at the butterfly before turning to me with a mischievous grin. "Should I be jealous that another male has captured your attention on our romantic outing?" He inched his hand closer to rest it on top of mine. My heartbeat immediately escalated.

I gave his hand a reassuring squeeze. "He'll only distract me for a moment, and then I'll return to doting only on you."

I studied the silver-studded blue as it continued to sit on the heather, its only movement the gentle folding and unfolding of its wings. Out of all the insects I'd observed over the years, butterflies were by far my favorite.

"Isn't it amazing how after a once seemingly insignificant caterpillar emerges from its cocoon, it completely transforms into something so beautiful?"

I glanced sideways at Liam, expecting him to look bored, but instead the look he gave the butterfly was rather pensive. "Considering it's been both a caterpillar and a butterfly, which one do you think it considers to be its real self?"

"I'm not sure." He seemed to be asking not about the silver-studded blue but about me. I felt very much like this butterfly—I'd started out as a common girl like it'd begun its life as a caterpillar—but unlike the butterfly, my transformation was a façade.

But now as I knelt in the grass beside Liam, sharing this moment with him, I desired more than ever to really be a butterfly. If I had wings, perhaps I could truly belong in Liam's world and never be forced to leave.

The butterfly chose that moment to fly away and we returned to our picnic spread, which contained all my favorite foods, save for strawberries. The afternoon passed pleasantly until Liam took it upon himself to begin eating not from his own plate but mine.

I giggled and twisted away as he made to snag one of my sandwiches. "How can the sweetest man who arranges a surprise picnic for his wife also be so mischievous as to steal her food during it?"

"I can't help it; your food looks better than mine." He succeeded in retrieving a piece of cheese and eating it with a triumphant smirk. "I win. And I was right—your cheese definitely tastes more delicious."

I seized a grape and tossed it at him; he caught it easily and simply popped it into his mouth.

"Why, I'd love a grape. Thank you for sharing, darling."

I rolled my eyes, but it was impossible to mask my grin. "I had no intention of sharing; I threw the grape at you simply because you deserved it."

He chuckled. "Naturally. You only go against your sweet nature when I fully deserve it."

"You're making it sound like you enjoy my tormenting you."

"Caught." He winked and immediately laughed. "Goodness, Lavena, you're blushing *again*. Am I really so skilled at flirting?"

That only deepened the heat filling my cheeks. "Are you *trying* to make me blush?"

He grinned rakishly as he began tossing and catching his apple. "Perhaps. I'm quite invested in that adorable blush of yours. It makes me hope you're as affected by me as I am by you."

Cue warmer cheeks. "You think I'm adorable?" I asked shyly.

The look in his blue eyes intensified. "Adorable, lovely, beautiful, gorgeous...not to mention incredibly sweet and delightful." With each compliment he scooted closer until he was only inches away. I could see each freckle that dotted his nose, the bit of his golden hair that flopped against his forehead, and the longing filling his eyes.

The moment was ruined when he unexpectedly smeared a glob of pink icing from his cupcake onto my cheek. I jerked away. "Liam!"

"Wait, don't leave. Goodness, that wasn't one of my better ideas." He seized hold of my hem, staring up at me with the most imploring look that caused me to immediately melt—a dangerous response, for my softening so easily would only invite him to cause trouble again.

"How can I trust you after you wiped icing on my face?"

He flashed a wide, boyish smile. "You likely can't. But even so, couldn't you possibly find it in your heart to forgive me? Please?"

I groaned and relented. "Why are you so charming?"

"It's one of my many talents, one I'll always employ in order to remain in my wife's good graces." He scooted back over and in my weakness I let him. "Now I have a new game in mind."

Humming cheerfully, he stuck his finger in the icing marring my cheek and started to draw. I kept very still.

"There." He licked the tip of his finger.

I stood to peer into the nearby fountain. My breath caught at the sight of my reflection. I spun around. "You drew a heart."

He only smiled, one different than his usual easygoing

grins, this one full of sweetness, tenderness, and something else that seeped into my fluttery heart. These feelings only escalated when I returned to Liam's side and he took a loose strand of my hair, using it to contentedly trace up and down my arm and along my face. Even something so simple caused me to fall more in love with him.

He leaned towards my ear, as if to share a secret. "You're blushing again." He beamed, as usual pleased by his effect on me. "Why are you blushing?" he asked, still whispering.

I wasn't sure how to answer. I couldn't very well tell him it was because of *him*. "It's a secret."

Desperate for a distraction, I lay back on my elbows and tipped my head back, enjoying the soft breeze caressing my cheeks. I felt so incredibly content and I knew it wasn't because of the beautiful sunshine, the glorious summer manifested in the spectacular palace grounds, or our delicious picnic—it was because of the man sitting beside me, a man becoming more and more dear to me the longer I knew him.

I peeked shyly over at him and found him staring at me, his eyes soft. "I'm hoping your blush is because of me." He playfully tapped my nose; his casual touch sent my heart aflutter. "Are you happy, Lavena?"

"I am." I'd never been happier. The only thing tainting my joy was the knowledge I was deceiving Liam and that our relationship would eventually come to an end. I severed our gazes and glanced out across the beautiful grounds.

Liam scooted closer. I shuddered when he brushed my dark hair aside. "You're so...*soft*." He lightly traced my cheek and I instinctively leaned against his fingers. "Before our marriage you seemed more hardened, more unhappy, so different than you are now."

My heart beat wildly, not just from the way his touch affected me, but from my ever-present fear—the fear that with every difference Liam noticed between me and the real Princess Lavena, our scheme would be exposed and I'd lose him forever. Only the fact that Liam wouldn't suspect his wife to be an imposter, especially since he didn't know the real Princess Lavena well, assured my secret was safe...for now.

He lightly brushed my cheek. "This is the real you. I wish I'd seen it earlier, for it would have made everything so much easier. But I see you now, and I'll never not be able to ever again."

I leaned closer, drawn to his sunshine and warmth that was so *Liam*. "Do you like what you see?"

"Very much."

My heart warmed. "And are you happy, Liam?"

"Extremely." He rubbed his nose with mine. "Now I have an idea. Would you like to cloud watch?"

He gently tugged me down beside him to lay on the lawn. I stared up at the blue sky, but before I could begin looking for unique shapes in the clouds, my view was blocked by Liam as he propped himself above me.

"Aren't we going to watch the clouds?"

"I have something better to watch instead." He stroked my hair. My heart ignited at his touch, at the tender look filling his eyes. "You know what, Lavena?"

"What?" I could barely speak, not with the smoldering way he looked at me.

"You surprise me."

I cupped his face, delighting in the way he leaned against my hand, as if my touch meant something to him. "I like surprises."

"I do, too. Are you ready for another?" And before I could prepare myself for it, he leaned down and, after a moment's hesitation, he kissed me.

It was the most beautiful first kiss—warm, soft, sweet,

and gentle, everything that was Liam and more. His fingers wove through my hair as he passionately yet still tenderly explored our kiss. I hesitantly joined him, shy about doing it wrong, but the way Liam groaned made me feel that perhaps I'd done it right after all.

I kissed Liam not as Princess Lavena but as Anwen. The ever-present pain that came from pretending faded away until there was only this moment with him, my wonderful husband, the man who had somehow stolen my heart and would keep it forever...the man who didn't even know the woman he called wife.

That thought caused me to yank away, ending the kiss. "What is it?" he asked. "Was that not—*Lavena!*"

He brushed away the tears streaking my cheeks, first with his thumbs, and then to my horror and delight his lips, a gesture which only made me cry harder.

He broke away. "Are you alright, darling? I'm sorry, I should have asked your permission before kissing you, especially after you'd resisted it the other day." He stroked my hair back in apology.

"That's not why I'm crying," I stuttered. "It's because—" But I couldn't tell him that the most beautiful moment of my life had been marred by the thought that while I'd been kissing him, the man I adored, he hadn't been kissing *me*, but instead a mask, a mask I'd never wanted to yank off more than I did now.

Liam sat us up, bringing me gently with him. He embraced me and began gently rocking me and soothingly rubbing my back. I melted at his touch.

"Then what's wrong? Was it...not a good kiss?"

"It was perfect. I loved it. Thank you."

"I loved it, too. I—" He stared into my eyes, his gaze smoldering once more. I knew the words he wanted to express, ones I both ached for and desperately didn't want to hear.

I pressed my fingers to his lips. "Not now. Please."

He obediently closed his mouth with a sigh. "As you wish, sweetheart."

Sweetheart.... My heart, if possible, cracked open even further.

"Can you just hold me?" I asked, needing his arms around me. He gathered me back to him.

"Of course." He nestled against my hair. "I'm sorry I didn't ask your permission; I got caught up in the moment. I won't kiss you again until you're ready. Alright, darling?"

I nodded before nestling myself against his shoulder, wishing I could express the desire of my heart—that I was ready *now*. But I knew that such a confession would only cause the pain from this façade to grow until I was certain it'd consume me completely.

How could the most beautiful moment of my life also be the most heartbreaking? For Liam hadn't kissed *me,* and he likely never would. Being so close to something I desperately wanted—but which I'd never be able to truly have—was akin to torture.

It was the last evening of our honeymoon. I couldn't believe how quickly the month had sped by, just like a dream. I felt as if the curtain of the first act of the production that had become my new life was drawing to a close—one that had started with so much fear, uncertainty, and tension but was now filled with beautiful memories, each like a precious jewel.

Especially the memory of our kiss, the shadow of which lingered on my lips and the memory of which graced my dreams. We hadn't kissed since—my tears had undoubtedly scared Liam away from trying it again too soon—but I sensed he wanted to, sensed there were words he yearned to share, words I hoped matched those filling my heart. I needed to hear these words yet couldn't bear the thought of receiving them when they were addressed not to me but to another woman. I was trapped in a play, so much about our relationship nothing but a performance.

I wandered the gardens alone. We'd just finished our last dinner together before returning to the Dracerian palace tomorrow, where instead of being alone in the world of just Liam and me—a place I wanted to reside in forever—we'd be surrounded by Liam's family, more people to have to pretend for, and with them a higher risk of getting caught. But the potential consequences for posing as royalty were no longer my greatest fear when the façade shattered—it was losing Liam.

I settled on a patch of lawn near a bed of azaleas, hugging my legs to my chest. Sunset had arrived to caress the sky in a palette of gold, ruby, and rose light. I became distracted from this beautiful vision when a moth fluttered nearby. I held my hand still, hoping the moth would heed my silent invitation. It did, perching itself on my fingertips.

"What kind of moth are you?" I carefully brought my hand closer so I could study it in the fading light. I gave a tiny gasp of delight. "Oh, you're a *thysania agrippina*, a ghost moth. I've always wanted to see one of you up close. Do you really have the largest wingspan of all moths?" Even from my casual observation, I could see that it did.

The moth wandered up and down my finger. If only it could converse so it could tell me all about itself. I recalled all the facts I'd read about *thysania agrippina* during my hours of studying entomology, hours that felt part of another lifetime.

"Moths are drawn to light. I wonder why you flew towards me, for there isn't much light within me at the moment, not when this sunset represents the ending of something that's been far more wonderful than I could have ever imagined."

"Who are you talking to?"

I gasped. My jolt frightened the moth and caused it to flitter away into the night. I swiveled around to face Liam, who stood only a few feet away, his expression curious.

"A ghost moth landed on me and I took advantage of my good fortune by conversing with it."

"And I interrupted your conversation and chased away your new friend? Not a very husbandly gesture." After an inquiring look seeking permission to sit with me, he settled beside me and leaned back on his elbows. "I didn't know you had an affinity for moths. You recognized its species?"

Oops, another mistake. Apprehension eclipsed the wonder that had filled me at having discovered a rare moth. "Even you would recognize a ghost moth after seeing an illustration. They're quite distinctive. I read about them in one of the books in the library."

His grin became mischievous. "A ghost moth, huh? Sounds interesting...and creepy. Should we capture it and use it to instill fear in our enemies?"

"Too bad you scared it away."

"I am rather frightening."

I giggled and scooted closer to rest my head on his shoulder. He nestled against my hair and together we watched the sky, still awash in its symphony of color. "I've always enjoyed the sky's masterpieces. I used to sneak out before the sun every morning in order to watch the sun rise."

I sensed Liam's smile even though I couldn't see it. "That sounds lovely. I'd love to watch a sunrise with you. Perhaps we can do it tomorrow."

"Not tomorrow," I said. "This sunset is concluding our time here, and tomorrow's sunrise will be the beginning of the unknown."

"It doesn't feel like the unknown any longer." Liam took my hand and began playing with each finger.

"Doesn't it?" I could scarcely speak.

"No." He pressed a soft kiss on the end of my pinky. "It's the beginning of our new life together, one I'm looking forward to experiencing."

I met his smoldering gaze with a shy one of my own. "Are you really? Because on our carriage ride here—"

"That Liam was an idiot," he said. "He didn't know you the way I know you."

But that was just it—he didn't know *me* at all.

"It's been the most fabulous discovery," he continued. "I was engaged to the most remarkable woman and I didn't even know it. What a delightful surprise to be proven wrong. I like surprises."

My pulse pounded in my ears. "Me, too."

He smiled before lightly kissing each of my fingertips, each touch of his lips causing me to lose yet another piece of my heart to him. When he'd reached my thumb he paused to peek up at me uncertainly. "Are you alright, dear? You've been so out of sorts since our kiss. Did I do something wrong?"

"No, Liam. That was a wonderful kiss."

He scooted closer. "Then what's distressing you? Because *something* is. You might have fooled the old blind Liam who never paid attention to you, but that Liam no longer exists. I've watched you the past few days, being followed by a shadow I can't see. Won't you share it with me?"

I ached to now more than ever. I wanted to share everything with him, especially myself. The contract ring sensed my desires and burned threateningly, a warning. Was there a way to be honest while still fulfilling the ring's sinister demands for my silence?

I chose my words carefully. "I'm being forced to hide

myself even though I no longer want to hide at all...especially from you."

He nodded slowly. "I felt that way at the very beginning of our marriage. I was like a sulky child throwing a tantrum, so instead of trying to make our marriage work, I played a game of hide-and-seek...until you found me. Perhaps I can return the favor. The question is: do you want to be found?"

"Very much so," I whispered. "But that doesn't mean you'll be able to find me, even if you look."

He tucked a loose strand of hair behind my ear. "I'm very good at hide-and-seek."

I hoped he was. I wanted Liam to come to know me, the *real* me, rather than the mask I wore, and since the ring prevented me from sharing too much of myself, he'd only be able to know Anwen if he found me himself. By the determined gleam in his eye, perhaps he'd succeed in this particular quest. But if he did, would he like who he discovered?

Twilight settled over us and with it came fireflies, glowing against the darkness. It would have been impossible for the old Anwen to have sat so still and avoided her favorite childhood pastime of trying to catch them, but the current Anwen found this experience far more engaging, especially considering Liam hadn't pulled his hand from my hair. He combed his fingers through it, his expression concentrated.

"I've had a wonderful time here with you," he whispered, as if the darkness required a certain reverence.

"I have, too."

He smiled and wrapped his arm around my waist to snuggle me close. Stillness settled over us. We cuddled as the sunset faded, leaving behind the starry night and the fireflies, golden bulbs of light that waltzed through the air.

There were so many things I wanted to ask Liam. Had he ever caught fireflies? Did he wish upon the stars? Did he know the stories behind the constellations found in the sky? But asking any of these questions would require me to speak, which would have broken the beautiful spell cloaking us like the silvery starlight.

We sat together for ages, and soon I began to drift off. Liam stirred to help me up, and without releasing my hand he led me back to the palace, playing with my fingers with each step.

Crimson darkened his cheeks as he paused outside my door. "Since you said you weren't averse to my first kiss... may I kiss you again?"

Even after my nod he hesitated before bridging the distance between us and lightly kissing me, his lips the softest caress. This kiss was far sweeter than our first and I almost protested when he pulled away.

"Lavena? I—" He took a deep, wavering breath, his eyes shy. "Are you ready for...more?"

My breath hooked. *Oh.* For a moment I couldn't speak. He shifted restlessly as he awaited my response, the crimson blush staining his cheeks deepening.

"You mean...*being together?*"

He avoided my eyes and nodded. "It is our honeymoon."

How I ached to say yes, for in my heart I truly was ready. But an emotion other than my love for dear Liam vied for my attention—fear, for if we were together in that way, it wouldn't be *Anwen* he was with, but *Princess Lavena.* I wasn't strong enough to give all of myself and have him give himself to another.

"No." As if that single word were a dagger, he winced and immediately dropped my hand. "I'm sorry," I whispered. If only I could convey how sorry I truly was.

He released a disappointed sigh. "Oh...alright. Have a good night. I'll see you in the morning." He started to turn, paused, and after another shy, longing look, he kissed my cheek and entered his room, leaving me alone in the hallway.

I stared after him before slipping inside my bedchamber, where the connecting door between our two rooms greeted me. I pressed my back against this door, my heart tightening as I remembered the pain that had filled Liam's eyes at my rejection. Unfortunately, tonight wouldn't be the last time I hurt him. How could I repeatedly inflict pain on the kindest, most wonderful man I'd ever known, the man I loved? The pain he felt now would be nothing compared to the stinging betrayal he'd experience when this charade I played inevitably crumbled.

These agonizing thoughts haunted me as the night stretched on, making sleep impossible. I kept staring at the connecting door dividing our rooms, the knowledge that I'd only keep hurting Liam twisting my stomach in knots, as did my regret for being unable to give him the answer I'd longed to: *yes*.

CHAPTER 14

*T*he carriage clattered down the road towards the Dracerian palace, but even the unpleasant swaying of the carriage was nothing compared to the awkwardness accompanying us on our journey. Liam had been unusually quiet during breakfast, clearly avoiding my eyes but still stealing several shy peeks anyway, as if he couldn't resist looking at me. My heart lurched each time our eyes met and I caught a glimpse of the pain I'd caused him last night.

Remorse gnawed at my heart as we traveled in silence. We sat side by side, so close that we briefly touched with each of the carriage's jostles. The heat from his nearness taunted me, making me want nothing more than to curl up with him, despite the distance that had sprung up between us at my rejection.

I fought this desire for the first hour before I couldn't bear it any longer. Since I'd been the one to hurt him, I had to be the first to make amends. With a wavering breath, I scooted closer until our sides touched. His breath hooked as did mine, for the contact sent a jolt through me. I melted into him.

When he made no move to reject me as I'd feared, I curled myself closer around his stiff form. He softened with a sigh, and then his arm wound around me to snuggle me close. I nearly sobbed in relief at his acceptance.

"Oh, Lavena."

I flinched at her name but it couldn't upset me completely, not with his arm looped around me. "I'm sorry, Liam. I didn't mean—"

His hold tightened as he nestled his head against my hair. "Please don't be distressed, my dear, I'm not upset with you."

I snapped my head back to stare incredulously up at him. I lightly traced around his eyes, which still swirled with pain. "Don't lie. I can see I hurt you."

"You didn't; you're far too sweet. It's your core trait."

"But I'm not sweet," I protested. "I rejected you last night." Heat enveloped my cheeks. I burrowed my blush in the crook of his arm.

"I'm not upset by that, darling. I'm glad you can be honest with me. I'd hate to push you."

I shyly peeked up at him. He lightly caressed my cheek.

"I do need to be close to you, but not at the expense of hurting you. Nothing is worth that. I need your happiness, my Lavena." I winced at her name passing his lips. He instantly dropped his caress. "What's wrong? Shall I slow down?"

I felt at war with myself between my desire for him to slow down and for him to not go slow at all. Each touch from him was both torturous and wonderful, given both to me and Princess Lavena. It was all incredibly confusing.

"Please don't slow down," I murmured. "I don't want you to."

"But you're still not ready?"

I was, but Anwen wasn't supposed to exist. I shook my head. "It's complicated." If only I could explain.

"Then we'll wait."

"You're not upset?" I asked.

"Not about waiting," he said gently. "It's just the thought that you'll never feel for me what I'm feeling for you that's unbearable."

I cupped his cheek and felt a delightful thrill ripple over me as he leaned against my hand. "You have no need to worry about that; I feel the same way towards you."

He grinned crookedly, causing the unhappiness that had cloaked him all morning to slowly fade away. "Really?"

I nodded. He had to know what the Anwen in me was feeling, even though her beautiful emotions were forbidden. His entire manner lit up.

"With that hope, I can wait as long as you need." He kissed the top of my head and pulled me closer, tucking me against his side. I rested my head on his shoulder with a contented sigh, and we passed the rest of the far-more-pleasant carriage ride cuddled this way.

LIAM'S FAMILY was waiting for us in front of the majestic Dracerian palace as the carriage clattered through the gilded gates. The awkwardness of their farewells lingered in my memory, and although they smiled, wariness filled their expressions—the queen's in particular. It was no wonder, for the last they'd seen us, Liam and I had both showed an undisguised lack of enthusiasm for our union.

Liam chuckled. "Just look at their faces. They're nervous for us. Shall we give them a delightful surprise?"

He gave me one final snuggle before bounding from the carriage. He helped me descend with a bright smile and didn't release me even after I'd clambered out with far less grace than the real Princess Lavena would have shown. He tucked my hand through his arm, causing Her Majesty's eyes to widen.

"Hello, Mother, Father, my favorite sisters." Liam bestowed a kiss on the cheek of each—save His Majesty, who received a firm handshake—before he turned towards me with feigned surprise. "And Lavena! Fancy seeing you here. Hello to you, too."

To my delight I also got a kiss, one that sent a shiver through me.

The queen glanced back and forth between us, her brows furrowed. "How was your honeymoon?"

I smiled and Liam sighed with obvious contentment that warmed me straight through. "Wonderful," he said. "We had a fabulous time, didn't we, dear?"

"We did."

Liam's sisters began giggling in a way that caused my cheeks to burn. The king rested his hand on Liam's shoulder. "I'm pleased, Son, that despite your years of complaining about your union, it's going better than you initially expected."

The queen gave him a disapproving look before casting me a worried glance. "Nonsense, dear. Liam was very excited to be marrying Lavena."

The king frowned. "But he wasn't. He said he'd rather—" He snapped his mouth shut at his wife's sharp glare and cleared his throat. "So you two had a good time? Excellent. We're pleased to hear that. Didn't expect anything else."

"Indeed not." The queen was all smiles again. "I'm so glad you enjoyed yourselves. We'll let you two rest from your travels before joining us for dinner in an hour. We have a private welcome-home feast prepared, during which we'd love to hear more details about how things went."

My stomach tightened. Our conversation with Their Majesties hadn't even started and already I felt overwhelmed at the thought of enduring it, especially considering I wasn't sure how well Liam's family knew Princess Lavena or how convincing an imposter I'd be.

Liam noticed my distress and wrapped his arm around my shoulders to pull me close enough to murmur in my ear. "You're looking weary. Would you like to rest from our journey?"

"Please."

"I read you accurately. I'm getting rather good at this husband thing." He led me up the front steps. "Lavena and I are going to rest for a bit. Stop sniggering, Elodie; I said *rest*. We'll see you later."

A footman opened the door with a bow. Just before we slipped inside, I heard the king mutter, "Don't scold me, darling, I have every right to be shocked. Liam acted like his marriage was his execution, and now they're not only civil towards one another, but seem utterly besotted."

The moment the doors closed behind us, Liam tipped his head back and laughed boisterously. My embarrassment melted away until I was smiling, too.

"That was fantastic. Did you see their faces? They expected us to emerge from that carriage scarred from many epic battles." He pressed me against his side as we ascended the grand staircase.

"They did seem rather shocked."

His grin widened. "*Shocked* is an understatement. I love surprising people. That was *brilliant*, Lavena. They weren't expecting us to be such good friends."

I smiled. We had become good friends, although I now considered Liam so much *more*.

It took several corridors before I noticed two guards discreetly following us. "Who are they?" I asked Liam in a whisper. He glanced over his shoulder.

"Oh, those are our personal guards. Yet another example

of being off our honeymoon: the guards at the summer palace kept more out of the way, but not the ones here." He sighed. "Our time alone will be more limited now that we've returned. Here we are, our quarters."

He opened the door to my room and bowed me through before following, closing the door behind him. My heart immediately flared to life. Liam was in my room. His presence made it feel as if the walls were closing in, shrinking the space.

Liam glanced around the marble, satin, and pastel-pink surroundings. "Feminine. It was just redecorated according to your desires."

According to *Princess Lavena's* desires. All the pink and lace made it far too frilly for my personal taste, but I forced a smile. "They did an excellent job." The room was luscious, far more than my bedroom at the summer palace had been. I slowly walked around, taking in every detail, Liam following close behind.

"I take it you like it?" he asked.

I hesitated. "It's so...grand. It can't possibly belong to me."

He frowned. "Did the decorators not remodel it to your wishes?"

"No, I meant—" I swallowed my condemning words; over the past month, I'd gotten much better at appeasing the sadistic jailer adorning my finger.

Liam's brow furrowed as he looked around. "I almost think the decorators did make a mistake. There's a lot of pink, a color you never seem to wear. You mostly wear green."

Because green was *Anwen's* favorite color, but as usual that was something I wasn't supposed to admit. "What an observant husband you are, Liam dear."

His puzzlement melted away as he chuckled. He stood to

come over and take my hands in his. "When I'm with you, it's impossible not to pay attention."

He lifted my hands and pressed a kiss on the back of each before lowering them and then rubbing them with his thumbs. He stared at me for a moment, his expression incredibly tender, before he glanced at something over my shoulder.

"I see they've uncovered the connecting door. My room is through there."

He motioned with his chin. My heart leapt as I glanced behind me. We could access one another's rooms as easily as crossing the threshold. The door had stayed resolutely shut during our honeymoon, but after Liam's admission last night that he was ready, I wondered how long I could keep that door closed here.

"It'll stay closed until you're ready," he murmured, as if he'd read my worry-laden thoughts. With each passing day he seemed to become more attuned to me. I felt my heated blush reappear. Liam caressed it with his fingertips. "Am I making you uncomfortable?"

"Never." I pressed myself against him and sighed contentedly when he embraced me and held me close, his head nestling against my hair.

We spent some time alone before the feast, a final taste of our honeymoon that I never wanted to end. We eventually wandered to the settee and settled on it, arms still wound around each other.

I laid my head on his shoulder. "Now that our honeymoon is over, I'll be getting responsibilities as the new crown princess, won't I?"

"Yes," he said. "Most will be similar to the duties you had as the Princess of Lyceria, with several new ones that you'll need to receive training for. Not to worry; Mother will take you under her wing and show you everything."

I took a steadying breath at the thought of the new tasks I'd be expected to perform, some I was aware of due to my service to the princess and many which still remained a mystery. But rather than feeling nervous for them, a flutter of excitement filled me. I liked to keep busy, and after helping the peasant family during our honeymoon, the possibilities of all the good I could do in this temporary role thrilled me.

"Could I perhaps choose additional duties?"

Liam hooked his fingers beneath my chin to raise my gaze. "Such as what?"

"The fire in the village caused me to ponder the state of your—I mean *our*—subjects. Is there something more we can do to help? Perhaps we can create charities, or visit some of the poorer villages in order to lend our aid, or..." I trailed off, my cheeks warming at the perplexed look Liam was giving me. "What is it?" I whispered.

He slowly grinned. "That's a fantastic suggestion. Goodness, just when I think I've gotten used to how wonderful you are, you continue to amaze me." He pressed a soft kiss to my brow. "May I join you in your project?"

"Certainly. In fact, you should be the one in charge of it."

He lifted his eyebrow. "Why? It was your idea."

It needed to be him, so that when Princess Lavena eventually returned, he could continue doing good for his people without me. "It'll help you realize what a fine crown prince you are."

His expression softened. "I'll accept as long as you're an intricate part of these plans. We'll do it together." He was silent a thoughtful moment. "You've just given me an idea for my own project; I can't let you be the only one to have all the fun."

"What kind of project do you have in mind?"

His eyes lit up. "Well, I thought I was rather handy with a

hammer when we rebuilt the village family's burnt cottage. I'd love to get my royal hands dirty building more useful things. Maybe we could go to each village and see what the people have need of—homes, a larger school, a nicer church...I could appoint men in each town to be in charge and show up when my schedule permits in order to help them."

I smiled. "What a wonderful idea; that would be perfect for you." Such a project would build up his confidence and give him the opportunity to make a difference as the crown prince. He'd undoubtedly make a fine king.

He gathered me close, and we settled into another comfortable moment of stillness, basking in one of the last moments alone we'd experience before rejoining the real world. Liam must have been thinking something similar, for he sighed.

"It'll take some getting used to, not having every moment be like this anymore. Starting tomorrow the honeymoon is truly over. I'll return to attempting to fill a role that was never meant to be mine and you'll have your princess duties to attend to. We'll have to steal moments throughout the day to spend together."

I nestled closer, resting my head against his heart. "I hate having to share you."

"You'll always be my priority, even when my attention is forced to be diverted...like now. It's time to get ready for dinner."

I scowled at the clock. "Time with you speeds by, whereas I'm certain the moments we're apart will slow to a crawl."

"At least we can use the time we're separated to plan more adventures for when we're together again." He stroked my hair. "I know it'll be difficult returning to the real world, but we have a lifetime together, and unlike before, it no longer feels like a sentence, but rather a marvelous adventure just waiting to unfold."

He pressed a soft kiss to my forehead before standing and going to the connecting door. I followed him, keeping my hand woven through his until the last possible moment. He paused in the threshold and turned to me.

"I'll return to escort you to dinner." He hesitated before dipping down and kissing me softly, this kiss more shy than our others, but just as lovely. I kissed him back, trying to communicate all the feelings in my heart that I couldn't express. By the time he pulled away, he was grinning. "I'll see you soon."

He disappeared into his room, his gaze lingering on mine until the door had closed, separating us. I missed him immediately. I stared at the closed door for a long moment before turning around to survey the room that was now *mine*. I frowned. Pink, frilly, and totally not to my taste.

I sighed and went to pull the cord that would summon my maid so I could prepare for the feast with Liam's family, for whom I was now expected to perform. Nerves knotted my stomach, but a single glance towards the connecting door reminded me of my motivation to continue the charade —*Liam*, always him.

CHAPTER 15

*B*y the time Liam arrived to escort me to dinner, my nerves had escalated, twisting my stomach into anxious knots. I took a fortifying breath before opening the door in answer to his knock and was rewarded when Liam's expression immediately brightened as he looked me over in clear appreciation.

"Why, Your Royal Highness, you look particularly lovely tonight."

I smiled. When Liam spoke my title, I sort of liked it; it almost made me feel like a real princess, one who belonged to him. I *looked* like a princess, at least, dressed up in my golden silk, jewelry, and fancy hairdo. Hopefully I'd be able to *act* like one as well—a task that felt daunting, especially when I was dining with the king and queen. My fear threatened to swallow me whole.

I took his offered arm and allowed him to lead me down the corridor. "Will only your family be at dinner?" I asked shakily.

"Yes, it's a private dinner, so thankfully we won't have to brave court."

Despite that small mercy, apprehension cinched my chest with every step closer to the scrutinizing audience I'd be forced to perform for. I'd managed to fool Liam, but could I fool the royal family of Draceria?

Liam hovered outside the door and peered inside, where his family chatted easily around the dining table as they awaited our arrival. He sighed. "As much as I love my family, I already miss our meals from our honeymoon when it was just us."

"It's not too late to escape."

He chuckled at what he undoubtedly considered a joke and squeezed my hand with a reassuring smile, which I managed to weakly return. Despite the daunting performance before me, at least I would face it with Liam by my side.

He escorted me into the dining room. His family looked up with "we can't wait to hear how your honeymoon really went" expressions. I stiffly sank into my seat at Liam's right, so different from how we'd sat across from one another at the summer palace.

I cast a nervous glance towards the king and queen, both relaxed and wearing friendly looks, which didn't change the fact they were the *King and Queen*—royal, regal, and formidable—and I was a common girl posing as a princess. My stomach tightened.

The interrogation began with the first course. The queen smiled at us as she took a dainty sip of soup. "Tell us about your honeymoon, dears. What did you do?"

"We went on all sorts of adventures," Liam said with his usual exuberance. "Didn't we, darling?"

Memories of our time together flittered through my mind like snippets from the most beautiful of dreams. *Adventures* seemed too inadequate a description, but I managed a brief nod.

"*Adventures* is so vague," Princess Elodie complained as she swirled her finger in her glass. "I want details."

Liam turned to me expectantly, inviting me to speak, but my throat had sealed up. When I remained silent, he turned back to his family. "We did many fun things—made paper boats, went on picnics, read in the library, watched the sunset, strolled the gardens, searched for haunted settees..."

I smiled at each of his recollections. As terrified as I'd been before our honeymoon, it had turned out to be rather incredible. I yearned to return to that magical time and the security I'd experienced when it had been just us.

Liam launched into additional details while holding my hand beneath the table and tracing swirls along my palm. Each touch escalated my heart, already pattering in nerves. The sensations soon became too much and I slowly withdrew my hand from his.

He paused in his recitation about our adventures tracking down the haunted settee to frown at me, confusion lining his brow. "Do you not like me playing with your hand?" he whispered, a whisper that was loud enough for his surrounding family to overhear.

My cheeks warmed as I cast another apprehensive glance at the royalty surrounding us. The queen leaned forward, eyes lined with concern.

"You're not eating, Lavena dear. Aren't you hungry?"

How could I possibly eat beneath their scrutiny when one wrong move would certainly expose me? Nausea swirled my stomach at the thought.

Liam's touch went to my cheek. "You're a bit pale, darling. Are you alright?"

I took a deep breath. I was being ridiculous. My nerves were only causing more attention to be directed towards me, attention I didn't want.

I nodded and shakily picked up my spoon. After a few

timid spoonfuls of the creamy chicken soup, I noticed that Liam's family's attention was still riveted to me. I froze. Was I using the wrong spoon? Slurping too loudly?

"What is it?" I squeaked. The queen tilted her head, studying me, as if searching for evidence of my authenticity.

"You seem...different tonight, dear. Are you sure you're alright?"

"I'm fine, Your Majesty." I wriggled in my seat, waiting for the accusations, which thankfully didn't come. One by one, each dropped their curious staring. I slowly released my pent-up breath.

The agonizing dinner continued. The food's tantalizing smells tickled my nose but I scarcely tasted any of it, too busy overanalyzing every gesture to ensure I didn't do anything to shatter the façade that I was Princess Lavena; picking at my food and remaining a silent observer quickly seemed the safest option. I knew I was doing a terrible job imitating the confident, chatty princess, but my nerves seemed to have paralyzed me; it was all I could do to not have a panic attack.

Our salad was swept away by the attending servants and the third course began. After a few more polite questions concerning our wedding trip—questions once again answered exclusively by Liam, while I remained mute and anxious beside him—the conversation turned to how Liam's family had spent the past month. I thought I could safely not participate in this particular topic, but unfortunately by the fourth course, my silence once again didn't go unnoticed.

The queen set down her fork. "Are you *sure* you're alright, Lavena? You're being so quiet. You're normally quite the conversationalist."

I frantically scrambled for an explanation, but words weren't forthcoming.

"Perhaps you're tired from your travels?" she asked.

I seized this excuse gratefully. "It's been a long day," I managed to squeak.

"Poor dear. We should have allowed you to rest longer before dinner. We were just eager to hear how your honeymoon went. We've been so anxious...but it appears we needn't have worried; you both look as if you had a wonderful time."

Liam grinned. "We had an amazing time, didn't we, sweetheart?" He wrapped his arm around me and I stiffened. Was such a gesture appropriate in front of Their Majesties? Furthermore, the real Princess Lavena would have shaken his arm off. Would my not doing so crack the charade that I wasn't really the princess I claimed to be?

I slowly tugged myself away. Avoiding Liam's surprised and wounded eyes, I cut up my chicken, my hands shaking so badly it took several attempts to get a single bite. When I was finally brave enough to raise my gaze, I noticed his family— the queen especially—once more studying me closely.

Don't panic, Anwen. I took several long, deep breaths to steady my nerves, but my pulse quickened and didn't settle even after they turned their perusal away and began conversing again.

Liam didn't join in; instead he cast me several confused and rather hurt looks. Guilt that I'd distressed him pierced my already clenched heart. When His Majesty began discussing an important meeting Liam looked all too thankful to have missed, Liam leaned towards my ear.

"You seem upset. What's wrong?"

I subtly shook my head, dismissing his question, and with a sigh he withdrew.

He didn't make another attempt to show me affection until the next course, when his arm wound back around me, much more hesitantly than the first time. The king's eyebrows rose in surprise and the queen and Liam's sisters all lit up in pleasure. Once again I stiffened, but I didn't have the heart to reject him again. When I made no move to pull away, he relaxed.

After several minutes when Their Majesties didn't scold us for sitting in such a way during the meal, I managed to relax my tense posture and snuggle closer to Liam. His snug embrace helped to steady my wild heartbeat and my tangled nerves.

I became even more calm when Liam began casually playing with a loose strand of hair that had slipped from my updo. With each twist of it around his finger, Princess Elodie and Princess Rheanna—who watched each of his movements with growing smiles—exchanged knowing looks and heaved romantic sighs, each of which caused my blush to deepen.

Despite my growing embarrassment, Liam's attentions helped me endure the rest of dinner. It was a relief when the king and queen finally rose from the table, formally signaling the end of the meal.

"Shall we adjourn to the parlor, dears, until your father and Liam join us?" the queen asked.

Me? Alone with Her Majesty and Their Highnesses? The panic that had been gradually dispelling immediately swelled once more, especially when Liam unwound his arm from around my shoulders. I seized his hand. "Where are you going?"

He gave an exaggerated groan. "Oh, just the traditional after-dinner drinks and dull political talk before rejoining you ladies in the parlor. Don't worry, I'll escape soon." He swept a kiss across my cheek—earning another happy sigh from Princess Elodie—but in my heightened emotional state I flinched away, causing Liam to frown. My heart wrenched that my nerves had inadvertently hurt him.

"I'll see you soon?" I asked hopefully. He managed a half smile.

"I'm looking forward to it." He kissed my hand—this time I let him—and followed the king from the room, casting me a confused glance as he left, leaving me feeling adrift in an ocean without an anchor, left at the mercies of his extremely royal and rather intimidating family. I turned to face them. What scene was next in this performance of mine?

It turned out to be an evening of embroidery. My slowly abating nerves not only returned at this news, but escalated into full-blown panic. I, a terrible stitcher, was expected to do embroidery in front of an audience who had undoubtedly witnessed Princess Lavena's unmatched skill. I may have fooled Liam on our honeymoon, but I could in no way fool the queen and her daughters.

I was going to be sick.

We entered the amber parlor and I rigidly perched at the edge of an armchair. I took in the bright, cheery room of pastel yellows, searching for any escape routes. The queen and three princesses relaxed into their seats, chatting easily, while I clenched and unclenched my fists in an attempt to keep my hands from shaking. They quickly became sweaty but there was no place to wipe them; my silk evening gown and the satin seating were both out of the question.

A servant handed me an embroidery hoop, but it remained untouched in my lap until the light conversation of my companions ceased and they turned towards me, their foreheads furrowed.

Princess Elodie lowered her gaze to my empty hoop. "What's the matter? Don't you want to embroider? I thought it was one of your favorite pastimes."

I struggled to control my frantic breaths. I was certain if I opened my mouth to respond I'd do something ridiculous such as cry. The queen, who sat nearest me, rested a gentle hand on my arm.

"If you're not in the mood to embroider, perhaps you'd be willing to entertain us on the pianoforte. I love your music."

I winced. Considering I couldn't even *play* the pianoforte and I could at least fake my way through my stitches, I opted for the embroidery. I shakily picked up my hoop and made as delicate stitches as I could muster in a pattern that I hoped resembled something floral but which, in reality, turned out looking like nothing more than a jumbled mess. I ignored the cheerful conversation surrounding me as I impatiently fiddled with my thread in a futile attempt to salvage the project.

"You're really being unusually quiet tonight, Lavena." Princess Elodie's comment caused my attention to snap back up.

"I'm sorry," I stuttered. "I—I'm just not up for conversation. I'm rather tired."

"And rather concentrated on your embroidery," Princess Elodie said. "It's no wonder; your skill is unparalleled. I always love seeing your masterpieces. What are you working on now?" She leaned forward eagerly and her expectant expression faltered as she took in the mess in my lap. "What is it?" she asked with an overly polite tone.

"Uh…" As had been my problem for most of the evening, no words were forthcoming.

Princess Aveline bit her lip, as if to suppress a laugh. "What a…*unique* design. You must be very tired."

My stomach churned. Would my obvious lack of talent for embroidery—so unlike Princess Lavena—reveal the truth?

Princess Rheanna stared at my embroidery, her expression surprisingly kind for how hideous it was. "I think it looks rather nice," she offered quietly. Bless her for her obvious lie.

Princess Elodie tipped her head from side to side, examining the piece from different angles—even readjusting its position so it was upside down at one point. "It must be a style I'm unfamiliar with. I suppose your skills are far too advanced for the average embroiderer such as myself."

Another far-too-kind statement, one that made me want to sob with relief that despite my horrible portrayal of Princess Lavena, the sweet Dracerian princesses were finding excuses to explain it away rather than assume an imposter. And why would they expect one? No one outside Princess Lavena's family and close servants even knew of the handmaiden who so closely resembled her. This thought caused the anxiety that had been tightening my chest to slowly loosen. Perhaps I wouldn't get caught after all.

Princess Aveline wrinkled her nose at my pattern. "What's it supposed to be, exactly?"

I was spared answering by the arrival of Liam and the king. My tension melted away at seeing Liam again. I beamed and he returned my smile, seeming surprised but undoubtedly pleased.

"Hello, darling." He settled beside me and smirked at my embroidery. "Another secret code?"

"No, another gift for my husband."

He laughed and wrapped his arm around me. Once again I let him; I felt more secure with him touching me. "Perhaps I'm too good at this husband thing if you're feeling compelled to gift me with another of your *delightful* creations."

"It's in your best interest to continue all the same," I said with a teasing smirk. "Unless you're feeling brave enough to face a displeased wife."

"So this is your way of telling me you're pleased with me?" All humor left Liam's eyes, replaced with a smoldering look.

"You're getting quite good at reading me."

177

His grin broadened and he placed a quick kiss at the tip of my nose. Although I welcomed his kiss, I remembered our audience and felt my shyness heat my cheeks and choke my voice. I lowered my gaze to my lap. Liam gave me a side squeeze.

"What is it, Lavena?"

If only I could explain. I cast an uncertain glance towards his family. Once again, the queen was surveying me with concern.

"You really do seem out of sorts tonight, dear," she said. "Perhaps you should retire early."

Although I felt much calmer with Liam beside me, I gratefully pounced on the invitation to end this anxiety-riddled evening. "Yes, Your Majesty, I'd appreciate that."

I rose and Liam immediately leapt to his feet. "May I escort you, dear?"

The worry filling his eyes compelled me to nod. I curtsied to the king and queen and bid them and Liam's sisters good night. Liam took my hand and led me from the parlor, but rather than escort me to my room, he gently tugged me into a tucked-away alcove, where he held both my hands close and studied my expression.

"You've been so different tonight, Lavena. You seem almost...*frightened*. Are you quite alright?" He caressed my cheek, which had a rather soothing effect on me, not to mention I felt considerably more calm finally being away from his kind but rather intimidating family.

"Not to worry, I'm feeling much better."

He frowned. "So you were feeling unwell?"

I glanced towards the parlor we'd just left. How could I explain my behavior? My nerves to accurately portray the princess had caused me to perform dismally, which only made me appear more suspicious.

Liam's frown deepened as he followed the line of my gaze. "Was it my family? Do you not like them?"

"I like them very much. It's just...I was nervous dining with them for the first time since the wedding."

His brows constricted. "Nervous? Whatever for? You've always gotten along with them in the past, I daresay more than you ever got along with me. Now you've been behaving as if they were strangers; I've never seen you so on edge."

Oh dear. "It must be my exhaustion. It's been a long day."

Remorse filled his previously worried expression. "Of course. I should be a better husband and escort you to your room rather than interrogate you." But he looked as if he wanted the interrogation to continue.

"I'm not too tired to pass up an opportunity to spend time with my husband," I said. "It's nice to be alone with you again."

I expected him to smile but instead he bit his lip. "Are you *sure* you're alright? Because it wasn't just your nerves around my family that's worrying me. You've been rather...aloof and cold, like you no longer welcome my affections, almost like you were before." He hesitated. "For a brief moment, I was afraid we'd lost everything we'd built during our honeymoon. I don't want to lose you."

I silently cursed myself. In that regard, I'd performed a bit too well as Princess Lavena. Remorse filled me that I'd given him such a wrong impression.

I cradled his cheek. "I'm sorry, Liam. Of course I welcome your affections. I was just shy about receiving them in front of your parents."

His face softened in relief at my explanation. "They don't mind, especially in a private family setting. They actually seemed pleased that things are going so well for us. My father even said so after dinner."

And then I'd made it seem like things weren't going well

at all with my ridiculous anxiety. I rested my hand against his chest, relishing the beat of his heart against my palm before I slowly hooked my arms around his neck.

His eyes glistened and he grinned boyishly. "Lavena?"

"It seems I owe my husband an apology for how I treated him at dinner." I stood on tiptoe and brushed my lips against his. Despite the gentle kiss I gave, I received a passionate one in return, one that ignited my heart. I pressed myself closer, thrilled when his arms tightened around me, as if he needed to keep me close. It was such a beautiful, heated kiss, one I wanted to last forever, but all too soon we broke away.

"Wow, it appears I have no need to worry that you don't welcome my affections." He kissed me again. "Why did you resist before?" he murmured against my lips. "Are you shy, Lavena? It's strange, but you were never shy before—"

I kissed him fervently, hoping to distract him from his suspicions, and by his responding groan and the way he eagerly burrowed his fingers in my hair, my ploy succeeded. I allowed myself to push my fears away and melt into his kiss, into *him*.

In this moment, everything was perfect. Despite my nerves causing my performance to be the complete opposite of Princess Lavena, I'd survived the first night in the second half of this production, although I hadn't emerged entirely unscathed—the many baffled and suspicious looks from Liam's family swirled through my mind. It'd take a miracle for me to fool them for much longer, and then the wonderful relationship Liam and I had created would come to an end, a thought even more unbearable than getting caught.

But for now we were together, and it was beautiful.

CHAPTER 16

*B*eginning the next morning, Liam became swamped in his duties as the crown prince, and I began mine as the crown princess. An advisor helped me learn my many responsibilities, and to my relief I found I was a quick study; at least in this one regard, it was easy to be convincing as Princess Lavena.

When my duties were finished, Liam still had many meetings he needed to attend to, which left me far too much time to miss him. During our honeymoon, Liam had eclipsed all my attention, but now the time apart from him prevented me from being distracted from another I missed fiercely: Archer.

Distress knotted my stomach; he was undoubtedly worried sick. I needed to write to him and assure him of my safety, even though the power of the contract ring brandishing my finger prevented me from telling him all that had happened to me. Still, if I could at least ease his heart that I was alive...

I sat at the desk in my room, toying with the end of my quill as I scribbled out my first attempt to write my brother:

Dear Archer, I'm so sorry to have disappeared so suddenly. I currently find myself in quite the predicament—

Searing heat spread from the ring and up my arm, forcing my silence. I groaned, crumpled up my failed letter, and started again: *Dear Archer, you're undoubtedly anxiously wondering what's become of me. I've been forced into a situation that—*

Once again, the ring's power overcame me, more burning than the last warning. I startled and dropped my quill, splotching my letter with ink. I growled in frustration, crumpled this failed attempt, and tossed it into the fire before pressing my head against the desk with a sigh. If I couldn't tell Archer where I was, how would I ease his worries?

I considered the problem from all angles before straightening and dipping my quill into my inkwell for attempt number three:

My Dear Archer, I'm so sorry not to have written before now, especially as my absence from Lyceria undoubtedly has you quite worried. Please be assured I'm safe, although I can't tell you where I am or what's become of me.

I blew the ink dry and read what I'd written so far. I frowned. It was too vague, leaving too many unanswered questions that would cause him to worry all the more and likely try to find me.

I sighed as I crumpled this most recent failure and tossed it towards the fireplace; the letter bounced off the mantle and landed on the hearth. Before I could retrieve it and burn the evidence of my attempts to soothe my frantic brother, someone knocked on the door.

My heart immediately flipped. It must be Liam, back early from his duties. I quickly checked my appearance in the mirror and nodded in approval. I looked quite lovely in my favorite fern-green gown...or rather, my favorite gown of the *princess's*. It was strange not only how accustomed I'd become to my new wardrobe, but how much I now enjoyed dressing up.

Perhaps I belonged here with Liam after all. Eager to see him, I fixed my hair and turned towards the door. "Come in."

The door opened to reveal not Liam but his three younger sisters—Rheanna, Aveline, and Elodie. They flounced in with smiles of anticipation.

"There you are," Elodie said. "You've been cooped up pining for Liam far too long, hence we're here to kidnap you for a fun distraction." She came over and tugged me to my feet, while Rheanna searched my expression with a concerned one of her own.

"Are you alright, Lavena?"

My cheeks heated. "I thought you were Liam," I admitted.

Elodie giggled. "And we just disappointed you, didn't we? I know we're not your dear husband, but would you welcome our company anyway?"

Instinctively, my nerves from last night flared, but I forced myself to push them away. Acting anxious would only rouse suspicion, not to mention the princesses seemed quite friendly. Although handmaidens didn't spend time with princesses, in this charade they were my sisters-in-law. I'd always wanted sisters.

I smiled shyly. "I'd love to spend the day with you until Liam is finished. Is he still in meetings?"

"He is, likely bored to tears," Rheanna said. My heart clenched with another worry that Liam suffered not just from boredom but from feeling inadequate as the heir. I ached to see him to ensure myself he was alright.

Elodie looped her arm through mine and practically skipped towards the door, her sisters following...until Aveline caught sight of the crumpled up letter to Archer. She scooped it up, wrinkling her brow. "What's this?"

"Wait, don't, that's—"

Too late. Before I could stop her, she unfolded the letter and read it. "*My Dear Archer?*" She glared at me. "Who's Archer?"

Elodie released me and scampered over to read over Aveline's shoulder. Her mouth popped open. "Are you writing a lover?"

My stomach lurched. Of course that's what this looked like. "Of course not."

"I think Liam needs to see this," Aveline said. "He deserves to know that his wife's pining for another man."

My cheeks burned at the implication. Why did I have to impersonate someone with such an unflattering reputation? "I swear it's not what it looks like," I stuttered.

"I'm sure it's not." But Rheanna bit her lip doubtfully.

"Of course it isn't." Elodie snatched the unfinished letter, crumpled it back up, and tossed it into the fireplace, where the flames consumed it. "Things are going too well with Liam for Lavena to want anyone else. She was likely writing to tell him off. Weren't you, Lavena?"

She didn't even wait for me to answer before she looped her arm back through mine and led me down several flights of stairs and out into the gardens. It was a sunny day, with the flowers in full bloom, an environment far too cheerful for the tension now festering between me and the princesses. Couldn't things ever go well?

But it seemed Elodie couldn't endure anything uncomfortable for long. As we entered the rose garden, her expression became mischievous. "Guess what I saw last night?" she asked in a singsong tone.

Aveline rolled her eyes towards the cloudless blue sky. "Not another one of your guessing games."

"That's not a guess," she said with a rather elegant pout. "Do you have a guess, Rhea?"

Rheanna shrugged. "Not really," she said in her usual quiet voice. Elodie sighed and gave me a hopeful look.

"You'll play along, won't you, Lavena?"

"Why would she? She's never done so before," Aveline said, causing me to swallow my own guess.

"Yes, but Lavena is different now," Elodie said. "We discussed it at length after you and Liam left last night."

I automatically stiffened.

"The first rule of engaging in gossip," Aveline said wryly, "is not to tell the victim of said gossip we were talking about her."

Elodie waved that thought away. "We didn't say anything *bad*. I promise, Lavena." She widened her eyes in such a way that compelled me to believe her. "And anyway, we were just discussing that you're much improved from how sour you used to be. Married life certainly suits you."

My quickening heartbeat gradually settled. Bless her for making excuses to explain my continued poor Princess-Lavena performance.

"We didn't talk about you for very long...except for when Liam returned from *escorting* you." A smirk tugged on her mouth. "He asked us to get to know you better so that you'd be more comfortable in our family, which is a strange request considering you've never seemed tense around us before." Her forehead furrowed in puzzlement before it smoothed out and she smiled. "Naturally, we don't need his invitation to get to know our newest sister more."

"Hence this stroll?" I asked.

Elodie brightened. "Exactly. It's the perfect pastime to engage in, especially on such a lovely day." She tipped her head back to soak in the sun.

"You're so easily distracted," Aveline said. "Weren't we supposed to be playing a guessing game with you?"

"Ha, I knew you were secretly interested."

Aveline rolled her eyes again while Elodie gave me a rather knowing look.

"Last night shortly after you and Liam left, I followed and caught you two...*kissing!*"

My face ignited while Rheanna frowned disapprovingly at her sister. "Oh Elodie, you were spying on them?"

"Yes, I was," she said without the tiniest hint of remorse. "It was a rather adorable display. I could clearly see you two care for one another." Her eyes lit up. "For as stiff you were being around him during dinner, I was quite surprised at the level of your affection...surprised but *delighted*. I'm so pleased. You two deserve a wonderful marriage, especially after your rough engagement."

Although I smiled at her sweet comment, it suddenly occurred to me that there would be more problems with Liam having three younger sisters than them merely being more people to perform for. I'd have to keep on my toes.

Rheanna eyed my anxious expression and thankfully changed the subject. "We shouldn't let this fine day go to waste. What would you like to do?"

Elodie tapped her lips before she lit up. "We'll pick berries. Perhaps we can make a game of it and see who can pick the most. I'll fetch the baskets, you three go on ahead."

She scampered off and Rheanna took the lead, guiding us to a clump of strawberries growing in a thicket against the surrounding gilded fence enclosing the palace. I froze, staring longingly at the plump, juicy red fruit. Why strawberries?

Rheanna chewed on her lip. "Oh dear, I'd forgotten you were allergic. Will picking strawberries aggravate your allergy?"

So much for hoping the princesses had forgotten Princess Lavena's allergy. My gaze lingered longingly at the fruit, hanging like ruby ornaments on the bush, as I fought not to imagine their juicy sweetness. "Picking them is harmless." Except for torturing me with their tantalizing nearness when I couldn't eat any.

Rheanna slumped in relief. "I'm glad. I know it's strange for princesses to engage in such an unroyal activity, but we've always enjoyed it." She cast Aveline—currently polishing her nails—a wary glance before she leaned closer, expression anxious. "Are you really not involved with Archer?" she whispered.

I wrinkled my nose at the thought she believed me involved with my *brother*. "I'm not, I promise."

"Because if you were, it'd break Liam's heart. I know how painful rejection can be, and I wasn't even in love with the one who denied me." Sadness filled her eyes at the memory. "Liam hasn't looked this happy in years. Please don't do anything to hurt him."

I wanted to assure her I wouldn't, but the knowledge that my deception would do just that if discovered made me realize this was a promise I couldn't give. The thought twisted my heart.

"Ooh, are we gossiping about our brother?" Elodie had returned with four baskets, which she handed each of us with giddy excitement.

"We're not gossiping about Liam," Rheanna said.

"But I heard his name. And even if we aren't gossiping about him, we should; there are so many stories to share with his new wife." Her grin became wicked.

My curiosity was immediately piqued. "What sorts of stories?"

Elodie settled on the lawn and began to pick strawberries. "All kinds."

She launched into her tales, mostly about Liam's many escapades and mischief throughout the years, but also several about his kindness towards his sisters. I soaked them all up, loving each revealed piece of my Liam. It made for a cozy afternoon—stories of the man I loved while picking my favorite fruit, whose sweet scent enveloped me, tempting me to eat each one I picked.

Elodie paused when she noticed Rheanna, slowly picking her strawberries as if in a daze. "Are you alright, Rhea?"

"What?" She blinked at her sister before giving a rather forced smile. "It's nothing. Just...thinking."

Elodie and Aveline exchanged looks. Aveline mouthed, *broken engagement*, and Elodie's face twisted in sympathy. "Were you and Lavena discussing your broken engagement?"

Rheanna stiffened, her answer. Elodie rubbed her sister's back.

"Poor dear. Are you really still so upset about it? It's been over a year."

"I was just warning Lavena to be careful with our brother's heart," she said before she pursed her lips and became extra occupied with plucking strawberries from the bush in rapid, rigid movements, signaling the end to the conversation. Elodie glanced uncertainly towards me.

"Rhea's right, Lavena; should there be anything between you and Archer, Liam would be utterly distraught. He's a happy person by nature, but I've never seen him so ecstatic about anything—or specifically *anyone*—until now."

My heartbeat escalated. Joy filled me at the thought I could make Liam as happy as he made me.

I recalled her words over and over again as we picked strawberries, tuning out Elodie and Aveline's chatter when it no longer revolved around dear Liam, while Rheanna remained quiet. The afternoon passed at a leisurely pace, pleasant enough with the princesses' enjoyable company, but it became even more so when my favorite voice drifted across the grounds.

"Might I join you, ladies?"

Liam. I beamed as he bounded over, eager for whatever adventure we promised him.

"Won't you?" I asked breathlessly, earning me a giggle from Elodie and a timid smile from Rheanna.

He lit up, as if hoping I'd ask him. "Of course. After all, you're the reason I'm here...although these strawberries are rather tempting."

He swept a kiss across my cheek before settling beside me, so close his cinnamon-scented warmth mingled with the fruity perfume of the strawberries. It was intoxicating and made me slightly dizzy.

Liam rested his hand on top of mine before turning back to his sisters with eyes wide in mock horror. "Sitting on the grass in such an unladylike manner? Whatever will Mother say?"

Elodie groaned. "You're not going to tell her, are you?"

"I might be persuaded to keep silent...for a price. Goodness, those strawberries look delicious." His gaze lowered to our nearly full baskets.

She rolled her eyes. "Blackmailing your sisters? That's not a very kind big brother thing to do."

He looked affronted. "You misjudge me. I have only your best interests in mind; after all, grass is rather frightening." He yanked out a handful and rained it over Elodie's head. She shrieked and tried to crawl away.

"Liam!"

He laughed. "The way you're shrieking, Elodie, you'd think it was poisonous."

"Or full of chiggers," I offered before I could check my words.

"Full of *what?*" All four of my companions gave me blank stares. Heat tickled my cheeks. Why couldn't I keep my mouth shut when it came to useless insect facts?

Aveline wrinkled her nose. "What's a chigger?"

"Oh, you know," I said in an offhand tone as I fidgeted with my warm ring, fighting to squelch my panic at yet another slip-up. "They're tiny red bugs that sometimes invade lawns and attach themselves to people in order to inject a liquid that dissolves the skin, which they then ingest."

The ring burned stronger in warning.

"*Ew!*" Elodie and Rheanna immediately leapt to their feet and shook their skirts, while Aveline pushed her basket of strawberries away as if she'd lost her appetite.

"No wonder Mother won't let us on the lawn," Elodie said with a disgusted moan. "Why are you still on the grass, Lavena? Get up before they get you."

"Don't worry, they're only found in grass near forests, orchards, berry bushes..."

All three princesses jolted away from the strawberry patch as if they expected an invasion of the red insects to descend at any moment. Liam calmly used the opportunity to steal Rheanna's abandoned basket and begin popping strawberries into his mouth.

He met my gaze with a crooked grin. "Aren't you going to abandon your strawberries, too?"

"I'm not frightened of chiggers," I said. "I'd actually find it fascinating if they—"

I swallowed my words. No, knowing about such an insect was one thing, gushing about how I wanted one to attach itself to me so that I could happily study it was a different matter entirely. Liam's eyes lit up at my comment, as if he'd just realized something, whereas his sisters' expressions twisted.

"*Fascinating?* I think you mean *revolting*." Elodie shuddered. "Oh dear, I feel all itchy; the creepy blood-sucking bugs are on me; I just know they are. Ew, ew, ew, ew, ew..."

"They don't suck blood," I said, my need to correct her eclipsing my need to stop digging myself deeper in my current predicament. "They inject a liquid into your skin in order to break it down and *eat it*. When they're full, they drop off." The ring seared stronger in protest. I needed to stop speaking; I was pushing too hard against my mask.

Elodie and Rheanna continued shrieking. I peeked shyly over at Liam, nervous for his reaction. To my surprise, he threw his head back and *laughed*.

"That's *awesome*. Who knew such an insect existed, right beneath our noses." He lowered himself eye level with the grass, as if intending to search them out. "Just think, an insect that starts *digesting* you as soon as it latches on. We should capture some and use them to refine the interrogation techniques of prisoners. Shall we consider it during our future reign, darling?"

He winked at me, seeming nothing but charmed by my random spout of insect lore. The love filling my heart for this man felt fit to burst. He must have seen some of this affection in my eyes, for his expression softened. He straightened and scooted closer.

"I've figured it out, you know," he whispered brightly.

"Figured out what?"

"Your secret." His warm breath caressed my ear. "You like insects."

I felt my ever-present blush return to creep across my skin. I ached to deny it, but the fact that I'd fought too long to hide this part of myself and Liam had discovered it anyway kept my ready lie from being spoken; in fact, I was secretly pleased he'd seen such a crucial part of Anwen.

I lowered my eyes shyly. "Do you find that strange?"

"Not at all, Lavena."

I peeked up at him in disbelief. His expression was both sincere and incredibly tender. "You don't?"

"I find it delightful you're interested in such a hobby, one I'd like to join you in pursuing."

I released a breath of relief, not realizing I'd been holding it as I'd awaited Liam's assessment. Of course Liam wouldn't care. It was so *Liam,* and I loved him all the more for it.

"Oh, Liam." I pounced on him, sending him toppling backwards onto the lawn, squeezing him so tightly I was practically strangling him.

"What is it, Lavena? What have I done to please you? Tell me immediately so that I might repeat it in the future. I definitely will, for such a reward as this."

"You're just so *wonderful.*"

I kissed him, right in front of his sisters. It was an incredibly sweet kiss, and upon further investigation I realized it was because he'd been eating strawberries. No wonder he tasted so good. My first strawberry since beginning this charade and what a way to experience it.

His fingers burrowed into my hair as he deepened the kiss...until quite suddenly he pushed me away with a gasp. "I've been eating strawberries. You're not going to stop breathing, are you?"

"If I stop breathing, it's for a different reason entirely," I panted. He chuckled as he ran his fingers through my hair as he stared up at me, eyes adoring.

"Just in case, I'll keep a close eye on you...at least more than usual." He placed the gentlest kiss on my brow before sitting us back up, keeping us intertwined in a rather cozy way. I was moments away from melting, and I was certain my entire face was crimson.

"That was *so* adorable," Elodie gushed, reminding me about the unwanted audience to our spontaneous passion.

"*Adorable* is a good word, but not the one I'd use to describe that moment of heaven." Liam reached out and curled a loose strand of my hair around his finger, his soft gaze not once leaving mine. "Is the strawberry-picking adventure over? Because if so, I have another one in mind with my charming wife." His gaze lowered to linger on my lips.

They seemed hesitant to return to their excursion now that I'd brought up the existence of chiggers, but after much teasing and cajoling from Liam, they returned to picking strawberries, with Liam fulfilling his proper older-brother role by frequently stealing from his sisters' baskets with a wicked glint in his eyes.

When the princesses had ventured a few paces away to a fuller bush, I used the opportunity to scoot back to Liam's side. He promptly kissed my temple. "Are you here for a visit, darling?"

"I wanted to ask how your meeting went."

"It was dull, of course," he said.

"But are you alright? I know you worry about your role as the crown prince."

His expression softened and he rested his hand over mine. "You were worried for me?"

"I don't want you to feel inadequate."

"Then let me ease your heart: I fared quite well today, although I missed you like mad." He smiled. "My role is actually getting easier knowing you believe in me."

He looked like he wanted to say more, but his chattering sisters returned, pulling him into their conversation. An ache filled my chest and I felt a strange sense of loss at having to share him with others. I longed for the intimacy we'd shared on our honeymoon, when nothing had existed except for us.

As if sensing this, although his polite attention didn't divert from his sisters, Liam took my hand and rested it on his knee, palm up, where he proceeded to trace pictures. My breath hitched. He grinned mischievously and leaned in close.

"Shall we play a game of 'guess that picture?'"

I nodded, breathless from each stroke of his finger as he traced something on my hand.

"What did I draw?" he whispered.

I hadn't even noticed he'd stopped. "No idea."

He chuckled quietly. "Are you enjoying my touch, Lavena dear?"

"I can scarcely breathe, actually."

"Excellent." His eyes danced merrily. "I'll draw it one more time so you can redeem yourself." He traced out the picture again.

"A heart?"

"Not just any heart, but *my* heart. Do you want it, Lavena?"

My own skipped a few beats at the beautiful intensity filling his eyes...and that's when I realized the truth: Liam had given me his heart; *he loved me*, just as I loved him. It was a realization that was both beautiful and painful, for I knew I couldn't claim Liam's heart as my own. But oh how I wanted it, more than I'd ever wanted anything.

Liam's smoldering gaze searched mine as he awaited my answer. I opened my mouth to tell him yes.

"Liam? *Liam?*"

Wide grin not faltering, Liam turned towards his impatient sister. "Yes, Elodie?"

She gave him a *look* that was both amused and exasperated. "Have you been paying attention to anything I've been saying?"

Liam's smile became guilty. "Honestly? Not really."

Elodie glared for a moment before brightening. "I see you're going to be inattentive whenever Lavena is around. I suppose that's to be expected from newlyweds."

"And even when she isn't around, I can only go so long without thinking of her. Indeed, I'll likely only be paying half attention to everyone from now on."

My heart fluttered at how open he was being with his feelings. I smiled shyly, which he returned with an enthusiastic kiss on my cheek.

I sighed happily as I tucked my head against his shoulder, allowing myself to bask in this perfect moment with him. Princess Lavena hadn't yet returned to claim Liam. Hope stirred within me that perhaps she never would. I'd happily continue to pretend as an imposter if only I could remain with my Liam forever.

CHAPTER 17

*O*nce again I found myself at my desk. I tapped my
quill as I stared at the blank piece of parchment.
We'd returned from our honeymoon a week ago, meaning it
had been over five weeks since Archer had heard from me—
five weeks of his fierce worry that I needed to ease as soon as
possible—but as usual when it came to trying to write my
brother, words weren't forthcoming, at least words the ring
would allow me to use.

I sighed, dipped my quill into the inkwell as if the act
could somehow summon inspiration, and posed with my
quill hovering over the page as I waited for the words to
come.

Nothing.

My grip tightened around the quill. I wouldn't budge
from this desk until I'd composed a letter that, while
undoubtedly vague thanks to the sadistic enchantment of the
contract ring, would at least assure him I was safe.

Determined, I re-dipped my quill into my inkwell and
began:

. . .

My Dearest Archer,

I'm so sorry for my neglectful correspondence. I know it's been five weeks since you've heard from me, and as such you must be worried sick. I regret I can't ease your heart completely and tell you where I am or what's become of me (for I find myself in quite the situation), but please be assured that I'm well.

I'm not sure when we'll see one another again—or whether or not we even will—which makes my heart ache. I miss you fiercely, and the thought I won't be able to see one so dear to me is unbearable. Please forgive me, dear Archer. If this is the last opportunity I have to write, please know how much I love you. I think of you and miss you every single day, and I pray that one day I can explain everything that has—

Someone gasped sharply behind me. I startled and swiveled around, nearly whacking into Liam, who hovered over my shoulder reading the letter. I'd been so engrossed in my writing I hadn't heard him knock or approach.

My stomach plummeted. I hastily flipped over the parchment even before my recent sentences had dried. But by the wounded look filling Liam's eyes I knew it was too late; he'd seen the letter.

"I thought you had a meeting?" I squeaked.

Liam stared at me, his eyes glassy, looking as if something precious had just been ripped away from him. He swallowed and opened his mouth but no words came out, while my own explanation, forbidden by the ring to be uttered, remained lodged in my throat.

Liam eventually found his voice and spoke in a devastated whisper that wrenched my heart. "My meeting got out early. I came looking for you, hoping we could spend some time together, only to find..." Pain twisted his expression as he glared accusingly at the turned-over letter. "Aveline told me she and my sisters caught you writing another man, but I didn't believe her; I knew you were too sweet to ever betray me like that. But now, after seeing this letter..." He took a shaky breath. "Is this man your...*lover?*" He seemed to choke on the word and my face enflamed at his implication.

I frantically shook my head, desperate for him to understand. "No, Liam, of course not."

"How can you deny it? I read your letter. You told this *Archer* that you're in love with him."

"I'm not *in love* with him." If only Liam knew he was my *twin brother*. It would easily explain away what was quickly becoming an awkward and escalating situation. The ring burned in warning, once again forcing my silence.

His expression hardened. "You told him you love him." He jabbed his finger at the letter as if he meant to skewer it. "You wrote 'please know how much I love you.'" He gave me a look that was both a challenge and a plea to deny it.

I silently cursed. Why had he seen *those* particular words of this incriminating letter? "I can love someone without being *in love* with them. You love your sisters, your parents—"

He raised a mocking brow. "Are you really comparing the relationship you have with this *Archer* with the one I have with my sisters?"

I clenched my fists in frustration. "Yes, I am." *Because Archer is my brother.* How frustrating I couldn't just *tell* him that, but the mere temptation caused the ring to burn more threateningly, keeping me from clearing up this misunderstanding with just a few spoken words. "You can't understand my relationship with Archer merely from snooping."

"Your *relationship.*" His mouth twisted on the word. "And the *situation* you refer to that you find yourself in"—he motioned to my letter—"is that you're married to another man, one you don't love, and therefore aren't free to pursue your liaison with this lover."

I shook my head. While finding myself married to Liam was certainly an unexpected situation, I loved him dearly. "No, Liam, it's not like that—"

"And the promise you made me on our wedding day that you had no past exploits and would honor our commitment to one another...that was nothing more than empty words."

Tears burned my eyes as I frantically shook my head once more.

"I didn't believe Aveline's accusation, just as I'd begun to doubt the rumors about your past reputation. But I was wrong to have faith in you." He squeezed his eyes shut, as if looking at me was physically painful. "I suppose I needed to believe you. I wish I still could."

"Liam..." I caressed his face. He allowed me to touch him for a few seconds before he severed our connection.

"Your *resistance* to me now makes sense," he said. "I foolishly thought you just needed time, when in reality your heart has already been stolen by another man. Yet you continue to toy with me as you cheat on him. What is our marriage to you, Lavena? Another game?"

I could no longer contain my tears. His expression momentarily crumpled at my distress and he reached out as if to brush them away, but then he dropped his hand and stepped back, as if he no longer wanted to be near me. My heart wrenched. I stepped forward, desperate to bridge the physical distance between us even as I desperately tried to close the chasm of our growing emotional distance.

"Please, Liam, our marriage is the most important thing in the world to me. I would never do anything to harm it. I'm not in a romantic relationship with Archer."

His jaw tightened and he remained silent.

"You have to believe me." I twisted the condemning ring

brandishing my finger, more desperate than ever to yank it off. "The only man I've ever been in a relationship with is you." I reached for his hand but he flinched away.

"*Relationship?* You mean the one you referred to as your *situation?* How awkward it must be to try and explain to a past tryst that you now find yourself married."

I flinched. I hadn't seen this Liam in a long time—the Liam who lashed out at me and cut me with his words. Only the raw pain filling his eyes made this Liam different from the one who'd been my husband at the beginning of our marriage.

"No, Liam," I said, weak from our fight but still desperate for him to understand. "I've never done such a thing with anyone."

A long, torturous moment of silence followed. "Well, I no longer believe you," he spat, his tone as hard as his fierce expression.

Panic clawed at my heart. What was happening? All we'd built between us was now in danger of crumbling before my very eyes. I'd wounded my dear husband and I wasn't sure how to fix it when the truth was locked away by the power of the ring. But I wouldn't give up, not when my husband was hurting so deeply.

"Please Liam, Archer and I are only...friends. We've known one another our entire lives."

"How touching," he said. "Well, by all means, invite him to the palace so you two can continue knowing one another for the rest of your lives. Don't let something like our marriage stand in your way."

I winced at the stinging implication. "Liam, *please.*"

But he was already stomping away. "Don't let me distract you from finishing your letter to your *Dearest Archer.*"

I scampered after him and seized his hand. He froze, breathing hard, before his gaze lowered to our connected hands. He stared at them unblinking before raising his wounded gaze to mine.

"Lavena…" The name came out as a strangled sob. He pressed my hand against his heart, as if desperate for me to reclaim it, even now.

"I know what this looks like," I whispered. "But I swear, Liam, this isn't what you think. Please, you have to believe me."

His hands tightened around mine. "How can it not be? I can see you love this Archer; the emotion is in your eyes."

"I'm not *in love* with him," I insisted. "It's different. Please, Liam, try to understand."

"Then why are you clearly distraught at being caught writing him?"

"Because of what it looks like!"

He took a long breath, his hold on my hand tightening. "If he's not a lover, then who is he?"

I struggled mightily to say *my twin brother*, but the words remained trapped in my throat as hot, burning pain spread up my arm. I gasped and instinctively yanked my hand away, a gesture which caused Liam's softening expression to harden once more.

"I see. You have no answer for me."

I clutched my hand to my chest, panting for breath, all while my tears of pain and frustration continued to fall. "Please, Liam."

He took a wavering breath before meeting my gaze, his swirling with too many emotions for me to try and decipher them all. "I've grown to care deeply for you, Lavena, an outcome I never would have imagined before our marriage. Now that I feel what I feel for you, I want our relationship to work, but how can it when your disloyal heart is prone to wandering? How many more *Archers* are there between us?"

He reached out and wiped one of the tears trickling down my chin, as if he couldn't help himself.

"I wish I hadn't grown to care, not when caring is so painful. Indifference is the most effective shield, but it's far too late for that defense." He slowly backed away. "If only I could stop caring. Perhaps it was better when we were enemies."

I gasped sharply. No, he couldn't mean…. His insult dug deep into my heart as he stormed from the room, slamming the door behind him, leaving me stunned and heartbroken.

I'd always known Liam wasn't mine, but with his departure, I still felt I'd just lost something precious—and I wanted it back, more than I'd ever wanted anything.

LIAM DISTANCED himself from me for the remainder of the day, something he hadn't done since our first week of marriage. When we were forced to be in the same room during dinner, he determinedly avoided looking at me, nor did he hold or play with my hand beneath the table like he normally did. The tension between us felt like a foreign stranger, one I was desperate to get rid of, but I had no means to do so as the ring guarded the key that could unlock our misunderstanding.

The king and queen retired early for the evening, leaving just me, Liam, and his sisters adjourning to the parlor. Normally, Liam and I curled up together in the same seat and had our own private conversation. Not tonight. While I headed for our usual settee just beneath the sunset-lit window, Liam settled on the opposite side of the room, a clear dismissal that nearly made me cry.

His sisters looked back and forth between us, Elodie scowling. "Whatever is the matter with you two?"

Liam didn't answer. Aveline raised her eyebrows. "It appears the newlyweds are fighting."

Elodie gasped. "But you can't be. Things have been going so well."

Liam glared at her. "Our marriage is none of your concern."

She withered slightly. "There's no need to be so curt," she said as she picked up her embroidery. "I'm just concerned, but if you don't want me to be, then I won't ask."

Following Liam's sharp dismissal, silence reigned in the parlor. Liam continued looking everywhere around the room except at me, while the princesses all quietly embroidered. I didn't embroider, too agitated to fake my way through my stitches. Instead I sat in misery, aching to get Liam to speak with me again.

"Liam?" I finally asked hesitantly.

He made no response, instead seeming rather occupied with the patterns in the ornate parlor rug. I took a shaky breath and pushed forward.

"I never got the chance to ask how your meeting went. Did it go alright? I know you were worried about it."

He remained silent. Both Elodie and Rheanna looked up from their embroidery to glance back and forth between us, their expressions growing ever more anxious the longer the taut tension stretched on.

"I'm sure you did a wonderful job," I shakily managed. "Especially since you prepared so thoroughly…" My voice trailed off as my words slipped away. Liam's fists clenched and he was now glaring at the rug, as if fighting to keep his gaze there.

More torturous silence followed my failed attempts to engage my wounded husband. Soon it became unbearable even for the princesses.

Elodie finally spoke up. "Liam, why are you ignoring your wife?"

Still no answer. She sighed and glanced at me in hopes I'd elaborate. My cheeks warmed as I lowered my gaze. Aveline snorted, the most inelegant sound I'd ever heard from her.

"Since the unhappy couple is failing to satisfy your curiosity, I'll happily oblige. Dear Lavena has reverted back to her old unfaithful habits."

My eyes burned at her accusation, the perfect incentive to keep my gaze resolutely locked on my lap. I shook my head. "No, I haven't."

"Liam caught her this afternoon writing a letter declaring her love for that Archer fellow," Aveline continued as if I hadn't spoken.

Elodie gasped. "But Lavena, you told us you weren't involved with him."

"I'm not," I said, my voice pleading. "I promise I'm not."

"Then why did you write Archer declaring that you love him?"

I wrung my hands in my lap. "It's not what it looks like. I swear."

"Maybe he's a cousin?" Rheanna offered quietly from her usual corner.

"There are no *Archers* in the Lycerian royal family tree," Aveline said with a smirk. "I've already checked. Now won't you tell us who he is, Lavena?"

I bit my lip but said nothing. At my continued silence, Aveline's smirk widened.

"In my research, I did find an Archer that works at the Lycerian palace, a peasant who's a member of the royal hunting party."

My cheeks burned, betraying me. Elodie gasped dramatically. "A peasant? Oh, Lavena. How could you choose a peasant over Liam?"

Liam stirred but I couldn't look at him. "It's not like that," I stuttered. Any moment now my tears were going to escape. I ached to explain that Archer was my twin brother, but that relationship belonged between Archer and Anwen, the handmaiden who no longer existed.

Aveline's eyes flashed in challenge. "Then why have we caught you writing him *twice*?

"I wish I could explain," I said as I fidgeted with my ring. "But I can't."

"You can't explain why you decided to break my brother's heart?"

I turned towards Liam, whose aloof expression had transformed into one of raw pain. "Oh, Liam...*please*."

His jaw tightened and he looked away, his rejection clear, and I couldn't contain my tears any longer.

Elodie gasped. "Don't cry, Lavena."

Liam's gaze snapped to mine, worry warring with his vulnerable expression, a look almost as painful as his disdain. I could no longer bear the distance that had sprung up between us, nor endure the confrontation from his protective sisters.

I stood and hurried from the room.

CHAPTER 18

*O*ur fight swirled through my mind like a recurring nightmare as I tossed and turned throughout the night. I frequently sat up to stare longingly at the connecting door dividing our rooms, knowing that Liam slept just beyond the threshold, so close yet having never felt so far as he did now. The pain I'd caused him haunted me.

You always knew you'd hurt him. But I hadn't expected to do it in *this* way. I collapsed back against the pillows and watched the long shadows dance across my canopy as I frantically spent the endless night trying to come up with a way to ease Liam's hurt. But I could see no way out with the ring's sinister grip on my tongue.

When morning finally dawned, I got ready as quickly as possible so I wouldn't miss Liam at breakfast. I was desperate for another chance to try and explain away our misunderstanding, but even though I waited at the dining table for an entire hour, he never arrived. My heart sank. He was undoubtedly avoiding me.

"Good morning, Lavena."

I looked up gloomily from staring at my eggs and toast as

Elodie skipped into the room, smiling cheerily. She made herself a plate from the sideboard and settled beside me. She frowned as she took in my untouched food.

"Aren't you hungry?"

I shook my head. I wasn't one to waste food—not when I'd spent so many times throughout my life hungry—but with my knotted stomach, I couldn't force myself to eat a single bite.

Elodie's expression softened into understanding. "Is it Liam?"

I managed the briefest nod. "Have you seen him this morning?"

She hesitated. "I briefly encountered him in the hallway. He claims he's not hungry."

He was definitely avoiding me. I sank several inches in my seat.

Elodie nervously swirled her eggs on her plate. "Is it true he caught you writing that servant, Archer?"

I ached to deny it. "I promise it's not what it looks like, yet I can't explain; he won't listen." Not that I blamed him. Given the real princess's reputation, was it any wonder I appeared guilty?

"Well, I believe you. He's being unfair…and rather ridiculous. How can you two resolve anything if you don't communicate?" She frowned and took a sip of juice. "But don't worry, he'll come around. Liam can't stay upset for long, especially with those he cares about…although admittedly he seems more *hurt* than upset."

My heart twisted. That was worse.

The door opened to reveal the queen, smiling warmly. "Good morning, girls. I'm pleased you're up, Lavena. I was hoping this morning I could tutor you in another of your duties as the new crown princess."

My pulse quickened. The unresolved contention festering

between Liam and me made the charade seem far too daunting to perform adequately, especially since I'd now lost my primary incentive to continue to pretend. But perform I must. I had no other choice.

I swallowed. "Today?"

"Yes. Do you object?" While her look was kind, it left no room for argument.

"Certainly not, Your Majesty."

Her smile returned. "Then it's decided. Don't look so frightened, dear; this morning's task is simple: receiving our subjects who've come to us seeking aid. You've surely done something similar in your role as Lycerian princess, so it shouldn't be difficult."

Even without the enchantment of the ring preventing me, I knew I'd never be able to form the words to tell her I had absolutely no experience in such matters. What little appetite I had left vanished. I pushed my plate away and waited anxiously until the queen had finished her meal.

By the time she rose from the table, the rest of Liam's family had arrived...save for Liam himself. I avoided the penetrating and accusing stare of Aveline as I followed the queen from the room. Nerves squeezed my heart with every step. It took me two corridors to realize the queen was speaking to me.

"We meet our subjects in the receiving hall once a week," she said. "It's important to remain in touch with our people and do what we can to assist them. Most cases they present are easily handled; some are more difficult. I'll allow you to deal with most this morning while I remain nearby in case you need me."

Little did she know she was dealing with someone who'd never trained to be a princess at all, other than the instruction the advisor had given me after our honeymoon. I felt she was throwing me into the ocean and expected me to instantly know how to swim.

"Will Liam be there?" He always had a calming presence, but I doubted he was keen on being near me so soon after our fight.

"Not today. He has business with his father." The queen eyed my expression with concern. "You're a bit pale. Are you alright, dear? Are you nervous or is something else troubling you?"

I couldn't bear to tell her that I'd broken the heart of the man I loved. "I didn't sleep well."

"I'm sorry to hear that. Perhaps we should begin your duties another day."

Despite the daunting task looming before me, it'd undoubtedly serve as a distraction; remaining alone with my miserable thoughts would be far more torturous than fumbling my way through my duties as crown princess.

I gave the queen my assurances I was feeling well enough, and in no time at all we arrived at the receiving hall. I froze in the doorway. The room was crowded with people, mostly peasants, but also members of the middle class and the court, all forming a line waiting for the privilege of addressing us.

My nerves escalated into panic as I followed the queen past the bowing and curtsying subjects to take our places on the thrones at the front of the room.

A middle-aged woman approached first with an exaggerated curtsy. "Thank you for receiving me, Your Majesty and Your Highness. I come seeking aid for my ill husband. He's been battling a fever these past several weeks and we haven't the herbs we need to treat him, nor the means to acquire them considering he's been unable to work."

The heartache and nerves weighing on me immediately vanished as my heart lifted. Thanks to my mother's tutoring, I was familiar with basic herbal remedies and knew how to make them cheaply. I arranged for the herbs she needed to care for her husband and promised to visit her family personally, a promise I fully intended to keep.

She curtsied gratefully before she was replaced by another seeking aid, followed by another, then another. Several hours sped by without my noticing. Most of the peasants had serious issues—having lost their crops in a recent hail storm, an illness in the family robbing them of their primary breadwinner, a stolen goat that had provided the milk and cheese that was their main livelihood.

With each assistance I rendered, I felt my heart stir, as if Anwen were awakening from a deep slumber. Before Princess Lavena had taken me as her handmaiden, I could have easily been one of these peasants. The queen watched me with a pleased smile, offering occasional guidance but mostly leaving me to my own devices.

While it was a joy to help the peasants with their humble yet earnest requests, most of the issues brought by the upper class were wearying, often full of greed and pettiness. One case in particular tested my patience as two lords presented a dispute over their property line, a case the queen graciously assisted with after realizing my ignorance with the laws and traditions of Dracerian landholders.

As she dealt with the squabble, my heart tightened at the heated exchange of words and the lack of listening done by either party. It was amazing how quickly their miscommunication had escalated. *Just like your fight with Liam.* The thought caused my energy and enthusiasm to wane, and it was all I could do to meet with the final two subjects. When the last finally exited the room, I sank wearily in my seat.

"You did very well, Lavena," the queen said. "I admit I'm pleasantly surprised."

"Thank you, Your Majesty. I enjoy helping people."

"That attitude made you very effective today. I'm very

proud of you." She scooted to the edge of her seat and rested her hand over mine. "Now that our subjects have been seen to, might I offer my help to you? I can tell something is bothering you, something more than a restless night. Won't you confide in me?"

She gave me such a sweet, motherly look, as if I were her own daughter. It had been years since I'd had a mother. This longing compelled me to share my burden with her.

My lip trembled. "Liam and I got in a fight. There's been a horrible misunderstanding, but Liam won't believe my explanation."

The queen's expression twisted in sympathy. "Poor dear. I wondered if it had to do with Liam." She patted my hand. "Liam is a very passionate person. Whatever emotion he feels, he does so completely. Because he's upset, it's difficult for him to focus on any other emotion—in this case, the compassion to talk with you and understand your perspective. But he will. He never remains upset for long. Try talking with him again. I can see that he cares for you deeply, and I'm sure he will open his heart if you just give him a little more time."

I ached to believe her, but I knew she wouldn't be so certain of Liam's forgiveness if she knew the extent of his hurt—that he thought his wife was being unfaithful.

Heart still heavy, I followed Her Majesty from the reception hall. We'd gone only a few corridors when we encountered Liam. He froze when he saw us, staring hungrily at me before he hastily looked away.

The queen frowned disapprovingly. "Good afternoon, Liam. Lavena and I just finished receiving some of our subjects. Lavena did very well. She has such a compassionate heart."

Liam's expression wrenched, as if her words caused him pain. "It's my favorite quality of hers." While his words seemed sincere, they lacked the warmth that usually filled his tone.

My heart tightened, but I refused to be like those disputing lords and give up trying to heal the pain I'd caused Liam. I took a wavering breath and stepped forward, brushing his arm.

"Can I talk to you, Liam? Please."

He didn't look at me as he nodded curtly. The queen excused herself and we ducked into a side room to sit down and talk. I perched nervously on the edge of my seat and took another steadying breath.

"Please forgive me for this misunderstanding, because I assure you a misunderstanding is all this is. Please believe me when I tell you that there's nothing going on between me and Archer."

He finally peeked up at me, his eyes swirling with pain. "How can you sit there and tell me that when there's clearly a relationship between you two? You told him you loved him." His mouth twisted at the words. "I thought his name sounded familiar. It took me most of the night to remember he's the Lycerian servant who arrived unexpectedly during our honeymoon, seeking a private audience with you." His look was both accusing and heartbreaking.

My stomach jolted. *Oh no*, he'd remembered that. He squeezed his eyes shut, as if the sight of my panic confirmed his suspicions.

"I can think of no other explanation for your relationship with a mere servant than—" He couldn't finish.

"So you're choosing to believe your assumptions rather than listen to me?"

"You said you love him," he repeated, his voice breaking.

"I know I said that, but I told you I'm not *in love* with him." *I'm in love with you.* "You have to believe me. Please."

He hesitated before reaching out to lightly touch the back

of my hand. "You have no idea how much I want to, but you must admit what this looks like. I don't want it to be true, but I'm terrified that it is."

"Believe me, I know exactly what this looks like," I said. "But I assure you it isn't what you think. I promise you that I was faithful to you even before our wedding, and have remained so since our marriage. I need you to believe me. Your pain is breaking my heart."

He said nothing at first, only continued to trace swirl after swirl on my hand. His touch was both wonderful and torturous. Then, quietly, he whispered, "You've already broken mine."

My heart wrenched at his admission and the tears I'd fought to keep back escaped. At my strangled sob, his gaze jolted up to meet mine, lingering on the tears now streaking my cheeks.

"Lavena?"

The heartbreak in his voice was too much. I wasn't strong enough to continue the confrontation. With another shuddering sob, I turned and fled the room.

I escaped to my usual garden refuge, where I tucked myself behind a manicured hedge, pulled my knees to my chest, and cried.

I wasn't huddled there long before I heard footsteps. My breath hooked as I waited for them to approach my hiding place. "Lavena?"

Liam. I didn't look up.

"Lavena darling, it's raining."

Was it? I peeked out from my knees to take in my wet surroundings. Only then did I notice the raindrops pattering my hair and the moisture seeping into my skirts. But the rain didn't matter. I reburied myself.

"Sweetheart, please come inside. I don't want you catching a cold."

Sweetheart? I peeked back up to see beautiful concern filling his expression. My broken heart fluttered in hope.

"Why do you care?" I mumbled.

He sighed. "Believe me, I've spent the past day trying not to care in an effort to protect myself from yesterday's...revelation. Instead, I only feel worse; avoiding you has caused me to miss you all the more." He advanced a hesitant step. "May I join you?"

At my nod, he settled beside me and I was immediately bathed in his warmth. In spite of my own promise to maintain distance from the man I'd inadvertently hurt, I snuggled closer and nearly sobbed in relief when his arm wrapped around me. Despite his cozy embrace I shivered. He tugged off his cloak to gently wrap it around me, immersing me in his intoxicating scent.

"Was there something you needed?" I whispered, desperate for an explanation for his unexpected closeness.

He began rubbing up and down my arm to warm me from the rainy chill, pausing to peer up at me, his expression intensifying. "I need you."

My heart lifted and I couldn't contain the smile that overcame me, the first since our fight. "You need...*me?*"

He nodded. "Always. I'm sorry about how I've treated you since yesterday, dear."

"*You're* sorry? I'm not the one who caught my spouse writing a letter to another."

"But I am the one who, in his hurt and anger, chose to ignore his wife's explanation." He cupped my chin, his gaze penetrating mine. "Are you currently or have you ever been engaged in a romantic relationship with this Archer?"

I stared into his eyes, desperate for him to believe me. "No. I swear, Liam."

He searched my gaze for a long time before the corner of his mouth quirked up, hinting at his adorable dimple. I softly traced around it with my finger, marveling at its appearance at such a time.

"Please believe me," I whispered. "I need you to."

"Then your wish shall be granted."

I gaped at him. "You believe me?"

He stroked my cheek. "Marriage is about trust, so I do. I need to. Besides, this misunderstanding doesn't fit you now that I've discovered who you truly are."

I stared at him in astonishment. *He sees me.* My pent-up sob escaped as I buried myself against his chest. He embraced me and I marveled at the feel of his firm, warm arms cradling me, holding me close. In them I felt home. "I missed you, Liam."

He chuckled and began to stroke my wet hair. "Not as much as I've missed you." He tilted my face up so he could lightly trace each of my features with his fingertip, his look attentive. "Although I feel as if I have every bit of you memorized, after forcing myself this past day not to look at you, I feel as if I'm seeing you for the first time. You're so lovely, Lavena." He kissed my brow.

I grinned and snuggled closer. A different silence settled over us, one absent of tension although still lingering with some hurt. But it was also a healing silence, and I knew that despite our fight, things would be alright between us.

Liam spoke first. "After my meeting today, I sought you out, needing to tell you, my confidante, all about it. I couldn't stand how things were between us any longer. It was agonizing playing the silent treatment with you."

"I never want to play that game with you," I said.

"Oh, Lavena, of course you don't." He released a long sigh. "Where's Archer's letter now? Did you ever send it?"

I shook my head. "I couldn't." For as anxious as I was to ease my brother's heart, I couldn't do it through *that* letter after it had caused Liam such pain. "I burned it."

"You did?" Relief filled Liam's expression. He cradled my cheek. "Even though I can see your honesty, I'm too curious not to ask: who's Archer?"

"It's as Aveline said—he's a common man on the royal hunt in Lyceria."

"And how do you know him?"

I nibbled my lip, deliberating how to answer. "I've always known him. We met in infancy. He's like a brother to me."

"A...*brother*?" He seemed to be testing the word and obviously liked it considering the smile that lit his face. "Really?"

"Yes, Liam. I promise. He didn't know about our marriage, so I fear he's worried about me. I was only writing him to tell him I was alright."

His brow furrowed. "He must have known, for he came to see you during our honeymoon." His frown deepened and his look became searching. "Not to mention, at the time of his visit, you told me you'd only met him a few times. Was that a lie?"

My cheeks burned. "It was, but I only gave it because I was afraid you'd assume the true nature of our relationship was more insinuating than it actually is...and I was right. I'm sorry."

He was silent for an agonizing moment. "If that was a lie, how can I be certain what you're telling me now isn't a lie too?"

"But it's not." I twisted the ring on my finger. "There's nothing going on between me and Archer. I promise."

Once more he searched my expression, his own anxious in his desperation for my words to be true. His own softened at seeing my sincerity even as his brows furrowed in confusion. "I'm afraid I still don't understand. Why would a princess be so well acquainted with a common man?"

"Well, as I mentioned during our honeymoon, he's my handmaiden's brother..."

I ached to tell him more. Ever since becoming bound by the princess's vicious ring, I'd never wanted to break its enchantment of silence more than I did now. Despite Liam's sweet trust, pain still lingered in his eyes, pain that had been caused by this ridiculous charade. I was tired of the lies, the misunderstandings, the hiding, and the pretending. If only I could tell him the truth, everything would become clear to him.

My jaw set in determination. "Because he's my—" The words *twin brother* were swallowed by my startled cry as white-hot pain laced up my arm, more burning than it had ever been since being forced to don the ring. My finger scorched and throbbed with the intensity, as if I'd stuck my hand into a flame.

"Lavena?"

I barely heard Liam, my senses eclipsed by the searing torture. Tears poured down my cheeks as I cradled my hand against my chest. Liam held me tightly, frantically demanding over and over what was wrong, but I couldn't tell him; I wouldn't risk angering the sadistic ring further, already punishing me mercilessly for my breach of contract.

"Lavena? *Lavena?*"

Liam shook me desperately. Dizzy with pain, I somehow managed to tip my head back to take in his frantic expression. He stroked me over and over, as if he could rub away the pain tormenting me.

"What is it, Lavena? Are you hurt? Please tell me." He sounded so desperate.

How could I explain that the ring brandishing my finger

was torturing me? So I said nothing, and at my submissive silence, the torment slowly began to dissipate.

I glanced down at the ring, glistening with sickly satisfaction that I'd understood its threatening message: remain silent. Play your part. Or experience fiery torment that would force me to comply with its cruel demands. I silently swore my allegiance to it. All thought of attempting to tell Liam my true relationship with Archer vanished, for I was too terrified of experiencing such agony again, certain that next time it wouldn't just be torturous, but unbearable.

"Lavena?" Liam's voice choked. He was near tears. I took several long, deep breaths, cradling my hand. Liam's gaze lowered to it and his face lit with understanding. "Your hand?"

He reached for it. I tried to jerk away but he seized it and examined every inch. Despite feeling like it'd been immersed in fire, it remained unscathed and unburned.

"Does your hand hurt?"

I ached to lie, but unfortunately my huge reaction could not be dismissed. "It's fading."

"What happened?" He stroked my hand, his touch a soothing balm for the pain thankfully slipping away.

I shook my head. "I can't explain." If only I could. I rested my forehead against his chest, suddenly weary, both from our earlier fight and the torture I'd just endured. Thankfully, he didn't press me for further details. He just held me close, rubbing my back as I took steady breath after steady breath, waiting for the fire that had laced through me to completely abate. It gradually faded, faded, faded...until it was nothing more than a throbbing memory.

I released a long breath. "I feel better. Thank you for comforting me." I tipped my head back. "I'm really sorry for our misunderstanding."

For a moment he looked confused before he let out a

strangled sob and pulled me closer, holding me tightly against his chest. "Oh, Lavena, our earlier fight seems so trivial compared to what just happened now. Watching you suffer, both because I refused to believe you and because of the pain in your hand...I can't endure that again."

He wouldn't have to, I'd make sure of that. At this silent promise, the ring gave a tiny little throb, as if smirking, for it knew that my trying to be honest with Liam would undoubtedly never happen again. Despite our reconciliation, this thought made me feel as if more distance had sprung up between us. As desperate as I was for our relationship to work, how could it when I wasn't who Liam thought I was?

CHAPTER 19

*J*peeked out the window and watched as the carriage bearing the Sortileyan royal crest rolled to a stop in front of the palace. My chest tightened. The Sortileyan Crown Prince and Princess were only two of the guests we were expecting for a series of meetings and a formal state dinner. While Liam dreaded the meetings, I was an anxious mess thinking about performing for royals and nobles who knew Princess Lavena. How well they knew her, I wasn't sure. I was about to find out.

"They've arrived." I let the curtain fall back as I turned to Liam, the picture of ease on the parlor settee.

"Thank you, my little watchwoman." He beckoned me over and I happily placed my hand in his. His reassuring squeeze abated some of my tension, although not all. "Are you alright? You seem nervous."

I took a steadying breath and forced a smile. "I'm fine.

"I don't think you are." Liam lightly traced the contract ring I'd been absentmindedly fiddling with. "You twist your ring when agitated. You see, I'm quite the observant husband." He frowned at the ring. "It's an unusual ring. Is it a gift from someone?"

With the insecurity filling his eyes, I knew he feared the worst—that it was a promise ring from one of the princess's past beaus. "It's a family heirloom." I didn't want him to question further, so I added hastily, "And you're right, I'm rather nervous."

"I can tell." He tilted his head. "You used to betray your nerves by fiddling with your hair, but you haven't done that in a while."

I stilled. It had been one of the princess's quirks I'd made an effort to mimic in the beginning of this charade, one that had been slowly eclipsed by my own. I hadn't even noticed I'd stopped. Which other parts of my mask had slipped away without my noticing? Enough for the scheme to be exposed? And why wasn't the ring protesting against these lapses?

I took a steadying breath. "I'm concerned about the dinner with the neighboring kingdoms' diplomats tomorrow. It's my first formal event as the crown princess."

His expression cleared into one of sympathy. "Don't worry, you'll be perfect." He playfully swung my arm back and forth. "You should be more worried about me as I'll be dying a slow and agonizing death cooped up in meetings all day."

"I have meetings, too." I'd been slowly gaining more duties as the crown princess, responsibilities I actually found I rather enjoyed. While the meetings could sometimes be tedious, I loved visiting with our subjects, organizing charities, and doing what I could for them. My favorite project was one the queen and I were doing together in establishing schools for the children in all the villages so we could increase the people's literacy; I looked forward to the afternoons when I could spend time in the schoolrooms teaching the sweet children their letters.

I almost felt guilty enjoying not just my duties, but every aspect of royal life. Was loving any part of this masquerade a betrayal to my true self?

"Yes, but you're clearly a natural at your position. You're doing so well." He looked both envious and incredibly proud of me. Despite this all being an elaborate charade, he was right. No one was more surprised than me that I was rather proficient at being a princess.

I squeezed his hand assuredly. "You're doing a wonderful job, too."

"Only because of you. I know I can accomplish anything with you by my side."

I felt the same, and it was his strength I was relying on for the new duties I faced today, for meetings weren't my only task with this diplomatic visit—I was also acting as hostess, for the queen wanted me to practice the duties that would one day be expected of me. Unlike the other duties I was gradually acquiring and growing used to, entertaining royalty sounded rather daunting.

Liam read the apprehension in my expression. "It'll be alright. Your brother will arrive tomorrow, and in the meantime, Eileen can keep you company. I know you're well acquainted with her and Aiden, so there's no need to fret."

"Well…" It came out as a question, for I truly didn't know the nature of the princess's relationship with the Sortileyan royalty, nor any of those due to arrive tomorrow. It made navigating the tumultuous waters of my upcoming performance all the more frightening.

Before I could spend too much time entertaining my worries, a footman entered the parlor and executed a crisp bow. "May I present Their Highnesses—Crown Prince Deidric, Crown Princess Eileen, and Prince Deidric."

We both stood in greeting, Liam tucking my arm securely through his. Prince Aiden—as he was known to Liam—and

Princess Eileen entered, with a baby several months old propped on the princess's hip. Liam's face broke into a wide grin.

"Welcome. You know I like surprises, and this is a splendid one. I'd heard there was a new prince of Sortileya." He beamed at the young prince. "It appears congratulations are in order."

Prince Aiden smiled with fatherly pride as his young son looked around with wide, blue-eyed curiosity. "We wanted to show him off at your wedding, but it didn't seem the appropriate time." He cast a nervous glance between the two of us, as if to assess how it was going. He took in our linked arms with a furrowed brow.

Liam noticed his friend's puzzlement and laughed. "It appears I have my own surprise. You can't be the only one to have all the fun." He wrapped his arm around my waist and nestled me against his side before turning another wide grin to the infant. "Deidric, is it? A surprising choice, coming from you."

Prince Aiden sighed. "I was outnumbered. It appears I'll never escape my given name."

"While it's not fitting for you, dear, it fits him perfectly." Princess Eileen stroked Deidric's dark hair.

Prince Aiden chuckled. "The name is growing on me considering how much my wife likes it. It does suit him." He stroked Deidric's cheek, earning a toothless smile.

Liam held out his arms. "May I hold him?" Princess Eileen relinquished him and Liam's grin grew as he cradled him close. "He's a strapping young boy."

He began to bounce him gently, earning a delighted giggle from Deidric and a warm smile from me. While Deidric was cute, it was nothing to watching Liam dote on the boy. He'd make an incredible father one day. Yearning to experience that with him filled me, but I tried to push the desires away, for it was yet another experience with Liam that wasn't mine to have.

Liam cooed at Deidric before turning an apologetic look to our guests. "It probably wasn't wise to bring him. Between him and my wife, I doubt you'll get little if any of my attention."

Prince Aiden raised his eyebrows at that. I couldn't blame him for his confusion, for last he'd seen us together, Liam had behaved as if our wedding were his execution. The prince glanced at me and did a double take, studying me closely.

"Princess Lavena?" he asked slowly. My heart tightened as cold fear trickled up my spine. I took a deep breath to steady my voice.

"Yes?"

He continued staring before blinking, giving a slight shake of his head, and offered a tight smile. "It's a pleasure to see you again."

"The pleasure is mine, Prince Aiden and Princess Eileen." I smiled at her and she hesitantly returned it. I took another calming breath, willing my heartbeat to slow. Hopefully, my hostess duties would prove an adequate distraction from my escalating nerves. "Please have a seat. I'll send for some tea."

They accepted my invitation. After I'd spoken to a servant, I sat beside Liam, who, seeming to sense my lingering nerves, promptly wrapped one arm securely around me while keeping Deidric on his lap. The boy became preoccupied with investigating Liam's shiny gold buttons.

Liam led the conversation, beginning with inquiring after our guests' journey, but I felt too on edge to join. Instead I analyzed each look the prince and princess gave me, each more bewildered than the last. I knew my shyness was only making me a less believable Princess Lavena, but I was too tense to play the game.

I shifted nervously on the settee and stole several peeks at Liam's face, each glimpse relaxing me further, and it didn't take long before he noticed. We shared a smile as he gave my hand an affectionate squeeze, a gesture not lost on Prince Aiden and Princess Eileen, whose perplexity only grew.

The conversation soon shifted to young Deidric, who was being rather spoiled with Liam's attention. "He's a good-looking lad," he said as he bounced the infant on his knee. "Aren't you, Dee Dee?"

Prince Aiden choked on his tea. "What did you call him?"

"Dee Dee," Liam said. "Come on, Aiden, Deidric is far too formal a name for such a child. As the boy's doting Godfather, it's my duty to remedy that."

Prince Aiden's expression darkened. "You'll do no such thing, Liam. I won't have *my* son be called such a ridiculous—"

"Oh, I think it's adorable!" Princess Eileen gushed.

Prince Aiden gaped at her in horror. "Are you in jest, darling?"

She gave him a guilty smile. "I'm afraid not. I think it's rather cute."

Liam smirked in triumph while Prince Aiden leaned his head back with a groan. "Thanks a lot, Liam. I'll get my revenge when *you* have a child."

Liam's smile grew, seeming nothing but delighted with the threat as he continued bouncing and cooing at Deidric. It was a rather adorable display.

"You're besotted with him," I said fondly.

"I can't help it." He pulled a funny face, earning a giggle from Deidric and another smile from me. He laughed and met my gaze, his own pleading. "Darling, we need one of these."

My face ignited and yearning once more fluttered in my stomach, a longing I was sure filled my eyes as we stared at one another for a beautiful moment. When we looked away, we found Prince Aiden gaping at us once more, clearly flabbergasted.

His bafflement only increased as Liam proudly told him all the details about his recent building projects. After he'd enthusiastically shown off every battle wound he'd ever received from his hammer, he began sharing my own accomplishments, and how at my encouragement we were planning to conduct regular tours to all areas of the kingdom. His praise caused my face to burn and Prince Aiden's gaze to become even more suspicious as he looked at me as if he'd never seen me before. Little did he know he actually hadn't.

After several more minutes witnessing our affectionate exchanges and hearing Liam speak of me with unabashed fondness, it seemed Prince Aiden couldn't contain his curiosity any longer. He turned to his wife. "Darling, you haven't had a chance to see much of the Dracerian Palace. The grounds alone are unparalleled. Perhaps Lavena would show them to you?"

Princess Eileen immediately picked up on Prince Aiden's subtle hint that he wanted to speak with Liam alone. "I do want to see the gardens." She stood gracefully and reached for young Deidric, still being bounced and cooed at on Liam's lap. "May I trouble you for a tour, Lavena, after I put Deidric down for a nap?" For the boy's eyes were beginning to droop.

"Can I play with him later?" Liam asked as he relinquished the infant with adorable reluctance.

Princess Eileen smiled. "If you survive whatever interrogation my husband has in mind." She swept a kiss across Prince Aiden's cheek. "Don't be too hard on him, dear."

"It's just a friendly chat." He squeezed his wife's hand where it rested on his shoulder before she led the way out of the parlor.

"We'll be in the nursery," Princess Eileen called over her shoulder.

I followed reluctantly, my curiosity compelling me to remain behind in order to overhear Prince Aiden's conversation with Liam. He undoubtedly planned to inquire how well things were going between us and I was quite anxious to hear Liam's response. But the bowing footmen closed the doors behind us, barring me from the private conversation I so longed to hear. The moment we were in the corridor, Princess Eileen gave me an expectant look, waiting for me to lead her.

"I'm afraid I don't know where the nursery is," I said.

"That's alright." She turned to one of the footmen. "May I trouble you to show me to the nursery?"

He obeyed with a crisp bow and guided her down the hallway and out of sight, leaving me alone outside the parlor. Temptation tickled my sense of propriety, encouraging me to seize the opportunity I'd just been given. Ignoring the baffled look from the remaining footman, I crouched on my heels and pressed my eye to the keyhole.

I could only catch glimpses inside the parlor, but they were enough to see Prince Aiden search Liam's expression, as if trying to decipher his friend's wellbeing through his perusal. He leaned forward, eyes concerned. "So how are things going between you and Lavena?"

"Wonderfully," Liam said.

Prince Aiden raised a skeptical brow. *Really?* You aren't just putting on a show for Eileen and me?"

Liam grinned. "Nobody's more surprised than me. At this point in my marriage, I expected to either be dead and buried or a murderer myself, but as you can see, things haven't turned out that way at all." His look became quite tender. "Things have actually turned out quite wonderfully, much differently than I'd expected."

Prince Aiden gaped at him before shaking his head. "I'm admittedly quite shocked, especially in regards to Lavena herself." His forehead furrowed, as if he were trying to work out a complicated puzzle. "Are you *sure* that's Lavena?"

I stiffened and scooted closer to the keyhole.

Liam laughed. "What a ridiculous question. Of course I'm sure. I know my own wife. Who else would she be?"

Prince Aiden was silent a moment, pondering. "She certainly *looks* like Lavena, but she's so...altered. Don't get me wrong, I'm happy for you. Eileen and I have been worried about how things were going. It's just that...she's completely different than the Lavena I know."

"Maybe it's her secret twin." At his snigger, the worry tightening my insides slowly eased knowing that Liam wasn't taking the prince's doubt seriously.

"Obviously, it has to be Lavena, but her change is certainly dramatic."

"I agree," Liam said. "But now that I understand her reasonings for who she was before, it all makes perfect sense. Like me, she became a hardened version of herself in order to try to wriggle out of an undesirable engagement. Now that we've married, we're both trying to make the best of it. And it's going well." Liam's expression softened. "Actually, it's going *extremely* well."

Prince Aiden smiled. "You genuinely care for her?"

"Very much. If I'd known who my wife really was, I never would have resisted our union, but would have made her mine as soon as possible."

Prince Aiden stared at Liam in disbelief. "You're falling in love with her."

Liam's grin grew and the most affectionate look filled his eyes. "I'm pretty much already there."

My heart swelled at his beautiful words and I beamed. Even though I'd suspected he felt that way towards me, I loved hearing his precious feelings confirmed. But as wonderful as they were, I ached to hear more. In my desperation, I pressed my ear even more against the keyhole.

"Lavena?"

I straightened with a gasp. Princess Eileen had returned from the nursery with surprising speed. "Yes?" I squeaked.

Her gaze shifted from me to the keyhole that up until moments ago I'd been pressed against. She raised her eyebrows. "Eavesdropping?"

My face burned in shame as I lowered my eyes. I ached to deny it but there was little point. "Yes."

"I see." Amusement rather than disapproval filled the princess's tone. "I don't blame you. I doubt I would have been able to resist myself, especially when the perfect opportunity presented itself." She crouched down to peek through the keyhole. "What are they talking about? Anything good?"

"Your husband wants to be sure Liam isn't suffering too terribly being married to me."

Princess Eileen peered up at me, a question in her gaze. "And is he?"

I beamed girlishly, unable to contain it. She smiled in return.

"I see. I suspected as much when I saw the way he looked at you; unlike Aiden, I didn't need to corner him for a private interrogation. Men." She rolled her eyes before peeking back through the keyhole. I shifted restlessly, itching to take another look myself.

"Are they discussing anything interesting?"

Princess Eileen sighed. "Unfortunately not. They've moved on to dull matters." She straightened. "At least you got the information you wanted."

My grin grew. "I certainly did."

She surveyed my bright expression, her own rather

confused. "I realize we don't know one another well, but you do seem a bit...different."

My smile instantly melted away. I nervously fiddled with my ring. "Different?" I squeaked. "How so?"

Her frown deepened. "You seem more...amiable, but it's more than that. I can't quite put my finger on it..." She pressed her thumb to her lips and surveyed me for a thoughtful moment before shrugging. "Forgive me, I'm being rather rude. I still haven't gotten the hang of this princess thing, even though it's been well over a year. Though it has gotten much easier, and I find myself enjoying it more than I used to."

I understood that all too well, for it was how I'd felt at the beginning of the charade. I saw in Eileen a kindred spirit. If only I could confess to Princess Eileen who I really was. The ring gave a threatening throb, dashing my wishes.

The princess was awaiting my response, almost with a look as if she expected an insult on her performance. "Liam says you're doing very well considering you've had no royal training before," I said.

Her eyebrows rose in disbelief and she studied me again, her look suspicious. My heart pounded. Too late I wondered if perhaps I was being too friendly towards her. If she'd ever interacted with the real Princess Lavena, I was certain the experience hadn't been a pleasant one. Yet although I was once more undoubtedly playing my part wrong, the ring remained strangely silent.

Thankfully, Princess Eileen's expression cleared. "Thank you, Lavena. Now, we better take that tour of the gardens before our husbands emerge from the parlor and catch us eavesdropping."

She looped her arm through mine and I let her lead me outside. With each step the tension tightening my chest slowly eased. I'd survived another encounter with someone who knew Princess Lavena. Each one gave me confidence that despite my fears, perhaps the façade wouldn't be exposed after all.

THE FOLLOWING DAY, I paced the sitting room, wringing my hands anxiously while Liam leaned back in his seat—the picture of ease—and watched me with amusement.

"Are you sure my parents won't be coming?" I asked for what must have been the dozenth time.

His lips twitched. "Yes, I'm sure. Shall I repeat the answer a few more times in response to the next several times you'll ask?"

I knew I was being ridiculous, but I couldn't help it, not when my nerves gnawing my insides made it impossible to relax. "But are you *sure*?"

"Yes, darling." His smile faltered and his previous amusement transformed into concern. "Do you really miss them so much?"

Oh dear, I hadn't meant for my agitation to make Liam believe I missed Their Majesties. Seeing them was the last thing I wanted. They'd detect my switch with Princess Lavena the moment they saw me, and then I'd lose Liam forever.

"Not particularly," I said, knowing the answer sounded rather heartless, but it was better than Liam arranging for a surprise visit with the King and Queen of Lyceria. He frowned, clearly puzzled that my words and actions contradicted one another. As he sat in confusion, I managed to pace the perimeter of the room a few more times.

"Your pacing is making me anxious. Come sit with me, darling."

He motioned me over and, despite feeling far too restless

to hold still, I joined him. He wrapped his arm around me as if to keep me from escaping and nestled me close so I was tucked quite comfortably against his side. As usual, he had a calming effect on my frazzled nerves.

"There. Feeling better?"

I rested my head on his shoulder with a sigh. "I will when this horrible state dinner is over. When is Nolan due to arrive?"

"Any moment now. Are you excited to see him?"

Yes and no, for I wanted to confront him about why he'd allowed this charade and at the same time ask him not to expose me. It was all a complicated mess, but the thought of losing Liam was my sole motivation to continue.

Liam was still awaiting my answer so I nodded. He smiled. "I had no idea you and Nolan were so close."

I didn't answer. Lying seemed more difficult when my nerves were stretched taut over tonight's dinner. All too soon a footman announced the arrival of Crown Prince Nolan of Lyceria and he was shown in. He froze when he spotted us snuggling together.

A grin filled his usual stoic expression. "Well, look at you two newlyweds; I see I've won the bet."

Liam's eyebrow rose. "Which bet?"

"At your reception I said you two would make a fine match. It appears I was correct."

Liam's expression softened. "Indeed you were. I've never been happier to be proven wrong." He brushed a kiss along my cheek. Prince Nolan's grin broadened.

"I'm pleased to hear that. I've been thinking a lot about you two, hoping things were going well."

He seemed to be addressing this last statement more towards me than Liam. His gaze was searching, as if by looking hard enough he could both discern my well-being and get an accurate assessment on my marriage.

He approached and extended his hand. "A stroll through the gardens, Lavena?"

"She'd like that," Liam said. "She's been in stitches awaiting your arrival." He gave me a final snuggle before withdrawing his arm. "Have a good time, sweetheart." He turned to Prince Nolan. "Bring her back quickly."

"I certainly will." Prince Nolan helped me to my feet before tucking my arm through his and leading me from the room. The moment we entered the corridor, he leaned in close and lowered his voice to a whisper. "Well done, Anwen. That didn't take long."

"Is that all you have to say to me?" I hissed.

He chuckled. "No, I have plenty to say, but I'm sure you have much more. Since I'm a gentleman, I'll allow you to go first."

I launched in immediately. "Why are you going along with your sister's dangerous scheme? Do you find it amusing? Should I be caught—and I will be—this will end in disaster for me."

He patted my hand reassuringly. "I won't let anything happen to you. You have my word."

His word did little to ease the fear squeezing my heart. "What if Their Majesties don't listen?"

"They will, especially once they they see this." He tapped Princess Lavena's ring brandishing my finger.

"Can you take it off?" I asked.

"Unfortunately not. Only Lavena can do that."

I sighed. His answer wasn't surprising, but it was disappointing all the same. We stepped outside, far too sunny and pleasant for my current mood. "You never answered my questions about your motivations to go along with the switch."

Prince Nolan smirked. "I already have; you just didn't

recognize the answer—I truly think you and Liam make a much better match. Are you suggesting I'm wrong?"

My cheeks flushed. There were no words to summarize all that I felt for Liam.

He smirked. "I can easily discern for myself how well things are going. I knew you were a sweet, charming girl, but even I'm surprised at how close you two have become in such a short amount of time. I've known Liam since we were children and I've never seen him happier. Not only are you two better suited, but I have no doubt Liam will be a much better king with you as his queen. For selfish reasons, a better King of Draceria will aid me when I'm King of Lyceria. You two are meant to be together."

I stared at him in disbelief. He chuckled.

"You doubt that?"

I didn't want to, not when it was my secret hope that Liam and I belonged together. "But my station, the political contract—"

"Ah, yes." His expression became grave once more. He was silent for several minutes as he escorted me through the garden of blooming daylilies and daisies, whose beauty was lost on me as I restlessly awaited his response. "I admit those are both obstacles," he finally confessed.

"The political contract is more than an *obstacle*, Your Highness," I said. "Isn't it in your best interest as the future Lycerian King to want the benefits of a union between your kingdom and Draceria?"

"It undoubtedly is," he said. "Don't get me wrong, I was slightly disappointed when I saw you with Liam at the reception. While I wouldn't wish Lavena on my good friend to achieve it, the benefits of her union with Draceria cannot be denied. However, at that point, the contract was already in jeopardy because of my sister's actions. There was little I could do except expose you publicly, and that would have harmed both you and Lavena, as well as soured the relations between our two kingdom."

"So you're merely delaying the inevitable consequences."

He frowned. "They're not necessarily inevitable. I'm hoping by the time Lavena's actions become known, I'll have uncovered a solution that will protect both you and the contract's benefits."

"And are you anywhere near finding this solution?"

He sighed. "Unfortunately not."

That wasn't reassuring. Prince Nolan saw my anxiety and gave my hand another pat.

"Please don't worry; all will be well. You forget there will be another fighting to protect both you and an arrangement that will allow him to keep you: Liam."

My heart gave a strange flutter. "Liam?" I squeaked.

"While Kian welcomed the arrangement, poor Liam has always abhorred it," Prince Nolan said. "As has Lavena. She looked forward to her union with Kian, but when he died... she became cold and bitter. I believe she resents Liam because he's not his brother, and he resents her for taking away his choice in whom to marry." He shook his head. "In any case, now that Liam has fallen for you, he'll like his arrangement with Lavena even less, hence he'll do all he can to break it."

"Fallen for me?" I stuttered.

"Come now, Anwen, surely you can see the way he looks at you—like a man who's lost his heart."

My already fluttering heart felt on the brink of soaring at the thought.

He smiled knowingly. "I see he's not the only one whose heart has been stolen."

I blushed and lowered my eyes to the cobblestone path. "Although you're correct, I'm not foolish enough to allow myself to hope. I know we'll never work."

"I disagree. You *are* working."

"He's a prince; I'm a goose girl."

"There is no law preventing such a match."

"There's no benefit to it either, except to Liam and me."

Prince Nolan nodded solemnly. "I can't deny that, but don't give up yet. Liam will fight for you, and so will I."

Liam had been fighting against his engagement contract for years. What made Prince Nolan believe he could find a solution now when he couldn't before? "But won't Liam be hurt when the truth is finally exposed?"

"He knows Lavena as well as I do. He'll know the one behind the deception and hold you blameless."

"You're assuming I wriggle out of a trip to the gallows." My blood chilled at the thought.

"I've already assured you no harm will befall you."

"But my union with Liam will ruin the contract."

Prince Nolan waved that thought away. "I'm still working on that puzzle, so you have no need to worry about that. Just enjoy your relationship with Liam and be assured that we'll do all in our power to allow you to keep him. All will be well."

I ached for the fairy tale picture he was painting to come true, but how could I believe it? Happy endings only occurred in stories...didn't they?

CHAPTER 20

*L*iam seemed quite excited about something, for he was extra wriggly during lunch, earning several smiles from me and puzzled looks from his family.

"Alright, I can't handle it anymore," I said when we adjourned to the parlor following the meal. "What has you so excited?"

His grin only grew. "Finally you ask. You have an annoying amount of patience."

I raised my eyebrow. "Is this a game?"

"Everything is a game with me." He held up a single finger —his silent instruction to wait a moment—before hurrying from the room.

"What on earth has gotten into him?" the queen asked.

Elodie shrugged. "Considering it's Liam, it could be anything."

"I'm pleased to see him so happy." The queen gave me a tender look, as if she thought me responsible for Liam's contagious joy.

Prince Nolan—who'd arranged to stay a week after the state dinner and diplomatic meetings had ended—gave me a knowing, almost smug look, as if he felt justified in going along with the princess's plot so he could play matchmaker. My cheeks warmed but I couldn't mask my pleased smile.

Liam returned in record time, holding something behind his back. "Shall we play a guessing game?"

"I couldn't even begin to guess what you're up to." I tried to shift in my seat to peer behind him, but he angled his body so I couldn't steal a peek.

"No cheating, dear."

I pouted. "But I'm curious. Won't you show me?"

Mischief flashed in his eyes. "I might be persuaded with a kiss." He leaned forward expectedly. I humored him and was rewarded with his dashing smile. "Payment accepted. Your surprise, my dear. Happy two-month anniversary." And he presented a package wrapped in shiny paper. My heart swelled as I stared at it.

"You got me an anniversary gift?"

He became bashful. "It seemed a fitting gesture considering how well things are going between us." He handed me the package. I spent a moment admiring it before Elodie gave an impatient sigh.

"Hurry up and open it. I want to see what he gave you."

I carefully unwrapped my present while Liam nervously crunched the hem of his shirt and watched. The wrappings fell away, revealing a wooden music box, carved with a simple yet elegant design of butterflies. I gaped at it as I lightly traced the patterns with my fingertip.

Princess Aveline wrinkled her nose. "Shouldn't you have given her something more grand, Liam? Jewels would have been a more appropriate choice."

Liam's face went bright crimson. "But Lavena likes bugs, butterflies in particular."

My gaze snapped up to meet his worried-filled one, my heart hammering wildly in my chest, as if it too were a butterfly on the brink of taking flight. How had he known butterflies were my favorite?

"You always notice them," he said in his rush to explain, still blushing adorably. "You point them out during every stroll."

I continued to stare.

"I had this made especially for you," he continued. "I thought you'd like not only this design, but that you'd prefer a more simple music box, one free from extravagant jewels considering you seem more simple in your own tastes. You always wear your simplest gowns and very little if any jewelry. And its melody…"

He motioned for me to wind it up. I complied and the most tranquil tune, which I immediately recognized, trilled through the air like a gentle waltz. My breath caught. The melody was the one Mother had sung to me growing up.

"Lavena?" Liam's voice was taut with worry, his fear that his most perfect of gifts had failed.

"The song," I stuttered. "How?"

"You're always humming it," he said. "I spent ages plucking it out on the pianoforte when I was supposed to be going over reports, and then I played it for the music box maker."

"Mother used to sing that to me. I don't even know if it has a name." I wiped away my embarrassing tears. "Oh Liam, this is perfect, the best present I've ever received."

"You really like it?" Hope pierced the worry marring his expression. It brightened further as I pulled him into a hug. He enthusiastically squeezed me back. "Does this mean I passed this particular husband test?"

"You certainly did. Not only is this the most beautiful music box, but you're right in that I love butterflies." It felt wonderful to make this Anwen admission, but that wasn't what made my heart soar. This was yet more proof that Liam could see the true me, even buried deep behind my Princess Lavena mask.

And I loved him all the more for it.

"I'm so glad you love it, sweetheart," he murmured into my hair before pulling back and placing a gentle kiss on my brow. "I hoped you would."

"It's my most cherished gift." How perfect it had come from the man I loved.

He smiled sweetly. "Then prepare for another, for this isn't the only surprise I've arranged—your parents are coming for a visit."

Instantly, my happiness deflated, replaced with raw panic. "My *parents?*" He nodded, grinning widely. My panic swelled into sheer terror, seeping over me like I was being dipped in ice. "They're *what?*"

He mistook my exclamation for one of excitement and his beam widened. "You kept asking for them before last week's state dinner. I realized you missed them, so I wrote and learned that they'd be passing through Draceria on the way to Sortileya for a meeting. They were pleased with the invitation to stay for dinner. Isn't this a grand surprise?"

Surprise was not the word I was searching for; this was a *nightmare*. I may have fooled Liam's family, Prince Aiden and Princess Eileen, the Lycerian dignitaries at the state dinner, and the servants, but there was no way I'd fool Their Majesties. It'd only take them one look to immediately know I wasn't their daughter, and then…

Fear churned my stomach and I felt on the brink of a faint. I exchanged a panicked look with Prince Nolan, who sat frozen, his tea cup raised halfway to his gaping mouth. He slowly lowered it. "Our parents are arriving today?"

"Yes." Liam was practically bursting with joy at his surprise. I would have found it adorable if I hadn't been experiencing a miniature heart attack. I widened my eyes desperately at Prince Nolan, who seemed at a loss as to what to do. Some help he was.

Liam leaned forward, his brow lined with concern. "Are you alright, sweetheart? You're looking quite pale."

"I feel sick," I muttered. "Please, I need to lie down."

Liam helped me to my feet. "I'll escort you back to your room. I hope you feel better before your parents arrive."

I most definitely wouldn't. Rather, I'd embrace this excuse to hide away in my room, for Their Majesties seeing me would ruin everything—the charade would be exposed, causing me to lose Liam, a thought I couldn't bear.

Liam began leading me from the sitting room, but I stopped him in the doorway. "Please wait a moment, I want to bid my brother good night." I practically scampered towards Prince Nolan, who rose and met me in the corner of the parlor. "Prince Nolan!" I hissed quietly. "Your parents— what am I going to do?"

He rested an assuring hand on my arm. "Don't panic, Anwen," he whispered. "I'll do all in my power to ensure they don't see you. Just try to remain calm."

His words did little to reassure me. My nerves only tightened as I turned away from Prince Nolan's own worried expression and returned to Liam's side, looping my arm through his so he could escort me to my room.

Once we arrived, it took much convincing before Liam would leave my side, and even after I'd won that battle, he still seemed reluctant to do so.

"Please let me stay. I'll go crazy with worry if I'm apart from you when you're not feeling well." He stroked my hair back. "Won't you let me be the doting husband you deserve and remain by your bedside?"

I was touched by his eagerness to remain close to me, but my fear of the inevitable discovery that would cause me to lose him permanently was stronger than my need for him now.

"Staying with me all day will make you restless," I said. "I insist you do something fun. You can tell me all about it after I rest."

He searched my expression and sighed in defeat when he realized my determination. "Very well, if that's what you need. I'll check on you soon."

He leaned down to bestow another gentle kiss before slowly backing from the room. The moment the door closed behind him, I released a heavy sigh and fell back against my pillows. The calmness I felt with Liam's presence disappeared, replaced with anxiety smothering my senses, much as I imagined the noose would feel like should I be caught.

No, I wouldn't get caught. I'd feign being ill until Their Majesties left. All would be well. Despite this assurance, the knots in my stomach only tightened.

Time slowly crept by. I stared up at my canopy, the patterns of the shadows of settling darkness doing little to soothe the tension shackling my body. A knock came at the door. I immediately rolled over to my side, praying it wasn't Their Majesties.

The door creaked open. "Lavena love? Your parents are here and…oh, she's asleep." Liam pattered over and stroked my hair.

"I'll inform her parents she's not feeling well," the queen said. "Perhaps her mother can check on her."

Liam and the queen tiptoed out of my bedroom. I waited a minute or two to be sure they were gone before I sprang from the bed. They were going to inform the Lycerian Queen that her daughter was ill and have her check on me? It was a problem I hadn't foreseen.

I swiveled to the mirror and frowned at the outfit I wore —a gown of silk, earrings donning my ears—a costume that wouldn't make me look any more like Princess Lavena to her mother. I yanked my disguise off before raiding my trunk, where I'd packed one of my old handmaiden outfits, just in case I encountered such a horrible situation as this. I slipped the familiar outfit on and quickly pinned my hair up in my simple servant's bun before peeking in the mirror once more.

My breath hooked as I stared at myself. *Me.* My eyes hungrily traced my reflection. It *was* me, looking so much like Anwen it was as if she'd never left. I pressed my fingers against the glass, meeting up with Anwen's fingertips, as if by touching hers, she would feel more like a real person rather than a mere reflection.

I stared at Anwen, a girl who had seemed to be slipping away bit by bit. But despite the charade I'd been forced to play these past two months, the real me had remained the entire time. It was an incredibly comforting thought.

I froze as a soft knock sounded at the door, reverberating through the room. "Lavena dear? Are you alright?" It was the Queen of Lyceria.

My heart skittered to a stop. I took a calming breath to quell my escalating panic. I could do this. I braced myself, trudged to the door, and opened it, sweeping into a curtsy. "Your Majesties."

Their eyes widened when they saw me before recognition filled the queen's eyes. "Anwen? Where's Lavena? We heard she's ill." She bustled into the room towards the empty bed, followed by the stern-looking king. Her brow furrowed as she scanned the room. "She's not here."

My heartbeat escalated. I fought to keep my breath steady. "No, Your Majesty."

She frowned. "Where is she? Liam told me she's not feeling well."

"I—" I twisted my ring anxiously as my mind scrambled

for an excuse. The king's look became penetrating, as if he sensed something amiss.

"You know where she is, don't you? Out with it, handmaiden."

My throat had gone dry. I swallowed before latching on to the first excuse I could think of. "Forgive me, Your Majesties, but she...snuck out."

A stunned silence followed, broken by the king's bellow. "She *what?*"

I lowered my eyes. Her habit of sneaking out had been a secret Princess Lavena had made me swear to keep, but it was a promise I wasn't bound to by the contract ring. "Yes, Your Majesty."

I regretted the lie almost the moment I gave it. What if Their Majesties spoke of it to a member of the Dracerian royal family, or worse, Liam himself? I took another steadying breath. It'd be alright. They wouldn't do anything to risk the union between Liam and Princess Lavena.

By their horror-filled expressions at my words, they feared that union was on the brink of crumbling. Tension hung thick in the air before the queen sighed and frowned at the king, whose eyebrow was twitching dangerously. "I told you she was sneaking out," she said.

So they already knew about Princess Lavena's rebellious habit?

"Yes, but you would think she'd have stopped such nonsense after her *marriage*. The foolish girl." He began to pace, his face reddening. "How dare she revert back to her old habits after our union with the Dracerian royal family?" He froze suddenly, going pale, before swiveling to face me. "Does Liam know?" His voice had lowered to a whisper.

"I don't believe so," I said shakily.

His Majesty's eyes narrowed. "You don't *believe* so? I

suggest you find out for sure. I need to know the extent of the mess Lavena's making."

The queen rested a hand on his arm. "Dear, how can Anwen know such a thing? She never sees Liam."

The king muttered something indiscernible as he resumed his pacing. "Foolish girl. How could she do this? If the Dracerian monarchy finds out, the relations between our two kingdoms that the betrothal contract strengthened will be in ruins. When I see her, I'm going to—" He made a rather violent gesture.

"Dear, really." The queen now looked quite agitated.

"Don't *dear* me now. That girl—"

"Do keep your voice down." The queen anxiously eyed the door, as if afraid someone was eavesdropping at the keyhole, ready to spread lewd rumors about Princess Lavena.

The king took a deep breath before turning a much more calm expression back towards me. "When will she return?" he asked. "I have a few *words* to exchange with her."

"Not until late, Your Majesty," I said. "It's usually long past midnight."

"Midnight?" His eyebrow was twitching again. "That's not acceptable."

I gave a helpless shrug. "Forgive me, Your Majesty."

"It's not your fault, Anwen." The queen glanced at the king. "Surely we can stay until she returns—"

"We don't have time." His voice was rising, and when he turned away from me to resume his prowling, I hastily seized the opportunity to retreat a step. "We're due in Sortileya by tomorrow morning."

"Can't we delay it? Lavena—"

"Is not here, is she? That girl..."

A string of obscenities spilled from his escalating voice. The queen turned her alarm towards me, as if afraid of how I'd perceive His Majesty in his undignified state. She needn't have worried; the only emotions I was experiencing were anxiety that they were still here and a fragile hope that perhaps they'd leave before the princess's charade was discovered.

Finally, it seemed the king had released enough of his wrath to straighten back to his usual regal manner, the only sign of his lingering emotions being the anger filling his eyes.

"I suppose spouting words to her bedroom won't reform the slippery girl. I refuse to wait around for her to return from another of her trysts; we're expected in Sortileya, and unlike her, I take my responsibilities seriously. Come, dear, we need to leave before the hour grows later." He strode towards the door.

"But we haven't seen Lavena yet," the queen protested.

"It's not my fault your daughter is rebellious." The king reached the doorway but paused as rushed footsteps sounded in the corridor.

At first I feared it was Liam, but it was Prince Nolan who burst into the room, panting and looking more flustered than I'd ever seen the normally serious, stoic prince.

"Mother, Father, I—" He froze when he saw me standing in my handmaiden's outfit. His eyes widened as he slowly raked his gaze over my uniform. Whatever he'd expected to find, it clearly wasn't me disguised as myself.

"What is it, Nolan?" the king asked. For a moment, Prince Nolan looked at a loss for words.

"I—where's Lavena?" He said her name hesitantly, as if unsure whether or not his parents were aware of her absence.

"She's snuck out. Again." The king actually snorted in his disgust. "Apparently, the fact that she's married is no deterrent, nor the fact that she could potentially ruin the relations between Draceria and Lyceria should Liam learn of it. Were you aware of her sneaking out?"

"I—no, Father." Prince Nolan continued to gape at me for a moment more before glancing back at the king.

"That girl only thinks of herself," the king muttered, his anger overcoming him once more. "Perhaps I'd better delay our trip to Sortileya after all so I can talk with her. I need to set her straight before Liam discovers her liaisons."

Panic set in at his words. I looked pleadingly at Prince Nolan.

"That won't be necessary, Father," Prince Nolan said. "Your meeting with the King of Sortileya is too important to delay. I'll remain in Draceria until Lavena returns in order to give her a proper talking-to about her duties as Liam's wife."

"That would undoubtedly be best," the queen said, eying the king's pulsing eyebrow with concern. "You'll likely be able to handle the situation with much more calm. Isn't that right, dear?"

The king hesitated before sighing. "Perhaps you're right. I'm in no state to handle that girl at the moment. But so help me, Nolan, if you don't talk sense into her…she must understand that this behavior of hers can't continue."

"Of course, Father." Prince Nolan bowed, his expression relieved, but his feelings couldn't exceed my own. Were Their Majesties really leaving without having detected the switch?

It appeared I'd been granted a miraculous reprieve, for the king stomped towards the door and yanked it back open. He nearly careened into Liam, who'd lifted his hand to knock. "Pardon me, dear boy." He stepped around him and stomped, grumbling, into the corridor.

Liam's anxious gaze immediately sought mine. "Is everything alright?" he asked, and my stomach sank to realize he must have heard the king's tirade. The queen seemed to sense this, too, for she gave Liam an overly bright smile that didn't reach her eyes.

"Of course, dear. Everything is fine. We're just... exhausted from the journey. I'm afraid we can't stay. Forgive us." And she bustled past him, Prince Nolan following closely behind, pausing only to wink at me.

"But Your Majesties—" Liam stared down the hallway, brow furrowed in confusion, before he hurried towards me. "What happened? Are you alright?"

I groaned and collapsed on the settee at the foot of my bed so I could lean my head back against the mattress. He sat beside me, rubbing my arms soothingly.

"You're trembling. Did something happen with your parents? I heard yelling and...Lavena?"

The tears I'd been fighting ever since the confrontation with Their Majesties began finally escaped. The fear tightening my chest was slowly abating, but it was an almost painful feeling, leaving me feeling wrung out and drained.

Liam wiped away my tears with frantic fingers, his expression twisted in worry. "Please tell me what happened. Did you and your parents get in a fight?"

It was as good an excuse as any. I slowly nodded. By the look in Liam's eyes, I knew he needed more explanation than that.

I found the perfect one. "We don't get along."

His brow furrowed. "You don't?"

I shook my head. Perplexity replaced his confusion.

"But *why*? You're wonderful."

I was too drained to say anything more. He stroked my wet cheek.

"I'm sorry. I wish I'd known your feelings concerning the matter. I never would have invited them here. But to think of the harsh way His Majesty yelled at you..."

His expression darkened as he pulled me into a hug. I burrowed against him, feeling safe in his arms. He began to rub my back but paused to pull away, staring at me as if finally seeing me since entering the room.

"Your hair…" He stared at my servant's bun before taking my hands to tug me to my feet, his bewildered gaze taking in my outfit. "Goodness, Lavena, whatever are you wearing?"

"A handmaiden outfit," I squeaked.

His raised his brow. "Why?"

Why indeed. I couldn't very well tell him I'd needed to dress as a servant for Their Majesties so they wouldn't discover I'd switched places with their daughter and he was married to an imposter. My mind swirled for another explanation, *any*, no matter how weak.

I bit my lip. "I thought…it'd be rather disrespectful to dress in such an outfit for my parents."

The astonishment that filled Liam's face made me want to sink through the floor in shame for such a dishonorable gesture. He continued gaping for a moment before, to my surprise, he grinned boyishly.

"You never cease to surprise me. And here I was beginning to think you were too perfect to be real." Chuckling, he pulled me into another hug. I stood stiffly in his arms, unable to believe his reaction.

"You don't hate me for such a horrible thing?"

"I could never *hate* you." His hold tightened protectively. "Your relationship with your parents must be rather tense for someone as sweet as you to do something so drastic. I must make it my quest to always stay on your good side." He kissed the top of my head. "Did you also feign your illness so that you wouldn't have to see them? If so, I must scold you for causing me to worry."

I burrowed my tear-streaked face against his chest. "I'm sorry, Liam."

He hooked his fingers beneath my chin to lift my teary

gaze. "Perhaps another one of your apologies is in order." He stared at my lips.

The fact that even after seeing me at my worst he still wanted a kiss made it impossible for me to deny him. I nodded and his lips captured mine. His arms tightened around me and my own hooked around his neck to burrow my fingers in his hair, pulling him closer, deeper.

The kiss was heated, beautiful, and felt so *right*, as if we truly did belong together. I melted into his embrace as his hands stroked up and down my back before sliding into my hair. He unhooked the pins so my hair tumbled down my back and he could weave his fingers through it.

As I heard the pins clatter to the floor, his actions registered—he'd pulled my hair from the style I'd worn as a handmaiden, which only reminded me I was dressed not as the princess but as *Anwen*. The mask had been removed, reminding me it was Anwen who kissed the prince, which explained why it felt both incredibly right and so horribly wrong. His soft lips suddenly burned on mine. I broke away with a gasp.

"No." The pain at my deception gnawed at me. This was wrong. I, a mere goose girl, wasn't supposed to be kissing Liam, no matter how strongly I felt towards him, no matter how much I ached for him to be mine. I was in Princess Lavena's place, a place that any day I was sure she'd try to reclaim, a thought that raked my heart.

"What is it, Lavena? Was that too fast?"

I squeezed my eyes shut at his sweet worry. It made me love him even more, something I couldn't afford to do, especially now. "I need to be alone," I said. "Please leave."

His breath caught and in his eyes I could see my request had hurt him. But I couldn't take it back. Princess Lavena had slipped away, leaving Anwen in her place, and I couldn't be me for him, no matter how much I ached to.

Liam sighed and glanced longingly at the bed behind me before he forced a smile for me. "As you wish, darling." He lifted my hand and kissed it before he left.

As the door closed behind him, I crumpled to the ground, feeling worn out from changing parts so frequently. I wasn't sure how much longer I could continue to endure this, but how could I possibly end the charade when doing so would cause me to lose Liam forever?

CHAPTER 21

Memories from the King and Queen of Lyceria's tension-riddled visit made sleep that night impossible. Even though I'd narrowly escaped being caught, the nerves and fear from the ordeal still tightened my chest. I tossed and turned, unable to quiet my mind or settle my anxiety. I may have gotten away with it this time, but surely the king and queen would visit again, and then I'd be expected to come up with more lies to explain my presence and the princess's absence. One day I'd run out of excuses, and then…

I sighed as I settled back against the pillows and glanced towards the connecting door separating my room from Liam's. He seemed so far away, especially after my earlier actions. I both understood my reasons for pushing him away and was frustrated by them.

Today's visit from the king and queen reminded me anew that I needed to maintain my distance from Liam. Continuing to get closer to him would hurt both of us in the end when the deception was inevitably exposed, but despite knowing this, that didn't keep me from falling deeper in love with him with each passing day. I ached to cross the threshold separating us in order to be near him.

Stop thinking of Liam, I firmly scolded myself as I glared at the canopy above me. But despite my firm orders and the heavy exhaustion pressing against my senses, thoughts of Liam and my anxieties continued to fill my mind, so that it took another hour before sleep eventually claimed me.

I dreamed of Liam. It wasn't the first time I'd dreamt of him, but unlike the ones that had recently graced my nights, this dream wasn't pleasant. Instead of revisiting one of our many wonderful memories together, I dreamt of the hateful look in his eyes on our wedding day, his disdain during our first week of marriage, his confusion and hurt whenever I pushed him away, and the hopeless feeling that he was slipping away from me. The more desperately I tried to bridge the vast distance between us, the more out of reach he became.

And then the dream shifted to the future event I so feared: Liam's discovery of who I truly was. I found myself at the gallows in my servant's garb as Liam sneered at me with a disgust that broke my heart.

Before I could plead for him to accept me as Anwen, I was pushed forward and forced to clamber onto a chair beneath the dangling noose, a noose that was draped around my neck, the rope scratchy against my throat.

"Please, Liam," I managed before the chair was kicked out from beneath me. The noose immediately tightened, suffocating, agonizing…and I felt my life slip away, all while Liam watched with cold hatred.

I sat up with a gasp, panting as I struggled for the air that in my dream I'd been so desperate for. Cold sweat covered my body and my heart beat wildly against my ribcage. I looked frantically around my darkened room, lit only by the silverly light of the moon tumbling through the window and the dying fire in the hearth.

A nightmare, only a horrible nightmare...yet one that had felt far too real. I held my hands up to my neck; I could still feel the horrific sensation of the rough rope tightening, see the disgust in Liam's eyes, feel the sharp pain lacing my skull as my life drifted away at the gallows...I shuddered.

With a whooshing breath, I collapsed against my pillows and pressed my hand to my chest in an attempt to still my pounding heart. Although it was settling, the memory of my dream lingered, haunting me. Even though Liam's disdain and my execution had only been a nightmare, it was still a future I feared would come to fruition.

I shuddered and snuggled deeper beneath the blankets, cocooning myself in a feeble act of comfort, but it wouldn't come. I stared longingly at the door between me and Liam. I'd craved his presence before, but I *needed* him now. Did I dare?

I slowly sat up, my gaze locked on the connecting door. In the darkness its distance seemed magnified, stretching far out of reach, just like I'd felt from Liam during my nightmare. I tugged my blankets securely around my shaking frame and slipped from bed to tiptoe across the room. The door seemed to drift further away the closer I approached, but eventually I arrived and placed my shaky hand on the knob. I took a deep, wavering breath before knocking. The sound echoed in the still night. Summoning my courage, I pushed the door open.

I'd never been inside Liam's room, but even though the moonlight tumbling through the window illuminated it enough to study it, my attention was eclipsed by his four-poster bed where Liam lay. He stirred and groggily sat up, brows drawn in confusion. His eyes widened when he spotted me standing in the doorway.

My cheeks burned as we stared at one another. I wasn't sure Liam would accept me after I'd once again pushed him away only hours before, but I should have known him better than that. He broke the awkward silence first, his voice as gentle as his softening expression.

"Lavena? Is something wrong?"

I swallowed my nerves and crept closer. His breath hooked as he caught sight of my tear-streaked face.

"Lavena?" He scrambled out of bed and approached, his hands hovering uncertainly over me before he rested them on my shoulders. Calm immediately penetrated the fear tightening my heart from the simple gesture. "What is it?"

My lip trembled. "I had a nightmare," I murmured pathetically.

"You did?" He carefully wiped the moisture clinging to my eyelids. I nodded.

"It was horrible." I stepped closer and relaxed against his chest, resting my head above his heartbeat, which flared to life at my contact.

Liam's arms wound around me and he rested his head on top of mine. "Oh my dear, you're shaking." He began rubbing the base of my back in soothing circles.

"It was so scary and seemed so real." I burrowed myself closer to him, his cinnamon-scented warmth gradually calming my taut nerves. "Can you sit up with me? I need you."

His hold tightened around me as he nodded but he didn't move, as if reluctant to release me. When he eventually pulled away, he kept his arm securely around my waist and led me towards my bedroom. I whimpered and wrapped my arms tightly around him, holding him possessively.

"Liam…" Just like my dream, he was pushing me away.

"It's alright, darling." He stroked my hair and I felt my

unease slip away with each touch. "I'm not leaving you. I just thought more familiar surroundings would help calm you."

I relaxed but didn't loosen my hold. He led me to the settee in front of my dying fire, where we settled. I snuggled closer to him, basking in the way he held me, caressed me, and murmured soothingly, comforting me so sweetly and attentively.

He pressed his lips in my hair. "Will you tell me about your nightmare?"

I shuddered. I could still feel it reaching for me, invading my mind with images of the gallows and losing Liam. "It was horrible."

"What was it about?"

I shook my head. I couldn't tell him, and even though this was just one of many examples of keeping secrets from him, it felt more frustrating now than it had before. I was tired of this constant battle raging war against my heart—between needing Liam and being afraid of getting too close to him. Such a paradox.

Liam began to rub up and down my arms. "You don't have to tell me if you don't want to. I just hope you know that you can always confide in me."

My heart swelled at his sweetness, which he always extended despite everything that transpired between us. "I do know that," I whispered. "That's why I came to you tonight."

He smiled. "We've really grown close these past several months, haven't we? It's hard to believe things are so different than what I'd initially imagined this marriage would be like." He hesitated. "I never want things to revert back to the way they were before, which means I must ask— what happened between us after your parents left?"

Too much of my real self had been unmasked, and in my fear I'd pushed him away. If only I could share this with him so he'd understand. My heart twisted at the thought that I'd hurt him. "I'm sorry," I said. "I wish I could explain."

"Do you not trust me?"

"There's no one I trust more than you. Again, that's why I came to you tonight."

"I'm glad you did." He nestled his head on top of mine. "Even if you can't share your nightmare with me, I want to help ease your fears."

The love already filling my heart blossomed even further. No matter how many times I pushed him away or hurt him, he remained constant. It made me love him all the more, a love that frightened me and caused me to cling more firmly to my disguise.

But as I sat in his arms now, I realized that my fear was of more than getting too close to Liam only for Princess Lavena to return and take him away—it was of my caring so deeply that I wouldn't be able to play the charade any longer. The closer we became, the less I wanted to pretend with him and the more I wanted to set aside my mask as Princess Lavena and show him Anwen. Yet showing him who I truly was would put my heart at risk for him to reject me, an outcome far more torturous than any other potential consequence that could befall me.

For a moment we sat cuddling in front of the fire with you, which had slowly died as the night wore on but still crackled merrily. The longer I sat with Liam, the more distant the nightmare grew, and the more beautiful this moment we shared became. I needed more perfect moments like this.

He broke the still and reverent silence first. "This is rather nice, isn't it?"

I tipped my head back, resting my chin on his chest to peek up at him. His cheeks were crimson and his gaze smoldering as it seeped into mine. *Mine*, not Princess Lavena's. She wasn't here. *I* was.

"It is," I whispered.

He pressed a soft kiss to my brow. "I've always imagined experiences such as us cuddling in front of the fire."

"You've always imagined sharing romantic moments with me?"

His lips tickled my cheek as he chuckled, causing me to shudder. "Admittedly no, but the moment in our marriage when I came to truly know you, everything changed. It's as if you're a completely different person from who you were before. Nothing pleases me more."

Normally, such words would cause anxiety to seep over me, but not tonight. I stared into his eyes, for the first time fully understanding his words. No matter what name Liam knew me by, he knew *me*.

What was wrong with allowing him to know Anwen? He truly didn't know the difference between me and Princess Lavena. Besides, she wasn't here; *I* was, and the name Liam knew me by didn't affect the relationship we'd forged together.

Lavena is only a name. For the first time since starting this horrible, deceiving charade, the truth finally settled over me. I beamed, feeling lighter and happier than I had in a long time. Liam's eyes lit up. He traced my smile with his fingertip.

"What is it, Lavena?"

I hooked my arms around his neck to stare adoringly up at him. I loved this man. My heart could no longer keep him at arm's length. While I was still terrified he'd reject me should he learn I was a goose girl, I knew he loved me enough to accept other parts of me, ones I could no longer keep hidden.

"I'm just marveling at how lucky I am," I said. "I'm

married to a man who will comfort me even when I wake him in the middle of the night due to a nightmare. You're a wonderful husband, Liam."

He grinned and pressed his forehead against mine. "And you're a wonderful wife. I do care for you, dear, more than I could have ever imagined."

My smile grew. His feelings had developed only *after* he'd met *me*, and thus existed only *for* me. It was such a wonderful, liberating thought. Why had it taken me so long to realize this?

He gave me an affectionate snuggle. "You seem more cheerful. Have I comforted you enough so you'll be able to fall asleep?"

I whined in protest and nestled myself closer. "I don't want to go back to sleep. I need more comfort. Comfort me all night." I never wanted this moment to end.

He chuckled and kissed me softly. "Then I'll happily stay up and give it to you, even if it takes all night, and once you fall asleep, I'll be sure to keep the nightmares away."

And that's what he did. We stayed up for another hour conversing, during which I opened up more and more about myself—sharing bits of Anwen throughout, while the ring remained strangely silent—until drowsiness eventually claimed me. I laid my head against his shoulder and felt myself drifting off. The last thing I remembered was Liam's soft kiss pressed tenderly against my temple.

I STIRRED AWAKE, feeling blissfully comfortable. Why was I so comfortable? My eyes fluttered open and I groggily took in my surroundings, bathed in rose and gold-tinted dawn. I lay curled on the settee in front of the fire, my head in Liam's lap, his arms wrapped snugly around me and his hand stroking my hair.

I'd fallen asleep on Liam. I blinked, trying to orient myself to the situation, all while my thoughts scrambled back to how I'd ended up in such a remarkable position. It slowly dawned on me—last night's nightmare, seeking Liam's comfort, our conversation in front of the fire, and eventually drifting off on his shoulder. No wonder I'd passed the most pleasant of nights.

But the wonder of the moment faded into burning embarrassment. I wasn't lying against his shoulder now, but using his lap as a *pillow*. This thought jolted me awake. I bolted upright. "Liam!"

He smiled, looking particularly happy. "Good morning."

"Good morning," I managed even midst my shyness. "Did you stay with me all night?" The words sounded both beautiful and mortifying.

Crimson caressed his cheeks. "I'm sorry," he said in a rush. "I didn't mean to—that is, you seemed so frightened and tired last night, so when you fell asleep, I was afraid moving you would wake you and..." He lowered his gaze to his lap.

"I didn't mind," I said.

He peeked up shyly, his smile hesitant. "Neither did I. I'm pleased you came to me last night." He stroked my cheek, his touch gentle. "Did you have any more nightmares?"

"You kept them away."

His soft smile became mischievous. "Of course I did; I take my husbandly duties seriously."

He kissed the tip of my nose before he unwound his arm from around me, his blush deepening as he took in my appearance in my nightclothes. He yanked his gaze away and swallowed.

"I should, uh, leave and allow you to prepare for the day."

He went to the connecting door, the barrier that had finally been breached, pausing to glance back at me, his smile shy. "I had a wonderful night, dear."

My own cheeks warmed. "I did too."

His smile grew. "I'll see you soon." He disappeared into his room, shutting the door behind him. I stared after him, my heart hammering, before I collapsed backwards onto the settee with an ecstatic smile.

Liam and I had passed the night together. I rolled onto my stomach to burrow my face in the cushion, where Liam's cinnamon scent still clung. I giggled girlishly even as I seized the pillow and rolled back over, holding it tightly to my chest as my toes curled in delight. Liam and I had passed the night together and it had been *wonderful*.

It took a moment for me to emerge from my fantasies about what it'd be like to spend every night with Liam in order to get up and dress with the assistance of my maid. Shortly after she left, a knock sounded on the door. I grinned girlishly. That'd likely be—wait. I frowned. The knock had come not from the connecting door but the one that led to the hallway. I opened it and gasped, my heart sinking.

There stood Princess Lavena.

It had happened, just like I always knew it would. But why did it have to happen *now*? I gaped at her, taking in her travel-worn yet still elegant appearance, hoping she was an illusion, for surely she couldn't be part of my morning that seemed straight from a dream, a dream she was rapidly transforming into a nightmare, as if last night's actual nightmare had been a premonition that everything was about to unravel.

It took me a moment to find my voice. "Your Highness?"

She smirked and flounced into the room. "Shut the door, Anwen. It wouldn't do for anyone to see us together."

I managed to thaw enough to do so, but I couldn't still my

heart's painful pounding in my chest. Princess Lavena *couldn't* be here, not now. Things had not only been going well with Liam, but I'd finally decided to stop holding myself back from him. She couldn't just come into my life—*our* life —and take him from me.

"What are you doing here?" I managed.

She raised an elegant brow. "Need you even ask? Our similarities made it an easy feat to get past the guards; they naturally assumed I was you, although they did look rather perplexed to see me enter the palace so early." She giggled and tossed her hair over her shoulder, as if all of this was some game. "As to why I've come, I'm here to relieve you from the charade. I know that's something you've been wanting ever since it began."

I wished I'd heard her wrong, but I knew all too well I hadn't. I swallowed. "Relieve me?"

"Yes. You no longer have to pretend to be me. I've had my fun." She wrinkled her nose. "If one could call it that. The life of a commoner isn't fun at all. I didn't enjoy traveling with that minstrel, but once I realized how dreadful it was, I was too far from home to make it back quickly. But I'm here now." She gave me a rather accusing look. "You should have warned me I wouldn't like living the life of a peasant."

If I hadn't been so shocked and horrified to see her, I'd have rolled my eyes and reminded her how many times I'd told her that very thing during my arguments against this ridiculous scheme. But the scheme didn't feel ridiculous any longer. I no longer wanted it to end, a desire that caused different arguments to burn on my tongue.

"Your Highness, we can't switch back now," I said. "Everyone will notice."

She rolled her eyes. "They won't. They obviously didn't notice you took my place, so they won't notice when I take it back."

"They didn't notice our first switch because they didn't know you well enough," I said. "They now know me. They'll know the difference the moment they see you. How will you explain it?"

She frowned. "Are you implying that they won't recognize the *real* Lavena?"

"It's not an implication," I said. "Because they won't. As far as they're concerned, *I* am now Princess Lavena."

Her eyes narrowed. "But you're not. I'm the real princess, whereas you're nothing more than my handmaiden and a goose girl. You don't belong in a palace. How you ever thought you could pass for royalty is beyond me."

I folded my arms like a shield. "The fact is I *have* passed for royalty. I've become Princess Lavena. It's too late for you to switch back without anyone noticing."

She stared at me. "Just what are you saying? That we *don't* switch back?"

I bit my lip. I couldn't well suggest that, no matter how much I wanted to. After all, she was the real Princess Lavena, and as I'd always feared, she wanted to take back what was rightfully hers. But that didn't change the fact that what was technically hers now felt like *mine*.

"Surely you realize, Your Highness, that the façade has gone on too long for our switching back to go unnoticed," I said. "However will you explain your sudden change?"

She stared. "What's gotten into you? With as much as you resisted before, I thought you'd be happy to take back your former position. What's changed?"

My gaze darted towards the connecting door behind which Liam was finishing getting ready. *Everything* had changed. I may have believed I'd lost Anwen, but I'd gained everything by getting Liam, and despite the mask I'd worn, he saw enough of me that I could happily continue with this charade for the rest of my life if it meant I got to keep him.

Princess Lavena's giggle tore my gaze away from the door. She pressed her hand over her mouth to stifle her mirth, staring at me as if I were insane. "Oh, it's *Liam*, is it? Do you fancy yourself in love with that ridiculous oaf? Oh Anwen, you've always liked strange things."

I tightened my jaw. "He's the most kind, wonderful man I know, and thus deserves someone better than *you*. You can't just come back after all this time and claim him."

Up went her eyebrow again. "You've certainly become more bold, but you forget that it's not about my deserving *him*, but *what* I deserve due to my birthright. Despite you filling my place these past two months, he's still my betrothed, not yours."

The thought of the princess being with Liam made me want to vomit. "But why would you want to bear the *burden* of being with Liam if you don't even like him?"

She shrugged. "It's true, I do hate him, quite a bit, actually, but with our marriage I shall become what I was born to be: queen. With the power to do whatever I want, I could put up with him."

My fists clenched. "You can't use Liam in that way. He deserves better."

"He's *Prince Liam* to you, handmaiden," she said with a nasty sneer. "And I'll use him in any way I see fit. He's mine, not yours. He's never been yours and he never will be."

Tears burned my eyes even as my desperation overcame me. "You will never convince everyone that you're the real Princess Lavena, especially Liam; everyone will think *you're* the imposter."

Her smirk widened. "Perhaps for now. You may think you've fooled everyone into thinking you're me, but we both know the truth: you're nothing more than Anwen, a handmaiden, whereas I'm a princess by birth, destined to become queen."

"Be that as it may, it's my word against yours. You have no proof as to your true identity. I suggest you leave." The brisk order passing my lips startled me, but I couldn't withdraw it, not when I was desperate for her to leave before Liam saw her. I wouldn't let her ruin everything.

She gaped at me. "Leave?"

I lifted my chin. "Yes. You made your choice when I took your place at the wedding, and it's too late to switch back now. Liam is my husband and it will stay that way."

"But...*I'm* Princess Lavena."

"Not anymore."

Her expression twisted. "How dare you. I order you to switch back with me."

"And I'm ordering you to leave."

Her disbelief sharpened into a glare. "*Excuse me?* Just who do you think you are, you—"

"For all intents and purposes, I am the Crown Princess of Draceria," I said. "And I'm never switching back with you. I won't let your selfish, manipulative cruelty anywhere near Liam." I waved my hand dismissively. "I suggest leaving before there's a scene. If you choose to make one, I guarantee Their Majesties will listen to me over you."

She remained unmoving, glaring at me with pure hatred. Then her look became calculating. My stomach knotted in fear, but I fought to maintain my composure.

"Very well, *Lavena*, I'll leave...for now. But don't think this is over. On the contrary, it's only the beginning. You'll regret your lack of cooperation when you realize you've just thrown away your last opportunity to leave quietly, for no matter how much you've deluded yourself, you're not the real Princess Lavena, a fact that I'll ensure is exposed no matter what it takes."

She glided to the door, pausing with her hand on the knob to give me one final skewering look.

"You may be foolish enough to have fallen in love with Liam, but he certainly doesn't love you. How could he? Underneath your finery, you're nothing more than a common goose girl."

She flounced from the room, leaving my heart pounding in fear. Even though I'd gotten her to leave, I knew she was right—I'd only delayed the inevitable, for if there was one thing I knew about the princess, it was that she wouldn't rest until she'd gotten her way.

CHAPTER 22

I was on edge the entire morning, expecting Princess Lavena to burst through the door at any moment, closely followed by armed guards who'd drag me to the dungeon...or worse. I wrung my hands anxiously in my lap, all while scolding myself for this morning's stupidity. Why hadn't I switched back when I'd had the chance?

"Are you alright, Lavena?"

My gaze shifted to Liam's, filled with such sweet concern, and my heart swelled with all the love I felt for him. *He* was the reason I didn't want this to end. But end it would. I felt the conclusion of our time together drawing nearer and nearer. I tried to cling to it, but it was rapidly slipping through my fingers like sand in an hourglass, impossible to hold on to, no matter how much I tried.

I needed a plan. I cast Prince Nolan several glances throughout tea, hoping he'd read the urgency in my expression and come to my aid. He tilted his head with a confused frown, but after the third desperate look from me, he motioned towards the corner, inviting me for a private conversation.

"What is it?" he asked the moment we were alone.

I took a shaky breath. "Princess Lavena arrived this morning."

He gaped at me. *"What?"*

"She wants to switch back." I twisted the contract ring on my finger. "I refused and managed to convince her to leave, but you know your sister as well as I do—she'll be back, likely soon. What do I do?"

Prince Nolan scrunched his forehead, thinking hard. "I'm not sure. Switching back now will not go unnoticed, but you can't pretend to be her forever."

"Exactly." Terror tightened my chest, more acute at Prince Nolan's obvious worry. "She'll expose the charade and everything will be over."

He rested his hand on my arm. "Don't panic. No matter what happens, remember I know the truth about the switch. I promise no harm will come to you. I'll think of something."

I tried to cling to his promise as we separated and I shakily returned to my seat, but his assurances did little to calm my pounding heart.

Liam searched my expression. "You're so pale. Are you alright, darling?"

How could I be? Everything was about to shatter, and I was powerless to stop it.

All too soon, the curtain to this beautiful production which had become my life closed. A footman entered the parlor where I sat with Liam's family.

"Forgive the interruption, Your Majesties, but a guest has arrived." His perplexed gaze darted towards me. "A Princess Lavena."

Silence followed this announcement. My stomach clenched. *Oh no*, she'd come sooner than I'd expected. Oh, why hadn't I switched back when I had the chance?

The king blinked in astonishment. "A *Princess Lavena*? You

must be mistaken. Lavena is here with us." He gave me a fatherly smile I thoroughly didn't deserve.

The footman fidgeted. "Forgive me, Your Majesty, but that's the only name she supplied."

Liam snorted. "Then our guest is delusional. There's no way there's another Lavena." He gave me a snuggle. If I hadn't been on the brink of a nervous breakdown, I'd have enjoyed what would likely be the last affectionate gesture from the man I loved. Instead I felt near a faint, darkness lapping against my senses.

The footman frowned at me. "Forgive me, but this woman claiming to be Princess Lavena looks uncannily similar to the real Princess Lavena. Permission to show her in?"

"How strange," the queen said. "Please do so that we may learn why anyone would make such an outrageous claim."

No, I silently pleaded as the footman bowed crisply and left the room. I ached to tell him to not bring Princess Lavena here to ruin everything. As much as I'd known it was inevitable, I didn't want the charade to end, for with it I'd lose the relationship that was more precious to me than any other.

I instinctively pressed myself against Liam's side. He searched my expression, his brow furrowed. "Are you sure you're alright, darling? You're awfully pale."

I couldn't speak; my throat had sealed, silencing the protests I longed to make. The door swung open and Princess Lavena entered, her eyes fiery. She wasted no time in pointing an accusing finger at me. "That girl is an imposter."

Tense silence followed her accusation. I sat frozen as Liam and his family looked back and forth between me and the princess with widening eyes. "Oh my heavens," the queen murmured. "The two are identical."

Liam studied us more closely. "No, they're not, but... they're rather similar." He glared at Princess Lavena, as if our similarities were her fault. "Who are you? What gives you the right to barge in on us making such outrageous accusations against my wife?"

"Because the accusations are true," she said. "I'm the *real* Princess Lavena, the woman you were supposed to marry before that handmaiden usurped me and stole my place."

My apprehension turned to full-blown terror as I realized what the princess's plan was—to force me to take responsibility for her plot. "No! I—that's not true. You—"

"Be quiet, Anwen; your lies can't save you."

"Don't speak to my wife that way," Liam snapped, his expression fierce, his hold around me tight and protective. "Your ridiculous accusations have no place here. I know my own wife."

Princess Lavena smirked. "Ask her yourself; I dare her to lie to you."

Liam rolled his eyes before turning to me with twitching lips, as if he expected me to laugh at what he considered to be an elaborate joke.

My heart pounded furiously as I stared into Liam's deep blue eyes, filled with such adoration, while my own love for him filled my heart. I wanted to believe that I could still keep him even after he learned the truth, but Liam had only known me as a princess. While I had no doubt he cared for me, would he still do so once he realized who I truly was—nothing more than a common goose girl? The thought of losing him was unbearable.

There was only one course of action my heart would allow me to take. I'd gladly sacrifice Anwen forever if I could keep Liam.

I stood regally. "I'm the real Princess Lavena. That woman is my former handmaiden."

Princess Lavena's mouth fell open in disbelief. Had she truly expected that with my love for Liam, the power of her contract ring, and the dire consequences for me should I accept her accusations, that I'd confess my true identity?

Liam smirked triumphantly "There. You see?"

"But—I'm the *real* Princess Lavena. She's—"

I lifted my chin. "You have no proof other than your word that I'm an imposter, whereas I have many witnesses to my identity." I gestured towards Liam's family.

"Indeed." The queen studied Princess Lavena closely, taking in her similar features. "You two do look quite a bit alike, but different enough that I'd have recognized if you two had switched places."

Oh, the irony that no one had.

Princess Lavena continued to gape. "But we *did* switch. Tell them, Anwen."

"Who's Anwen?" Liam asked.

"*She* is." She jabbed her finger towards me. "She's my handmaiden. Anwen, tell them who you are." She gave me a desperate look.

Had she really forgotten that her ring forbade such a confession? I folded my arms. "I'm afraid I must disappoint you, for I'm Lavena."

"No, you're not; *I* am."

I raised a challenging brow and she shrieked in a most undignified manner. Elodie giggled at the display, whereas the queen covered her mouth.

"Oh, my goodness." She turned to Prince Nolan, who was watching the entire spectacle with his usual serious expression. "Nolan, you must clear this up. Which of these women is your sister?"

My stomach sank. I'd forgotten about him. My gaze snapped to his, my own pleading. He stared long and hard at me before shifting his attention to Princess Lavena, who glared at him.

"Don't just stand there. Tell them, Nolan. Don't let that handmaiden get away with her deception."

Prince Nolan cocked his eyebrow. "*Nolan?* Don't you mean *Prince* Nolan?"

Princess Lavena's mouth fell agape. "What—"

Prince Nolan strode towards me and stood by my side. "This is my sister, Lavena."

I fought to hide my astonishment. Whatever plan I'd expected from the prince, it hadn't been to side with me against his own sister.

Liam laughed in relief as he wrapped his arm around my waist, claiming me as his. "There. You see?"

Princess Lavena gaped at her brother in disbelief before she swelled in indignation. "I'm the *real* Lavena and you know it. Tell them, Nolan. *Tell them.*"

"If you were the real Lavena," he said smoothly, "then you'd have been at the wedding fulfilling your engagement contract like you were *supposed* to." He gave her a challenging look and her face darkened. "But you weren't; *she* was. Therefore, she is Lavena."

"Nolan!" Her voice was escalating. "How could you do this? I'm your *sister.*"

Prince Nolan said nothing. Princess Lavena continued to glare before she lifted her chin defiantly.

"Fine. If this is the game you want to play, then it's time for me to reveal my trump card." She gave me a nasty smirk that sent a wave of icy fear straight up my spine. She strolled to the door and poked her head into the corridor. "You may come in now. I know there's someone here you've been anxiously looking for."

All eyes were on the door. I had no time to wonder what the princess's newest plan could possibly be before Archer burst into the room, his expression marred with worry. My heart skittered to a stop. "Archer..." I breathed.

His desperate gaze scanned the parlor before settling on me. He gaped at me for only a moment before in a few strides he reached me and pulled me into a suffocating hug.

"Where have you been, Anwen? I've been worried sick looking everywhere for you." He pulled away just enough to scan me in order to determine my well-being. "What's happened to you? Why are you dressed like that? Are you alright?"

I shook my head, having lost the ability to speak. Archer's expression hardened as he slowly took in the confused expressions of our audience before his eyes narrowed at Liam.

"What have you done to my sister?"

"Your *sister*?" Liam's gaze snapped to mine, pleading for me to deny my connection to Archer. I lowered my eyes and remained silent.

"Archer, is this woman your sister, Anwen?" Princess Lavena asked.

"Of course she is, Your Highness," Archer snapped. "What brother doesn't recognize his own sister?"

"Indeed." Princess Lavena glared at Prince Nolan before her expression faltered and vulnerability overshadowed her. "I can't believe you didn't recognize me."

He sighed. "Of course I recognized you, Lavena. I detected your switch with Anwen immediately, at the wedding reception."

She stared at him, her eyes glassy. "Then why did you side with her?"

"So she wouldn't be punished for *your* scheme. What were you thinking, Lavena?"

She tossed her hair over her shoulder. "I had nothing to do with this; I was the victim of that usurper and am deter-

273

mined to reclaim my rightful position." She narrowed her eyes at me once more. "Don't think you can get away with this, Anwen. You're unfit for the royal position you've been masquerading in. It baffles me you managed to remain undetected for so long when you're nothing more than a common goose girl."

I ached to find the words to deny her accusations, but panic pressed against my chest and my mouth had gone dry. "I—I—"

Liam's expression crumpled at my hesitancy. "Wait, it can't possibly be true. You're Lavena, my wife."

I stood mutely, unable to defend myself with the power of the contract ring still binding me. The crushing helplessness caused the tears burning my eyes to escape.

Princess Lavena smirked. "Your silence is as good as a confession. You realize you've lost, haven't you? In the end you can't escape who you really are—nothing more than a servant—nor the fact that you've participated in this condemning scheme. Admit it: you're an imposter who, along with your brother, orchestrated our switch in order to usurp the Dracerian throne."

My swelling panic unclogged my throat. "Archer had nothing to do with it!"

No matter what fate befell me, I needed to protect my brother, even if my own escape was impossible. How could I have deluded myself into thinking I could deny the princess's accusations? It made me appear even more guilty. Now no one would believe me when I told them it had all been her idea, but even so, Archer wouldn't take the fall with me.

Princess Lavena's smirk widened, making her look very much like a spider who'd just caught a fly in her web, one she would devour mercilessly. "Your protectiveness of this peasant only confirms you're not the real princess, for only *Anwen*, his sister, would care what fate befalls him. There's no use in pretending; your continuing to deny your true identity will only further condemn you."

She was right. There was no use lying any longer. It was over. I slumped in defeat.

Liam's eyes widened. "No, it can't be true. Tell me it's not." He glanced back and forth between me and the princess before he stroked my cheek, wiping a few stray tears with his thumb. "Lavena, love? Tell her she's wrong. You're not this Anwen."

I leaned against his touch. "I'm so sorry." An apology, at least, wasn't forbidden by the sadistic ring.

Liam shook his head, his expression frantic. "Please, it can't be true."

"It is, Liam," the princess said. "She's not Lavena, *I* am."

"I don't believe you." Liam's gaze returned to mine, desperate and pleading. "Tell them who you are, darling. You're Lavena, my wife."

"I—" I ached to tell him everything, explain why I'd deceived him, but the power of the ring prevented the words from forming. It burned my hand, pain I was now numb to compared to the torture being inflicted on my breaking heart at Liam's distress. "I can't."

He set his jaw. "I don't need your confession; I know who you are." Liam spun on Prince Nolan. "She's not a handmaiden; she's Lavena, just as you said."

Prince Nolan bit his lip. "I'm afraid I was mistaken."

"You were *mistaken*? How can you not recognize your own sister?" Liam grabbed my shoulders and turned me to face the prince. "Tell me this is Lavena."

Prince Nolan hesitated before his usual confident, regal manner slumped. "I'm sorry."

"*No!*" Liam spun me back around to face him. "You're *Lavena*. I refuse to believe anything else. Tell me, Lavena, tell me that's who you are."

My heart broke at the despair in his eyes, that my deception was hurting him as much as I'd always feared. More tears trickled down my cheeks, but I couldn't answer. Each time I tried, the searing ring once again forced my silence. I whimpered and cradled my throbbing hand to my chest.

"Why aren't you saying anything?" Liam demanded.

"She can't, Liam. She's bound by a contract of silence, but I assure you that despite how this looks, she's done nothing wrong." Prince Nolan gently took my hand and turned to the princess. "Take off the ring, Lavena."

"No," she said.

"This has gone on long enough." Prince Nolan's tone was hardening. "Take it off and allow Anwen to defend herself… or are you too afraid of what she has to say?"

The princess stuck her chin in the air, her refusal.

"Take off the ring." This fierce command came not from Prince Nolan but the king, who'd been observing the entire scene alongside the queen and Liam's sisters.

Princess Lavena flinched. She hesitated before stomping over with an exasperated sigh to yank the scorching ring off. The relief was instantaneous, for it wasn't just the white, fiery pain that vanished, but the burden of deceit I'd been forced to carry finally lifting from my shoulders.

I extended my hand and stared at my ringless finger, bearing no sign of the burning it'd endured these past several months.

"Does that feel better, Anwen?" Prince Nolan asked kindly.

I nodded. "Much better."

Liam gaped at me in disbelieving silence while Archer seized my hand and examined it front to back before raising his glare to the princess. "You bound my sister under that sadistic ring?"

Princess Lavena merely shrugged. "It was rather effective."

Archer muttered a curse that I considered unwise to direct towards royalty. "Effective? Is that all you have to say for ruining my sister's life?" I rested a calming hand on Archer's arm but he shook it off. "You've always forced Anwen to do all sorts of horrible things, but this is the worst —having her switch places with you for an arranged marriage? I curse fate for giving her looks so similar to yours."

"Archer, please," I whispered urgently. "Upsetting Her Highness will only make our situation worse."

Archer tightened his jaw and obediently fell silent. Liam stared at my hand resting on my brother's arm before slowly raising his gaze to mine. "I still don't want to believe it."

I took a wavering breath as I took his hands. Without the ring, I could now finally speak freely and tell him the truth he deserved to hear. "I'm so sorry, Liam, but it's as Her Highness said: I'm Anwen, former goose girl and the princess's handmaiden."

He shook his head, as if he couldn't make himself believe it, even after my confession. "No, you're not, you can't be." He pressed my hands to his chest. "Please."

"I'm so sorry, Liam." How I loathed the truth. The torment filling his eyes squeezed my heart, his anguish as acute as my own. "Please believe me: I never wanted to hurt you, but I was trapped. The princess's enchanted ring bound me by a contract that forced me to pretend to be her. I had no choice."

"So it was all a lie?" Liam glanced towards the real Princess Lavena. "Since when?"

"Since the wedding," she said. "This little pretender had her brother Archer kidnap me so she could take my place and marry you in order to become queen."

"That's not true," I said. "Archer had nothing to do with it. I only took your place because you *forced* me to so you could elope with your minstrel."

She laughed coldly. "Your story is ridiculous. Why would I throw away my birthright for a peasant? I had nothing to gain from our switch, whereas you had everything. You wanted to entrap the prince in order to get the throne."

At her words, Liam dropped my hands, wrenching my heart further. "Is that true? You took her place because you only wanted what I could offer you?"

"No!" How could he think that after all we'd been through? I rapidly shook my head. "I'd never do that to you, Liam."

He bit his lip in doubt. "You did initially lie when she first accused you of being an imposter. Why would you do that if you were innocent?"

"The ring wouldn't let me tell you the truth," I explained. "Besides, I didn't want to lose you."

He was silent for a moment. "Me or my crown?"

"Of course you, Liam, please believe me." I ached to say it was because I loved him, but I was a common girl again, meaning my feelings towards him were ones my lower station forbade me to express.

He searched my face earnestly, as if desperate to find something precious to him, looking so confused and hopelessly lost. "Why would you lose me?"

"Because I was afraid you wouldn't want me if you knew I wasn't a princess."

His expression softened, causing my heart to lift in hope. If he didn't hate me for my horrible deceit, I could face whatever consequences came.

"You've heard the handmaiden's confession," Princess Lavena said. "Now the usurper deserves to be punished. It's against the law for a commoner to pose as a royal. Now that you realize Anwen is an imposter, she must face the conse-quences—imprisonment or even death."

Icy fear squeezed my heart. I whimpered and buried my face in my hands. Liam's breath hooked and he embraced me, his arms tight in his desperation to protect me. "She won't be punished for a plot of *your* making. I know my wife. She'd never engage in anything so deceitful of her own volition." He pressed my hands to his chest and gazed earnestly into my eyes. "Nothing has changed, Anwen." He said my name hesitantly, but oh how I loved hearing him say it. "You're still my wife; the real Lavena isn't the one I married, *you* are. It doesn't matter that you're not a princess. I still want you. Always."

"I'm afraid it *does* matter, Son," the king said gravely. "If she was not the real Lavena at the time of the wedding, then the marriage is void. And the initial contract still stands—you are bound to marry Princess Lavena, the *real* one."

"*No!*" Raw panic filled Liam's face. He pulled me close, holding me in a suffocating embrace. I burrowed against his chest, savoring the feeling of what would likely be the last time I felt his arms around me. "You can't do this to me. I don't want to marry Lavena." He glared at her with pure hatred.

The princess smirked in triumph, her previous disdain for the match seemingly forgotten. "You have no choice," she said. "Our two kingdoms have a contract. I will be Queen of Draceria."

"I refuse to marry you. Anwen is the only one for me." Liam turned a desperate, pleading look to his parents. "It's void now, isn't it? Surely the contract was broken when she forced Anwen to take her place."

The king, looking regretful, shook his head. "I'm afraid not, son, not when she's now returned to fulfill it."

Liam gaped at him in horror. "No! I refuse to go along

with this." He turned his despairing look to his mother, whose face was streaked with tears.

She turned to the king with a frown. "After Lavena's horrible actions...surely we don't have to honor it, dear."

"I'm afraid we have no choice." The king gave Princess Lavena a sharp look. "But until it's fulfilled, I will fight to find a way to void it. She doesn't deserve to be queen."

"You have to find a way," Liam said, his voice desperate. "Because I won't marry her. I can't." He stared down at me pleadingly. "Why did you have to be the fake Lavena?"

"I'm so sorry," I said. "I never meant to hurt you."

Liam searched my eyes. "Was any of it real?"

I cradled his face. "It was all real, Liam."

He pressed my hand against his cheek. "I know, yet now we're losing everything we've built together and you're being stolen from me." He slowly pulled away, looking utterly defeated. "This is too much. I—I need a moment alone."

And without another word, he slumped from the room, taking the pieces of my broken heart with him, for I knew I wouldn't see him again. I'd lost him, for he wasn't mine. He never had been.

I glanced at Liam's family. The queen and his sisters were in tears, while the king looked heartbroken on his son's behalf. I turned and glared at Princess Lavena, smirking wickedly in triumph. Hate burned through my veins, both for the pain she'd caused Liam and for her stealing him from me, the man I couldn't have.

"I suggest you leave, Anwen," Princess Lavena said. "There's nothing for you here."

"Unfortunately, she's right," the queen said. "It'd be best for you to leave for poor Liam's sake." She frowned at the closed door where he'd departed. "I don't know how he'll ever recover from this."

The king rested a hand on her shoulder and turned to me.

"I agree, Anwen. While you certainly won't be punished, your remaining here will make everything more difficult." He beckoned to an attending footman. "I'll prepare a missive, which you'll immediately arrange to be delivered to the King and Queen of Lyceria. We need to inform them of what's happened." He turned his cold gaze onto Princess Lavena. "What you've done is a complete disgrace. I will speak with your father and do everything in my power to see that the contract is broken. You will not be Queen of Draceria if I can help it, not after you've proven yourself unworthy of the title."

"They won't break the contract," Princess Lavena said smugly.

The king gave her a piercing look. "That matter will be between us." But by the defeated look on his face, I could tell that he knew the King of Lyceria would never agree to it, not when Princess Lavena's union with Liam would be too great a benefit for Lyceria to break. Which meant I'd really lost Liam after all.

And suddenly I needed to be as far away from him as possible. I couldn't stay and endure the agony of watching Liam forced into an unwanted and miserable marriage with such a horrible woman. Being sent away would actually be a mercy.

Yet the thought of being so far from the man I loved shattered the last piece of my heart, a heart that after today I doubted would ever fully heal.

CHAPTER 23

"*A*re you sure you're alright, Anwen? I can't believe everything you've been forced to endure these last two months. When I think of it..." Archer's fists clenched.

He hadn't left my side since leaving the parlor where the charade had finally ended and I'd said a tearful goodbye to the king, queen, and Liam's sisters, who'd become my family. I yearned to say goodbye to Liam, but he hadn't returned after seeking a moment alone.

As much as I longed to see him, perhaps it was for the best. Saying goodbye to him would make our separation feel all the more final, and leaving was unbearable enough as it was.

I resisted each step towards the palace gates, for once I walked through them, I'd leave behind the life I'd come to love. In Lyceria, I'd try—and likely fail—to forget everything that had happened. I paused and looked back at the palace one final time. It was lit with the golden light of the setting sun, a sunset that represented an ending I'd hoped would never come, but which I'd always known was inevitable.

"Anwen?"

Archer's voice was taut with worry. He gently brushed my arm, beckoning me to turn to him and ease his concerns. But what could I possibly tell him? I *wasn't* alright. I doubted I ever would be again. My heart tightened as it desperately tried to keep all its broken pieces together. I hoped that the pain would lessen with time, that the memory of the hurt and betrayal filling Liam's eyes would stop haunting me, although I knew it would be impossible to ever forget him completely.

"Anwen?" Archer's voice wrenched me from my thoughts and I finally turned to his worry-marred expression and forced a smile I didn't at all feel.

"I'll be fine."

The look Archer gave me showed he wasn't fooled by my lie. My lip trembled and all my foolish attempts to be brave faltered, causing the tears I'd fought to keep back to finally escape.

Archer pulled me into a hug, his firm, brotherly arms protective. I buried myself against his chest and cried. He stroked my hair.

"You're clearly not fine, Pillbug. Won't you tell me everything that's happened? I can't even convey how worried sick I've been."

"I'm sorry," I said, even though an apology was inadequate for the torment I'd put him through these past two months.

He released a shuddering breath. "I thought you'd *died*."

"In a sense I had, for I had to lock myself away." But as I considered, I realized that wasn't entirely true. I'd *tried* to bury Anwen, but despite my efforts she'd still survived and occasionally emerged. What a beautiful thought that one couldn't lose themselves completely, no matter the circumstances.

Archer pulled back to once more scan my body in order to more accurately assess my well being. "But are you alright?

Did that *prince* hurt you?" His question came out as a fierce, protective growl.

I shook my head rapidly. "Oh no. He would never hurt me."

Archer's jaw tightened, clearly not believing me. I ached for him to understand.

"He was so respectful, so kind, so..." *Wonderful.* An ache clenched my heart to be thinking of Liam. I buried myself back against Archer. "I love him." If only I didn't. It'd make everything so much easier.

He sighed. "This is quite the mess."

It was, but as much as I'd initially longed to escape it, now I'd give anything to return.

Liam...

My sadness threatened to engulf me, for I'd lost what had been the most precious part of my life. I needed to let him go, for I was Anwen again, and she wasn't meant to be with Prince Liam, no matter how much she yearned to be.

Archer seemed to sense the direction of my thoughts and managed a tight smile. "It'll be alright, Pillbug. It may take time, but you've always been resilient and optimistic. You'll feel better after we return home. I've been back to check on your geese, and although they've been well cared for these past several years, they obviously miss you. Not to mention the insects have remained undisturbed for far too long and are in need of serious studying."

He cupped my chin with a look like he wanted me to smile. But I couldn't. As much as I'd missed my home and had thought of it often while surrounded by the elegant and opulent scenery of my charade, I wasn't sure whether it'd feel like home any longer, considering the man who'd brought me the greatest joy would be missing from it.

Not to mention, *I* myself had changed. I could no longer return to the Anwen I'd once been. I wasn't even sure I wanted to. I liked the woman Liam had made me. I allowed his face to fill my mind, despite the heartache remembering him brought me. If only I'd had a chance to fully apologize, to say goodbye, to confess that while I'd pretended many things, my feelings for him had been real.

I loved him.

"Anwen?" Archer's concerned tone once more tugged me from my melancholy. I took a wavering breath. Even if home didn't feel like home any longer, I wouldn't rest until I made it so. Despite my heartache, I needed to move forward as best I could.

It would undoubtedly be difficult, for I'd see Liam everywhere, even in a place he'd never been. He'd be in the warmth of the sunshine, the free spirit of the butterflies, the playfulness of the geese...and especially in my heart. Home wouldn't be a haven any longer, yet I still wanted to return there and do my best to make it so once more.

"Let's go home," I said.

I'd no sooner taken a fortifying breath and braced myself to walk through the palace gates and away from Liam forever than from behind me—

"Anwen!"

My heart flared to life. That voice...I spun around to see Liam sprinting across the lawn towards me, expression frantic. I stared. It couldn't be Liam. Last I'd seen him, he'd left me after I'd hurt him, as if he couldn't bear to see me anymore. How could he be here now? Would I be forced to say goodbye to him after all?

He slowed when he neared me, eyes shy. "Anwen?"

He said my name like a question, as if testing it out on his tongue. My heart warmed to hear my name spoken in his sweet voice.

"Can you say it again?"

His brow furrowed before he managed a boyish smile. "Anwen."

I closed my eyes, basking in the sound of my name spoken by him, before my smile melted away. I was Anwen again, a common girl standing in the presence of royalty. I swept into a curtsy. "Your Highness."

Sadness twisted Liam's expression. "Please don't do that, Anwen." He took another step closer. "It's Liam."

"Forgive me, Your Highness, but I'm a peasant and you're a prince. I can't address you so informally."

I knew Liam wouldn't care, but *I* needed to do it in order to remind myself of my place in the world and in Liam's life. It'd make it easier to let him go…even though doing so felt utterly impossible.

He gaped at me, eyes wide and wounded, seeming at a loss for what to say. I rose from my curtsy and waited for him to speak. He didn't. The silence filling the space between us was unbearable.

He stirred first, glancing towards Archer, who watched our reunion with a protective stance. "This is Archer?" Liam asked.

"Yes, my brother." It was wonderful to finally explain the true nature of our relationship.

He nodded, looking relieved to finally understand. "May I speak with Anwen alone?"

Archer's jaw tightened and he looked for a moment like he would refuse Liam's request. "Please, Archer?" I asked. His gaze flickered towards me and he immediately softened.

"If you wish it, Pillbug." He glared at Liam. "But I'll remain close by, watching you *very* carefully."

He sauntered several yards away, giving us only a small bit of privacy, but it was enough. For a moment we both just stood in silence, staring at one another. I couldn't speak, even though I was desperate to. If this was to be our goodbye, there were a multitude of feelings I needed to share, but even without the contract ring, the words still wouldn't come.

He found his voice first. "I only left you for a moment. I needed to consider all that had happened and the situation I'm facing now, but when I returned you were gone, without even saying goodbye." Emotion swirled in his eyes. "Are you really leaving?"

I hesitated. "Yes. I don't belong here."

"You do." He took another step forward, slowly bridging the distance I ached to cross. "You belong with me."

His words both lifted my heart and crushed it. He shouldn't be saying them, for his sweet endearments would change nothing about our impossible circumstances. I squeezed my eyes shut; it hurt to even look at him.

"You can't say that," I said. "Not when you know it's not true."

I sensed him close the remaining space between us and I was awash in his cinnamon warmth. My breath caught and my eyes fluttered open to meet his, seeping into mine with a look I'd come to know well—adoration.

"It is true, Anwen. You know it is. You told me it was all real." He caressed my cheek and I leaned against his soft touch, allowing myself one last taste of what I knew I couldn't have.

But I wanted it, and in my weakness I couldn't resist. "Oh, Liam."

I'd no sooner whimpered his name than I was in his arms. He pulled me possessively close. I nestled into his embrace, savoring the way he clung to me. I held him tightly in return, nestling myself against his warmth, his sweetness, all for the last time.

"Liam." I rested against his heartbeat, loving the feel of it against my cheek, even as I hated myself for allowing myself to bask in Liam once more.

He cradled my face, his blue gaze seeping into mine. "Anwen."

The way he said my name—like a caress—caused my heart to swell. I closed my eyes and allowed my own name to wash over me. "I love hearing you say my name."

"I love saying it," he said. "I'll never call you another name ever again. Anwen, Anwen, Anwen…"

I smiled and nestled myself back against his chest. "Why are you here?" My voice cracked, betraying the emotion I desperately tried to hide.

He pressed his lips against my hair. "For you. Can I be here for any other reason?"

"But the façade has shattered," I said. "You know who I truly am now—nothing more than a common goose girl and a handmaiden, an imposter who deceived you." The memory of the raw pain filling his eyes returned to haunt me. How could he be holding me now after all the hurt I'd caused him?

"None of this was your fault," Liam said. "I hold no blame against you."

"Be that as it may, I've spent our entire relationship pretending to be someone I'm not."

His hand went to my hair. "You haven't been pretending anything that truly matters. Otherwise it'd be impossible for me to feel what I do towards you."

I whimpered. "Don't Liam, it'll make it so much harder to—"

"Please, Anwen, I need you to know how I feel about you."

He began stroking the back of my hands with his thumbs. The sensations softened my fear enough for me to swallow and nod wordlessly. I prepared my heart for both the pain and joy it was about to feel, for by the earnestness filling Liam's eyes, I knew the words he hadn't yet shared.

He took a deep, wavering breath and pressed my hands to his chest. "I love you, Anwen."

How could the most beautiful words I'd always yearned to hear—especially from him—be so painful as to break one's heart? Deep down I'd already known his feelings, but hearing them made them all the more real. His sentiments both created cracks and instantly healed them, before my fierce happiness eclipsed every other emotion.

With a whimper I pressed myself into his arms and melted into his embrace as he held me impossibly close. I closed my eyes and for a moment allowed his beautiful confession to wash over me.

"I've wanted to say those words forever," Liam murmured against my hair.

As beautiful as his words were, they caused my heart to crack once again. "To who you thought was Princess Lavena."

Liam yanked away to cradle my face. "No, to you. Only to you. You're the one I've been with, not her."

"But how can you truly love me if you don't even know *me*? You only know the part I was forced to play. Anwen doesn't dress up in elegant gowns, she's not allergic to strawberries, she's terrible at embroidery, she's incredibly shy..."

Liam scrunched his forehead. "Does any of that matter?"

I'd opened my mouth to list more differences but now snapped it shut again. "Doesn't it?"

"Of course not, Anwen." He cupped my chin. "I may have known you by a different name, but a name is just a name; it doesn't change the relationship we've built or all that you mean to me, nor does it change the fact I know *your* heart. You're incredibly sweet, kind, shy, gentle, fun, brave, thoughtful, and you help make me a better man. You can't fake those traits, dear."

He withdrew the music box he'd given me and handed it to me. I cradled it close, tracing the engravings of butterflies in the smooth wood until my touch trailed down to the key to wind it up. The sweet, lovely melody that Mother had always sung to me filled the air. Tears trickled down my cheeks as I looked up at him.

His arms enveloped me to nestle me close. "I know you, Anwen. I saw more of you than you think, and I won't rest until I've uncovered every last piece. I don't want it to end. Please don't make me lose you."

I shook my head. "I ache to stay, to be with you, but you know it's impossible."

"It's not impossible, not with what we feel for one another," he said. "After all, it was all real. Wasn't it?"

Raw vulnerability filled his eyes as he awaited my confirmation, and even though confessing the depth of my feelings would only bring both of us heartache, I needed him to know. I cradled his face and stared deeply into his eyes so that he couldn't miss my sincerity.

"All I feel for you is real, Liam. Every endearment, every touch, every kiss was from Anwen, even though she was buried beneath the mask."

His bright smile lit up his eyes. "That's how I know we'll be together. Perhaps not right away, but one day we will. I'll find a way."

I ached to believe in the future together I yearned for. I choked back a sob. "But I'm a peasant, you're the crown prince. How can we possibly—"

He cradled my face to wipe away my lingering tears with his thumbs, just like he'd done during our first carriage ride together, the moment he'd stolen the first piece of my heart. "Somehow, sweetheart."

"But the contract—"

Liam's expression twisted. "I admit that's quite the problem." He pressed his forehead against mine. "But there has to be a way. Every contract has a loophole. Just because I couldn't find one before doesn't mean one doesn't exist. I won't give up. Then I can marry you, for real this time."

My breath caught. "You want to marry me?"

"Yes, dear Anwen. I'll marry no one but you. Please have faith. It'll work out." He pressed the softest, sweetest kiss on my brow and I nearly melted at the tenderness of the gesture.

I stared into his eyes before I forced my gaze away towards the gate, where Archer stood with his arms folded and a protective look as he watched us with riveted attention. "As much as I want to, I still can't stay, not until we find a way to be together. It's better this way."

He sighed and caressed my cheek, the yearning in his expression softened by his usual tender understanding. "Then I shall use the time we're apart to my advantage. It'll be the perfect opportunity for me to not only find a way out of the contract, but to come to know the real you even more."

I furrowed my brow. "How?"

He grinned boyishly. "It's a surprise."

"Excellent. I like surprises." I pressed my hand to his heart. "Keep this safe for me, won't you?"

"Always." He pulled me into a hug, holding me so tightly he lifted me off the ground. In his embrace, all the despair, heartache, and uncertainty I'd been experiencing didn't completely fade away, but hope filled me all the same. I wasn't sure how, but perhaps we could still be together. Even if at the moment it felt impossible, I needed to believe it.

CHAPTER 24

J'd been home just over a week, surrounded once more by my gabbling geese, when the first letter arrived. I immediately recognized the untidy handwriting. Heart pounding, I hastily broke the royal seal and unfolded it to bask in my Liam's words:

My Dearest Anwen,

Surprise! My brilliant plan is to court you via letter. You see, I'm really quite clever, Anwen darling, and thus would make an incredible husband for someone as wonderful as yourself. I shall write you dozens of letters assuring you of how much I know and care for you while convincing you to disregard all sense and marry me, for I'm determined—I will *be your husband.*

It's only been a few days and I already miss you fiercely. I knew it'd be impossible to let you go and I'm determined I won't have to... although admittedly, the fight to break my horrible engagement has so far proven unyielding.

We've met with the King and Queen of Lyceria several times, whom I now view as my jailers considering they refuse to break the

*chains binding me to their horrible daughter. No matter our argu-
ments about how Lavena is unfit to be Draceria's future queen,
they remain unwilling to bend; they're even threatening war if we
back out of the agreement, so desperate not to lose the treaty's benefits or the opportunity for their daughter to become queen.*

*But I refuse to give up. If there's one thing I learned in our
evenings of reading together, it's that any dragon can be conquered,
especially considering I have quite the team of knights on my side.
My parents and sisters all support our union, and they—along with
Prince Nolan—have spent hours searching for a means for me to
escape. We've consulted with the advisors, pored over dozens of
volumes, and repeatedly attempted to negotiate.*

Unfortunately, so far we've been unsuccessful.

*Lavena watches our efforts with a constant dark smirk. What-
ever hatred I harbored towards her before was minuscule compared
to what I feel for her now, especially when I only want you. Thus
I'll never marry her. Father has only avoided Their Majesties'
insistence for a hasty wedding—and bought us much needed time—
by insisting Lavena still needs to prove herself trustworthy.*

*She's attempted to demonstrate a change of heart, but no matter
what she does, she can never prove herself to them and especially
not to me. My parents finally see her for the horrible person that
she is and agree that she's not only a terrible match for me, but
would make an irresponsible, selfish queen. Yet still the contract
binds us with its unrelenting chains. But I refuse to give up hope
that there's a way to be together. I need to believe it.*

*I'm writing this letter in your room...or rather, what was your
room. Being here makes me feel closer to you, even though it
doesn't seem like your room at all, considering Lavena chose its
style rather than you. I'm trying to imagine how you'd have deco-
rated it and am frustrated that I can't. For as much as I feel I know
you, there are still too many mysteries whose answers I long to
discover. I want to spend hours talking with you until I know
everything about you. Please share yourself with me, even the*

smallest thing, like...what's your favorite color? Perhaps I can guess.

Your favorite color is green.

I wish you hadn't gone home, even though I understand why you needed to. You had to return to the life you love rather than continue to play a part you never asked for. But I know you belong here with me, because your absence has left a gaping hole that can only be filled by you.

Until we're reunited, please satisfy my curiosities: are you enjoying being home? What is it like there? Lavena keeps referring to you as "that goose girl," and I confess I know next to nothing about what such an occupation is like. Won't you share it with me? I truly want to know every single detail, and even then it will never be enough.

Please write back. I ache to hear from you. In the meantime, I will continue to research as I strive to find a way to free myself so that I may be yours forever.

Affectionately Yours, Liam

Dear Anwen,

I've spent the week attempting to come up with a way to make time go faster while anxiously awaiting your response. I was convinced you wouldn't write back. Even though you've assured me that your feelings were real in the charade you performed, the longer it took for your letter to arrive, the more I'd convinced myself you couldn't possibly feel for me what I feel for you.

But then your letter came and it was well worth the wait. I've accepted a challenge to memorize it so that I can silently recite portions whenever I'm especially missing you. I'm unhappy to report there's been no progress in breaking my engagement contract. This dragon is proving quite the formidable beast, but we won't let him beat us, will we, my dear?

Anwen. I had to pause in this correspondence to write your name after you reminded me in your recent letter how much your name means to you. I'll write it a few more times—Anwen, Anwen, Anwen—and strive to better weave it throughout my letter. Another challenge accepted. I like challenges.

I miss you more than ever, Anwen. Our separation is made more torturous due to Lavena's thoroughly unwanted presence. You two are not identical by any means—for now that I have your face memorized, the differences between you two are obvious and jarring—but you're uncannily similar enough that each glimpse of her makes me think of you.

You both have the same dark brown hair, deep chocolate brown eyes, heart-shaped faces, upturned noses...but as to your differences: your features are softer; your eye color is a deeper brown, not to mention light fills your eyes while only scorn fills hers; you dimple when you smile; you have a darling array of freckles along your nose; your smile is brighter; and you yourself are the embodiment of sweetness and compassion, a woman who makes me better in every way.

I hate seeing Lavena and resent the fact I can't escape her while she and her family are visiting. It's as if she's donned the correct costume but plays her part all wrong. She's such a— (Forgive me for that blot on the parchment; I couldn't resist writing a particularly nasty word before feeling compelled to cross it out, but oh, it sure felt good to write it.) She's driving me insane. My intolerance for her is really pushing me past my breaking point and—

Ugh, I detest that woman. Lavena just interrupted, flouncing into the library with her usual smirk. I knew I should have taken refuge in my room...or perhaps even the dungeon would have been a better choice, considering she's taken to knocking on my door several times a day in an attempt to gain an audience with one of her false smiles. Perhaps I can at least entertain you by telling you of my torture in story form.

The moment Lavena interrupted me, she narrowed her eyes at your letter. "Who are you writing?"

I debated taking the silent treatment approach before realizing she'd likely pester me until I satisfied her annoying curiosity. "It shouldn't matter to you."

"Of course it does, Liam. I'm to be your wife, after all."

"More like my torturer," I muttered.

She pattered closer—undoubtedly to try and steal a peek at the letter. I hastily flipped it over. She pouted. "Considering we're to be married, it's wrong for us to keep secrets from one another."

I rolled my eyes. Her words were undoubtedly part of her speech she'd likely rehearsed several times. "Your act can't fool me."

Her feigned politeness faltered and she scowled. "Why shouldn't it? You're gullible enough, for my handmaiden's did."

I stiffened. Just hearing any reference to you caused my heart to pound furiously. "Anwen?" I stuttered.

She smirked. "Yes, Anwen, the little pretender who toyed with your emotions."

"You have no idea what occurred between us," I snapped. "You weren't there." Thank heavens for that.

"I didn't need to be. I've seen you mooning over her ever since she left. It's sickening how you're pining for a nobody." Before I could stop her, Lavena snatched my letter. She wrinkled her nose. "You're even writing to her. How pathetic."

"Give that back." I snatched it from her hands and smoothed out the edges. "She's not a nobody."

Lavena sneered. "She certainly is. She's nothing more than a common goose girl, whereas I'm a princess. Why would you want her when you can have me?"

"She may be a goose girl, but she's more of a princess than you'll ever be," I said. "Not to mention she makes me a better man, whereas you tear me down every chance you get."

Her smirk vanished and her eyes widened in shock before they narrowed dangerously. "So it's true then? I thought you merely missed her, but what you feel is something deeper. How disgusting."

Too late I realized she'd been baiting me in order to discern how

I felt about you. I tightened my jaw and didn't answer. She laughed coldly, no humor in her twisted expression.

"I don't believe it. You've deluded yourself into thinking you care for her, a mere peasant. You really are a fool. You need to let her go. She'll give you nothing, especially compared to what I could give you."

"The only thing you give me is a headache." I rubbed my temples. "Go away."

But she wasn't finished. "Why? Does it hurt you to be around me?" She sounded delighted by this fact.

I gripped the edge of the desk until my knuckles turned white. "It only hurts because you're a weak imitation of her."

She rolled her eyes. "We don't look that much alike."

Lavena was right about that. You two are nothing alike, yet far too similar in appearance for me to be at peace around her when it's you I long for.

"Go away," I repeated firmly, and this time (although most definitely not soon enough) she obeyed.

But she couldn't resist one last parting retort. "I know what I want, and you're the only one who can give it to me. I'll win you over yet."

"Don't count on it," I grumbled before the door shut blessedly behind her, leaving me free to finally finish my letter. But now that she's gone, the words won't come, not when my doubts and fears prevent me from writing anything cheerful.

I want to keep hoping, but that conversation with Lavena was so draining, not to mention she made me miss you more than ever. I ache for when we can finally be reunited.

Your Liam

Anwen Darling,

I'm begging you, put me out of my misery. Lavena is going to be the death of me. I've actually entertained myself by coming up with the most elaborate murder plots during particularly slow parts of this week's meetings. It'd certainly take care of the problem of my betrothal, wouldn't it? While I'd never actually murder anyone, she sure is tempting me...

She's actually making good on her parting words from our last confrontation that she'll "win me over," and I now realize with horror what they actually mean—attempting to woo me. I suspect this is her backup plan should we miraculously find a way to break the contract. But there's no doubt she wants nothing more than my throne, and in her attempts to gain it she flirts with reckless abandon. Several times a day I wonder if her advances will actually make me sick.

I'll share with you snippets: fluttery eyes, coy smiles, swirling her hair around her finger as if she thinks the gesture is appealing (it's most definitely not, at least when she does it), false compliments, accidental brushes against my arm...the list is endless, as is the torment.

At first my approach was to drive her as insane as she's driving me, which was the game we used play. I stack my plates at every meal in elaborate towers that she glares at with a look like she wants to knock them over; I ramble about nonsense and watch her fight not to yawn; and I goad her at every opportunity. Nothing works; instead, she redoubles her efforts to "win" me. So now I do all I can to avoid her, but somehow she finds me. I feel I'm trapped in an endless game of hide-and-seek.

This afternoon, despite my taking my lunch in the most obscure corner of the palace, she managed to track me down. She immediately gave me a coy smile and brushed against my elbow, causing me to jolt away from her so forcefully I upended the small table where I'd been eating.

I swore and Lavena's mask faltered. "Liam, you clumsy oaf. You are the most pathetic prince who's ever—" She snapped her mouth shut and forced a sickly smile. "Poor clumsy dear, you seem rather rattled by my presence."

I glared at her. "Quit the act, Lavena. And stop touching me."

Her eyes narrowed. "You let the handmaiden touch you."

I couldn't bear to hear her refer to you in that way. "Just leave me alone."

I stomped down the hall. The noise attracted my parents, who'd been in a nearby room going over reports. They frowned at me from the doorway. "Liam, what on earth—"

I jabbed my finger in Lavena's direction. "We need to break that contract before she's the death of me."

"We're trying, Liam," Mother said with a stroke of my hair. "But if we can't manage it, you'll have to try to make it work with—"

No, I wouldn't even entertain such a repulsive thought. "I won't," I said. "I already played that game with Anwen, and now it's too late to play it with anyone else; I only want her. Contract or not, I refuse to marry Lavena." I went to the library, where I redoubled my efforts to find a way out of my upcoming prison sentence. Still nothing. It's unbelievably frustrating.

But I won't give up. I may have consigned myself to honor and duty before I met you, but now I can't be the dutiful prince I'm supposed to be. I've never wanted this, but now I definitely can't accept this arrangement after having experienced love.

I'll close with writing your name again: Anwen. I love your real name. It fits you perfectly. I miss you, Anwen. I miss all the adventures we had, seeing your smile, enjoying our long conversations...everything. Please write back soon.

Your Liam

My Anwen,

I adored your recent letter and have already read it a dozen times. I love how each of your letters reveals more pieces to the Anwen puzzle I'm happily constructing. The more I learn about you, the more I care for you, not to mention your advice on how to deal with Lavena was both humorous and helpful. For now, I'll do my best to ignore her.

Still no progress with my horrible engagement contract. The longer our efforts are thwarted, the tighter the chains binding me feel. It's not only put me in a foul mood, but my motivation to be a good crown prince is faltering, especially considering you—the one who inspired me to embrace my role—are missing.

My parents have noticed my increased apathy, and seem both disapproving and worried. After a meeting when I was particularly inattentive, Father sat me down.

"What are you doing, Liam? You'd made such progress and now you're regressing."

I slumped in my seat. "What's the point? I'm a terrible heir anyway."

"No, you're not," he said fiercely. "In the past you've merely been a lazy one, but the last several months you were different—you've been flourishing, only to revert back to your old habits. Why the change?"

I sighed and stared unseeing out the window. "Because the one who made me different is no longer here."

He was silent a moment. Then, gently, he asked, "The handmaiden?"

"Her name is Anwen."

Father nodded with a look like he was going to make an effort to remember it. "You miss her, don't you?"

"I see her everywhere," I confessed. "I miss her so much."

"I'm sure you do. She's a sweet girl. It's a shame..." He rested his hand on my shoulder. "You know your mother and I support your desires to marry her, but we're still in quite the bind."

Yes, the engagement contract I curse.

"I know this is hard for you," Father continued. "But you need to keep making an effort to live up to your role."

"I'm trying," I said. "But it's so hard without her."

Father managed a smile. "She'll make you a better king."

"And she'll make a wonderful queen herself."

"I don't doubt that." He patted my shoulder. "We're doing all we can. Don't give up. Anwen wouldn't want you to."

I know he's right. You'd want me to push forward like I always do. It's strange how easy it was to do when we were together, but it seems so much harder now that you're gone. But I'll keep trying to be the man you believe me to be.

And our seemingly hopeless situation just got worse, for the King and Queen of Lyceria have insisted on a deadline—if we haven't found a loophole by the end of the month, the wedding between Lavena and me will take place. In order to maintain our relations with Lyceria, my parents have unfortunately agreed. The impending deadline feels like a noose.

But I'll never give up trying to find a way to keep you, the only woman I've ever wanted.

Your Liam

$\mathcal{I}$ giggled as my geese waddled around my ankles, alternating between nuzzling against me and investigating my hands for clover. When they failed to find any, they nipped my fingers in disappointment.

"No need to be cross, dears," I scolded half-heartedly. "You have plenty of meadow to wander and graze, you spoiled darlings."

They seemed to be paying me no mind as they continued to poke their beaks against my hand, investigating. They honked in protest at discovering no tasty morsels, and I soothed them by stroking their feathery heads.

How I loved being back with my geese. I'd missed them these past several years I'd served as Princess Lavena's handmaiden. They'd been adorably animated to see me upon my return. Their reaction had helped ease some of the pain of my aching heart, although not enough.

The tiny, affectionate, and extremely fluffy goose Bumblebee fluttered about excitedly in the way she always did when she wanted to be held. I settled in the grass and pulled her onto my lap. She snuggled up to me as if she were a cat.

"Did you need some love, sweetheart?" I cooed as I pet her feathers. My spoiling was interrupted when the geese suddenly began fluttering about, honking in agitation. "What's gotten your feathers ruffled? There's nothing to be —" My words died in my throat when I caught sight of Liam, standing at the edge of the meadow.

My breath hitched as I stared at him. Despite loving his wonderful letters, I'd been trying hard not to think about him, to instead treasure the beautiful memories we'd created together and move on. But it'd been impossible.

And now he was here. How could he be in Lyceria, and in my small, inconsequential village? As happy as I was to see him, his presence would deepen the wounds our separation had created, for despite his assurances that we'd find a way, our being together still seemed utterly impossible.

But he looked at me as if none of that mattered. He stared hungrily, his gaze stroking my face like he was committing it to memory. My cheeks warmed as I realized how I looked— tangled, windswept hair; a simple peasant's dress; dirt-covered hands; bare feet—so unlike how he'd known me at the palace. For as much as I'd yearned for Liam to see the true me, I now wanted to hide, terrified he'd reject me, and then I'd lose not only him, but even the *hope* of him that had been sustaining me since our separation.

His expression softened into the most tender look. "Oh Anwen, I've missed you."

I couldn't hold myself back from him any longer. I sprang to my feet—dislodging poor Bumblebee from my lap—and ran to him. He met me halfway and seized me in a tight hug that lifted me off the ground. He spun us around, both of us laughing in our joy. When he set me down, I burrowed my face against his neck.

"Is it really you?"

He chuckled. "I'm not sure. Do you recognize me?" He stepped back so I could take in his clothes.

I wrinkled my nose. "Whatever are you wearing?"

"It's my disguise." He extended his arms so I could get a full view of his peasant attire, looking too new and clean to convince anyone—not to mention his distinctive golden hair, bright blue eyes, and charming smile that gave him away as the Crown Prince of Draceria.

I giggled. "It's not a very good one. You don't exactly blend into your surroundings."

He frowned down at his outfit. "What's wrong with it?"

I perched my chin on my fist and examined him more carefully. "You're far too clean, as if you haven't done a single day's work in them." Which only reminded me of how unclean *I* was. Liam wasn't used to seeing me not groomed and elegant like a princess. I nibbled my lip. What must he think of me?

As if sensing my paranoid thoughts, Liam tilted his head and examined me more closely. I blushed and ran my fingers through my tangled hair in an attempt to tame it. He smiled sweetly as he tucked a loose strand behind my ear. "This look suits you. It reminds me of how you looked the day of the village disaster. You're as beautiful to me now as you were then."

I released a pent-up breath, his sweet words dispelling the insecurity tightening my chest. I felt strangely shy being around Liam in this way. As much as I knew him and cared about him—and despite our letters—a lot of Anwen was still a stranger to him.

Bumblebee fluttered at my ankles, seeking my attention once more. I picked her up and settled back on the grass, her warm, soft body helping ease my nerves. Liam crouched beside me and caressed my cheek. "It's truly wonderful to see you again, Anwen." He lightly traced my smile with his fingertip. "You look happy."

I started to fiddle with my hair but caught myself; I wasn't pretending to be the princess any longer. "I do love my geese." Talking about the geese felt safe in this new relationship of ours. I gave Bumblebee an affectionate snuggle.

"You spoke of them often in your letters. I'm eager to finally make their acquaintance."

"I'm afraid they don't know how to behave for a prince," I said, my attention not on him, but on stroking up and down Bumblebee's back.

"But I'm not a prince," he said. "I'm merely a man wanting to spend more time with a wonderful woman named Anwen. Perhaps you've met her?"

I managed a smile. "She and I used to be great friends before she had to leave for several months. We've since been getting reacquainted."

"And how is it going?"

I paused in my petting to consider. "I'm not sure."

I looked around the meadow, with its lush grass and dapples of wildflowers. Nearby was the creek I'd spent my childhood both wading in and investigating for water insects, and on the edge of the meadow was the grove of trees I'd spent years exploring, all encircled by the majestic mountains Lyceria was known for. The surroundings were so familiar, yet I almost felt separate from them, considering the person I used to be seemed so different from who I was now.

"Anwen?"

I smiled as I turned back to Liam. "I love hearing you say my name."

"It truly is lovely, just like you."

He settled more comfortably beside me and looped his arm around my shoulders to nestle me against his side, a position so familiar from our marriage. I happily snuggled closer and rested my head on his shoulder. But despite finally being back with Liam, it felt different now that I was no longer pretending to be a princess. Now I was simply goose girl Anwen. Could I ever really belong by his side?

Liam sobered as he searched my expression. "Are you alright?"

"I'm always happy to see you." I hesitated before slowly reaching for his hand, knowing I wasn't *supposed* to hold it anymore, but wanting to all the same. He happily relinquished it, giving my own hand an affectionate squeeze.

"As I am to see you." He stroked my cheek, beckoning me to turn my face towards his own. "Even though you seem pleased to see me, something is clearly bothering you. Won't you tell me what it is?"

Out of habit, I reached for the contract ring that I'd always twisted on my finger in my agitation, only it was missing. Its absence reminded me I could now be completely honest with Liam. "I'm feeling as if I've become two people: Anwen—who happily tends her geese and enjoys her life of simplicity—and Lavena, the one who adapted to your world of elegance and the life of a princess."

Liam's lips quirked into a mischievous smile. "I hate to contradict you, darling, but I don't recall ever seeing Lavena when I was with you."

My brow furrowed. "But she was who I was pretending to be."

He cupped my chin. "And I'm afraid you did a rather terrible job of imitating her. You see, I'm acquainted with both Anwen and Lavena, and you two are drastically different."

All the love I felt for this dear, wonderful man returned

anew, made even sweeter by his acceptance of me—he genuinely cared for *me*. At that sweet reminder, hope filled my heart. Could he be here now because...

"Have you found the loophole?" I asked breathlessly.

His cheerful expression faltered. "No, I haven't. I've written Aiden, Prince Ronan, and even Prince Briar, seeking their assistance, but they, like everyone else, are at a loss."

My heart sank. "Perhaps there isn't even a loophole." I hated saying the words, for if they were true, it wasn't right for Liam to be here with me.

"Don't say that," he whispered. "There has to be."

"But your wedding is only a few days away. How can we—"

"We'll find a way." Determination filled his expression. "I won't rest until we do. I thought perhaps we could look together. Maybe you'll see something we've all missed." He motioned to his satchel, stuffed with documents and books.

Despite the doubts squeezing my heart, I nodded. Bumblebee shifted in my lap to nestle her head against my neck, providing a much needed distraction from our somber conversation. I giggled and kissed the top of her fluffy head. "Are you feeling neglected? You do like your affection, don't you, Bumblebee darling?"

"It appears I'll have to compete for your attention," Liam said. "Shall I attempt to befriend her?" He reached out to stroke Bumblebee, but she nipped him. "Ow!"

"Oh dear, she's normally quite friendly," I said. "Bumblebee darling, you shouldn't harm the prince."

Bumblebee ignored my scolding. Instead, she nuzzled up against me, as if to appease my irritation and reclaim my affections.

"Oh no, you don't. You shan't try and humor me out of my disappointment in your behavior."

She kept nuzzling and I naturally softened, just as I

always did. I gave Liam an apologetic smile. "Now you can see who's clearly in charge here. I'm wrapped around their… wings." I examined Liam's finger, red from Bumblebee's mischief. "Did she hurt you?"

"Just my pride. I thought it'd be easier to get in her good graces."

"You are rather charming, so I have no doubt you'll win her heart in the end, but in the meantime, let me help." I took his hand and rested it on Bumblebee's back. He hesitated before beginning to stroke her. When she made no move to attack him again, his tension melted away, replaced with my favorite boyish smile.

"I knew I could charm her. I charm all the ladies." He winked at me.

"Do you now?" I pretended to be affronted.

"I do," he said, unabashed. "But there's only one I flirt with."

He nuzzled his nose with mine before placing a sweet kiss on the tip. Then his gaze, glinting with purpose, lowered to my lips. It was a look I knew well, one I'd previously loved but was frightened of now. He'd no sooner begun to dip down than I pulled away.

He sighed. "I know why you're resisting, but it feels wrong for us to be in the same place we started at the beginning of our marriage."

"I'm sorry, but it's inappropriate for us to kiss when you're betrothed to someone else. Besides, the more I give you, the more painful it'll be to lose you."

He cradled my face. "Is that why you resisted me during our marriage?"

I nodded, relieved to finally be allowed to share the reason. "I knew Princess Lavena would one day return, and thus I could never keep you. Yet you captured my heart anyway. That's what makes this so difficult. Why are you here, Liam? I'm both happy to see you and terrified of allowing myself to get closer to you."

He grinned widely. "It was a joint effort by all who are invested in our relationship. Elodie came up with the idea, and after I wrote a letter to Aiden pleading for him to send a fake invitation to invite me to Sortileya for business, I was able to escape Lavena while also having the opportunity to see you again so that I may court you to my heart's content."

That sounded wonderful...and painful. "But Liam, as lovely as that would be, it'll make it so much harder to let one another go should this end in the way we fear."

"We won't have to let one another go," he said fiercely, determination in his eyes. "We'll find a way out of my engagement contract. I promise. In the meantime, we need to spend time together." He snuggled me closer. "I want to be with you in your natural habitat like you were in mine."

How could I resist such an invitation? So even though I knew doing so was unwise considering our circumstances, I allowed myself to nestle against him. He began tickling up and down my arm, and in this cozy position we remained... until my geese considered themselves neglected for a bit too long. They waddled over, honking and ruffling their wings.

"You spoiled things," I scolded gently. "You can never go long without my attention, can you?"

Liam leaned down to whisper into my ear. "They seem pretty loyal to you. Perhaps the solution to our dilemma is to train your geese as our army to storm the castle and frighten Lavena away." He tilted his head and studied them. "Are aggravating, spoiled princesses part of a geese's diet?"

"Liam!" I smothered a laugh with my hand but it escaped anyway.

His grin broadened. "Yes, Anwen darling?" he asked, far too innocently. "Do you not approve of my plan?"

"My geese mean a lot to me. I don't want them to get indigestion."

He tipped his head back and laughed. "Oh, Anwen." He pulled me into a hug, his expression adoring. "You've always been willing to play along with my nonsense."

"I love everything about you, nonsense and all."

"And I love everything about—oh dear, I don't like sharing you." He glared at my geese as they waddled closer, once more vying for my attention.

"They're merely reminding me of my duties—I am supposed to be watching them." I reluctantly untangled myself from Liam. He leapt to his feet to help me up.

"Then I'll watch them with you. I want to know everything about your life as a goose girl. But first, might I have the proper introductions?"

I entwined our hands and led him to each goose in turn. "We own seven geese—two ganders and five females—and all are named after some of my favorite insects. You've met Bumblebee, so now I'll introduce you to Mantis, Aphid, Spider, and Dragonfly. They're rather attention-seeking birds at times, but I adore them."

Liam listened to each name carefully, as if trying to commit them to memory, even though he likely couldn't tell them apart. Most couldn't.

I pointed to the smaller gander, watching us curiously. "This is Cricket, always trying to attract the females' attention."

Liam bowed to him with all the solemnity of meeting a fellow royal before looking around. "You've only shown me six geese. Which one is missing?"

"Hornet, the other gander, who likes to think himself in charge."

As if his name had been a summons, Hornet waddled over with a distinctive gleam in his eyes that indicated he was about to cause mischief. He was the only goose with a black head, making him easily recognizable amongst the rest.

I frowned. "I think he's about to cause trouble."

"How can you know that?"

"I know my geese."

"Well, he's not causing trouble now, so perhaps—ow!" Hornet had made his move, nipping at our connected hands, as if he disapproved of our affection. All humor left Liam's expression as he glared at the goose. "He's rather sinister."

"He's normally quite friendly," I said.

"You keep claiming that, so you and I must have very different definitions of the word."

Liam led me several yards away but Hornet merely followed, as if he'd appointed himself chaperone. After a wary look at Hornet, Liam took my hand again. Hornet made another attack, causing Liam to drop my hand and nurse his now red and swollen fingers.

He glared at Hornet. "There's something wrong with that goose."

"So much for your irresistible charm," I teased. "Hornet dear, don't bite Liam."

Hornet's feathers ruffled and he honked in protest. I gave Liam an apologetic look.

"I'm sorry, I'm not sure what's gotten into him. Perhaps he's jealous."

I knelt in the grass and beckoned Hornet over. He obediently came and allowed me to pet him, honking when I withdrew my hand and reached for Liam's. Hornet nipped him again.

"That's it," Liam muttered. "That bird is going to be the main course at our wedding feast."

"He's just protective," I crooned as I stroked Hornet's head.

Liam gaped at me. *"Protective?* I'm beginning to think he's an enemy to the crown bent on my assassination."

"Well, he is being rather meddling." I gave Hornet a half-hearted disapproving look. Liam managed to chuckle.

"Like the rest, you're wrapped around his wing. How can I compete with a gander?"

"Don't worry, dear, there's no competition."

We strolled away, leaving Hornet behind strutting around the meadow like a peacock. Liam grinned down at the other geese waddling cheerfully around our ankles. "Now these birds I can handle. Will you initiate me into your world of being a goose girl, or in my case, a rather dashing goose boy?"

"You're really interested?" I asked.

He nodded enthusiastically. "Certainly. I can watch a few geese. How hard can it be?" And like with everything else he did, he jumped into this newest adventure with his usual exuberance. I showed him how to tend and gather them, explained some particularly interesting geese facts—such as how they sometimes ate pebbles to aid their digestion—and encouraged him to hold and pet each one. He did everything with a wide grin.

The afternoon melted away, full of sunshine and the ease we'd always enjoyed in one another's company when we were married. Being with Liam felt so *right.* Occasionally, Hornet—whom Liam quickly deemed his nemesis—would appear. He did seem to be keeping quite a close eye on us, almost as if Archer had put him up to spying. Luckily, the other geese took to Liam and he to them. With each of his smiles, I felt as if he not only saw me, but approved of me as well. It was an incredible feeling.

"What are they doing now?" Liam asked when Dragonfly and Aphid took it upon themselves to gently tug at his shirt sleeves.

"Oh, they're starting to like you. See? They're grooming you, similar to how they do with each other." I motioned to Mantis and Spider nearby, nipping at one another's feathers.

Liam raised an eyebrow. "I'm being *groomed?*"

"You don't need to be," I said. "You're already far too regal to pass for a peasant."

"Perhaps you can help me better blend in."

I took his hand and led him to the creek, where some of the geese were happily playing. I dipped down for a bit of mud, which I dabbed on Liam's clothes and streaked along his face before he caught my hands in his. He wiped some of the mud off my finger so he could use it to trace his fingertip on my face.

"What are you up to?" I asked breathlessly.

"Playing connect-the-dots with your freckles, like I promised one day I would," he murmured. "I've missed your freckles. Lavena doesn't have them, you know."

"The sun ruins a princess's complexion."

"Except for yours." He lowered his hand, leaving me longing for his touch, and extended his arms to the sides. "Do I look more like a goose boy now?"

"Almost." I burrowed my fingers in his thick hair to rumple it. "There, much better." Despite having finished, I didn't remove my fingers from his hair. His hands hooked around my waist and he gently pulled me closer.

"Anwen," he murmured, sounding as if he was in pain. He leaned down and this time I let him, my resistance weakened from the lovely afternoon we'd spent together and from missing all we'd once shared. He lightly brushed a kiss on my lips, his own soft and fluttery, and I'd just barely begun to kiss him back when…

"Get your hands off my sister."

Archer had returned from a day of hunting. I supposed it had been too much to hope to spend an entire day without his protective presence. We broke away with a gasp and turned to face my brother, who promptly seized Liam by the shirt.

"What are you doing to my sister?"

"Archer!" I tugged on his arm but he didn't release Liam. "Let him go. He's a prince."

"I don't care who he is. No one hurts you."

"It was just a kiss—" Liam began.

Archer's grip tightened. "Just a *kiss*? A kiss is rather dangerous when you use it to give Anwen false hope that you two could ever possibly be together."

I winced. He was right. I'd allowed my defenses to crumble when really I should be building them higher in order to protect my heart from further pain.

Liam took my hand. "I have only the purest intentions towards your sister. I intend to marry her."

Archer's eyes narrowed. "And how do you, a prince engaged to someone else, intend to do that?"

Liam frowned. "I haven't quite worked out the details yet."

Archer snorted. "Exactly. Until you do, I'll be keeping a close eye on you. I won't let you hurt Pillbug. You've already done enough of that."

He finally released Liam and stomped away, but not far, staying within view so he could act as our sullen and disapproving chaperone, which meant we wouldn't be able to steal any more kisses. It was likely for the best; I was already playing with fire by toying with the emotions of my heart.

"Are you alright?" I tried to smooth out Liam's collar where Archer had gripped it.

"Of course I am." Ever the brave one, Liam glanced warily at him before forcing a smile for me. "First Hornet, now your brother. You have quite the team of protectors. And I thought courting you would be easy, but it'll definitely be worth it." After another hesitant look at Archer he tentatively wrapped his arms back around my waist to pull me into an embrace.

I pressed myself closer to him as he held me and stroked my hair. "He's right. We can't do this. This will make it so much harder should we not be allowed to be together."

His hold tightened. "Don't say that. It's not over yet. We'll be together somehow. I promise, Anwen." He sealed it with a soft kiss on my brow.

And despite our seemingly hopeless circumstances, I believed him, for I was desperate to, no matter how impossible our situation seemed at the moment.

For several minutes I allowed him to hold me. I felt so complete in Liam's embrace, as if there was nowhere else I was meant to be.

"Anwen?"

I tipped my head back to see that his cheery, boyish expression had settled into one that was uncannily serious.

"There's another reason I'm here beyond needing to see you." He cupped my chin, his thumb caressing my cheek. "As we discussed earlier, the deadline for finding a loophole is only a few days away."

My heart tightened. "I know."

He pressed his forehead against mine. "Despite trying to assure you and myself otherwise, I'm beginning to fear there isn't a loophole, which leaves only one solution—I need to abdicate the throne so I can elope with you."

I gasped. He couldn't really be saying…was he serious? By his determined expression, I knew he was. As sweet as his sacrifice was, I knew he couldn't make it for me. My heart both lifted and wrenched at the thought.

"You'd do that for me?"

His eyes blazed with emotion. "I'd do anything to be with you. Please say you agree."

I ached to. The thought of Liam and I running away together sounded wonderful, but could I really be so selfish as to take him away from his people who I knew needed him? Selfishness was Princess Lavena's way, not mine.

"I love you, Liam," I whispered.

His eyes lit up, believing my words were my agreement, but before he could dip down to kiss me—

"But don't you see? We can't do this."

He froze inches away from my lips. "We have to, Anwen. I won't marry that wench, especially not when I'm in love with you. Let me stay with you. I make a rather dashing goose boy, don't I?" He attempted to smile, but it didn't reach his eyes.

"You have a duty to your throne, your subjects."

"But I'm not the only one in line," he said. "I have three younger sisters. Rhea can become the future queen. She'll undoubtedly do a better job than I ever could, and most certainly better than Lavena."

I caressed his cheek, relishing the way he leaned against my touch. "You'll make a remarkable king. Besides, abdicating and eloping would seriously harm your kingdom's relations with Lyceria."

His hopeful expression faltered, his acknowledgement of my logic. "But I need you, Anwen. I can't live or rule without you by my side. Please."

"It's not over yet," I said. "We still have several days to come up with something. And until then, we can spend time together."

Liam forced a smile as his arms looped back around me and he dipped down to whisper into my ear. "You may have won this battle, but I'm determined—nothing you say will ever make me let you go."

My heart both swelled and sank at his devotion. As much

as I yearned to be with Liam, I knew he couldn't sacrifice his kingdom for me. Surely, he'd quickly realize I wasn't worth all he'd have to give up. After all, I was nothing more than a goose girl, and goose girls didn't end up with crown princes, no matter how much they loved them.

CHAPTER 26

*L*iam spent the next several days with me, only separating at night when he returned to the local inn to sleep. We spent hours poring over the books and documents he'd brought, desperately searching for the ever-elusive loophole, but no matter how much time we dedicated to the task, the solution remained a mystery. With each passing moment my fears that there wasn't a way for us to be together increased, but I tried not to dwell on them, not when I was so desperate to be with Liam.

The time we didn't spend searching for a way to be together we spent in a second courtship of sorts. With each passing day, I showed him more of Anwen. It was one of the most frightening parts about love—to share every bit of one's heart—but something that was incredibly rewarding. Across dozens of conversations and various spontaneous adventures, I fell more in love with dear Liam, and the more he saw of common, insect-loving, geese-adoring Anwen, the more he seemed to care for me, dispelling my previous fears that he wouldn't love the real me.

It was dusk of the third day Liam had spent with me. I'd

just finished gathering the geese for the night, giving each a kiss before closing the paddock and accepting Liam's extended hand.

"I love watching you with your geese," he said. "You're so kind-hearted and gentle. You'll make the perfect queen." He'd brought up my capabilities multiple times during his visit, as if trying to get me used to the idea of an outcome he believed to be set in stone.

I raised my eyebrows. "You're suggesting I treat your subjects the way I do my geese? I don't believe they'll appreciate being locked in a paddock every night."

Liam laughed and squeezed my hand. "You never fail to make me smile. I've really enjoyed our time together these past few days. No matter how much time I spend with you, it's never enough."

"As have I." Although *enjoyed* was such an inadequate word for the pleasure I'd experienced from being with my Liam.

We paused outside the door to my cottage, both reluctant to part from one another. As was the case every night, Liam came up with an excuse to extend our time together. "Are you opposed to a walk before I'm forced to leave you?" he asked hopefully.

"An evening walk sounds lovely." We headed towards the meadow, passing Archer along the way, who as usual watched us through narrowed eyes in his usual chaperoning pose.

"Liam and I are just going for a walk," I told him. He nodded curtly but said nothing.

Liam glanced over his shoulder as we walked away. "His scowl isn't quite as pronounced as it was before. Perhaps I'm finally earning his good favor."

"I hope so," I said. "He really isn't as surly as he's seemed these past few days; he's simply protective."

"As he should be. I'm quite the shady character. I'm afraid I'm incapable of holding back my spouts of mischief, even from you."

I'd give anything to be subject to Liam's mischief forever if it meant I could keep him.

We continued our stroll hand in hand. The settling dusk bathed the meadow in ruby-rose light. I slowed as we approached the nearby grove, my breath catching when I caught sight of the dancing golden balls of light. "*Lampyridae.*"

Liam's brows furrowed "*Lamp...*what?"

"Fireflies." I opened my mouth to share all manner of interesting facts about them before closing it again with a heated blush, still shy to share my *bug obsession* as Archer liked to call it. Liam grinned, proving once again I had no need to worry.

"I love how you use fancy terms for your insects. It's just like a secret code. We should create an insect army, using their proper names to discuss them like generals strategizing for battle; no one will know what we're talking about, providing us the element of surprise when we attack."

I giggled. "You're only proving that you're indeed quite the shady character."

"It keeps life interesting." His attention quickly became recaptured by the fireflies. I watched them too, marveling at their beautiful glowing waltz against the night.

"Have you ever caught fireflies?" I asked.

"As a boy and admittedly as an adult as well." He grinned mischievously. "Have you?"

"All the time." Memories flittered through my mind like the surrounding fireflies. "Archer and I used to spend hours watching them. There's something magical about creatures that are able to shine in darkness. I've spent hours studying their patterns and the various uses for their light. As larvae, it's used as a warning to predators; as adults, while it's sometimes used to lure their prey, its primary function is to attract mates."

Liam grinned as his arms looped securely around me. "If I catch some, perhaps I can use it to attract *my* mate." He traced his finger across my warm blush, likely deep enough to be seen even in the fading light. "I love how you blush for me." He leaned down to lightly kiss both of my blush-coated cheeks before lingering inches away from my lips. "Anwen…"

His saying my real name gave me the confidence to meet his soft kiss. I hooked my arms around his neck and held him closer, basking in him and the beautiful moment we shared.

A mischievous glint filled Liam's eyes when he eventually pulled away. "Shall we have a friendly competition to see who can catch the most fireflies?"

"If you don't mind losing."

He chuckled and pressed another soft kiss to my brow. "It appears my Anwen is going to be a formidable opponent. That ought to make things interesting."

"It'll make things *very* interesting. Is your princely ego prepared for such a defeat?" I reluctantly untangled myself from him. "I'll go fetch the nets."

"I can get them. Where are they?"

I explained where to find them in the shed and smiled as he bounded off with enthusiasm to fulfill his quest. As I waited, I stared out into the settling night. The fireflies' glow flickered in and out as they waltzed against the velvety darkness. It was mesmerizing. I became so lost in their hypnotic dance I didn't even hear Liam return.

His arms looped around me from behind and he burrowed against my neck. "I brought some jars," he murmured. "And the nets."

"And my Liam back." I snuggled deeper into his hold,

loving the feel of his firm chest against my back. "I feared he'd run away from me because he's frightened of fireflies."

He snorted as he handed me my supplies. "Not in the least."

"Then he's frightened of a common goose girl besting a dashing prince?"

An adorable boyish eagerness filled his face. "A challenge. One last kiss before you become my temporary enemy in this competition of ours." He kissed me fiercely before pulling away with a hungry gleam in his eyes. "Ready to lose, darling?"

"I have no need to be ready for an outcome that will never occur."

And I scrambled off. I was an expert at catching fireflies, having done so countless times in order to study the various species and their habits. By the competitive glint filling Liam's eyes, he'd undoubtedly be a formidable opponent, but despite his own practiced skill, it quickly became apparent I was the superior firefly catcher, as I knew I would be.

Poor Liam quickly realized this and changed tactics from playing fair to playing dirty. When even his attempts at sabotage failed, in his desperation he became sloppy, swinging his net haphazardly without success.

He scowled at my jar of fireflies. "How many do you have?"

"Seven." I tauntingly wove the jar. "How many do you have, dear? Zero?"

"Three," he grumbled, taking another swing of his net and missing by inches. He mumbled a curse before throwing his net down and turning to me. His grin became wicked. "New game. Whoever catches the biggest firefly wins. Let's see if I can catch *my* firefly."

He began to advance and my heart flared in excitement. "Challenge accepted."

I broke into a sprint and he gave chase. Our laughter rang through the night as we ran through the meadow. With his longer legs, he quickly caught up and tackled me. We tumbled to the ground and rolled a few times before Liam propped over me with an impish grin.

"I've captured you." He pinned me gently and I wriggled weakly in protest, not really minding the feel of his knee against my stomach. "Now darling, I'll take this." He seized my jar and made to unscrew it.

"No Liam, please don't release them, not when I haven't yet studied them. It's been years since I've studied Lycerian *lampyridae.*"

He paused mid-screw. "There are different species?"

"Over two thousand."

His eyes widened. "That many? Looks like we have a quest throughout our upcoming marriage to capture every single one. Very well: your jar, my dear. I don't need to win this competition now that I already have my prize: *you.*"

He leaned down and softly kissed me before gathering me close and laying us down on the soft grass. I rested my head against his heartbeat as we watched the waltz of the glowing fireflies beneath the canopy of glittering stars.

I didn't realize my fingers were fiddling where the ring used to be—until Liam glanced down at my fidgeting. "Is it strange not wearing the contract ring anymore?"

"It's such a relief," I said. "I hated how it forced me to deceive you."

Liam picked up my hand, his thumb lightly tracing my finger where the ring used to be. "In a sense I miss it; it connected you to me." He raised his gaze, his fingers tightening around mine. "I have the perfect solution."

He reached inside his pocket and pulled out a lovely ring, the band smooth except for a dainty gold butterfly with one small diamond resting on each wing, simple in design yet still elegant. My breath caught.

"A promise ring, until the contract will no longer stand in our way." He started to push it onto my finger but paused. "I want you to choose to wear this ring. After all you've been through, I could never force you."

I smiled at him. "I'll happily wear your ring."

He grinned and slid the ring onto my finger. Its presence dispelled the lingering shadow of the contract ring, connecting me willingly to him.

Thunder rumbled through the sky, forcing us to return to the cottage. The rain began moments before we took shelter, quickly soaking us.

We ducked inside the cottage, where Archer started a fire while I frowned at the leaking ceiling. Unease that this wasn't the proper shelter to offer a prince flared in my chest as my insecurities returned.

I fiddled with my new promise ring. "I'm afraid the cottage is in need of repairs."

"I don't mind a bit of rain," Liam said with his usual cheerfulness. He rested his hand over mine, stilling the twirling of my new ring. "Please don't be afraid, Anwen. I'm not going anywhere."

His words eased the tightening in my chest.

Archer finished stoking the fire and straightened. "I'll check on the animals and move your geese to the barn." He strode to the door, pausing to glare back at Liam. "If I return and find you've so much as laid a finger on her…"

He let the threat hang in the air before stepping outside, slamming the door behind him. I led Liam to the hearth, where we settled side by side. He wrapped his arm around me to rub away the cold. I leaned into him and smiled as he took my hand. I flipped mine over beneath his and stroked his palm.

We stayed in this cozy position, keeping our hands clasped, until the door swung open and Archer entered, dripping water and carrying an armful of firewood. We hastily yanked our hands away but not soon enough. Archer paused in the doorway and narrowed his eyes at us, as if measuring the space between us. We must have passed, for he merely grunted and shut the door—blocking the howling wind—and deposited the wood near the fire.

"Your mischievous charges are safely cooped up," he said.

I sighed in relief. "Thank heavens. And is Spider doing alright? The poor dear is frightened of her own shadow."

Archer shrugged. "No idea. I can't tell your geese apart."

"She's the second smallest. She has a bit of grey just below her beak."

Archer gave me a blank stare. I started to stand.

"Perhaps I should check on the poor dear, make sure she's—"

"You're not going out in the rain, Anwen, not even for your *children*."

"But—"

"No, Anwen." Archer's tone was fierce. "It's pouring. I don't want you catching a chill." He gave me a *look* that forbade any further argument. I reluctantly sank back down on the hearth.

"The way you mother me you'd think I was a child."

"You're a child to me," he said. "I'm seven minutes older."

"Those seven minutes will forever haunt me."

He rolled his eyes but his lips twitched, revealing I wasn't truly in disgrace. I frowned out the window, where the heavy rain beat against the windowpanes. My stomach knotted in worry. "Poor darlings. I do hope they're alright. I so want to check on them."

"You're not going out in the storm," he snapped.

"I'm only going to worry, you know."

"I can handle a worried Anwen, but I can't handle an ill one. As if I haven't already worried about you enough these past several months."

Despite his annoying mothering, I couldn't resist smiling. "I love you, too, Archer."

He grunted in reply and ruffled my hair, his way of saying he loved me, too, before he stood to remove his worn coat, wringing the water out over the basin before laying it out to dry. I watched with a frown.

"I worry, too, you know, so come warm yourself in front of the fire before *you* catch a chill."

I patted the spot next to me and he obediently came over. When he'd settled, I got up and bustled around the kitchen preparing cups of watery tea, casting several anxious glances out the window, where rain and wind beat against the glass.

My nerves weren't lost on Liam, who frowned worriedly at me as he accepted his cup. "Are you alright, Anwen?"

I nodded, even though it was a lie, and settled beside him. As we drank the warm yet nearly flavorless liquid, my gaze was repeatedly drawn to the raging storm outside, my mind eclipsed by my geese. Were they warm enough? And how was poor Spider faring? The poor dear was a frightened thing. If I could only check on her…

"It's Spider, isn't it?" Liam's concerned voice drew my attention away from the window.

I gnawed my lip. "I know it seems silly, but I'm really worried about her."

"It's not silly at all." Liam reached out to tuck a wet strand of hair sticking to my cheek behind my ear. "You're compassionate. It's what I love most about you."

My heart fluttered at his words…until it began beating wildly when Liam drained his cup and stood. "What are you doing?"

"Spider is the second smallest with a bit of grey tuft beneath her beak?"

"Yes, she is, but...surely you're not planning on—"

He bent down to kiss the top of my head. "You stay cozy and dry while I go on an adventure for my princess." And before I could stop him, he bounded into the storm.

"Liam!" I scrambled to my feet, but the door had already slammed behind him. I ran to the window to peer out, but it was too splotched to see anything. I spun around to gape at Archer. "He went out into the rain."

Archer grunted. "Either the man is insane or he's in love with you."

I warmed at the thought. My Liam was braving the storm for common me. His sweetness only caused him to steal another piece of my heart he couldn't afford to.

I fidgeted with my ring as I began to pace, only stopping when Archer tugged me to a stop, his eyes narrowing at the ring. His jaw tightened. "What's that, Anwen?"

"Liam gave it to me."

Archer sighed and dropped my hand, and I continued pacing the tiny room as I waited for Liam to return, repeatedly looking out the blurry window to search the wet outdoors. I couldn't see him.

"He's been gone too long," I said. "Where is he? Will you go out and try to find...*Liam!*"

The door swung open to reveal a soaked and shivering Liam. I flung my arms around him. "Anwen, you'll get soaked," he said midst his chattering teeth.

"Oh Liam, did you really go check on Spider for me? How is she? Is she...what's that?" Something wriggled between us. I pulled away to see something fluffy shuddering beneath Liam's drenched coat.

"I pray this is Spider," he said. "Especially since she made it her mission to try and eat each of my fingers, but the sacrifice was well worth it if I got the right goose."

I gently picked up the huddling goose. "It *is* her. Oh, Liam."

I flung myself at him again to kiss his cheek. I wanted to give him a proper kiss, but Archer's protective hovering compelled me to suppress that impulse. Spider wriggled between us, forcing us apart. I stroked her shaking body. She honked in agitation and nestled closer to me, taking comfort from my embrace.

"She does seem rather frightened," Liam said.

"Hence I was worried." A new worry flared to life at his violent shiver. "You're freezing. Come, let's warm you up." I laced our hands together and led him back to the hearth while still holding a rather wet goose. "You're quite the hero," I said. "Spider is rather difficult to catch, not to mention hard to distinguish from the others to those who aren't familiar with my geese. However did you manage it?"

"Determination. I knew how important it was to you. I considered it a quest." He rubbed his hands in front of the flames, revealing several red fingers where Spider had bitten him. I lightly stroked the marks. He forced a smile. "Don't worry, it was worth the sacrifice of a few pieces of my flesh, although unfortunately, there were consequences." He leaned close. "Your precious darlings have now been exposed to all manner of foul cursings."

"That does sound serious," I said gravely, all while fighting my smile aching to emerge. "Since you're so wet, it'll be easy to wash your mouth out with soap." His shiver melted away all my amusement and my worry returned, tightening my chest. "I need to get you warm. Here, hold Spider."

I plopped the agitated goose on his lap and went to fetch a blanket and towel from the loft. I returned and took off

Liam's coat before draping the blanket over his shoulders as he wrestled with Spider, trying to keep her from escaping. I picked her up and patted the other half of my lap not occupied by my goose.

"Rest your head here and I'll dry your hair."

He grinned and eagerly obeyed. I began to work the towel through his soaked hair, and he closed his eyes with a contented smile. "I think I like being chilled if this is my reward."

"Except for a worried Anwen." I brushed a kiss along his cheek. When I'd finished with the towel, I ran my fingers through his wet hair. I could stay in this moment forever—the warmth from the flickering fire, the sound of rain pattering the roof, a goose in my arms, and especially Liam lying on my lap. I wished for more moments like this with him. Was such a future really a possibility?

Archer cleared his throat in warning, breaking the spell. Liam sighed and reluctantly sat up, his tender gaze resting first on me, then on Spider. "She seems to be settling."

I reluctantly turned my attention to Spider and tickled beneath her beak. "A bit, but she's still frightened. Poor thing." I kissed her head.

Liam's grin grew. "You mother her as if she really was your child."

"I've had her since she hatched."

"So we'll start our marriage with seven children? A fine number, which I hope to add to."

I flushed and Archer cleared his throat again, this one accompanied by a sharp glare. Liam leaned towards me.

"Does he not like the idea of us marrying?"

"He doesn't want me to hope for the impossible and get hurt."

"It's not impossible," he said firmly, whether for me or himself I wasn't sure. I didn't want to think about our seemingly hopeless situation, not when this moment was too special. Once again Spider provided ample distraction. I cradled her shaking form close.

"She still seems agitated. Perhaps music will calm her. Would one of you fetch my music box on the shelf near the door?"

Liam leapt to his feet before Archer could even stir. He carefully picked up the music box. "You still have it?"

"You chose the most perfect gift for me."

Liam beamed. "I was rather good at that husband thing. I hope with practice I'll become even better." He returned to my side, handing me my music box.

"You were very good."

"I'll be an even better one once we can be together."

Another reminder of the obstacle keeping us apart, one I couldn't dwell on now. Desperate for a distraction, I wound my music box and opened it. The music floated through the air, blending seamlessly with the sound of the storm outside. Spider calmed with the music enough to hop off of me and waddle around the room. I rested my music box on my lap and traced the butterfly patterns.

Liam watched with a soft smile. "Why do you like butterflies so much?"

"They're the most lovely *metamorphosis* insect. It's fascinating and wondrous how a seemingly insignificant caterpillar can transform and become not only a beautiful butterfly, but also develop wings to fly."

Liam's smile became knowing, and the look he gave me was as if he could see straight into my heart, a rather pleasant notion. "Ah, so you see yourself in the butterfly. The question is: do you still believe you're a caterpillar when nothing could be further from the truth?"

"But it *is* true," I protested. "I'm a common caterpillar, but unlike them, I can't change who I am."

"You're wrong," he said gently. "A person's identity isn't forever tied to their birth. You've already demonstrated the royal within you and that you'll make a remarkable queen. I've seen it time and time again—your kindness towards me at the first of our marriage, your compassion towards the village family whose house burned during our honeymoon, the natural way you embraced your duties as crown princess…. You might not have been born a royal, but you've become a princess who's meant to be the future Queen of Draceria. Once a butterfly has transformed, it can never go back to being a caterpillar."

My lips quirked up. "Nor can a crown prince ever return to being the spare when he's destined to be king. You've grown into your role."

"As have you," he said. "While you falsely believed you were merely pretending, you embraced the role and truly became my future queen."

I pondered his words as I traced and retraced the butterfly carvings on the music box. "You really believe I've become a butterfly?"

"I know it."

I smiled. Perhaps I had. Perhaps that's why I couldn't fully return to who I used to be. I *had* changed, even if I hadn't been able to see it until now. But was it enough? One look into Liam's adoring gaze and I knew it didn't matter. Liam saw me for who I truly was. He believed in me and loved me. *I* was enough.

Archer cleared his throat, once again interrupting our moment. "I noticed the ring on Anwen's hand," he said gruffly. "I've had enough of enchanted rings and I want to be assured that this is one contract Anwen is willingly entering into."

Liam's usual boyishness melted into a rare serious expression as he turned towards Archer. "I know you care for your twin and want what's best for her. I'm an older brother to three sisters and know what that emotion feels like. Rest assured, I will always care for her. You have my word."

Archer stared at him, jaw taut, before his expression softened. "I've been watching you these past few days and can see that your feelings for my sister are genuine. If you can wriggle out of your contract, then you have my blessing, Your Highness."

Liam gave me a triumphant grin. I extended my hand to stare at my ring, glistening in the flickering light of the fire.

"Do you like it?" Liam asked.

"I love it." Saying the words only escalated the fear filling my heart—this beautiful gift changed nothing of our circumstances. I sighed and let my hand drop. "Giving me this ring was a mistake, Liam."

His grin vanished. "Of course it wasn't." He took my hands and held them close. "Performing my duty is impossible without you. If we can't break the engagement contract, then I'll abdicate and we'll elope. I won't lose you."

"Oh, Liam." I cradled his face, relishing the way he leaned against my touch. "As much as I need you, you know I can't let you make such a sacrifice for me. You're the crown prince."

He pressed his forehead against mine. "You don't understand. I can only be king with you by my side."

The hopelessness of our situation tightened my heart. "But we can't," I stuttered. "What we feel for one another can't break the contract, and I can't let you abdicate for me."

"There has to be a way." But his words were without hope. The deadline was in two days, making tonight likely the last we ever spent together since tomorrow he returned to Draceria and his engagement to Lavena.

I couldn't respond, certain I'd unravel completely if I did.

"I can't live without you, Anwen," he continued desperately. "I don't believe fate would be so cruel as to have us meet only to tear us apart." He pressed several soft kisses along my hairline, causing me to cling to him even more fiercely. "We have to find a way so that I may keep both my throne and you."

"Which means the engagement contract must be broken."

We were back to the original problem that had vexed our entire relationship. I forced myself to push away all the painful emotions in order to consider the problem anew. It seemed far too strange that any contract, even a political one, could be so...*permanent*.

"Are you sure you and your advisors have looked everywhere?"

"We've searched every book in the library, but we've uncovered nothing."

I wrinkled my brow, considering the puzzle. It was hard to believe that in as vast a library as the one found in the palace, a loophole couldn't be discovered. "That doesn't make sense," I said. "Are you sure you've checked *every* book?"

"Yes," Liam said. "Most more than once."

"Even the books in the summer palace?"

Liam opened his mouth to respond but paused to consider. "No, I don't believe so. The books in the summer palace are mostly archaic volumes; many are centuries old. When the main palace was built, only the important books were transferred over."

"But there are several books about political contracts there," I said.

Liam frowned. "How do you know?"

"Because during our first week of marriage, I spent every spare moment searching for a way to break the contract I was bound to by the princess's ring."

Hope brightened Liam's expression. "And did you find anything?"

I scrunched my forehead, struggling to remember that far back. "I found a lot of nothing in regards to my contract, but I'm afraid I wasn't looking for information in regards to yours."

Liam slumped. "This is so frustrating. If it weren't for the fact that our marriage was made void due to it being performed under a false name, I wouldn't still be bound to that horrible Lavena and we could be together now."

That was true. It was amazing how even something as binding as marriage had been made void simply due to a name...

And then I remembered something, a faint recollection of a snippet from a book I'd stumbled upon at the summer palace. I gasped. Could it be...

"What is it?" Liam asked.

I stared at him in wonder. "I may have found the loophole."

$\mathcal{W}$e were forced to pass a restless night before we could leave the following morning for the summer palace, a carriage ride that would take most of the day. I sat beside Liam as the borrowed carriage rattled down the road.

"Won't you share your epiphany with me?" Liam pleaded once more.

I hesitated. "I'm not even sure if it's a solution. I don't want to give you false hope only to be wrong."

"At this point I'll take *any* hope." He cradled my face, his expression earnest. "Please, Anwen."

As usual, I couldn't resist him. "It's something I vaguely remember skimming during my research into the contract ring during our honeymoon," I said. "Your mentioning the fact that our marriage was void made me think of it. Despite reciting our vows, a contract as binding as a marriage was broken simply due to it being performed under a false name. It occurred to me that your situation is similar."

"How?" Liam asked, his previous frustration and despair

cloaking him once more. "Unlike our marriage, my betrothal contract wasn't created under a false name."

"No, but it was created under a *different* name."

"You mean Kian's?" Liam asked. "That shouldn't make a difference. It was created using his real name, and is thus binding, even when I inherited it upon his death and—" His eyes widened in understanding. "Wait..."

"Exactly," I said. "You *inherited* the contract. It was made with Crown Prince Kian, not Prince Liam. Was it redrawn when you became the heir?"

Liam scrunched his forehead, considering. "No, I don't believe it was. But I don't think it needed to be. I believe it was made between Princess Lavena of Lyceria and the Crown Prince of Draceria, not Kian specifically, despite him being the one who currently inhabited the role."

I nibbled my lip. "That's true, but I'm hoping that perhaps it still makes a difference. That's what we need to find out."

The endless carriage ride continued, and just as the sun began to dip below the horizon and darkness settled, we arrived at the palace.

I expected to enter by the front doors, but Liam took my hand and led me around to the back. "Where are we going?" I asked.

"The fewer servants who know I'm here, the better, just in case we can't find what we're looking for and they alert those at the main palace we were here. I'm afraid the moment the Lycerian royal family knows of my return, they'll immediately insist on the marriage."

He picked his way through the shadowy garden and approached the palace, where he pushed aside the crawling ivy and ran his hands along the stone wall, searching. He gave a triumphant cry as the wall turned inward, revealing a dark and dank passageway.

Liam grinned, basking in his victory. "I made it my

personal quest as a boy to find all the secret passageways in this palace. I'm glad my childhood mischief was good for something."

"May I ask why you didn't show me these passageways during our honeymoon?"

"A valid question, my dear, and clearly an oversight which I hope to remedy right now. Are you ready for an adventure, darling?"

Despite the rather spooky and ominous shadows of the passageway, I nodded as I tightened my hold on his hand. He led me deeper into the secret chamber. The wall closed behind us with a resonating *thud* that caused fear to creep up my spine.

I swallowed. "I'm assuming you know the passageways well?"

"You assume correctly," he said. "I needed somewhere to hide over the years whenever duty arose."

"So your previous irresponsibility is helping us now?"

His chuckle echoed off the surrounding stone, a welcome sound midst the cold, musty tunnel air that smothered us and caused me to shudder. Thankfully, Liam knew the passageway well, and several long corridors and seemingly random turns later, he pushed against a wall. It slid open to reveal the majestic library, lit up beneath the glowing moonlight tumbling through the tall windows.

Liam found a tinderbox next to a lantern and lit it. The soft, pale light illuminated the library, casting long shadows from the dozens of towering shelves, which were stuffed to the brim with books we'd have to go through. The task felt insurmountable.

Liam wasted no time. He led me to a section bursting with stuffy-looking volumes, many titles familiar from my search of the summer palace library several months earlier, though most were new to me.

He cast me an uncertain glance. "Do you happen to remember where you saw it?"

"I don't."

"We won't let that stop us." He took a fortifying breath. "We'll search all night if we need to."

We examined the faded titles by the pale lantern light caressing the worn spines, occasionally pulling out several to skim. An hour crawled by, then two, and soon three. My eyes became heavy with exhaustion and the pile of books we'd gone through grew into an unsteady tower, but still we pressed on.

As the fourth hour melted away, Liam groaned in frustration. "Where is it?"

"I just remember seeing it, though I can't recall which book I read it in." I yanked out *Laws and Traditions* from the shelf and began flipping through the pages, searching... searching...my breath caught as my gaze settled on a paragraph.

Those who inherit a title are honor-bound to fulfill all existing responsibilities associated with that title. In the case of contracts between parties or kingdoms, it is formal practice that all contracts be redrawn when a title is inherited by either party... I read the paragraph rapidly, only to reread it, and then read it again, my heartbeat escalating with each read through.

"Anwen?" Liam's urgent tone drew my gaze to him. He searched my expression hungrily, grinning at seeing the joy slowly filling it. "What is it? Have you found something?"

I beamed and held up the book. "I do believe I have."

THE CARRIAGE RIDE to the main palace felt endless, even though I knew it was only a few hours. Liam and I once more shared the same seat, my head resting on his shoulder as I stared out the window. The scenery was swallowed in inky blackness at first, but as the morning broke, the darkness began to fade, and soon the beginnings of golden twilight peeked above the horizon to slowly rise and stain the sky with the soft rosy hues of dawn.

Liam pressed his lips to my hair. "We're finally watching a sunrise together. I remember on the last day of our honeymoon you told me you loved sunrises because they represented new beginnings. This is our real beginning."

His confidence stoked the hope filling my heart, causing it to burn brighter. My hold tightened on the stack of papers and books in my lap from our research, which had extended a few more hours after stumbling upon what we believed to be the answer. Through our additional research, we'd discovered that this seemingly insignificant, archaic law was still in force, though tradition had usurped it.

"Do you really believe it'll work?" I asked.

Liam's arm looped securely around my waist tightened, keeping me snuggled close. "I do. Tradition is all well and good, but the law is the law."

His belief caused hope to warm my heart. I relaxed against him. It was easier to allow him to hold me now that we'd uncovered what could very well be the solution we'd been searching for, meaning I could keep him. This would work, and when it did, there would be no more obstacles between us—no engagement contract, no scheming Princess Lavena, and no feared rejection from Liam, for he'd seen the real me and he loved me.

The sun had fully risen by the time the carriage rolled through the gilded palace gates. Liam immediately leapt down and helped me descend. Keeping our hands intertwined, we ran up the palace steps.

The guards flanking the front doors rose their eyebrows in surprise—likely at both Liam's unexpected arrival and his peasant attire—but they bowed and opened the doors. "Welcome back, Your Highness."

Liam ignored their greeting and led me into the foyer, pausing only to address a footman. "Where can I find Their Majesties?"

"I believe they're still in their private quarters."

It was unsurprising given the early hour, but it was still disappointing that we'd be delayed in presenting our case. Liam, as usual, seemed undeterred as he led me to his parents' suite of rooms. It was wonderful to be back within the familiar corridors of the palace I now considered home.

Liam paused outside a large gilded door and turned to me. "Wait out here. I'll speak with my parents and request a meeting with them and the King and Queen of Lyceria." He pressed a gentle kiss along my knuckles before giving my fingers an assuring squeeze. "I'll be right back." He disappeared through the door after the attending footman opened it for him, and I leaned against the wall to wait.

I wasn't waiting long when I heard footsteps at the end of the corridor. I turned to see Princess Lavena. I gaped to see her awake at such an early hour, and in her dressing gown nonetheless. "Your Highness?"

She offered me a tight smile. "It's wonderful to see you, Anwen."

I narrowed my eyes. "Is it?"

"Of course." She paused in front of me. "I would like to speak with you. Might we walk together?"

I frowned at the door where Liam had disappeared through. "I'm waiting for—"

"Liam?" The princess rose an elegant eyebrow. "Yes, I suspected that. My new handmaiden saw you two arrive together and informed me. She knows how anxious I am to speak with you. Please, Anwen?" Her eyes widened imploringly, and despite myself I softened.

"Very well." I followed her into the next hallway, this one abandoned, granting us privacy. She immediately turned towards me with another smile.

"I've been giving the matter a lot of thought, and I think you and Liam are well suited for one another. I've decided to consent to breaking the betrothal."

I frowned. "That's very...amiable of you, Your Highness." A bit too much so, and completely out of character for her. Immediately, suspicion flared in my chest.

"There's no need to look so shocked, Anwen. Though I would certainly like to be Queen of Draceria, I really can't tolerate Liam in the least. I detest the man and have never wanted to be married to him, but when things didn't go well with my minstrel, I momentarily believed that even a life with him was better than the peasant life I was currently living."

I scrutinized the distaste twisting her mouth. Her words did fit my image of the princess. Perhaps she was sincere after all. "So you're withdrawing your claim on him?"

"Yes. I also apologize for entangling you in my scheme, although you really should be thanking me, considering you actually love the oaf." She extended her hand. "Might we be friends?"

Before I could even respond, the princess seized my hand, pulled me closer, and shoved the contract ring onto the finger next to the one that held my promise ring. The familiar burning spread over my hand. I gasped and yanked away, but it was too late—the ring was already in place, entangling me in another contract.

"What did you do?" I gasped, already desperately trying to wrench off the scorching ring, but as before it remained unyielding.

She laughed, a cold sound that caused icy fear to seep over me. "You're so gullible, Anwen, always determined to believe the best of everyone. Did you really think I'd ever relinquish my birthright to the likes of *you*? I'm a princess who is to be queen, whereas you're *nothing*."

I gaped at her while I continued to tug at the ring, but my attempts to free myself were futile. White hot pain throbbed through me at each desperate pull. "But you don't even want to be queen. The responsibility—"

"—is something I don't have to do. Queens can do whatever they want."

"But you don't even like—" My throat closed up around Liam's name, and try as I might, I couldn't say it. Each attempt to do so only caused the ring's burning to intensify. My panic grew. What contract had the princess placed me under? I glared down at the ring before raising my horrified gaze. "What did you do?"

She smirked. "Oh, that's just the new contract I placed on the ring, one that will ensure you stay far away from Liam. You won't even be able to say his name."

Despite her words I tried again, but the attempt only sealed my throat and caused another sharp pain to spread through my hand, as if I were clutching a hot poker. My anxiety rose, suffocating me. "Please, you can't do this."

She coyly lifted her brow. "Can't I? That's where you're wrong, for it appears that I *am*." My stomach twisted at her sickly triumphant look. "Now, here's what's going to happen —you're going to leave and never return, and I'm going to inform dear Liam that you considered the responsibilities that come with him too difficult for you to handle, so you've run away."

I glared at her. "He won't believe you."

"Won't he?" Her smirk widened. "He may think he cares for you, but he's undoubtedly secretly worried about whether you're fit for the role of queen. You're so common, Anwen. Love may have temporarily blinded him to that fact, but it won't be long before he regrets marrying you when he could have someone like *me*, a true princess."

For a brief second I believed her...until I remembered my time with Liam in the cottage during the storm, specifically the adoring look that had filled his eyes as he'd assured me I was *his* princess.

"He loves me," I said. "He wants me, no matter how common I may be. We belong together."

The princess snorted. "Then he's a fool. Even if he's deluded into believing that now, I'll be sure to change his mind. We have a lifetime together. Our wedding is today, and this time he can't wriggle out of it, especially when you're nowhere to be found."

As if her words were a command for the ring, I felt myself tugged down the corridor, away from Their Majesties' suite of rooms where Liam was. I gasped and struggled to resist the pull, but it was as if I were a puppet whose strings were being manipulated by the sadistic ring.

Desperate, I glanced behind me, where the princess watched with that cold, calculating look of hers. "Please, Your Highness."

She gave me a mocking wave. "Leaving so soon, Anwen? Sorry I can't see you off, but I have a wedding to prepare for. Don't worry, I'll be sure to take care of Liam." And with a sinister laugh, she turned and walked in the opposite direction, disappearing around the corner that led to Their Majesties' quarters while I was forced to retreat.

This couldn't be happening, especially now that I knew how much Liam cared for the real me and we'd finally found the path to being together. I struggled to turn around and return to him—or even to stop walking, but each attempt only caused the pain in my hand to intensify.

No! I struggled to shout for Liam, to even speak to the passing servants of my plight, but both actions must have fallen under the princess's new contract, for my throat sealed each time, forcing my silence.

I stumbled down the grand staircase. At my approach, the footmen opened the front doors with a bow. Again I tried to speak, but once more the ring's power prevented me. I found myself outside and heading for the ornate gate, a portal to a world I no longer belonged in. I glanced back at the palace, lit up with the rising sun that glistened off the gilded marble. When I'd first arrived months earlier, the palace had seemed formidable, part of a world not my own. But Liam had made it not just my world but my home. I couldn't lose it—or him—now.

I was nearing the gates, which I knew I couldn't pass through. I couldn't leave Liam. I loved him. I loved his kingdom and his people. I couldn't subject him or them to Princess Lavena's cold cruelty, not when he and I belonged together. I knew it with every fiber of my being. I wouldn't let the ring tear us apart. Surely there was a way to stop it; after all, every contract had a loophole.

My mind flickered back to the night of my nightmare when I'd shown more of my true self to Liam and the ring had remained strangely silent. Why hadn't it protested that breach of my contract or any of the previous times Anwen had slipped out? Could it be that I'd given the ring greater power over me than it really possessed?

The truth slowly dawned on me: contract or no contract, the ring didn't determine my true identity; *I* did.

I exerted all my energy and struggled to stop. The ring sensed a shift in my thoughts and attacked anew. I forced myself to speak through the throbbing pain. "I belong with Liam."

His name came out choked and sent a wave of pain so fierce it pierced my head, causing an excruciating headache to pulse against my temples. But I'd breached the ring's contract and spoken his name. Hope flared in my chest, spurring me onward.

"I love Liam," I said more forcefully.

In retaliation, searing heat flashed through me, so acute I thought I'd faint, but then it began to fade, as if the contract on the ring was weakening. I continued to struggle, fighting against the intensity, the headache, and most of all the compelling power of the ring trying to force me to do its horrible bidding that would tear me away from the man I loved.

I gritted my teeth against the pain. "I am the true Crown Princess of Draceria."

With those words, the pain vanished so instantly I felt I'd been doused with water. I collapsed onto the grass in exhaustion. For a moment I just lay there, staring up at the sky, dazed with the absence of the burning that had consumed my senses.

I slowly rolled over to my knees and sat up. I glanced down at the ring, the metal now cold, its usual malevolent glisten faded, as if it'd died. I yanked it off and held it in my palm, staring at it. Had I broken the contract? It appeared I had. I closed my hand around the ring in triumph.

I stumbled to my feet and ran towards the palace. As I neared the front doors, they opened and Liam hurried out, his expression frantic. He was halfway down the steps when he spotted me. "Anwen!"

I beamed and increased my pace. He met me halfway and scooped me into a tight hug, burrowing his face against my hair. I basked in his embrace. This was where I belonged.

"My Liam." I tipped my head back so I could stare up at him. He stroked my cheek, his eyes adoring as he caressed my face.

"Lavena told me you'd left, but I didn't believe it. Yet you were nowhere to be found. What happened?"

I extended my hand so he could stare at the ring on my palm. "Another sinister contract, one that would force us apart. But I broke it."

His eyes widened. "You did? But how?"

I smiled. "Every contract has a loophole. This one happened to be true love and belief in my true identity." I cradled his face. "We're meant for each other, and nothing will ever separate us again."

He grinned my favorite boyish dimpled smile. "I couldn't agree more." And he sealed his words with a heated kiss that left me no doubt that he wanted me, common handmaiden and goose girl. But now I was also Liam's princess and Draceria's future queen.

I was right where I belonged.

CHAPTER 28

*H*and in hand, Liam and I made our way to the meeting room, where Liam's parents and the King and Queen of Lyceria were waiting for us to present our case that would finally break the unwanted engagement contract. Liam held the books while I clutched the papers close to my chest as we took the grand staircase two steps at a time.

"Have you told your parents what we found?" I asked.

"Not yet. I wanted us to do it together. I merely told them I wanted to meet with them and the Lycerian king and queen. I can't wait to see Lavena's expression when she sees you. We'll wipe that gloating smirk right off her face." He seemed almost giddy at the prospect.

We arrived a few minutes later. "Shall I announce you, Your Highness?" The guard standing outside the meeting room began, but Liam ignored him and pushed the door open himself.

Inside, Liam's parents, the Lycerian royal family, and several sleepy-eyed advisors from both courts were already seated around a large circular table. The Queen of Draceria anxiously rose first.

"There you are, Liam." She hurried forward and hugged him. "I hope whatever you've found is strong enough for us to finally break the contract." She pulled away to take in our connected hands with a frown. "Do you think it was wise to bring Anwen to the palace before we have this all sorted out?"

"Yes, for she's the one who discovered the loophole."

The king stood. "So you found one at last?"

Liam beamed. "I believe so."

He led me further into the room towards where the Lycerian royal family sat. The King of Lyceria scowled, Prince Nolan smiled, and Princess Lavena stared wide-eyed.

"What are you doing here?" she hissed. "I thought I'd—"

"Gotten rid of me for good? Would you like your ring back, Lavena?" I triumphantly extended my hand, palm up, where her ring rested. She stared at it in disbelief. "Unfortunately, you failed to consider one thing when you attempted to bind me with another one of your contracts."

Princess Lavena continued gaping at the ring. Prince Nolan reached out and plucked it from my hand. "I'll be taking that."

At his words, her shock dispelled enough for her to glare at me. "How could you possibly have broken its enchantment?"

"Because every contract has a loophole, both your ring's and your engagement contract."

She paled. "You couldn't have found one, not when Draceria's advisors have searched everywhere."

Liam merely smirked. "Everywhere except the Dracerian summer palace library."

"The Dracerian summer palace?" the king asked. "Did you find anything useful in those outdated volumes?"

"We did, in fact." But before he could say anything further, the King of Lyceria spoke.

"Considering your apparel and the fact you've been gallivanting off to the summer palace, I take it you weren't actually engaged in meetings with Prince Deidric, as you told us you were? That lie was exposed when I sent an advisor to investigate when you were gone too long. I thought you'd run away from your duty."

"No, that type of offense is only committed by your daughter." Liam glared at Princess Lavena.

"Exactly. That's the crux of our argument for breaking the contract." The King of Draceria turned once more to the Lycerian King and Queen. "For the dozenth time, Princess Lavena has broken her end of the agreement, an offense that proves she's unfit to be Draceria's future queen. Why do you repeatedly insist on overlooking that fact?"

"Be that as it may, the integrity of her actions cannot void our contract," the King of Lyceria said. "I still don't understand why you no longer desire the coveted benefits of our union merely because of a single transgression, especially when she's returned to atone for it."

The King of Draceria's eyebrow twitched, a sign of his disapproval. The Queen of Draceria used the opportunity to speak up. "We're concerned that due to her past actions, Lavena has shown that she places little value on the responsibilities that she'll carry as the future queen. Thus we cannot in good conscience pass the crown to her."

The King of Lyceria pounded his fist on the table. "Enough of this. We've hashed this out for weeks. There is no loophole, and we refuse to break the contract. There are too many benefits for Lyceria to do so, and unless both parties agree, it's still binding."

"Might I be allowed to present our case?" Liam asked. Everyone turned to him. He took the documents I'd been cradling protectively and set them with his books on the table. "Your arguments are now irrelevant, considering the contract is already void. In fact, it was void upon Kian's death."

Shocked silence followed his announcement. Liam's mother spoke first, her eyes glassy. "I don't understand, Liam. How?"

He tapped his finger on the top document. "For the simple fact that the contract was drawn up not between me and Lavena, but between Lavena and the *Crown Prince of Draceria.*"

I waited for understanding to fill the others' expressions but they merely looked confused. "We know that, Liam," Princess Lavena said, scoffing. "But it changes nothing."

Liam smirked. "It appears you fail to see what Anwen was the first to realize—the engagement contract was drawn up between Lavena and the crown prince, which at the time was Kian."

"Yes, dear," the queen said. "But after his death, you inherited his title and all that came with it."

Liam's grin widened. "That's what we have all been erroneously assuming from the start—that I inherited everything from Kian when I became crown prince, including his engagement contract. But though I did inherit his title, I did not inherit his betrothal."

"This is nonsense," the Lycerian king muttered.

Hope filled the King of Draceria's expression. "What are you saying, son?"

"Had I inherited Kian's contract it would be ironclad, but we've discovered that contracts are an exception to the law of inheritance. According to our research, a contract has to be drawn up again if there is a change in title with either party."

He lifted another document we'd uncovered during our late night library research.

"We found in the first edition of *Laws and Traditions*—which our kingdom followed several hundred years ago—that every contract inherited along with a title needs to be formally redrawn, something we failed to do when I became the new crown prince following Kian's death." He glanced down at the document he held. "We did our research. Over time, that formality fell out of practice, and tradition dictated that to ensure a smooth transition, those who inherited titles were honor-bound to accept all that came with it, including any contracts between parties or kingdoms. But *technically*, it's still law that *formality* needs to be followed—in this case, redrawing up the engagement contract, something we failed to do."

The King of Draceria grabbed the document and began reading frantically.

"True, it's a rather archaic law," Liam continued. "One that hasn't been enforced in several hundred years. But it's still law."

The king's eyes widened as he continued to read before slowly looking up with a proud grin. "Well done, Liam." And with his words, I knew we'd won.

My heart lifted and Liam wrapped his arm around me. "Anwen was the one who first realized the solution to our dilemma could be found in examining the laws surrounding the inheriting of contracts."

The king gave me a fatherly look of approval. "Then well done, Anwen. You'll make a fine queen."

I blushed but couldn't help smiling. While the thought of being queen was still rather daunting, with it came Liam, a man who, despite everything, would finally really be mine.

The King of Draceria turned back to the Lycerian monarchy. "Liam and Anwen are correct. While for years we've upheld the inheriting of contracts as tradition, law dictates that when Liam inherited Kian's title of crown prince, the engagement contract needed to be redrawn. It wasn't, which means—"

"The engagement contract is void." I'd never seen Liam so happy, the heavy burden he'd carried for years lifted at last.

The King of Lyceria stood and snatched the document to read it for himself. With each word, he slumped in defeat. "Such an archaic law shouldn't have to be honored—"

"Archaic or not, the law is still the law," the King of Draceria said with a firmness that forbade any further argument.

"But to have a mere technicality break such a coveted—"

"This *mere technicality* is sparing my son from a horrible marriage and our kingdom from a woman unfit to be its queen."

The king sighed, his acquiescence. Princess Lavena's expression turned sour. "It can't be true."

The King of Lyceria rested his hand on her shoulder. "You have only yourself to blame for this, Lavena. If you hadn't run off several months ago, you'd now be the Crown Princess of Draceria."

Princess Lavena sneered at me. "But how could a common goose girl with no formal education have discovered such a loophole?"

"I obtained the knowledge several months ago when I found myself quite invested in researching contracts due to a certain one that *you* placed me under." I pointed to my finger, where up until a few minutes ago, her contract ring had been.

Prince Nolan laughed. "You dug your own grave, my dear sister. Perhaps in the future you'll start taking more responsibility and not make such foolish choices."

Her scowl deepened but she didn't say anything more. The Queen of Lyceria, however, still had plenty to say. "If this contract is void, then we can simply draw up another, perhaps one with greater benefits as an incentive for you to reconsider a union with our kingdom."

"I'm afraid we're no longer interested in an alliance that would involve Princess Lavena," the King of Draceria said dryly.

The princess's expression darkened. "But there would be no advantage to Draceria by having a handmaiden as queen."

"Anwen offers many benefits to my kingdom that may not be as tangible as a contracted alliance," the king said. "She's proven herself worthy to be Queen of Draceria by her compassion and willingness to serve her subjects, whereas you've only put your self-interest above all else."

"But—" Princess Lavena stuttered. Prince Nolan wrapped his arm around her shoulders.

"It'd be wise to cease speaking before you make even more of a spectacle of yourself," he said. "I propose a calming stroll through the gardens. Come, Lavena." He led her towards the door, sending Liam and me a smile of congratulations over his shoulder, whereas Princess Lavena cast us one final glare.

"How did you break the ring's enchantment?"

I lifted my chin with a smile. "Throughout our switch, I came to learn that being of royal birth doesn't make one a princess; true royalty is compassion and service, not just sitting on a throne. Once I realized I was the true Crown Princess of Draceria, the ring's contract broke."

Princess Lavena scowled at me as the door closed behind her.

The King of Draceria rested his hand on Liam's shoulder. "I'm proud of you, son. Anwen may have found the loophole, but you presented it in a dignified manner worthy of a future king. You're finally embracing the role I've never doubted you could fulfill."

Liam lifted his chin. "Because I've finally accepted that I am the Crown Prince of Draceria, and as such I'll do all I can to fulfill my responsibilities to my kingdom to the best of my abilities."

"I have no doubt you'll succeed." He patted Liam's shoulder before stepping aside so the queen could embrace him.

"We're so proud of you, dear."

Liam's grin became mischievous. "I did do a rather fantastic job, didn't I? Perhaps a reward is in order? I have only one in mind—a hasty wedding to Anwen, preferably today."

The queen smiled. "I think that could be arranged. What do you think, dear?" She turned to her husband.

"I believe that would be wise so that we can put this matter behind us as soon as possible."

Liam beamed and gently tugged me towards the window overlooking one of the gardens. He held my hands close, his eyes adoring. "Now that we've overcome all our obstacles, nothing will stand in the way of a lifetime of adventures." He scooped me in a tight hug. "We won, Anwen, which means we can finally marry, for real this time."

I hugged him back, feeling dazed. Despite all odds, we'd fought for and achieved our happily ever after, and in this moment of victory, I wanted to enjoy all I'd won—not just Liam's heart, but the privilege of getting to keep it.

I beamed with happiness. "We can really be together? You want me?"

"I want no one but you." He lifted my hands and kissed them softly. "I want my goose girl, the woman who is so sweet, intelligent, kind, and caring, the woman who not only makes me a better man, but who makes me unbelievably happy."

My smile grew. I hooked my arms around his neck and

stood on tiptoe to press my forehead against his. "And I just want my Liam."

"Does that mean you'll marry me in a quick, private ceremony as soon as Archer arrives so that you can officially become my future queen?"

I smiled. "As long as I'll always be your Anwen first."

"That's all I want you to be, and I'll love you forever for it." And he leaned down to seal the promise with a tender kiss.

EPILOGUE

"*I* think I found one, Anwen."

I looked up from combing my own section of flowers to see my husband's face lit up with his usual boyish enthusiasm. He lay on his stomach in the garden of the summer palace, where we were nearing the end of our month-long—and this time real—honeymoon. Due to royal duties and obligations, our honeymoon had been delayed two months, but it had been well worth the wait.

Liam stared with intense focus at the orchid in front of him, his jar at the ready. "Is this a flower mantis, Anwen?"

Excitement fluttered within me as I crept closer and leaned down. "It is."

"Then we have prevailed in our quest. We couldn't have left our honeymoon until we'd succeeded." Liam's excitement faded into a thoughtful frown. "Perhaps we should let the flower mantis escape so we finally have an excuse to extend our honeymoon indefinitely."

"That's far too drastic. Hurry and catch it before it gets away."

He did so, angling the jar carefully before successfully

capturing our prey in one swoop. "Success! Now, my dear, may I present the distinguished Sir Flower Mantis, captured by your adoring husband for your enjoyment."

He bowed and handed me the jar with great ceremony. I lifted it so I could better study its colors, which matched the orchid it had been perched on.

He scooted closer and peered into the jar. "They are rather fascinating insects. Do you think we can manage to catch all twelve species?"

I gaped at him. "How did you know there were twelve?"

He smirked. "I've been studying. After all, it's only fitting that my wife's favorite hobby become one of my own." His expression softened as he pressed his forehead against mine. "My wife."

I smiled. He made an effort to call me that almost as often as he found excuses to use my name.

He kissed me and as usual I melted into him, only breaking the kiss when something captured my attention. A few yards away, tucked within the grass, was an orb web. I craned my neck for a better view, hoping to see...yes, an orb-spider, an *argiope bruennichi* by the looks of it from this distance. I itched for a better look.

Liam sensed my wriggling. "What is it, darling?" He glanced over and his eyebrows raised. "Oh..." It came out as both a moan and a sigh of wonder.

"I need to get a closer look."

"Very well. Go hunt, darling."

I tugged out of the comfort of his arms and crawled over to eagerly study the black-and-yellow spider. Oh goodness, its web was so beautiful, a perfect orb with a zigzag shape in the center—likely used to aid camouflage and lure its prey— with the magnificent spider residing at the center.

"Liam! Come look! It's an *argiope bruennichi*, a wasp spider."

Liam, bless his heart, came over and peered down at it in interest. "Tell me about it," he said.

"It's an orb spider. It builds a new web every day—usually at dawn—after consuming its old one in the middle of the night, and then it lives in the center. Fascinating, isn't it?" I peeked up at Liam with a wicked grin. "These spiders are cannibals, almost always consuming their mate during reproduction."

He chuckled as he rested his hand reverently on my stomach. "I'm grateful you don't take that particular habit to heart, my bug-loving darling, else I'd be in trouble." He leaned down to press the sweetest kiss on my stomach, where we suspected new life already resided.

I rested my hand right above where he'd just tenderly kissed and he placed his on top of mine, beaming at where our hands resided with his usual boyish enthusiasm. "I told you, Liam, I'm not completely sure I'm with child." Though my suspicions were only being confirmed with each passing week.

"I'm betting you are, and my guess is it's a girl."

I hoped that was true. We'd waited long enough to marry for real, so how wonderful it'd be if we didn't have to endure the wait to become parents.

He bestowed another kiss on my stomach. "I'm going to be the favorite parent, I just know it."

I giggled. "Quite likely. You always know how to charm the ladies."

"While that's true, there's now only one lady I'm interested in charming, and her name is Anwen."

I smiled contentedly at the way he said my name, just like a caress. I closed my eyes a moment to savor it. "I never tire of hearing it from you."

He smiled tenderly. "I know, Anwen."

Liam gently took my hand and led me to where we had a

picnic set up. We settled on the lawn, where he looped his arms around me and pulled me securely against his chest before offering a basket filled to the brim with my favorite fruit, one of the only foods that didn't make me nauseous— another reason I suspected I was pregnant.

"Strawberries?" I eagerly accepted one, but I'd no sooner eaten the juicy fruit than he handed me another. "Can't forget the baby."

I took a sweet, juicy bite of my strawberry. "If I really am pregnant, your family is going to be ecstatic."

Mischief flashed in his eyes. "They will when they find out. Shall we play a game?"

"What sort of game?"

His grin became wicked. "Let's not tell anyone you're pregnant and see how long it takes them to notice."

I raised an eyebrow. "Isn't that rather mean?"

"Come on, Anwen, you know it sounds fun."

My lips twitched. "Fine, we'll play on the condition that you take the blame when your poor mother realizes we kept the secret for so long on purpose."

He chuckled. "Deal. This will be fun." He pressed his lips to my hair. "Now, how about another story about when you were a goose girl. Those are some of my favorites."

Thinking of my little darlings reminded me of one of the surprises Liam had arranged—having my geese brought to the palace. Unfortunately, Liam had insisted they not join us on our honeymoon as he was adamant that nothing eclipse our time together.

"Do you think the children miss us?" I asked.

He chuckled. "I'm sure they're getting along just fine... except perhaps Hornet; he's likely starving not having any of my fingers to eat."

"He's growing fonder of you."

"I'll win him over in the end," he said. "Considering my

goal is to be the favorite parent to *all* our children, not just this one." His hand lowered once more to my stomach. "This picnic reminds me of the day I discovered your picking strawberries with my sisters and you told us about chiggers. It was one of many clues into your true identity."

"You were really good at discovering those; I gave far too many hints about Anwen. I just couldn't keep myself from occasionally slipping out. I suppose one can never fully lose oneself." It was such a comforting thought.

"You were afraid I was falling in love with a mask, but it was only the glimpses of the real you that stole each piece of my heart. There were so many hints of my Anwen, each discovery causing me to fall more in love with you." He hooked his finger beneath my chin and lifted it so our eyes met. "I see you."

His words enveloped me, as warm and tender as his embrace, and they were more than a fact—they were his assurance. "You do see me." And I knew he always would.

He kissed me with the usual sweetness that was my Liam before he helped me to my feet. "Now Anwen, we've spoiled our baby, discussed the children, searched for insects, and had a picnic complete with strawberries. What other adventures shall we plan for today?"

I squeezed his hand. "Anything, as long as it's with you."

"Then I have the perfect one in mind. Even though I've already found my greatest treasure, how about a treasure hunt all the same?" He pulled out a hand-drawn map and wriggled his eyebrows. "Do you trust a pirate to lead you on a quest?"

I hooked my arms around his neck and stared up at him in adoration. "I trust my Liam to make our life together the greatest adventure of all." And hand in hand, we returned to the palace to continue what promised to be a lifetime of living happily ever after together.

ALSO BY CAMILLE PETERS

Pathways
Inspired by "The Princess and the Pea" and "Rumpelstiltskin"

Spelled
Inspired by "The Frog Prince"

Reflection
Inspired by "Snow White"

Enchantment
Inspired by "Beauty and the Beast"

Voyage
Inspired by "King Thrushbeard"

THANK YOU

Thank you for allowing me to share one of my beloved stories with you! If you'd like to be informed of new releases, please visit me at my website www.camillepeters.com to sign up for my newsletter, see my release plans, and read deleted scenes—as well as a scene written from Liam's POV.

I love to connect with readers! You can find me on Goodreads, Instagram, and on my Facebook Page, or write me at authorcamillepeters@icloud.com.

If you loved my story, I'd be honored if you'd share your thoughts with me and others by leaving a review on Amazon or Goodreads. Your support is invaluable. Thank you.

Coming November 2019: Princess Rheanna's story, *Reflection*, inspired by *Snow White*.

ACKNOWLEDGMENTS

I'm so incredibly grateful for all the wonderful people who've supported me throughout my writing adventures.

First, to my incredible mother, who's worn many hats over the years: from teaching me to read as a toddler; to recognizing my love and talent for writing and supporting it through boundless encouragement and hours of driving me back and forth to classes to help nourish my budding skills; to now being my muse, brainstorm buddy, beta-reader, editor, and my biggest cheerleader and believer of my dreams. I truly wouldn't be where I am without her and am so grateful for God's tender mercy in giving me such a mother.

Second, to my family: my father, twin brother Cliff, and darling sister Stephanie. Your love, belief in me, and your eager willingness to read my rough drafts and help me develop my stories has been invaluable. Words cannot express how much your support has meant to me.

Third, to my publishing team: my incredible editor, Jana Miller, whose talent, insights, and edits have helped my stories blossom into their potential; and Karri Klawiter, whose talent once again created a stunning book cover that's beyond my imagination, one that is still one of my absolute favorites.

Fourth, to my wonderful beta readers: my dear Grandma, Charla Stewart, Alesha Adamson, Mary Davis, Emma Miller, Holly, and Emily Flynn. I'm so grateful for your wonderful insights and suggestions that gave my story the last bit of polish in order to make it the best it can be. In addition, I'd like to thank all my ARC readers, who were so willing to give my book a chance and share their impressions. Thank you.

Fifth, to my Grandparents, whose invaluable support over the years has helped my dreams become a reality.

Last but not least, I'd like to thank my beloved Heavenly Father, who has not only given me my dreams, talent, and the opportunities to achieve them, but who loves me unconditionally, always provides inspiration whenever I turn to Him for help, gives me strength to push through whatever obstacles I face, and has sanctified all my efforts to make them better than my own.

ABOUT THE AUTHOR

Camille Peters was born and raised in Salt Lake City, Utah where she grew up surrounded by books. As a child, she spent every spare moment reading and writing her own stories on every scrap of paper she could find. Becoming an author was always more than a childhood dream; it was a certainty.

Her love of writing grew alongside her as she took local writing classes in her teens, spent a year studying Creative Writing at the English University of Northampton, and graduated from the University of Utah with a degree in English and History. She's now blessed to be a full-time author.

When she's not writing she's thinking about writing, and when's she's not thinking about writing she's...alright, she's always thinking about writing, but she can also be found reading, at the piano, playing board games with her family and friends, or taking long, bare-foot walks as she lives inside her imagination and brainstorms more tales.

Printed in Great Britain
by Amazon